Praise for

The Princess Plot

series

"Engaging, clever, quick-paced — and well stocked with royals! Jenna will put readers firmly on her side."   —*Kirkus Reviews*

"A fun, attention-keeping read. For readers who dream of being a royal or singlehandedly saving an entire country from ruin, Boie's story will hit the spot."   —*Publishers Weekly*

"Well crafted, intricate, and suspenseful. For readers who want more from their princesses than sumptuous clothes and first kisses."   —*BCCB*

"One part political drama, one part mystery, and one part fairy tale, all included in a very fun read."   —*TeensReadToo.com*

The Princess Trap

KIRSTEN BOIE

TRANSLATED BY DAVID HENRY WILSON

Chicken House

SCHOLASTIC INC.

NEW YORK   TORONTO   LONDON   AUCKLAND

SYDNEY   MEXICO CITY   NEW DELHI   HONG KONG

Original text copyright © 2007 by Verlag Friedrich Oetinger
English translation copyright © 2009 by David Henry Wilson

All rights reserved. Published by Scholastic Inc. Originally published in hardcover in 2010 by Chicken House, an imprint of Scholastic Inc. SCHOLASTIC, CHICKEN HOUSE, and associated logos are trademarks and/or registered trademarks of Scholastic Inc. www.scholastic.com

ISBN 978-0-545-22262-4

12 11 10 9 8 7 6 5 4 3 2 1   12 13 14 15 16 17/0

Printed in the U.S.A.   40
This edition first printing, June 2012

The text type was set in Lino Letter.
The display type was set in Marketing Script.
Book design by Becky Terhune and Kristina Iulo

The
Princess Trap

PROLOGUE

Scandia was celebrating.

Flags fluttered over the palace, and crowds of people clustered around the stalls and booths lining the boulevard.

"To the king!" they cried, raising their glasses. "To Scandia, united at last! And to a future full of joy and justice for all!"

Children of all backgrounds were playing in the palace park, which had been opened to the public for the first time in the country's history. Balloons of all colors, dangling messages of goodwill, rose high in the sky, while music blared from loudspeakers up in the trees. Small boys and girls twisted and turned to the tunes, oblivious to everything around them, while older children played ball games on the lawns, yelling at the tops of their lungs and getting grass stains on their best clothes, though today their mothers didn't seem to mind.

In the midst of the throng stood King Magnus and his sister, Margareta. They shook hands, smiled, and exchanged friendly words with the crowd, while their bodyguards kept a respectful distance. The two princesses — Malena, tall with short blonde hair, and Jenna, brunette and smaller — had separated from them, and were happily waving to people and laughing as children plucked at their skirts or nudged them with their elbows so that they could later say they'd touched royalty. The two girls hummed along with the music from the loudspeakers, and graciously accepted bouquets of flowers, which they then discreetly passed on to their bodyguards.

Just a few paces away walked a dark-haired boy, his eyes always fixed on the smaller of the two girls as she acknowledged the cheers.

"Isn't it wonderful!" whispered a woman, her head bent over a paper plate on which she was balancing a frankfurter while trying not to spill ketchup over her dress. "Who would ever have thought things would turn out so well after we saw the king go to his grave less than a year ago!"

Her husband skillfully turned over some more franks on a portable barbecue, and took a bottle out of the well-worn cooler he'd put down on the grass beside him.

"When we *thought* we'd seen the king go to his grave!" he said. "Good to see how happy the little princesses are now, after all they've been through. But you're right: Who'd have thought it?"

The woman stuck the rest of her hot dog in her mouth, looked furtively around to see if anyone was watching, and then quickly licked her fingers. "Is there another one ready?"

she asked. "Thank you. And north and south united! Justice at last for the northerners!"

Her husband passed her the ketchup. "Some people won't be too happy about the election results," he said. "In fact, some people are going to be very unhappy. They think there are far too many northerners in the government now."

"Who cares what they think?" the woman said. "There are more northerners in Scandia than southerners, so we've just got to get used to it. As our king keeps telling us, we in the south must learn to share our wealth. And now you can see just how happy the country is."

The man pursed his lips. "Let's hope so," he said skeptically. "Let's just hope so."

Some distance away from the hustle and bustle, standing in the shade of the tall old cedar trees, a group of men in elegant suits and uniforms gazed out thoughtfully over the lawn as the king came toward them.

"To the happiness of our country!" they said, raising their glasses to the king. "And to our entry at last into the family of free, democratic nations. Long live King Magnus! Long live Princess Margareta! Long live the two princesses!"

"And long live the great and the good of Scandia," said the king, also raising his glass, "who have so courageously supported these reforms." Then he turned once more to the crowd and waved them a swift good-bye.

The men watched him go, and no one noticed the wary

glances they cast behind his back as they spoke to one another in lowered voices.

The two princesses would have been the last to notice such things anyway. In their billowing dresses they raced across the lawn, almost delirious with joy; they linked arms and laughed and waved to the right and the left, and they thought nothing could go wrong.

PART ONE

1

As soon as the alarm went off on his cell phone, Jonas was alert. There was no moment of transition, no gray area between asleep and awake, no recollection of a dream.

Almost noiselessly, he swung his legs out of the bed and put on his track pants. Sneakers in hand, he tiptoed to the French door that opened out onto the spiral fire escape. One of his roommates turned over with a soft sigh, and Jonas froze for a second. They still had exactly forty-five minutes' sleep left, and the others would kill him if he robbed them of it.

The cold metal steps beneath his bare feet still came as a shock. *But it's getting easier*, thought Jonas as he reached the last step and stooped to put on his sneakers. *These days I'd feel there was something missing from my life if I didn't go running before school.*

Jonas had the world to himself. The air was pure, with the last streaks of morning mist rising knee-high above the wide lawn, behind which stretched the forest. The first wispy clouds seemed to be hanging motionless in the sky, and although the sun's light was still glassy, almost cool, he could already sense the dawning heat.

He covered the first quarter mile with long strides, pumping his arms in wide circles so that his whole body felt alive; then he began a slow trot. Behind the boys' wing, the grass sloped gently down over several hundred yards into the valley, where it came to an end as it reached the dense forest. For a few seconds every morning, Jonas stopped to enjoy the view: The forest was dark and endless, but farther off the landscape was dotted with occasional summer-green fields and red-roofed farmhouses, which shone in the morning light. There were lakes, too, large and small, whose surfaces now glittered in the sun. And on the horizon, a yellow-gray haze that hardly ever dispersed, behind which lay the capital and the sea.

Scandia is beautiful, he thought, and began to run a bit faster. *Scandia is never so beautiful as it is first thing in the morning.* Then he stopped himself. *For goodness' sake, Jonas, focus!* he thought. *Stop with the sentimental! That's the last thing you need to be right now.*

He pushed himself a bit harder, his springy steps making tiny squelching noises as he ran over the damp grass. He estimated that he was moving faster than on the previous day, and he felt as fresh as if he had only just started out. *I'm improving*, he thought. *Every day. Next time I speak to my dad, I've got to tell him. Liron always says it's important that I be prepared at all times. He can only mean by getting fit, by keeping my eyes open. Well, I'm certainly doing that, and how else can I prepare except by training?*

He finally reached the edge of the forest, and started out along the narrow, shadowy path that led through the trees and around the school campus. The security fence was concealed behind the thick foliage, as were the guard posts, which had been doubled since Jenna had arrived almost a year ago. If he had not already known about them, he could have thought there was no one else around for miles.

Last summer, as they had driven to the school, Liron had talked to him about what would happen to the country now that the king had been returned to power. Jonas had been surprised when, halfway into the journey, his father had suddenly swung the car sharply to the right and brought it to a standstill on the sandy shoulder of the road.

"Don't imagine that it's all over now, Jonas," Liron had told him, turning off the engine so that there was no sound other than his voice and the roar of passing cars. "Don't assume that we're going to live happily ever after just because the good king is back. It's only been eight weeks since he was rescued. And this is no fairy tale."

Jonas had waited, realizing why his father had insisted on driving him to the boarding school himself, without a chauffeur or bodyguards. It wouldn't have been wise to let them overhear such a conversation. On the blacktop, trucks thundered past, together with a stream of well-polished family sedans out on weekend excursions.

"You must always be prepared, Jonas," Liron had said. "Just because you can go back to school now and it looks as if the world's been put right — or is about to be — that doesn't mean we can relax. We have to be on our guard at all times."

And then at last he explained to Jonas what he should have told him weeks ago: that the threats to Scandian unity weren't over yet.

"The king is getting across his message about equal rights for north and south," he said. "Reform will come. Even the southerners can see they stand to gain by it. And, thanks to you and Jenna and Malena, the immediate crisis is over. But the greedy rich southerners who backed Norlin and helped kidnap the king are still here, and they're still just as anxious to destabilize the country."

"But why?" Jonas asked. "And who?"

"If we knew that, I'd feel a lot safer," Liron answered, and turned on the ignition again to make his way back into the traffic. "I'm going to try to find out. There are a few clues, but not enough. That's why I keep telling you to be prepared. Anything can happen at any time, and as my son . . ."

"What happened to Bolström and Norlin?" Jonas had said.

"They're in exile somewhere in South America."

"And the rebels?"

"Nahira has sent them all home."

"What about Jenna?" Jonas asked, and felt a blush rising all the way up his neck.

Near them on the road, the exhaust from a tractor-trailer belched out thick gray clouds, and Liron closed the windows. "Jenna," he said. "Yes. That's the only reason I'm happy she's going to the same school. Keep an eye on her, Jonas."

Jonas nodded. The road led upward, and around the next bend they would be able to see the school.

"Why are you telling me this now?" asked Jonas. "Why didn't you tell me before? Why did you let me go on thinking that everything was going to be OK once the king was free again?"

"I never had the chance. It was hard enough borrowing the cook's car to drive you here so we could talk safely. I had to tell her I fell for a girl years ago in exactly this model car — I saw someone use that as a reason in a movie once! The cook's car won't be bugged, you see, Jonas, so we're safe. But where else could we be sure that every word isn't reaching ears that we don't want overhearing us?"

Liron had not taken his eyes off the road. "Listen very carefully to what I'm going to say now, Jonas, because I shan't be able to repeat it. You mustn't tell anyone, and maybe what I'm about to do is crazy." He said nothing for a moment. "But just in case anything should happen to me . . ."

They had reached the top of the hill, and the green countryside stretched far and wide before them; they could already see the gate, with the flag of Morgard flying. "Listen carefully. But don't tell anyone!"

"But why . . . ?" Jonas had asked.

"If something happens to me, just think about these three questions," Liron persisted. "One: What came three years after the kingdom of Scandia conquered North Island?"

"What are you talking about?" asked Jonas. "Are you giving me a history lesson now?"

"Just think about these questions if something happens to me," Liron repeated. "OK? Number two: Which was the highest building in Scandia for a long time, and why?"

"So it *is* a history lesson!" said Jonas. "Dad! You may as well just tell me now . . ."

Liron put the car into a lower gear. "And the last question is: What have dwarfs and wonders got in common?"

"Dwarfs and wonders?" repeated Jonas. "You cannot be serious! Does this have to do with fairy tales or something?"

Liron smiled. They were almost at the school gates, and Jonas knew he was not going to get any more information out of his dad. "Don't forget the questions!" was all Liron said.

They had reached the school, and Jonas had spent the rest of the trip in silence. After the liberation battle in Saarstad, he had really thought it was all over, and that they had won — for good. How stupid he'd been.

Or maybe he hadn't.

Jonas was now running at a steady pace through the forest. *That conversation was more than six months ago*, he thought, *and nothing bad has happened since then.* He was beginning to think that Liron had been paranoid, imagining another plot. Besides, his father never actually said a word about *how* he should prepare, or *what* he should prepare for — nothing except that he had to remember those three crazy questions!

For a few yards, the path through the trees ran close to the security fence, and between the trunks Jonas could see barbed wire stretched above the outward-leaning spikes. Then he was back again in the depths of the forest.

Dad has spent most of his life living in fear, and he sees ghosts around every corner, Jonas mused. *But nothing bad has happened recently. The elections have come and gone. We have members of parliament from north and south. The new government has started passing laws to make things fairer, and he'll soon get everything he's ever fought for. Anyway, he hasn't said another word about it since that conversation. So maybe everything's all right now. Maybe there's no need for me to get up at the crack of dawn every day to go running.*

Jonas could see the school lake shimmering through the trees. He upped the pace for the homestretch. As he came closer, the whole campus lay before him: the main building behind the lake, with the girls' wing to the right and the boys' to the left, the tennis courts, lacrosse and football fields, the track, and the 25-meter swimming pool. Through the open windows on the ground floor came the sound of cutlery on china, as the first students sat down to breakfast in the cafeteria.

Outside the boys' wing, he put his hands on his knees and breathed deeply. *Come on, admit it,* he thought. *You're not just training for Dad. If you were, you'd have started right back in the autumn after he gave you that warning, not waited till the spring. So admit why you really get up and go for a run so early. Can't you be honest, at least with yourself?*

Jenna.

Why shouldn't he keep an eye on her? Liron said he should. And Jonas knew she sometimes went running before breakfast. He'd heard the other girls sneering about how she was trying to get rid of her "northern fat."

He went through the front entrance of the building. He was breathing easily now, so maybe he should increase the distance tomorrow. All the corridors were buzzing with life, voices, laughter. If he was late, Perry would save a place for him in the cafeteria.

Jenna. He thought about her again, and was shocked at the effect her name had on him.

2

The midday sun blazed high above the suburban gardens — already way too hot for early June. Heavy-headed roses hung limply from their bushes, and only heavy-duty watering in the evening could prevent them from withering on the branch. Jasmine and hawthorn poured out their scents all across the yellowed patches of parched lawn.

"Don't be such a girl!" said Bea. "If you insist on whining *sans cesse* about how all things princess are forever stressing you, then just jail-break out the window with me already! Let's be, like, *normal* for a whole afternoon, without your body-guards breathing down our necks."

"What do you mean, 'whining *sans cesse*'? And I don't need a translation!" Jenna replied. She flung herself down on Bea's bed. "I only just got here yesterday!"

"Yes, but ever since you arrived it's complain, complain, complain!" said Bea, opening the window. "Whoa. It. Is. Hot! Look, I was superpsyched when you texted that you were coming to visit, but now all I get is . . . Let's just say it rhymes with *itch*, 'kay? So c'mon, let us blow this proverbial Popsicle stand, shall we? Climb out the window, sneak off through the backyard — we'll be over the fence in under a minute and your designated goons will be none the wiser. Are you ready to make your own rules, Your Royal Highness? Or do you want to be a good girl? In which case, here's *my* ruling: No more moaning!"

Jenna sat up and smiled. She was already warm enough on the outside in the early summer heat wave, and now she was starting to get a warm feeling on the inside, too.

"Oh, how you've changed — not!" she said, and for a moment it seemed as if maybe her old life was still ready and waiting for her, or at least some small part of it. "Remember how you used to nag me? *'Your mom's a nervous wreck. You just have to train her right. She's practically packed you in bubble wrap.'* Remember, Bea? You were so on my case!"

"Hello, back then I didn't know *why* your mom was always so freaked out," said Bea. "Now I do. Anyway, stop wallowing in the past. We can stroll down memory lane in our orthopedic platforms when we're blue-haired and eighty. But today"— she leaned so far out the window that Jenna jumped up in fright —"carpe diem, girl! As predicted, the coast is clear. Let's outie!"

Jenna laughed. *Bea's still Bea,* she thought, *and, more important, we're still besties; nothing's changed between us.* It had taken Jenna a long time to persuade her mom to let her come and stay with Bea once they'd finished their tour of Scandia.

"All right," Jenna answered, looking up at her friend, "let's!"

Bea hoisted herself onto the windowsill and dangled her feet toward the drainpipe. "Good thing I got an A in PE!" she said. "This jump will be beyond easy. You know, I always wanted to do this. Climb out a window and into the world! Just like in that old movie — what was it called? Or one of those storybooks I used to love when I was ten . . . ack!"

Jenna rushed to the window and looked down into the flower bed, aghast.

"Oww-M-G!" Bea exclaimed, grimacing as she rubbed her arm. "It's not that far a fall, just make sure you don't land in the roses!" Even from up above, Jenna could see the thin red scratches on her skin. "I'll be scarred for life!" Bea declared dramatically as she plucked a thorn out of the palm of her hand.

Jenna knelt on the windowsill and reached for the drainpipe. *No, it's not very high at all,* she thought. *Not like the balcony at Osterlin that I jumped from last summer, with rabid dogs at my heels. This, by comparison, is a piece of cake.* She launched herself from the window and landed on her feet.

"Ta-da!" Jenna said, bowing to Bea. "Yikes — you *are* a mess!"

Bea tapped her forehead (she always tapped her forehead, even back in the day) and made straight for the hedge that ran all around the little garden, concealing the wire-mesh fence behind it. "You all right?" she asked over her shoulder.

"But of course!" Jenna whispered, following close behind.

Once she was standing in the narrow road on the other side of the fence, brushing the leaves out of her hair with her fingers, she was suddenly overcome with a feeling of lightness and joy that she hadn't experienced for weeks on end. *Now it really is like it was before*, she thought. *At least for one afternoon — no hat, no sunglasses, no disguise, no alias, no gorillas watching every move I make.*

She'd been majorly looking forward to these two days. For weeks she'd thought of nothing else — and her countdown kept her going, every morning when she'd wake up to face disdainful looks from Ylva, and every school period when she'd enter a classroom to the sound of stone-cold silence. As she fell asleep each night, Jenna would picture Bea's house, Bea's room, dinner with Bea's parents. Everything, she imagined, would be exactly as it had always been.

But of course it wasn't. Instead of having dinner in Bea's cozy, cluttered kitchen, Jenna had to go to a banquet that her old school held in her honor. They'd even invited the press, and suddenly everyone had become either remarkably shy or unnaturally chummy: *Hi there, Jenna, back to see how the other half lives?* Wink, wink, nudge, nudge. No matter where she went, they pushed and jostled around her, and she pretended not to notice that every single one of them made sure they got a photo with her: Philippa and Jenna; Britt and Jenna; Eva and Jenna . . .

No, nothing, absolutely nothing, was the same as before, when shy, boring little Jenna could disappear into the crowd and drop the fixed smile. *I'm definitely not dull and conventional anymore,* she thought. *Those days are so over.* So why wasn't she happy that everything had changed? Why wasn't she proud?

At least Bea remained the same.

"Where shall we go?"

"Pizza?" Bea suggested. "Bet you don't get much deep dish up there on your 'lonely island.'"

"Seriously!" said Jenna.

The little six-seater glided across the blue summer sky, heading north; no clouds above, and a clear view of the open sea below.

"I shouldn't have let her go by herself, Peter!" fretted Jenna's mother, her face still turned to the window. Her blonde hair was elegantly coiffed and her deceptively simple dress was, in fact, expensive enough to feed a North Island family for several months. "It's not safe! And it's not suitable. She's got to learn—"

"Margareta!" Peter Petterson interjected, taking off his jacket. Jenna's mother's new boyfriend, a wealthy South Scandian lord, was growing exasperated. He tossed the jacket over the two seats behind him, then loosened his silk ascot and undid the top three buttons of his shirt. "Our people are with her twenty-four hours a day. You've yet to get over your fears for Jenna, and I can understand that — you spent so many, too many, years in hiding — but what could possibly happen to her now?"

Margareta didn't answer, just looked down over the sea. Ahead she could see the shore of South Island, just a black line at the moment. The flight to Scandia was short — even in this little plane, the journey took barely two hours. In a few minutes they would be descending over the lakes and forests. Margareta felt a warm glow in her heart: She had yearned for so long to return to Scandia that even now, almost a year since she'd come out of exile, she still felt a surge of pleasure every time she approached her country from the south. She was back. She was home.

"Jenna's got to learn that her life is different now," she said at last, turning to look at her companion for the first time. "Yes, Bea was important to her while we were living there, and I'm not saying she should just cut herself off from her completely, but a close friendship with someone like . . . like that . . . just isn't appropriate anymore. There are plenty of other girls at her boarding school for her to make friends with, aren't there? She's not making enough of an effort to adapt to her new position, Peter. You have to keep in mind —"

"Margareta." Petterson leaned over to give her a quick peck on the cheek. "Give the girl some time. You've got to remember that she grew up there — it's home to her just as Scandia is home to you. You longed for years to be back in Scandia, but for her it's the other way around. And just as you couldn't forget your earlier life, she can't forget hers."

Margareta leaned back, angry. "There's no comparison!" she snapped. "I gave up my comfortable life in the palace for one of poverty and insecurity! But Jenna has a privileged life now. Sometimes I get the feeling that she doesn't understand the responsibilities that go with it."

"Now, now," said Peter, placing his hand on her knee. "That's all fine and well, but you can easily feel like a stranger in a new place, however luxurious your way of life. You didn't have many close friends back there, did you? Because your heart was always here in Scandia. Unfamiliar situations make people long for the world they know, and why should Jenna be any different?" He smiled. "Anyway, I'm glad I decided to fly back with you, Greta. You obviously need some cheering up. Business can wait."

"Oh, Peter!" Margareta sighed. "I'm not just afraid for Jenna — it's not simply because something might happen to her. I'm worried that *she* might do something that would be bad for her — and for us."

"Us?" he asked, furrowing his brow. "What sort of something would that be?"

The sound of the engines suddenly changed, and Jenna's mother looked out the window again at the forests of Scandia, the dense, dark forests, broken here and there by the glint of sunlit lakes. Soon they would be landing.

"Particularly now," she muttered, "when things are getting difficult again. With the press already turning against us . . . We've talked about it often enough."

Petterson laughed. "Do you really think that whatever Jenna does or doesn't do will make any difference? That the escapades of a teenager, still scarcely more than a child, are going to affect world history? Methinks you might be imagining things!"

"They've already done it once," Margareta murmured. "If it hadn't been for Jenna, Norlin would now be on the throne, and the north would not be free. I've learned not to underestimate children, Peter."

Petterson said nothing. They heard the wheels release and click into position; the runway lights were almost directly below. Not long now and he'd be able to have a cigarette.

"She'll be back tonight, anyway," he said. "For goodness' sake, Greta, as if there isn't enough to worry about in this country of ours, all you can think of is your daughter!"

The wheels hit the concrete as the plane touched down.

"Whereas you . . ." Margareta paused. "As far as I'm concerned, you don't talk enough about your son." She was sitting very upright now.

Lord Petterson sighed. "We're home" was all he said.

The pizza place was just off the main road, at a spot that trucks had to pass on their way to the nearest highway entrance ramp.

"Seriously?" Jenna said again. "Here?"

"It's not as bad as it looks. Let's go in and sit down," Bea answered. "It just reopened and the food's good. You're thinking of the dump that was here before. The Health Department shut them down for violations — ugh, now *that* be nasty!"

Large square awnings with the logo of the pizza chain threw shadows over little wooden tables; the cushions on the seats looked clean; and terra-cotta pots with shiny green plants separated the entrance from the dining area, almost giving it the atmosphere of a bistro.

"Well, if you say so," said Jenna. "Where's the menu?"

A man came out from behind the counter and headed toward them — he was probably in his midthirties and had dark olive skin. *I used to wonder about my own ethnic background,* Jenna thought, *because of my darker skin tone and Mom's refusal to tell me who my father was. The truth ended up being way more complicated than I ever could have imagined . . .*

"The menu," the waiter said with a friendly smile, and handed one to each of the girls. "Have you decided what you would like to drink?"

"Can you give us a few minutes?" Bea asked.

The man smiled again and left. At a neighboring table, a heavyset customer waved his hand to indicate that he wanted to pay. *Truck driver,* thought Jenna. She looked back at the menu.

"Um, yay? And yum! They've got four-cheese pizza," she said. "Do you know how long it's been since I had one of those?"

"Frankly, darling, there's not much I *do* know about you since you started moving up in the world!" said Bea. "In case you haven't noticed, you've yet to actually download much info."

"There's always so much to do!" Jenna began. "For real, you cannot imagine . . ."

The waiter returned, holding a small notepad. "Ready to order?" he asked.

"The four-cheese pizza," said Jenna, "with a Diet Coke, please."

"The Cobb salad," said Bea, "and a chai iced tea." Then she looked disapprovingly across the table at Jenna. "Your skinny Coke won't make up for the other ten thousand calories, you know. Four-cheese pizza! The only person I know who eats that is my dad!"

"Don't even, because I'll be fat no matter what I eat," said Jenna, and pressed the flat of her hand against her stomach. "As you can see."

"You are not fat now, you were not fat then, you are not fat, period!" Bea said with exasperation. "I thought that by now you might be over all your neuroses, Jenna. Or have you forgotten that it was you they cast in the movie?"

"Oh, please," Jenna said. "That whole thing was just a scam, and you know it."

Bea shrugged. "Fine, whatevs! Anyway, come on, spill. I'm dying of curiosity. Life as a princess? Tell me already! Then, afterward, I'll treat you to dessert — an ice-cream cone."

Jenna giggled. "An ice-cream cone? My hero! Thank you so much for riding to my rescue in the battle against the bulge!"

Al Patel, manager and currently sole waiter of Pizza Heaven, looked out through the spotlessly clean window. Only two of the tables were occupied, one by a man on his own, the other by two girls. *Business is slow*, he thought. *Maybe I'll give the girls dessert on the house. If they're happy and they tell their friends about the place, sales might pick up. The school isn't far away.*

He went out and put the drinks on the table.

"The food will be ready in a moment," he said. "The chef always makes the salads fresh, so it might take a little longer."

"That's cool, no worries," said Bea. Al smiled at the girl. She was slim and blonde and could have got herself hired by any lucky modeling agency. The other girl was curvier, and looked familiar somehow. She stopped talking to her friend and simply smiled at him. Where had he seen her before?

Al went back into the kitchen, where the chef was cutting up tomatoes and cucumbers for the salad, and adding a few olives. The pizza was baking in the oven.

"Take a look through the door for a second, will you?" Al asked him. "Has the shorter one been here before?" He pointed outside. "The dark-haired girl? Her face looks familiar. Think we've got our first regulars?" His heart beat a little faster at the thought.

The chef at Pizza Heaven had stopped chopping the salad

and was standing motionless, staring at the two girls through the window, his knife in midair.

"I've definitely seen her before!" he said. "And just recently. But it wasn't here . . ." He put down his knife and, with trembling fingers, leafed through the daily paper. "Look! If I'm not mistaken, we have a princess sitting in our restaurant!"

3

*A*l looked at the newspaper photo of the dark-haired girl. Then he left the kitchen, carrying the salad, and put it down on the table with the pizza in front of the girl, smiling straight at her. Once again she stopped in midsentence. It seemed as if she was the one doing all the talking. Her friend was just listening, apart from asking the occasional question.

It is *her*, he thought as he went back to the kitchen. He glanced again at the photo. But was it really possible? Could a princess just wander in off the street and eat pizza at one of *his* tables? Princesses didn't eat pizza. At least not in public. And a princess wouldn't be caught dead in an average little place like his.

"Al!" The chef beckoned him excitedly. He had just opened the latest issue of *People* magazine, bought for customers.

"Look, she's in here, too! It's got to be her! 'Princess Jenna of Scandia.' And it says she was actually here yesterday, visiting her old school . . ."

"But why doesn't she have any bodyguards?" said Al. "Surely a princess wouldn't just go off on her own?"

The chef shrugged. "I'm not saying I know *why* she's here," he said. "I'm just saying *that* she's here."

The customer at the other table was waving his wallet impatiently. "I'll go and get his check," said Al, "and then I'll talk to her. I can at least say hello, right? Maybe she'll let us take a photo of her in the restaurant — and then one of her with the two of us."

"I've got a better idea," whispered the chef, turning to the telephone mounted on the wall in the kitchen. He flicked quickly to the masthead of the paper. "Here. Call the news desk."

"Hey!" shouted the man at the table. "You having a party or what? I've got to get going!"

Al hurried outside. They couldn't afford to offend a customer. By the time he reached the table, his face was wearing a smile once more. "I'm so sorry, sir, I didn't realize you were waiting," he said.

The man flapped his hand in annoyance. "Typical!" he said, pulling a bill out of his wallet.

The girls at the neighboring table were in animated conversation. The pizza lay untouched on the plate, and must have gone cold by now. *It is her*, Al thought again. The man didn't tip him. *It's definitely her. If Chef is right, it'll be such good publicity* . . .

As he passed, he smiled at the girls. What a lucky break!

"I mean, most people would think being a princess was totally cool," Jenna was saying wearily, sipping her Coke. "I thought so, too, at the beginning. *Princess Jenna of Scandia*. And I'd helped uncover the plot and free the king . . ."

"Just like in a movie!" said Bea. "My dad said no one would believe something like that could happen in real life. There you were, pigging out at our place year after year . . ."

"Thanks!" said Jenna, giggling. But it was pretty much true. Some of the best times she'd had in her life were dinners at Bea's.

". . . and you were always so shy that we could hardly get a word out of you, while your *mom* was the snootiest, craziest mother ever . . ."

"Mom's not snooty!" said Jenna. They'd had this conversation over and over in the old days. Why couldn't Bea just drop it already?

"Well, that's the impression she always gave," Bea said. "All that silly etiquette business, and you never being allowed to do *anything*, and always having to be home by six!"

"Because she was afraid someone might kidnap me!" Jenna tried to explain for the umpteenth time. "Because I happen to be the daughter of Princess Margareta of Scandia, even though none of us knew it back then. They could have used me to blackmail the king!"

"Don't get all defensive. I know the whole story," said Bea. "I'm just saying, you weren't the most exciting girl in the world, were you? But now all of a sudden you're a princess. Like I said: Hollywood movie."

Jenna looked down at her congealing pizza. Suddenly she wasn't sure that she wanted anything to eat.

"So?" asked Bea. "Is it really like that? Like a movie, I mean?"

Jenna attempted a forkful of pizza. The cheese was cold and claggy. It stuck to the roof of her mouth. She should have ordered a salad instead, like Bea.

"Honestly?" she said, putting down her knife and fork. "It's not like that at all. I mean, I'm still me, Bea. But my life has done a total one-eighty. It's totally different."

"Well, give *me* a gig as a princess and *I* wouldn't complain," said Bea. She'd almost finished her salad.

Jenna shook her head. "It's not as nice as you think. You're never alone, for one thing — there are always bodyguards with you. And the cameras! I'm supposed to smile and be on my best behavior all the time, polite and 'dressed appropriately.' Because if I'm not, you can bet it'll be in all the papers and all over the web. Everybody's interested in me, everybody wants to talk to me, to be photographed with me so they can pretend they know me."

"I guess you can't blame them," said Bea. "Take me, for example. It's all I talk about most of the time. 'By the way,' I say, 'Princess Jenna of Scandia just happens to be my best friend.' My cred has gone through the roof at school. Not to mention everywhere else."

"You know I don't mean you, Bea! Why do you think I was so desperate to come see you? Because you always were my best friend."

"Were?"

"Still are, I hope. I know you like me for me, for who I was pre-princess, and not because you can show me off. Everyone else only seems to like me because I'm, you know . . . royalty."

"Like the poor little rich girls in TV movies," said Bea, "never sure if a guy is in love with them — or their money."

"Something like that," Jenna agreed. And if she really wanted to be honest with Bea, she'd tell her it was worse. No one even wanted to be friends with Jenna the princess. "And it'll be the same if *I* ever fall in love with someone." She felt herself turning red. The tabloids had already picked up on that. How sweet — a princess who blushes on cue! Nobody wanted to read things like that about themselves. Or comments about how they came across in public. "Princess Jenna, Still the Ugly Duckling." "Princess Jenna Looking Helpless at State Reception." After too many headlines like those, she stopped looking at the papers, but that didn't keep the other girls at school from reading them — and then ripping out the articles and leaving them spread across her bed.

"Excuse me, Your Highness?" Bea broke into her thoughts. "Is there something — or some*one* — I should know?"

"What are you talking about?" Jenna asked distractedly.

"Boys!" said Bea. "You're very quiet all of a sudden. Is

there a prince for the princess?" She giggled. "'And will they live happily ever after?'" she pronounced dramatically. "Sorry, Jenna, I couldn't resist! But that guy who came to our place last year with you and Malena — he was kind of cute."

"Jonas," said Jenna, feeling herself turning a deeper shade of red. "He's been Malena's friend forever — since they were in kindergarten."

"How unfortunate," said Bea. "I thought he had hottie potential. But I guess cousins can't go stealing each other's boyfriends, can they?"

"No," she acknowledged, neglecting to add, *As if someone who can have Malena would want me instead.*

"Anyway, you'll probably have plenty of guys to choose from," said Bea. "That's how it is with royalty, isn't it? You can have a prince, you can have a millionaire, you can have a movie star, you can even have a boring old nobody, if that's what you want. Not like me." She rolled her eyes up to the heavens. "*I'll* probably end up with a boy who plays accordion in a klezmer band."

"Poor you!" said Jenna, laughing. "Oh, why do I have to go back tonight?" The thought made her feel slightly sick.

"Can't you change your schedule?" asked Bea. "Stay another day. Two or three, even."

Jenna shook her head. "The day after tomorrow is this big summer party," she said gloomily. "Thrown by the family of the girl I share a room with — Ylva."

"But do you really have to go?" asked Bea. "Wouldn't she give you a pass?"

Jenna pushed her plate away. She'd eaten almost nothing — meaning fewer calories, at least: Every cloud had a silver lining. "Ylva couldn't care less whether I was there," she said. "But her father's very high up in the army — a general or something, I don't know."

"And that's why you have to go?" asked Bea, puzzled. "What does the military have to do with you?"

Jenna shrugged and picked up a slice of pizza. She gave it an angry bite. "It's because of the press," she mumbled. She took another mouthful. "Newspapers, TV, they're all going to be there, and it'll be shown all over Scandia — 'the social event of the season.' So I have to be there. It's called 'making an appearance,' which is what I have to do all the time." She bit into the pizza again. A string of melted cheese trailed down her chin. It tasted awful. Everything was awful. She didn't want to go back to the palace.

"Oh, Jen!" said Bea, and put her hand on Jenna's arm as if to comfort her and to stop her from shoveling any more food into her mouth at the same time.

At that moment, Jenna heard the *click!* of a shutter. A man was leaning out the window of a black SUV that had stopped at the traffic light. He was taking photo after photo. On the door of the SUV was the logo of the local newspaper.

"Oh no!" Jenna cried, raising her hands to hide her face. "Not again!"

4

O*n Saturdays,* school in Morgard went until noon, but then, thankfully, everyone was free for the rest of the weekend. Saturday classes were less demanding, too — just a couple of hours of art and the weekly check-in with the guidance counselors.

Jenna was awake long before the first beep of the alarm clock. She'd been tracing all the cracks in the ceiling with her eyes, and silently reciting the words of every nursery rhyme she could remember. Anything to stop herself from thinking.

When she'd flown back to Scandia the previous evening, she finally had to face the fact that her earlier life was gone forever. Even if she climbed out the window and escaped from her bodyguards, there would always be someone who would track her down or recognize her. *A princess belongs to everyone, Jenna,* her mother had said when she'd first complained that she couldn't do anything or go anywhere on her own. *That's the price you pay.*

"Just put a wig on!" Malena had said. "And a pair of sunglasses. A hat. All the celebs do it. No big deal."

But Malena had been a princess all her life. She didn't know what it was like to sit and daydream in a coffee shop, undisturbed for hours; or to be in a bad mood and bite your friend's head off in public without all the newspapers turning it into an international crisis the next day; or even to burst into tears if you felt like it — because you could, because you belonged to yourself, not to the press and not to the crown and not to the entire country.

In the opposite bed, Ylva wriggled out from under her blankets, yawned, then grabbed her plastic bucket of toiletries and headed out to the showers.

Jenna kept her eyes closed. She would only get up when Ylva left for breakfast in the cafeteria. She couldn't bear the sneer on her roommate's face when she went to the door in her nightshirt, or the snide remarks spoken softly enough to seem as if they weren't meant to be heard: *Northern blubber, bounce like rubber* . . .

A few weeks ago, Jenna had started to starve herself so that she could at last become more like a southerner, slim and graceful. She soon gave up, though, when she realized she'd have to bleach her hair blonde as well, and wear high heels all the time to make herself seem taller.

Jenna looked across at Ylva's bed. When she'd first come to the boarding school nearly a year ago, no one had been nicer. Ylva had even blown off her own best friend in order to share a room with her. So why hadn't it worked out? Why was there no one in the whole school who hated her more than Ylva?

It's because I'm not what she expected. I'm not remotely glamorous enough — not even close.

She looked at the photos on the wall above her bed, tightly packed together: Jenna with Philippa, sitting on the back of a bench with their feet on the seat, each with an ice-cream cone in her hand. She was sticking her tongue out at Philippa's mom, who was taking the picture. Another one of her at ten years old, with the neighbors' dog, which was almost blind and had a funny smell, but which she loved so much that, when it died, she couldn't stop crying all day long. Another with Bea in a photo booth, having photos taken for her passport — she'd only needed one, so they'd made funny faces on the other three.

Jenna took down another photo of Bea. She was in her back-yard, on the hammock in her bathing suit, drenched, laughing and raising her fist in mock anger. She was pretending to rage at Jenna for dousing her with the garden hose. *Oh, Bea!* thought Jenna. *If only I could come back and stay with you!*

The door was flung open and in came Ylva, fresh from her shower. Her long blonde hair hung in wet strands over her shoulders, leaving a trail of drops across the wooden floorboards.

"Sorry, am I disturbing you?" she said mockingly. "On an imaginary date, are we?"

Jenna looked down. It would make no difference whatever she said, and so she said nothing.

"Poor little mousey!" said Ylva. "Crying for her girlfriend."

She put on her school blouse, the pleated skirt, and the blazer. Her hair was still dripping. When she had slammed the door shut behind her, Jenna put the photo down on the bedspread and slowly lowered her feet to the floor.

The banquet hall at Osterlin was far too big for just two people.

"Have you seen this, Peter?" cried Margareta, passing the newspaper across the table. They were sitting together at one end. There was room for at least thirty more people on each of the long sides. A page fluttered down into the basket of rolls, and one corner stuck in the jar of honey. "A whole page attacking Jenna!"

Since she'd returned to Scandia, Margareta had made it a habit to read the newspapers over breakfast, or at least skim through them and weed out the important parts. And now Peter was here with her, doing the same thing. They had so much in common. It hadn't been easy to go back to Scandia after all those years in exile, but falling in love had made it so much better. It had been her brother who had introduced her to the wealthy lord, and they'd hit it off right away.

"Just look at this photo! When I phoned her yesterday after she'd got back to school, Jenna didn't even mention it! Now I know why."

"I'm afraid it's everywhere, Greta," said Petterson. "Look.

'Roly-Poly Princess Goes Abroad to Pig Out.' 'Princess Jenna in the Land of Milk and Pizza.' 'Princess Jenna: A Model for Our Young People???' With three question marks, and the same photo in all of them. It was probably the ugliest one they had."

On every front page, six columns wide and reaching down to the middle, was the same picture: Jenna, bending low — far too low — over a plate, her hair virtually hanging into it, with a trail of cheese across her chin and her mouth gaping wide. Above it, in giant letters, the headline: "The Pizza Princess!"

"Good grief," said Margareta, "the stupid girl! Doesn't she realize what she's doing to herself? To all of us?"

Peter had picked up another paper. "It's hard for her, Greta," he said. "I'm sometimes surprised at how little you understand her. To be suddenly thrust into a completely different world . . . Oh, for heaven's sake! Wretched journalists. On the front page of the *Financial Times* as well? As if our country didn't have enough problems!" He threw the paper across the table, and Margareta caught it before it landed in her coffee.

"What's the matter with our press, Peter?" asked Margareta. "In the old days they never would have —"

Petterson's phone began to trill out a song from a famous opera. He took it from his pocket and switched it off. "You know very well what's the matter, Greta" was all he said.

As she made her way down the long paneled corridor to the cafeteria, Jenna could already hear the usual morning hub-bub: laughter, the clatter of plates, the scraping of chairs.

Friendly noises, thought Jenna, *so why do they make me feel so nervous?*

She tried to open the heavy door without making a sound, so that she could slip into the room unnoticed. At breakfast, you could choose your own seat, and for weeks now she'd sat behind the waist-high partition wall with its ugly pots of flowers, in the area where the younger students sat. There she would eat her breakfast, hunched up as unobtrusively as possible, among the twelve- and thirteen-year-olds.

The door snapped shut behind her. Heads turned, and faces confronted her. In the corner farthest away from the door, by a window overlooking the campus, sat her classmates.

"Jenna!" cried Paula. Her voice sounded so friendly that Jenna had to make an effort not to trust it. "There she is at last! Come and sit with us! We've been waiting for you!"

Quiet fell at all the other tables. There was just the occasional giggle or whisper. Jenna saw that all eyes were now on her.

What's going on? she wondered apprehensively. *It's always bad, every morning, but now they're all staring at me, as if they're waiting for something. I haven't even been here for the last few days. Nothing has happened, so why are they all staring at me?*

She went around the partition wall and squeezed between the tables. If only she could find some other place to sit, not with her classmates, not with Ylva. She'd pretend she hadn't heard Paula.

"That seat is taken!" said a thin, red-haired girl when Jenna pulled a chair out from under the table. The child looked straight at her, an insolent expression on her face. "My friend's sitting there!"

"No room here, either!" screeched a girl at the next table. "My friend's sitting here, too!"

"No room, no room!" came the cry from all around, as the children patted the seats of the empty chairs. "All taken, all taken!"

The cafeteria ladies in their white aprons looked up from their pots and pans at the noise. Jenna took a deep breath. The women pretended to be counting their plates, their knives and forks, and the buffet dishes. Not so long ago, those dishes had been full of eggs and bacon, hash browns and sausages, to give the girls strength for the day ahead. But now they were empty. The women weren't going to help her.

She straightened her back and squared her shoulders. *I'm Princess Jenna of Scandia*, she thought. Slowly she made her way to the table where the rest of her class was sitting — it didn't matter if they were all watching her. It was only breakfast, and it would only take a quarter of an hour, so no need to turn it into a drama. She was just being childish.

"I kept a place just for you," said Paula with a smile, pointing to a chair beside her. "We missed you so much."

Someone giggled.

"I hope you had a nice time in your old home country," Rachel said in a chatty tone. Jenna could see right away that the only food on the table was white toast topped with thick red jam. "Stuffing yourself stupid again, Your Highness, was that it? While the rest of us were suffering here, with your friends from the north in charge of the country?" Rachel held a piece of bread with two fingers, then let it fall onto Jenna's plate. "Two weeks and nothing but this cardboard for breakfast! In the old days, not even you northerners had to eat stuff like this! Amazing how quickly a new government can ruin the whole economy!"

Jenna stared at her. *What does the new government have to do with me?* she wondered. *Just because I'm half-northern, that doesn't mean . . .*

"But at least Your Highness got a chance to carb-load for a couple of days," said Ylva. "Afraid you might get too thin, I suppose."

The younger girls at the nearby tables laughed out loud. *Now I can't even go and sit with them anymore*, thought Jenna.

"No danger of that." It was Linda this time. "Who cares if everyone else is starving, as long as the royal family can jet off and stuff their royal faces?"

Then a newspaper appeared on the table. How could Jenna have thought that the pizza photos would go no farther than Bea's town? Of course the photographer was going to make the most of his scoop — how often would he get the chance to earn so much with so little? In seconds, he had uploaded his picture and it had gone online to every newspaper desk in the world, and they'd all snapped it up — she was on display from Tokyo to New York, from London to Los Angeles.

She stared at the photo. The girl she saw looked repulsive, a portrait of greed. Grease dripped down from the pizza, no doubt touched up with the help of Photoshop. And above the picture, that headline . . .

And now the whole country's looking at it, thought Jenna. *What happened? How did it go so wrong? They loved me at the beginning, but now they're printing photos like this.*

"Oh well, at least *you* got enough to eat," said Ylva with a friendly smile. "That's the most important thing, isn't it? We can't have our princess going hungry! After all, she's so skinny, isn't she?" Then, just like Rachel had done, she held up a piece of toast and jam by her fingertips and, with a grimace, let it drop onto Jenna's plate.

Behind her, from the younger girls' table, a clear voice rang out: "Pizza Princess!" There was laughter, as if it were someone's birthday party. "Pizza Princess!" they sang.

"Come on and sit down," Paula taunted. "Or is our Scandian food no longer good enough for Your Highness?"

"Pizza Princess!"

Jenna turned and ran.

5

On the way to his room, Jonas took off his tank top. He was late, so he had to hurry. He'd thought he might bump into her today, so he'd dawdled, running extra slowly, but there'd been no sign of her. He sat on his bed, tugged off his shoes and socks, and reached for his towel. Just when he'd grabbed some fresh clothes out of the closet and tucked them under his arm, Perry came through the door.

"Man, you're late!" he said. "You'll have the showers all to yourself."

"So how come *you're* still here, Mr. Punctuality?" asked Jonas.

"Whoa, sorry. What's your problem? That time of the month?" said Perry.

"Shut up," said Jonas. "You're not exactly Joe Happy yourself. So what's *your* problem?"

Perry looked at him. "Later, Jonas, OK? We've got to get to class," he said.

"No deal," said Jonas. "I'm not moving till you tell me what's up. So spill it."

"No way," said Perry. "So hit the showers — you reek, by the way." He turned toward the closet and pulled out a clean school shirt.

"No kidding, I went for a run," Jonas answered. "But seriously, why are you acting so weird?" Then suddenly it dawned on him. "Your dad called."

"Jonas, give it a rest!" Perry snapped, and yanked his blazer off its hook. The loop at the back of the collar broke, but Perry didn't seem to notice. "Just . . . mind your own business."

"Hey, dude, I'm only trying to help," said Jonas, shuffling his feet impatiently.

Perry looked at him with a frown, as if he was thinking things over. Then he took a deep breath, and when he spoke again, his voice was almost normal.

"Dad's going to force me into the army if it's the last thing he does, *apparently*. He rants on and on about family tradition, letting the family down. But what about me, Jonas?" He angrily tried to force his arm into the sleeve of his jacket. "I really hate him sometimes. I mean, do I *look* like a soldier?"

Jonas didn't respond. Perry was short and slim, certainly no action hero. Ever since Jonas had known him, he'd been useless at sports and regularly suffered the indignity of being the last one picked for any team. And he got endless grief about it from his father as a result.

"Yeah, you'll make a good soldier," Jonas said eventually.

He really needed a shower now; the sweat was running down the back of his neck.

Perry didn't look up. "Uh-huh, right," he said. "You know I suck at sports. I've got no muscles, I've got no stamina, and I *hate* games!"

"But you're, like, a thinker! A strategist," said Jonas. "The world needs brainiacs way more than it needs musclemen."

Perry laughed. "The world, maybe!" he said. "But that doesn't include my father! Or the military academy! How do you think the other cadets are going to treat me when they're all doing their thirty push-ups and I can only manage three? I'll collapse halfway through the night marches. I'll sink in the mud. I won't be able to climb over their walls . . . What do you think is going to happen to me there? They'll . . . they'll do . . ." He thought for a moment. ". . . what the girls here do to Jenna! I won't go! I don't belong there."

He grabbed his books and was gone.

"That's it?" Jonas yelled after him. "You've been saying that forever! There's something else, isn't there, Perry?"

Silence was the only response. With a sigh, Jonas made his way to the showers. It didn't matter how late he was now. He'd definitely missed her.

Jenna had been afraid that she'd be late for class. *Pizza Princess.*

As she entered the school building, she could hear muffled sounds. Most of the doors on the ground floor were closed, except at the far end, where a little girl in a very short pleated skirt came darting out of a room, only to disappear again with a startled look as soon as she saw Jenna.

Jenna went upstairs. Art was good. You didn't have to answer questions in art — you could just keep your head down and concentrate on your own drawing or painting or whatever. The door to the studio was still open, so at least she wasn't late. She could hear laughter, but then it stopped. A single voice was talking, loud, passionate, and then there was more laughter. She stiffened her shoulders and went in.

Immediately everything went quiet. She tried not to look at anyone, although she could sense that everyone was looking at her.

She put on a couldn't-care-less expression. *I'm Princess of Scandia*, she reminded herself once more. *A hundred years ago, I could have had them all beheaded.*

She put her bag next to a vacant chair and sat down.

Patty, who was sitting on the chair next to her, leaped to her feet. "Eww!" she yelled. "Any spare seats anywhere else?"

Someone giggled. *Does eating pizza make you that disgusting?* Jenna wondered. This was getting childish.

"There's no one sitting here," said Paula. "Come and join me and Rachel."

Jenna cast her eyes around the room. Now what was up?

In front of the class, next to the teacher's desk, stood Ylva, surrounded by a group of smiling girls. They were all looking at something in Ylva's hand.

"Oh, it must have found its way into my bag somehow," said Ylva, and took a step toward Jenna. But Jenna still couldn't see what she was holding. "From your bed. Do you sleep with her, Your Highness? I know you're always kissing the glass, it's all sticky, and you keep on talking to her . . . but actually going to *bed* with her . . ."

"Ugh!" cried a voice from the crowd.

Ylva raised her hand with fingers delicately poised, as if whatever she was holding was quite disgusting. The girls stepped aside, and now Jenna could see what Ylva had been talking about — though by then she had already guessed.

"Give me the picture," she said in a hoarse voice.

"Don't worry, Your Highness," said Ylva. "You can have her back. Do you think any of us want your little lover-girl? We all prefer boys, just in case you hadn't noticed!"

She stretched out her arm, offering the photo to Jenna: Bea on the hammock in her backyard, soaking wet in her bathing suit, laughing. In the tense silence, someone scraped a chair.

"Give me the picture," Jenna said again, and took a step toward Ylva.

"Look out, Ylva, she's coming after you!" said Patty. Her voice was shrill. The others screeched and laughed, and Jenna saw Ylva open her hand almost carelessly, so that the frame slipped from her hand and fell to the floor, where the glass shattered into a thousand pieces.

"Oh, I'm so sorry, Your Highness!" said Ylva. "I went and dropped it! I must try not to be so nervous about you coming to get me. It's keeping me awake at night, just knowing you're there in the same room . . ."

"Eeeek!" cried a dozen voices in mock horror. Someone laughed. On the floor lay the shattered frame and the countless splinters of glass, with Bea's photo underneath.

"You bitches!" cried Jenna, and bent down. *Don't cry,* she told herself. *Don't cry! Don't give them that satisfaction.* She reached for the photo beneath the shards of glass.

"Ooh, she got her GF back!" said someone.

At that moment, a loud voice spoke from the doorway. "Jenna?" said the art teacher. "See me after class. Certain words are strictly forbidden at this school."

The man had drawn the curtains to keep out the morning sun, and now he sat in the wing chair with his feet resting on his desk. He was exhausted. He needed some peace and quiet. It wasn't easy constructing a plan of this complexity . . .

The ringtone from his cell phone startled him out of his reflections. It was his second phone, the one registered in his chauffeur's name. Who had he given this number to?

"Captain?" said the voice at the other end impatiently. "I haven't heard from you for days!"

"Ah, Bolström, I should have known it was you," he said, taking his feet off the desk. "I'm sure you know what I've been up to. Or don't you have newspapers over there under your Brazilian palm trees?"

"Do you really think you're that important?" said the other man irritably. "Now listen, Captain, Norlin and I are coming back, and don't try to tell me why we shouldn't. I know why we should, and that's what matters most for me."

"So why should you?"

"You need me," said Bolström. "Didn't I manage everything perfectly last time?"

"No, you didn't! Pretending that the king was dead when really you'd kidnapped him — that was a shrewd move, I'll grant you. And your miserable little puppet Norlin was an excellent pawn in the game. But the fact that those kids and the rebels were able to . . ."

"Mistakes were made, I'll give you that," Bolström cut him off. "But who would have imagined clumsy little Jenna actually finding out where Magnus was being held? And escaping from us to boot? Fate was against us, Captain, but now we shall put things right. I'm coming back."

"You're crazy."

Bolström laughed. "On the contrary, Captain, on the contrary. Even though your antics may be too insignificant for the newspapers of this wonderful country to report"— he paused and then laughed —"the reforms in Scandia are not. I still own a mine in the north, remember? And a bit of oil. And I'm not prepared to give it all up."

"I have a mine, too, you know," said the man. He had stood up now and begun pacing to and fro. A ray of sunshine squeezed between the gap in the curtains and into the room, drawing a bright, shimmering circle on the polished parquet floor. Little grains of dust danced in the light. "And sheep. And oil." He lit a cigarette as he paced. "But they still belong to me, Bolström, just as yours still belong to you. Even the new government won't dare take our possessions away from us so soon!"

There was a moment's silence. "Let's not talk about what they will and won't dare do, Captain," said Bolström eventually. "Let's talk about what they've already done. Look at the schools. Every wretched dark-haired brat in the north now has the same right to education as our sons and daughters in the south! Do you want your son working for some swarthy northerner when he grows up? And then there's health care. Before we know it, there'll be doctors all over the north, access to hospitals. And who's paying for it? Who's paying for all this, Captain?"

"Calm down, Bolström," said the man. He dragged on his cigarette. "I know. It's us paying for it — you, me, and everyone else who's got more than the northerners think we ought to have. How much do you think I earn on a ton of bauxite or a barrel of oil since the new taxation laws went into effect? Not to mention the price of wool . . ."

"So why don't you do something about it?" yelled Bolström. The man held the receiver away from his ear. "Didn't I tell you what needed to be done? So why don't you get on with it? All right, I've seen on the news that you're beginning to introduce emergency rations — wonderful, at least you've paid some attention! But for the —"

"Bolström," the man interjected, "will you just listen for a second! We've seen to it that all of a sudden there's no more pork, vegetables, milk, and heaven knows what else. And what you may not have heard, while you lie there sunbathing on the beach in your sunshine state, is that everybody in this country is now convinced that it's all the fault of the blackheads. Those barbarians are not ready to be in parliament. The press are already accusing them of creating an economic crisis, even though they're only sharing power." He gave a snort. "But you don't care about that, do you? The fact that we've got the press on our side . . . Stupid of the king not to take control of the media last year, when you idiots let him escape — didn't I say then that a quiet execution would have saved us all a lot of trouble, Bolli? And the blackheads are making the same mistake! It's incredible! Democracy! Liberty! They really believe in those things! And what's more —"

The telephone on his desk rang, and he could see from the flashing light that it was his secretary. He held the cell aside and picked up the buzzing receiver in his other hand. "Yes?"

"There's an urgent matter to attend to," said the secretary. He always sounded so high-strung and pressured. Why did he put up with him? "Apparently the rebels have launched

an attack. An oil pipeline in the north of South Island —
fortunately not a vital link —"

"I'm coming," said the man, and hung up the desk phone.

When he put the cell back to his ear, there was a laugh at
the other end. "Yes, that's all good stuff, Captain, no doubt
about it," Bolström was saying. "The blackheads are naïve.
But unfortunately this government has the legal right to stay
in power for a long time still, and what do you think —?"

"I'm truly sorry to interrupt you, Bolli. I'd really like to
continue this conversation," said the man. On his way to the
door, he opened the curtains, and sunlight flooded the room.
"But my secretary is waiting for me. Turn on the news and
you'll see why. So you can stop criticizing us for not doing
anything. We'll resume our little chat at a more suitable time."
He switched off the cell phone without giving Bolström a
chance to reply. Who knew when he'd switch it on again? And
Bolström wouldn't dare contact him on any other line.

Or perhaps having Bolström back in Scandia could be useful. Either way, no one could stop him from returning; that
man would do what he wanted, regardless. And he had always
been the brains behind the southern movement — nobody was
as good at summing up situations or planning campaigns.

He hurried downstairs.

6

*T*he *talk with the art teacher* had been laughable, and no one ever paid any attention to her, anyway. Teachers weren't the problem — the other girls were.

If only she'd sent me to the principal's, thought Jenna, *then maybe I could have escaped to detention this afternoon, so I wouldn't have to go with the other girls on the* de rigueur *Saturday outing into town — shopping, movies, strolling around, whatever.* Those few hours breathing the air of the big, bad world — which in the case of the local town was neither big nor bad — and then back to the snug, safe cocoon of the boarding school. *Except that it's not safe or snug for me.*

Of course, she sat by herself on the bus, as she did every week, but today she was more isolated than ever. Not only was the seat next to hers empty, but so, too, were those behind her and on the opposite side of the aisle. Instead, the girls were huddled together in the back. Jenna's bodyguards sat a few rows behind her, and when the bus stopped in the large parking lot behind the department store to let everyone off and out into their Saturday freedom, Jenna was left alone with them.

She took a deep breath. The bodyguards always stayed a few feet behind her — big, fair-haired, arrogant men, who had learned to act as if they didn't exist. *Maybe we could have a conversation*, thought Jenna. At least that would be something different. *Hi, guys, what d'you feel like doing today?* Maybe they could all go together to the tiny movie theater on Main Street and share a bucket of popcorn, and they'd all laugh afterward about whatever movie they'd seen. But during the first few weeks, she'd tried talking to the bodyguards as if they were her equals and she'd been shocked at their contempt.

And so once again she was on her own. *I'm getting to know this town like the back of my hand*, thought Jenna. It wasn't very big, really — there weren't any big cities in Scandia apart from Holmburg, and toward the north the towns were even smaller.

She could sense the men behind her. So where should she go? Apart from the main strip with the shops and the cinema, there was nothing worth seeing. So Main Street it was. Up and down, up and down, standing for a quarter of an hour in front of each store window to pass the time. Jenna sighed. She walked from the parking lot to the rear entrance of the one and only department store, right across the ground floor toward the main entrance, which led out onto Main Street. But there was something odd about the place. Was this how it had always looked? She stopped.

Of course. The shelves were bare, and there were no piles of brightly colored goods on the display counters. *What's wrong?* Jenna wondered. *What have they done with everything?* Shortages happen, but the store looked as if it had been looted, or was about to close down.

"But surely you've got shampoo!" an elegant lady was saying to the young salesgirl, who was shaking her head in embarrassment. "Any brand! I can't believe that something as ordinary as shampoo is out of stock, even in this backwater town." She frowned. "Are you trying to tell me I've got to go to Holmburg in order to get some shampoo?"

The young salesgirl turned red, and continued to shake her head.

"I'm afraid it's not likely to be any better in Holmburg, madam," an older sales assistant interjected. She had obviously recited her speech to plenty of other disgruntled customers, and spoke in a calm, friendly tone. "We've been told by company headquarters that they're completely out of the same products at the flagship store. Evidently something's gone wrong with getting raw materials to the factories and finished products to our warehouses. It appears that the government has been unable to coordinate the shipping required. The food situation is the worst of all."

"Since when has the government been responsible for coordinating the shipment of shampoo?" asked a short man who had just loaded several bottles of laundry detergent into his shopping cart. "What does shampoo have to do with them?!"

"I'm afraid I must ask you to put back seven of those, sir," said the senior salesclerk. She was beginning to look a bit weary. "All of our customers are trying to stock up on whatever's left on the shelves, and so we've had to limit everyone to a maximum of three of any item. If you'd be so kind . . ."

Jenna tried to make herself invisible behind a column as she listened to the exchange. Just what was going on?

"Then I'll take three of those as well," said the elegant lady who had failed to find her shampoo. "You never know! Would you mind passing them over?"

The man handed her three bottles, then put four back on the shelf. "I'll just have to send my son later," he said. "And my daughter. That way we'll get nine between us. But you can't just keep blaming the new government for everything, you know!"

The saleswoman shrugged her shoulders. "I can only give you the information I've received from corporate office," she said, irritation creeping into her voice. "But you know yourself that all these restrictions have only happened since the northerners were allowed into government. We never had problems like this before."

The elegant lady nodded vigorously. "Scandia's going to the dogs," she said. "And the next elections won't be for another four years, so who knows what those barbarians will have turned us into? We'll probably all have starved to death by then!"

You don't look like you're starving to me, thought Jenna. She kept her head turned away as she slipped past them. Behind her she could hear the footsteps of the bodyguards. *Please don't let anyone recognize me!*

When the sliding doors to the street closed behind her, she took a deep breath. All she wanted was to get away — not to hear any more complaints. Why did these things make her feel so guilty? What did it have to do with her? Just because she was half-northern and the king's niece . . .

She continued down Main Street. She hadn't been here for two weeks because of her trip back home. How could a town change so much in such a short time?

"All empty!" she murmured, gazing at the display cases in the coffee shop.

That was a bit of an exaggeration: There were still a few goods, though the gaps were more prominent. In the window of a clothing boutique, three of the mannequins stood stark naked, helplessly waving their slender plastic hands, while two others were only dressed from the waist down, looking almost ashamed of themselves. The last one, leaning forward slightly, wore nothing but a flowing blouse that hung down over its naked legs — the dummy seemed to be tugging at it, to cover up. Between all these, on the floor with its artistic folds of artificial satin, lay a handwritten notice:

We must ask our valued customers for their indulgence as, owing to current supply restrictions, we have nothing but remnants in stock.

But there were no valued customers even bothering to cast a glance at the pathetic scraps.

There were, however, crowds of people reading the reports posted outside the offices of the local newspaper. Jenna couldn't remember noticing anything like that before she went away, either.

"It's scandalous!" declared one man, tapping on the glass pane. Jenna couldn't see what disaster was being announced in the evening edition, and she didn't want to know. "My wife has cleared all the shelves in the cellar," he continued, "and now we're going to buy just about everything we can get our hands on!"

"There's still some dishwashing liquid in the hardware shop!" cried a woman carrying two heavy shopping bags. "But it's limited to two bottles a person. If you hurry, you might still get some."

WTH is happening? thought Jenna. *This can't be true!* But outside the supermarket there was a line stretching all the way to the street corner. "No more butter or margarine!" announced one woman, coming out of the market with bulging bags on both shoulders. Two little children followed her, also carrying bags. The younger one was crying. "Hardly any cheese left, and all the cans are gone!"

"*All* the cans?" echoed another woman near the front of the line. "You can't be serious!"

The man behind her laughed harshly. "Cans can be stored indefinitely!" he said. "At times like this they're always the first to go — it's obvious!"

"But I've got small children at home!" cried the woman. "How am I going to feed them if things go on this way?"

Jenna stood there listening. *How has this happened?* she thought again. *What's going on?*

"To think I supported the changes!" said a gray-haired woman at the back of the line. "I trusted the king when he said there should be equal rights for everyone! I didn't mind when a northerner was appointed Minister of the Interior. But who'd have thought it would come to this? And have you heard? Two hours ago they blew up some pipeline somewhere! We all hoped that with members of parliament from both north and south, this government would manage to keep the rebels under control, but . . ."

She stopped and looked at Jenna. "What are you standing there gawping at?" she asked. "If you want to buy something, get in line."

Jenna was taken aback. She shook her head. *Thank goodness they didn't recognize me*, she thought. *Without any makeup, and with my dark hair, they think I'm just another northerner. We all look the same to them.*

And if the north was responsible for everything, why should they be nice to her?

7

*S*earchlights illuminated the valley, and
in their glaring beams the emergency vehicles raced
around, unfurling their hoses and feverishly digging broad
ditches as firebreaks.

"Nahira!" Liron hissed into his cell phone. He hadn't made
contact before; there had been other more urgent things to
attend to — telephone calls, talks with the rescue teams and
the press. As Minister of the Interior, the man in charge of the
country's internal affairs, he'd had no time to himself.

The searchlights were hardly necessary. Behind him the
flames were still roaring as high as they'd been a few hours
ago, when he first reached the scene of the attack. They lit
up the night in a blaze of yellow and red. The pipeline ran
on raised girders across the valley, like some riveted metal
monster wending its way between the trees. At one point the
huge pipe had been blown apart, and the flames leaped far
above the tops of the oaks and beeches. On each side of it,
wide firebreaks had been dug into the ground.

The fire brigades did what they could, pumping water onto the trees while small planes circled over the area, dousing the flames from above. There had been a succession of explosions, and even from a distance the heat and the stench were almost unbearable. Luckily there were no towns in the vicinity, and this pipeline was the least important in Scandia.

"Nahira, can't you keep your people under control?"

He looked around, but there was no one within earshot. It might be a national emergency, but he hadn't expected the military to turn up. He had told General von Thunberg he was going to contact the king. He'd just have to hope the general didn't ask to be in on the conversation.

It seems as though everybody in Scandia has at least one secret cell phone these days, thought Liron. He moved a bit farther away from the fire, and realized the intense heat had made him incredibly thirsty. *And everyone seems to be spying on everyone else.* This would have to be a quick conversation — under no circumstances must anyone suspect what he was doing.

"'My people'!" Nahira replied indignantly on the other end of the line. "Liron, you can't be serious! I've seen it on TV. Don't you realize they're up to their old tricks? It's those rich southerners again, you know perfectly well it is! How crazy do you think 'my people' are?"

"Someone was crazy enough to do it!" said Liron. The general had broken away from the group of officials he'd been conferring with and was now heading toward him. "And whoever it is means business. It's an inferno here! Nahira, I've got to go. We'll . . ."

"Wait!" said Nahira. "Lorok thinks he's discovered something, Liron. He's keeping a daily watch. If what he suspects is right . . ."

The general was standing right in front of him. Liron flipped the cell phone shut.

"Did you speak to the king?" asked von Thunberg.

"So far I haven't managed to get ahold of him," said Liron. He slipped the cell phone into his pocket. "I've told his head of security, so I hope he'll call back right away."

At that moment, a ringtone sounded in his pocket. He knew from the tune that it was his official mobile phone and that the king would be on the line.

He reached into his pocket and fingered his two phones. He picked out the one that was ringing, and hoped the general wouldn't notice that it was different from the one he'd just had in his hand.

The double doors leading out onto the large roof terrace were wide open, but even now, in the early evening, there was scarcely a breath of cool air. Far below the balustrade, the tropical sea was shimmering, and beyond the bay the mountains were turning blue in the evening light. From down below came the voices of the sunbathers, calling to each other and laughing — the sounds of summer.

On the terrace, looking a little out of place, were two lounge chairs with broad arms and thick upholstery; on one was a pile of newspapers, and on the other was Norlin, his left arm hanging loosely down to the floor beside an almost empty glass. He was snoring so loudly that the sound could be heard in the bright, high-ceilinged room behind him, where Bolström had just turned on the television.

He flicked through the local stations showing Brazilian soap operas and variety shows until at last he found an English-speaking news channel. He flopped into a chair and used the remote control to increase the volume. From the terrace, Norlin let out a loud grunt and turned over, accidentally knocking the near-empty glass. It tipped over and began to roll, spilling its remaining contents onto the marble tiles and finally coming to a halt up against the balustrade.

"Norlin!" shouted Bolström. "Wake up! Stop that infernal racket!"

The man on the chaise longue went on snoring. His face was red and bloated, his mouth half-open.

The images on the TV screen switched rapidly from a motor race somewhere in Italy to an attack on a bus in the Middle East, while the crawl at the bottom silently announced the latest stock market figures.

And then there were flames.

"Norlin, come here if you want to see what's going on! They're really getting down to business now!"

The man on the terrace woke up with a start.

"What did you say, Bolström?" he asked. His eyes were bloodshot. He anxiously scanned the terrace for his glass, but finally gave up and reached instead for the bottle, which was just an arm's length away.

"Stop drinking, Norlin!" said the man in the room. "I'm surprised you can even stand on your own two legs. Just come in here and look at this! Things are really heating up, you could say!"

On unsteady legs, Norlin stumbled shakily into the room.

"That's Scandia!" he said. His speech was slurred, and he held on to the back of a chair for support.

"Yes," said Bolström, "our friends are on the move at last. Stopping the oil supply is a good idea. But they'll have to knock off a few people — I told them that from the start. Not long now and we'll be able to strike. We're flying back, Norlin. Remember? Has that information got through to your sozzled brain?"

"Who do you think you're talking to?" said Norlin, still clutching the chair. "I'm Viceroy of Scandia. I'm . . ."

"You're an incurable drunk, Norlin, and that's all you are," said Bolström, and went on watching the TV. The flames soared upward, and the reporter spoke into his microphone. "This," said Bolström, "is history in the making. Your nettle-some daughter and her friends got us into this mess, but now at last we're beginning to get the upper hand again. Take a good look. My phone calls to the old captain worked after all! The food shortage wasn't nearly enough. But this is good. This is really good."

"How come you're suddenly on the side of the rebels?" whined Norlin. "I thought we were trying to root them out. Now they've even set fire to our oil!"

"Precisely, my friend," said Bolström, and hurried across the room to the telephone. "That is precisely what people will say. It's starting to work. And gradually the ignorant voters of Scandia will be forced to realize what sort of government they've saddled themselves with, so it won't be long before they're cheering wildly as our tanks come rumbling in. Which is why we're flying back." He rummaged through a pile of notes that lay scattered near the phone, and keyed in a number.

Norlin held his bottle up to the light and gave it a little shake. Not a sound. "Have we got any whiskey left, Bolström?" he moaned. "Some of it must have spilled."

"That's right, Scandia," said Bolström into the phone. "Exactly. Two tickets. Thank you. I'll pay by credit card." He turned around.

"We're on our way now, Norlin," he said.

Breakfast had been served in the king's dining room. He had introduced these working breakfasts last year, soon after he had been freed. They were not official sessions, and no minutes were kept: He simply invited whomever he wanted, and the guests varied according to the problems that had to be discussed. Magnus alone made the choice, and today his guests were Liron, the Minister of the Interior; General von Thunberg, the commander in chief of the army; and his future brother-in-law, Lord Peter Petterson, representing the aristocracy and the business class.

From the buffet table came the scent of freshly brewed coffee; the tea was already in the pot; and the croissants had just been served, warm and crusty from the oven. Next to the scrambled eggs were strips of crispy bacon, links of savory sausage, and thin slices of fried tomatoes. There were jams for the bread; milk for the coffee; and granola, yogurt, and fruit. The French doors were wide open. It was another glorious summer morning.

The mood at the table, however, was subdued.

"Who else could it have been?" asked von Thunberg, taking a bite out of his buttered croissant. A crumb fell onto his tie. "I can't think of any other culprits. It's as clear as day, Your Majesty. The reforms are moving too slowly for the rebels. A coalition government makes decisions slowly and the rebels don't like it. The northern parliament members and the southern ones have very different views. Besides, they don't want to work with us: They want revolution! The rebels have gone back to being rebels! It's exactly the same problem as before."

"Nonsense!" said Liron. He was standing next to the buffet table, leaning against the frame of the open doors, with just a cup of coffee in his hand. "I'm sorry, Thunberg, but why would the rebels do such a thing? They'd only turn everyone against them and wreck the reforms they've been fighting for all this time. It doesn't make sense! It has to be in their own interests to work with us and make sure all changes happen peacefully, so that there'll be no excuse for the military to be brought in against them . . ."

"Your Majesty," said von Thunberg. He crossed to the buffet table, picked up a large plate, and loaded it with food. He evidently had no difficulty eating and talking at the same time. "It's time you let me bring in my men! We could search the premises of everyone we suspect of being in league with the rebels. All over the country, Your Majesty, in the south as well as the north. And at the same time we could protect any potential targets that the rebels might want to attack, like the pipeline yesterday. We need soldiers on the streets! Show the people we're not prepared to sit back and let ourselves be attacked. Otherwise, won't they get the impression the government's simply doing nothing — or even that some members of parliament are on the rebels' side? People are already talking."

"You forget, General, that I can only order the military to intervene in internal affairs in the event of a national crisis," said the king. "And can we honestly call this a national crisis? Times have changed in Scandia, thank goodness."

"But the mood of the country is changing, Magnus — we can all sense it," said Petterson. "Even the people's respect for the royal family has been dwindling over the last few months. All those articles recently about your niece! The free press is full of criticisms of current policies, what with all these shortages — you must have seen that for yourself — and they're holding you responsible, too. And now the pipeline. You've got to take action! Let Thunberg bring in his men before it's too late!"

The king looked down at his steaming cup and blew on it before taking a sip. Then he made a face. "Too hot," he murmured.

"I'm against it, Magnus!" said Liron. "Totally against it. As Minister of the Interior, I do not want to see this country suddenly swarming with soldiers. We could easily lose control. We're on the right path now, but we need more time."

"You think so, Liron?" asked the king, looking thoughtfully at him. "Of course, that's what I'd prefer."

Margareta entered the room through a side door. As she passed, she kissed Petterson on the cheek.

"Why don't you make a speech to your people, Magnus?" she said without any further greeting. "Try to explain the problems of transition to them. Ask them to be patient, the southerners as well as the northerners. You're king — they'll listen to you."

"Should I inform the TV stations, Magnus?" asked Petterson. "Maybe tonight, after the news? The people of Scandia usually spend Sunday evenings watching TV, now that the reception is so good everywhere."

The king nodded reflectively. "Maybe," he murmured.

"But don't wait to bring in the military until it's too late, Your Majesty!" urged von Thunberg. "There's a lot of resentment building up."

The king looked at his watch. "Thank you, gentlemen," he said. "I'll have to bring this discussion to a close. I have an appointment. And, Thunberg, I'm sure you want to get back to your estate as soon as you can — I'm sorry I had to send for you on such an important day."

8

*J*onas sat on the white-painted fence next to the little gatehouse in Morgard, waiting to be picked up. Cars drove along the narrow road that ran past the entrance to the school grounds. Sunday. In the school's front parking lot, where mothers, fathers, and chauffeurs dropped off the day students every morning and picked them up again every afternoon, there were now just two cars; their hoods were covered in sticky lime blossoms, and the sweet scent hung heavily from the trees in the hot and hazy air.

It's crazy hot, thought Jonas. The von Thunbergs had lucked out with the weather again.

He turned and looked over the school campus. In the oppressive heat he could see the flagpoles on either side of the gravel drive that led to the main parking lot; the alternating flags of Scandia and the school coat of arms hung down limply. On the gate and along the fence, colorful triangular pennants fluttered briefly in the breeze whenever a car passed by.

Jonas leaned forward in the hope of spotting Liron's car the moment it turned around the bend.

Amazing to think I'm back here, at the top school in the country, when this time last year I was in hiding. He looked at his brown legs, tanned even darker by the sun. *There's hardly a southern noble or oil tycoon or mine owner or real estate magnate who wasn't once a student here. And now,* he thought cynically, *they've finally let in a few northerners as well.*

His mother had insisted that Jonas must go to Morgard, even though she had left him and his father soon afterward in order to marry a wealthy nobleman from the south. She'd always been obsessed by getting in with the rich southern families, despite being a northerner. *How completely and utterly pathetic*, thought Jonas.

Then, when Malena had been sent to a boarding school farther to the north of South Island, Liron had protested that they should be allowed to stay together. "What about Jonas and Malena? They're like brother and sister. Why do you want to separate them now?"

At Malena's school the children were mainly middle-class, and some students, on scholarship, even came from poor North Scandian families, because the king wanted her to get to know people from different backgrounds. But it had been impossible to reason with his mother, and Jonas had been sent to Morgard to "mix with the right people." It had taken a long time to get used to life without Malena. Liron was right; she had been like a sister to him, and now he was shut away with the sons of rich southerners while she was at a school with real people. She raved about it with shining eyes: the freedom! She would tell him at length about where all her friends came from, the strange jobs their parents had, the way they lived. Two girls in her grade — one of them top of the class — actually came from the north, and their parents didn't even have enough money to pay for them to go home for a weekend!

"I do know what it's like, Malena. I come from the north, too," Jonas had said.

"Oh, you!" Malena had replied with a dismissive wave of the hand. Jonas was Jonas — she'd never really thought about where he came from.

But it's a whole 'nother deal at Morgard, he thought. He remembered the way they had stared at him at first. If it hadn't been for Perry, who couldn't have cared less about all that social status stuff because he was so shattered by his mother's death at the time — *if I hadn't been in the same dormitory to talk with him during those dark nights of our first year*, Jonas thought, *who knows? I might not have a single friend at this school.*

And for a long time Perry was the only friend. Jonas was still a blackhead as far as the other boys were concerned — the barbarian from the north. It didn't matter to them that his father was the king's advisor. In fact, that just made it worse, as their parents were suspicious that his father was putting all kinds of northern ideas into the king's head.

Cars drove past him and turned to go up the driveway. Where was Liron? He had said explicitly that they should go to the party together because there was a lot to talk about.

At last a limousine flying the Scandia standard rounded the bend.

"Liron!" shouted Jonas, jumping down from the fence. "Liron, over here!"

The man was just wondering whether in this heat it wouldn't be better to put on a linen suit rather than the ceremonial uniform he usually wore to garden parties, when his cell phone rang. The Toreador Song from *Carmen*. It was the phone he'd registered in his chauffeur's name, and he knew exactly who was calling him.

For a second he thought about not answering, but then he decided it would be better to find out what Bolström had to say. After all, that was the only reason he had turned on the phone this morning.

"Bolli," he said, "sorry, not a good time. The party's about to begin. The condensed version?"

"Oh, I'll get straight to the point, Captain: What were you thinking yesterday?" hissed the voice on the other end. "Hanging up on me like that! You think you can manage without me?"

"We've always managed without you, Bolli," the man said coolly. He would wear his ceremonial uniform. It was important in his position to radiate authority. "Trust me, we've got everything under control. It's getting better every day. Didn't you see for yourself yesterday?" He held up the hanger holding his shirt. *Bother*. He'd have to wear a tie as well. He hated these sudden heat waves. Up here in the north of the island the summers were not supposed to be so hot. The days should be long, clear, sunny, just as they were when he was a child. Wispy white clouds floating across the blue, picture-postcard sky, the air just warm enough to make it a sheer pleasure to take a dip in one of the island's many lakes . . .

"Yes, yes, the pipeline wasn't a bad move," said Bolström, breaking into his thoughts. "But things have got to go faster, old friend, or we'll never be able to get rid of these northerners. There are more of them than us southerners, and they're always going to vote for their own people if we don't slam the door shut now! There were good reasons why they were never given the vote before!"

The man took out the silver cuff links he'd been given for Christmas, an expensive gift from a child. He would wear them to show he appreciated the thought, even though he didn't particularly like them. He sighed. "Listen, Bolström," he said. "The king, curse him, still has far too many supporters for his reforms, even here in the south. They think, 'Oh, human rights, wonderful! It's only *fair*. We really *want* to see the northerners prosper. *One united Scandia, and justice for all!*' They think it would be *good* if our universities were stuffed with blackheads. That's what they call justice, Bolli! They really believe in it!"

There was a pause at the other end. "And the military?" Bolström asked in a low voice. "How far have you got with them?"

"You think we're not working on them?" hissed the man. "How stupid do you think we are? All of us sitting here waiting, ready to go. After all, they're hardly likely to be against us. Every single general comes from a good southern family. But it's still too soon to strike. First we have to soften up all the naïve idealists, and that's what we're doing now. When they can't get enough decent food to feed their children, even the most liberal southerners will soon change their tunes, believe me. Then they'll cheer every machine gun we use to blast the blackheads out of parliament!" He pressed a half-smoked cigarette into an ashtray on the glass top of the desk, and lit another one.

"Don't you tell me what you have to do! I'm the one who planned it all!" said Bolström. "But now we need to have soldiers all over the country. And what about the king? He's the one who landed us in this mess in the first place! What are you doing to undermine him and his family? Nothing! It was the same when we were at school together — you were always such a time-waster, it drove me crazy. You've got to tighten the screws!"

"It's all fine and well for you to talk. You can just sit there in your tropical paradise, relaxing from dawn to dusk, and whenever you get bored, you pick up the phone to give me a long-distance lecture."

"Captain!" Bolström yelled in frustration. "The time to act is now!"

"Look, the press is working on whipping up dissatisfaction. People over here are getting angry, only you don't hear about it all the way on the other side of the world. The royal glamour is already getting nicely tarnished — in case you hadn't realized, I'm doing more than my share on that front, too. Be patient. Rome wasn't built in a day."

"Say what you like, Captain, I'm coming back," said Bolström. "Things are reaching a crisis point, and I need to be there. Just make sure that I can enter the country without any hitches — have some of your people among the border police. I'll let you know the time of arrival so you can see to it that the right people are on duty at the airport."

The man said nothing for a while. "And Norlin?" he asked at last. "Are you going to leave him behind?"

"There's nothing I'd like more," said Bolström. "We've got no use for him now. The whole country knows he was involved in the king's kidnapping last year. Besides, he's drinking more than ever. But he knows too much about us, Captain, he knows too much. I can imagine just what he'd do if he realized I'd returned without him — he'd notify the press over here, and then it'd be curtains for us all. For the time being, we have to keep him in tow. Later we'll see about the best way to . . . cut him loose. Perhaps an unfortunate 'accident' . . ."

"Whatever it takes, eh, Bolli?"

Bolström gave a rueful laugh. "I'm committed to the cause," he said. "Completely. And while we're at it, we'll think up a nice 'exit strategy' for the king and his family, too. Use your imagination. I'll see you soon."

9

There wasn't a cloud in the sky, and it was too hot to go running.

Jenna could feel the sweat on her forehead, and wiped her brow with her forearm. She really didn't want to go to the summer party, and no one had officially invited her — but of course she was expected to go. When the commander in chief of the army held his annual garden party, it was simply taken for granted that the whole royal family would gather there, to stand on the lawn and chitchat in the sunshine, while the fountains sprayed and the caterers glided smiling and silent among them. *Presumably with trays full of disgusting little jam sandwiches*, thought Jenna, *as there isn't anything else to eat in the whole country. Great!*

Until this morning, she had avoided even thinking about the party. By now she knew precisely how these events proceeded: She'd be expected to circulate among the different groups, talking and smiling, saying nice things to everybody while everybody said nice things back to her. *You're a princess,*

Jenna! Our country looks up to you! And the future of our family depends on what you do!

She sat on a boulder by the edge of the forest in her tracksuit and sneakers, breathing heavily. She'd run twice around the outside of the school campus, but there had been no sign of Jonas. Big surprise, since nothing ever went right for her these days.

Jenna looked at her wristwatch: three o'clock. She'd skipped lunch, and breakfast as well. Strange that she didn't feel hungry at all. She'd have liked to bump into Jonas, even though she knew she'd turn bright red as soon as she saw him — she felt sick at just the thought of it.

A wind rustled the leaves. Maybe there'd be a thunderstorm; it was definitely hot enough for it. Then, boohoo, the party would have to be canceled. That would serve the von Thunbergs right! Jenna looked up at the sky.

When she lowered her eyes, she saw one of her bodyguards coming toward her across the grass.

"Princess?" he said. How was it possible to say the word in a tone that made it sound like the worst possible insult? "Your mother has come to get you. She's annoyed that you've made her wait."

Jenna stood up. She had to pull herself together. She had to go to the party whether she wanted to or not. *You can't make the world, or even the von Thunbergs' party, disappear, by covering your eyes like a silly child*, she told herself.

"I'm coming," she murmured, and began walking back toward the school.

Liron got out of the car and signaled to the driver to do the same. "Take a walk, why don't you, Carlson?" he said. "I get so few opportunities to talk privately with my son."

He and Jonas wandered a short distance away, and Liron affectionately ruffled his son's hair. Then he gave him a quick hug. "Jonas!" he sighed.

For a fraction of a second, Jonas laid his head on his dad's shoulder, then lifted it again self-consciously. He was too old for such things now.

"Thanks for stopping," he said.

"I don't think you'd have been waiting for me, son, if you didn't have something important to tell me," said Liron.

Jonas nodded. "It's about Jenna," he said. He felt himself turning red — it was the heat, that's all, he told himself. "I'm worried about her, Liron. She . . . It's getting worse all the time."

"Tell me," said Liron, taking off his jacket and hanging it over his arm.

"I don't know everything that's going on," said Jonas. "The boys' wing and girls' wing are kept pretty separate, so I only see her occasionally, when we're out of school. But it's obvious that she's more and more miserable. And she's got no friends; not one. I get the feeling that the other girls are being deliberately mean to her. Why did her mother have to send her here of all places — the worst school she could possibly go to?"

"Because until a year or so ago, she was just an ordinary girl — in fact, a poor girl — and now suddenly she's supposed to be a princess. Morgard will educate her for her new life. She has to learn to adapt. I'm afraid we can't let her change schools. The only person who may be able to help her is you."

There's nothing I'd rather do, thought Jonas.

Every so often, another car would drive past them, raising a cloud of dust. Liron took a couple of steps onto the grass, which despite the heat wave was still a shiny green.

"There are plenty of people who'll do anything they can to make a fool of her, Jonas. In public, too, if possible. If they make her look like a mockery, it'll help them to undermine the authority of the royal family. And they're using every method at their disposal to do precisely that. Jenna is just a means to an end." He looked around. "But they're planning something much bigger than just humiliating the royal family, Jonas. I'm sure of it. There are more and more signs."

"Who are?" asked Jonas. "What are you talking about?"

Liron stopped. There was no one on the lawn, and there were no trees or bushes nearby in which someone might have planted a listening device. It was safe to talk. "All those behind the plot against Magnus."

"But that was Norlin's plot!" said Jonas. "*He* was the one who kidnapped the king! He was power-hungry, you said so yourself! He wanted to be king, or at least viceroy."

"True, Norlin was power-hungry," said Liron. "But on his own he never could have . . . Think about it, Jonas: Who exploited Norlin's regency? Who would have benefited if it had gone on any longer?".

"You mean the rich southerners, like Bolström," murmured Jonas. "So where do you think they all are now?"

Liron shrugged his shoulders. "We don't know exactly who else was involved in last year's plot against the king. Bolström and Norlin fled the country, and we didn't know who else to interrogate in order to find out. But there are still traitors in Scandia, Jonas, cheering the king, clinking their champagne glasses with him at the palace, dancing across the lawns at Osterlin during his summer balls, and making speeches about how wonderful it is to have justice across the land and free elections! But take my word for it, secretly they're all hoping to turn back the clock and reverse the reforms, and they may well have been hatching their plans for months."

"I guess I should have expected it," said Jonas. "Why would they want to give up their privileges? It would be a miracle if they did."

"You see where I'm coming from, then," said Liron.

"At school the rumor's that you're in league with the rebels," murmured Jonas. "They think I can't hear what they're saying — or maybe they want me to hear. They say it's government by and for the north, and that you never broke off your contact with the rebels."

Liron's cell phone rang, and he reached for it in his jacket pocket.

"Liron!" Jonas pressed. "Is it true?"

Liron put his finger to his lips and listened. "No, everything seems to be in order here," he said into his phone, and looked around. "The clock on the gatehouse is working, and if it's not a generator they've . . . So it's just in Holmburg? I see, the cables across the dam. In that case I presume there's no chance of the king making his speech on TV tonight." He nodded. "Right, as soon as possible," he said. Then he closed his phone.

"Dad!" Jonas insisted.

"Someone's cut the power supply to Holmburg," said Liron. "There'll be no electricity till the lines are repaired. And today's the day when Magnus was going to make a speech asking both north and south to be patient."

"You think it's them?" said Jonas.

Liron shrugged his shoulders. "Everyone will say it's the rebels," he said wearily. "But how many people knew about Magnus's plans?"

"Well, the TV people did," said Jonas.

Liron nodded. "Indeed, you're right," he murmured. "And who is in control of them, I wonder . . . Come on. Let's go. Von Thunberg doesn't like to be kept waiting."

He beckoned to Carlson. The chauffeur stamped out his cigarette and pulled his key from his pocket.

"Wait!" said Jonas, grabbing his father's arm. "You never answered my question. Are you still in contact with the rebels?"

Liron looked at him. "Nahira is an old friend, not just the rebels' leader," he said, gently loosening his son's grip. "You know that, Jonas."

10

*T*he car traveled almost soundlessly through the summer haze. Even on South Island, there were narrow back roads winding their way up and down the countryside, through endless stretches of forest or between thick hedges, behind which the cornfields waited to be harvested before the first thunderstorms flattened them. Here and there you could still see the odd wild rose among the foliage — a white speck amid the dappled green — occasional poppies and clumps of chamomile. Sitting in the back of the car behind closed windows, Perry could imagine the scents and the summer atmosphere in a boundless silence so still that you could hear it.

He pulled his cell phone out of his coat pocket. Every summer he had to go to the von Thunbergs' garden party, and the weather was almost always as hot as today. He leaned back in his seat and searched through the photos on his phone.

He found what he was looking for. *She* would be there. That was the only reason why he hadn't protested when his father had called to say he'd be sending a car for him. Malena would be there.

Maybe I'm just jealous of the von Thunbergs, thought Perry. *Their perfect lives and perfect parties on perfect summer days. Maybe I should just admit it: I don't like them because I'm small and weak and I suck at sports — and everything else, for that matter. And now Dad's sending me to a military academy and I'll fail there, too.* He'd rather emigrate than go there.

He looked at Malena's photo. He'd taken it when watching the girls play a game of volleyball a few months ago. It was from a distance, of course. It would be way too embarrassing if anyone found out, let alone her! In fact, it was only because he knew it *was* her that he could actually identify her — raising her arms up in victory after the game. As if she wasn't the least bit tired and there was nothing in the world that was too big for her to tackle. He ran his fingertip over the display, outlining the figure behind the glass.

She'd be at the party — she was there every year. Even when he was just a little boy, he'd dreamed about her: the motherless princess, as beautiful and as friendly and as smart as a fairy-tale princess. *Yeah, right. Wake up, Perry*, he thought. Those kind of dreams were OK as long as you didn't keep thinking they might come true.

Maybe, right from the start, that had been one of the reasons why he'd made friends with Jonas. Jonas had grown up with Malena, and even now he spent the holidays with her, so he knew her better than anyone, and he talked about her as if knowing her was no big deal: how they'd gone fishing and Malena had fallen into the stream; they'd gone riding and Malena had jumped every obstacle; they'd hidden in the palace at night, and no one could find them, and there'd been all this drama afterward.

Now, however, Perry felt nothing but anger when he saw Jonas. Why did Jonas even have to exist? Perry would never dare tell Malena how he felt. It was bad enough knowing that she never wasted a thought on him, but at least he'd never have to listen to her rejecting him: *Oh, gosh, Perry, you know I've been friends with Jonas forever.* And afterward she and Jonas would laugh about him. *How on earth could he think that I'd go out with him? His own father's ashamed of him!*

No, Malena would never say that. Not sweet, kind Malena. It would be Jonas! Good thing Perry had never told his roommate what he felt for his childhood friend, the princess. He didn't even crack yesterday morning, when Jonas kept on asking him. Let him go on thinking that all his stress was about the military academy.

The limo passed through the gate of the Thunberg estate as the clock on the bell tower struck the quarter. His father had sent the car to Morgard, although Perry could easily have traveled to the party with a group of other students. He probably wanted to lecture him again before the party. Why else go to the expense of sending a chauffeured limousine just for him?

They stopped in front of the outbuildings: weathered yellow sandstone covered with roses; clematis and wisteria clinging to the trellises between the narrow windows. From here you had a view over the vast grounds. Among the sturdy native beeches were cedars, ginkgos, and other exotic trees. Now, in the baking summer sun, they threw oases of shade over the carpetlike lawns.

"Glad you managed to get here early," said Perry's father, bending down and opening the door for his son.

Like I had a choice, thought Perry.

"Over the last few weeks, we haven't had much of a chance to talk, Perry. So this is a good opportunity, and we've got quite a lot to talk about. I'm sorry you couldn't join Margareta and me for my birthday."

Perry didn't respond. *Why would I want to be there, when you're so wrapped up in her?* he thought. *And now you just want to talk about the logistics of shoving me into a military academy.*

"You know I've been concerned for quite a while about your future, Perry. Morgard itself is certainly the best school in the country . . ."

"I'm not going to your military academy," Perry stated bluntly. Figured he'd spare his father the bloated introduction. A startled bird flew up out of the rosebushes.

His father's tone now sharpened. "The fact is, Perry, that's not your decision to make. As long as you're still a minor, it's mine. And it's my duty as a father to ensure that my son gets the best possible education. Until now, for a Petterson, that's always meant going to the military academy."

"For a Petterson!" Perry repeated, his voice tinged with sarcasm. *"Always.* But for this Petterson here"— he pointed at himself —"why can't it be different? Scandia has changed, so why can't the Pettersons change? Someday I'll have to take over all your businesses — oil, bauxite, wool — so what good is military training going to do me?"

His father said nothing for a while. When he did speak, Perry knew for sure that nothing would alter his intentions.

"Scandia has indeed changed," he said. "And we're going through a difficult period. There's nothing more important at the moment for our country than an efficient army. And my son should be trained for that purpose." He tried to put his hand on Perry's shoulder, but the boy ducked away. "I have no intention of even discussing with you whether you should or shouldn't leave Morgard at the end of the school year, Perry. It's already decided. The only question is when you should start at the academy. And fortunately it's turned out to be sooner than I'd expected."

"What?" cried Perry.

"As you can imagine, I've been a bit concerned as to how you'll cope with conditions there," said his father. "It's no secret — you're not very strong. You've got no stamina — or dexterity, for that matter. I had my doubts . . ." Now he did succeed in grasping Perry's arm. "This year, for the first time, they're running an introductory course for new students. Over eight weeks in the summer they'll prepare you for everything you're going to learn during the following year. During those eight weeks, you'll have the chance to get yourself in shape, go on long-distance marches under tough conditions, conquer the obstacle course . . . show your mettle and harden your muscles! After eight weeks, you'll be a different boy."

"Eight weeks?" cried Perry. The staff from the catering firm were hurrying back and forth across the lawn, setting up little clusters of chairs and tightening the tent roofs. They pretended not to notice the outburst. "That's the whole summer!"

"My chauffeur will take you there next week," said Petterson. "You'll thank me later."

"Thank you?" shouted Perry. A waiter in a white shirt and black pants looked up, then quickly went back to counting the knives and forks. "For getting rid of me? Just because I'm in your way now that you're with the king's sister? You just don't want me hanging around at home anymore. Well, I don't care. I'm not going!"

"As I've just explained, Perry," he said over his shoulder as he walked away, "you have absolutely no say in the matter." Then, with outstretched arms and a smile on his face, he went to greet a couple who were just getting out of their limousine.

I'm not even worth arguing with, thought Perry, watching him go. *I'm irrelevant — it doesn't matter what I think or feel. He just has to shuffle me off somewhere so I don't interfere with his life.* His *life is what counts, not mine.*

With surprise, he realized that he didn't need to think anymore. He knew exactly what he was going to do without even having planned it in advance. He looked across the grounds to where the first guests were slowly making their way toward the main building. General von Thunberg would soon make his welcoming speech from the steps, as he did every year, once the Minister of the Interior and the king's sister had arrived. Perry would leave then, while they were all distracted. There was just one thing he had to take care of first. From now on, he had nothing to lose.

"Jenna!" said her mother. She was sitting in the headmaster's study on a chair embroidered with *petits points*, a cup of tea perched on the little side table next to her. Of course, when Princess Margareta made a surprise appearance, she couldn't possibly talk to anyone but the headmaster himself, even on a Sunday.

"You knew perfectly well that I was coming to pick you up! And what do you look like? Now hurry up and put on something sensible. Everyone's waiting for us!"

Jenna nodded. "I was out running and lost track of the time," she murmured.

The headmaster gave her the most radiant smile he had ever given her. "These things happen," he said. "But get a move on now." It was the tone he used to talk to first-graders — did he really think she wouldn't notice?

Half an hour later, she was sitting next to her mother in the backseat of the limousine, behind the escort car, and she knew exactly what was coming next.

"For heaven's sake, Jenna!" her mother said. The motor sprang to life and with a quiet hum the car moved down the gravel driveway and off school grounds. "Can't you be punctual for once in your life? I can understand that you're having difficulty adapting to your new role. Peter keeps telling me that it must be hard for you . . ."

Like he cares, thought Jenna.

". . . but you should at least be capable of keeping an eye on the clock. The garden party's been scheduled for months now."

"I just lost track of time," mumbled Jenna again. "I went running."

"Running!" said Mom. She pressed the control that closed the glass screen between them and the driver, waiting in silence until it was all the way up. Jenna was shocked to see how angry she was. Could a half hour delay really be such a big deal?

I suppose it could, if you're a princess, thought Jenna. *Because you're not just any old guest at a party, who can slip in unobserved. Everybody's waiting for you.*

"Listen, Jenna, you must have seen that recently the press have been using every opportunity to take potshots at all of us."

"But why?" asked Jenna. "What have they got against us all of a sudden? They were so happy when the king returned last year!"

"Just how naïve can a girl of your age be?" Mom snapped.

An animal ran across the road, maybe a rabbit, and the car braked sharply and swerved a little to one side. Their shoulders almost touched. "If they can make the royal family look ridiculous, then they can also make the king look ridiculous, and he's on the side of the north. A blow against the king is a blow against the reforms. That's what it's all about."

She didn't shout. Even when she was so furious that she might have lashed out, she still didn't. She was a real princess. She was everything Jenna would never be.

"Well, at least try to behave properly at the party. And why on earth did you put on that dowdy blue dress?"

"At home you always said it looked chic," whispered Jenna. She'd deliberately picked out the dark blue dress to please her mother. "I never wanted to wear it, but you always said it looked 'simple and unpretentious'. . ."

"At home?" said Mom irritably. "*This* is home now! And you're a princess! And you're going to a garden party in a cheap blue dress that's much too small and makes you look like a waitress!"

Jenna felt the tears welling up into her eyes. But she would not cry.

They'd arrived. A servant opened the car door. Ten feet away stood the general, welcoming them with a smile.

11

*N*ahira *sat* *on* the threadbare sofa, a cup of steaming coffee in her hand. *Much too hot in this sweltering weather,* she thought as the first drop burned her lips. *But I'll never get through the day without it. I don't get enough sleep. Too much to think about.*

She switched on the old television. It took a while to warm up.

Piece of junk, thought Nahira. But at least now she had a satellite dish she could carry from outpost to outpost and still have some idea of what was being broadcast.

It was a shame that they'd had to abandon their headquarters last summer, because she'd loved that house. Hidden in the forest but so near to the sea that you could smell the salt. Now they constantly had to keep on the move. Still, losing that house wasn't the worst thing that had happened in the past year.

After she, Malena, Jenna, and Jonas had freed the king and his sister from the clutches of the conspirators, Nahira had hoped for a while that all of this would come to an end — living in remote safe houses, waging a daily struggle to gain equal rights for the north, constantly in fear of some of her own people who thought she was too cautious, too accommodating, and kept demanding more and more violent action. They said she was a coward, and they had stopped listening to her. She didn't like to think about what they might do next.

And yet it had all looked so promising! thought Nahira. The king free, the country celebrating his return and outraged by the kidnapping. They had quickly acceded to the first reforms.

But now the original plotters were fighting a different fight with different methods. They'd had to change their tactics, and it was difficult to judge what they might be planning next.

Since last summer, she and her people had moved from place to place, never staying long in any one spot, though many of her followers had long since returned to their families in the hope that, after the elections, there really would be the justice, equality, and secure future they had fought for.

There were others, however, who did not trust all the new promises. Nahira stared at the TV screen. Who had set fire to the pipeline and disrupted the electricity supply to Holmburg? Could it have been them? Had she finally lost control over her people?

All she could do was wait, and watch, and try to understand what was really going on in the country.

The fact that she was still in contact with Liron was dangerous. If he was under surveillance, she might be caught that way. She was still regarded as the leader of the rebel movement, and she had never been forgiven for the bombing of parliament last summer, even though that had been a symbolic act — she had deliberately avoided causing any damage or taking any lives. But now there was the pipeline incident, and the disruption of the power supply.

Liron is running even more of a risk, she thought. Merely communicating with the rebels constituted high treason, and that was punishable by imprisonment or even, since he was Minister of the Interior, by death.

The last time she'd spoken to him, she'd told him she suspected there was a spy close to the king. He'd said, "Don't worry, I'm ultracautious. My cell phone's secure. And I have to know what information you've got, Nahira, what to expect from your people, what we must do to keep peace in the country. It's a risk I have to take."

"So you're cheating on your people, and I'm cheating on mine," Nahira had said wryly. "Maybe we're both in the wrong position, Liron."

He'd been dismissive. "And what would the right one be?" he'd asked.

She hadn't known how to answer him.

The theme music introducing the afternoon news brief began playing on the TV. The image flickered. Nahira turned up the volume.

". . . another problem in Scandia now?" the newscaster was saying with a grim expression on her face. Despite the change in government, it was the same woman who'd anchored the news a year ago. "Scandian customs have been asking this question after an unexplained and disturbing incident at Holmburg airport this afternoon." On the screen were blurred images of the inside of the terminal, with panic-stricken people rushing around while soldiers fired submachine guns. "Passengers from at least three incoming aircraft were allowed to bypass passport control and exit the airport without any form of clearance or documentation; all customs posts in Terminal A were left unoccupied for almost an hour. It was not until an alert passenger noticed strange noises coming from a storeroom and informed the airport police that five customs officers were found bound and gagged. A sniffer dog had been drugged." Now the screen showed the face of a young man in the green uniform of the Scandian immigration office. His eyes were still full of fear as he spoke into the microphone. "They had stockings over their heads," he said. "There were too many . . . They overpowered us in no time. They were definitely rebels, and we . . ." His face faded out, and the anchorwoman turned to another man in uniform, who was linked to the studio via satellite. Nahira recognized General von Thunberg, commander in chief of Scandia's army.

"Based on initial reports from the scene, our preliminary conclusion is that this attack was launched by members of the former North Scandian rebel movement," he said. "We have feared for some time that they might try to disrupt the stability of the current political situation by committing acts of violence, and recent incidents appear to support this theory. Airport officials have yet to confirm a specific reason why customs was targeted, but the obvious deduction is that this afternoon's attack was for the purpose of smuggling contraband into the country."

"Are you suggesting the illegal importation of controlled substances?" asked the news anchor. Her expression was now not merely grim, but positively distressed.

The general nodded. "Until today, Scandia has set an example for the rest of the modern world," he said. "Because our borders were more difficult to cross than those of many other countries, Scandia had been virtually drug-free. Inevitably, opening up our borders was bound to make it easier to import illegal substances, and the rebels can use the profits from their illicit trade to finance the acquisition of weapons . . ."

"What?!" Nahira exclaimed out loud, though there was no one to hear her. "What kind of journalism is this, when the commander in chief of the military can go on national television and make these outrageous and unsubstantiated accusations!" Whatever the real reason for the attack on the customs officials, though, Nahira knew it was yet another public relations disaster for her and her men.

She heard a familiar sound in the distance. The TV was now showing scenes of people lining up outside shops in various towns across the country — nothing new. She turned away from the screen and went outside. With screeching brakes, her ancient pickup truck came to a halt on the weed-covered driveway.

"Nahira!" cried Lorok. The door of the truck rattled in protest as he opened it. One day it would fall off its hinges. "Nahira, I was right! We've got them now!" He slammed his hand down on the hood, and quickly jerked it away again because of the heat. "Criminals! But we're onto them. We know what they're up to with their trucks!"

No one at the party mentioned pizza to Jenna — at least not directly. After all, they knew the rules of decorum, how they were supposed to behave at such a party, and around royalty to boot. But three times, people had come up to her and nodded toward the buffet table with a smile. "Aren't you going to get yourself a little something to eat?" they'd asked. Jenna was pretty much the only person wandering around the manicured lawns without a plate or even a glass in her hand.

The third person to ask had been Ylva's mother, the hostess herself, and when Jenna merely shook her head and moved away — how rude! — she was almost certain that Mrs. von Thunberg's next remark to the other guests was about her: "Well, as we all know, she's been eating her fill, anyway."

The buffet spread, Jenna noticed as she walked past it, was as lavish as it had always been at these parties: platters of fish, fowl, and roasted meats, tureens of summer soups, bowls of mixed greens, vegetables tucked in pastry, or caramelized, or grilled.

In between were exquisitely carved ice sculptures: swans; the von Thunbergs' coat of arms; the skyline of Holmburg with the palace in relief. And for dessert, various fruits from the south — pineapple, mango, guava — had magically been turned into strange animals by some clever chef. That is, if they weren't already baked into the wide selection of pies.

Where had all the food, all that fresh produce, come from? Jenna wondered. What about the shortages that had customers lining up outside supermarkets? She caught sight of another guest, and turned quickly away. The man standing by the desserts, wearing a loose-fitting linen suit and holding a glass in his hand — wasn't he the editor in chief of one of those awful tabloids? She couldn't let him see her here, anywhere near the buffet.

After the official greetings, she had made her way through the chattering groups toward the fringes of the party. Slowly, unobtrusively. She didn't want to talk to anybody.

Why had Mom left her standing there on her own? She was talking to someone near the broad flight of steps down to the terrace. Jenna could hear her laughing. She saw Ylva crossing the lawn, her blonde hair flowing over her shoulders, nodding to the right and nodding to the left, exchanging air kisses and passing comments to all and sundry. Oh, to be as confident as Ylva, or Malena, to feel at ease during parties, as she had back at home . . . Well, actually, if she was honest with herself, she had to admit that she'd never felt entirely at ease there, either.

Where *was* Malena, anyway? Jenna's gaze wandered all around the grounds. It was plain to see that the von Thunbergs were among the oldest and wealthiest families in the country. *Maybe that's why Ylva hates me so much*, thought Jenna. *Because of the reforms, her family will lose some of their wealth, and she blames the northerners. She blames me.*

Malena had to be somewhere. Malena, or maybe Jonas. All Jenna wanted was someone she could walk and talk with, someone who knew how you were supposed to behave — who would help her get through the afternoon.

It was strange that she hadn't yet spotted Malena. She was always on time; she was obliged to be at the reception, making small talk with the important guests, as was her royal duty. But where? All the women were fair-haired, all the women were slim, and they all wore loose-fitting summer dresses in pretty pastel colors. All except her.

Where are you, Malena? thought Jenna, feeling desperate. She was now completely alone at one end of the lawn, and the voices of the guests sounded muffled, as if they came from far away. *If I can't find her or Jonas, I'll just have to wait here till this horrible party is over — not that anyone will even notice that I'm gone.*

Just a few steps away was a summerhouse of weathered white wood, with wild roses climbing up its sides to its mildewed copper roof.

As pretty as a picture-book illustration, thought Jenna. *A bit like the pavilion at Osterlin where I eavesdropped on Norlin and* the chief of police last year. *Stop — don't think about that, don't think about Norlin, my horrible father* — she managed to shove him out of her mind most of the time since she'd learned the awful truth. She focused her attention back on the summerhouse. *I'll just sit inside, nice and cozy, and wait out this hideous party.* It had to end eventually. She could even practice her irregular verbs to pass the time: Then the afternoon wouldn't be a complete waste.

She listened. Nothing stirred in the undergrowth. No one spoke, no one laughed. No one was there. And yet somehow she had the feeling she was not alone . . .

Cautiously, Jenna leaned forward and peered through one of the glassless windows. Then, startled, she pulled her head back. On the white-painted bench that ran the length of the interior sat Malena and Perry, in a close, silent embrace.

Malena! thought Jenna in total disbelief. *So she* is *here! But how come she's with Perry? It's always been Jonas who she . . .*

Her heart began to pound. She tried not to make a sound. She had to see what was going on in there! But how could a girl like Malena be with a boy like Perry?

Malena was gently stroking Perry's face with her index finger, from his forehead down to his nose. Then her fingertip rested for a moment on his lips.

Stop looking! thought Jenna. *Oh God, what am I doing? Imagine if someone did that to me! Someone watching if Jonas and I . . .*

Jonas.

Deep inside her, Jenna suddenly felt an unbridled surge of joy. She had to stay there, at least for another moment or two. She had to be absolutely certain . . .

"Did you really think I didn't like you?" Malena was whispering. Again she gently stroked Perry's face and looked straight into his eyes, ran her fingers over his lips, and bent forward until her mouth was almost touching his.

Now Jenna was able to turn and run away.

1 2

Nahira had gone with Lorok in the rattling pickup. They'd avoided the roads and followed the forest tracks instead, and she was constantly surprised at how Lorok knew exactly where he had to turn off along the narrow paths, at how he coaxed the old vehicle and its protesting engine to get them up one slope, and then let it roll gently down another. Sometimes she had the feeling that he was even talking to it, as if it were alive.

At one point, where the tops of the trees thinned out and the undergrowth was particularly dense, Lorok let the truck coast into the bushes. Brambles scratched the dented hood, which had long since lost its polish after years of dusty roads and nights parked out in the rain.

"We'll have to go the rest of the way on foot," Lorok said. "It's too dangerous to drive from here on in."

Hunched over, they hurried through the undergrowth, never once stepping onto a path. After just a few minutes, they could suddenly hear the roar of engines — loud and steady, as if from a highway, and the farther they went, the closer it came. "The north–south beltway," said Lorok.

He has all the road maps in his head, thought Nahira admiringly. *Amazing. I need directions just to find my way to the dentist!*

"Now — can you hear it?"

Nahira stopped. She could now hear the engines of powerful tractor-trailers, and somewhere nearby they were pulling to a stop, with one final roar before the brakes screeched and the hydraulics wheezed to a standstill.

"What is it?" she asked.

Lorok put a finger to his lips and beckoned her to come closer. "The old concrete factory!" he whispered.

She peered through the bushes. Though it was difficult to make out from this distance, she could now see the hangars, each at least fifty feet high, with plenty of room between them for the trucks to maneuver. The factory dated back many years, to when quarters were being constructed on the outskirts of Holmburg to house the northerners arriving in increasing numbers to South Island in order to do the jobs that southerners found too dirty, too strenuous, or too low-paying. It was here that the slabs had been made for prefabricated housing projects that could be assembled like children's building blocks. But when the influx of northerners had first been cut and then stopped altogether, the factory had been closed, and now it lay derelict, with weeds sprouting everywhere.

"So that's what they've been doing," whispered Nahira.

"Stockpiling the goods of Scandia here!" One massive truck after another passed through the open gate only to disappear between the hangars. "Why did no one realize it before?"

"Maybe because no one was supposed to," Lorok said bitterly. He turned to leave. "Because no one wanted to. Imagine how many more abandoned warehouses just like this, all across the country, are being piled high with Scandia's goods as we speak? I think it's time you updated your friends in the government."

Nahira nodded. "But not from here," she whispered.

On the drive back they did not speak. If Liron learned about this, it could change everything.

Jenna hurried across the lawn, farther and farther away from the party and from the summerhouse. Malena and Perry deserved to be left in peace. Nobody would disturb them there.

How could her mood change so completely in just a few seconds? Utter despair a moment ago, and now such happiness! Malena and Perry — their names sounded like music. Malena and Perry, not Malena and Jonas! How stupid she'd been! *Malena's not in love with Jonas at all,* she thought. *Malena loves someone else, so I don't have to keep trying to get over Jonas! Malena and Perry! And Jonas and . . .*

She stopped by a bench overgrown with jasmine. The scent was sweet and heavy. The world was a beautiful place after all.

Then a note of caution sounded in her head. She sat down. She needed to think.

Malena being in love with Perry didn't mean that Jonas wasn't in love with Malena, she realized. The smell of the jasmine suddenly seemed cloying. *Don't jump to conclusions*, she chided herself. It wasn't Jonas kissing her, was it? And Malena didn't actually kiss Perry, did she — at least not while she was watching?

Oh, stop it! Stop it! Jenna thought in frustration. *Why do I always have to twist everything? I have a chance with Jonas!*

She stood up. She had to suppress the urge to let out a cry of joy and twirl around in circles. Why had she been so nervous about this party? *I don't care who talks to me*, she thought, and walked back across the lawn toward the crowds of guests. *Laugh at me all you like, snooty rich people! I'm Princess of Scandia, and no one can make me feel small. I may not be perfect, but I can learn. And as long as the things that matter work out, I'll be fine.*

Jonas.

He was standing with his back against a cedar tree, on his own. Jenna's heart throbbed.

"Hi, Jonas," she said. How simple it was. Maybe.

Jonas looked startled. "Oh, hi, Jenna," he said. "I couldn't find you anywhere." He nodded miserably. "I couldn't find anyone to talk to but boring old people. So I've been kind of blowing off the party."

"Me, too," said Jenna. It didn't matter that she'd started

blushing, as usual. Suddenly, it all seemed so simple. She was happy.

"And Perry's disappeared, too," said Jonas. "And Malena. What's going on? I've been looking for both of them."

Jenna shrugged. Would it be a betrayal if she told him? Maybe it should be Malena herself. Or Perry.

But since he was going to find out, anyway . . .

"They're back there in the summerhouse," she said softly. She looked down at the ground. She hadn't given away too much. That was all right, wasn't it?

"What?" asked Jonas in surprise.

Then again, maybe not.

Jenna shrugged her shoulders. Her face burned an even deeper shade of red. "They're together, in the summerhouse," she said.

Jonas stared at her. "Get out!" he whispered, and to her enormous relief Jenna saw a grin spreading across his face. The news hadn't made him unhappy — not at all. "Malena and Perry?"

Jenna nodded.

Jonas punched his open left hand with his right fist. "So that's what he's been all hung up about!" he said. "I was wondering what his problem was! Malena and Perry — I wouldn't have guessed that one!"

"You don't mind?" Jenna ventured cautiously. "I mean, you and Malena . . ." She blushed all over again. Why did she have to keep doing that?

"What? No! It's awesome!" said Jonas. "My two best friends! Things couldn't have turned out better. Perfect!"

So he only thought of Malena as a friend. How could she have been so dumb? But she couldn't let herself get carried away, either . . .

"I always sort of thought you and Malena . . ." she whispered. She must have been the color of an eggplant by now, but it didn't matter. "You and Malena . . ."

She couldn't look at him. But she didn't have to. Jonas's laugh was so happy that she didn't need to see his face.

"No way!" he said. "Not Malena! She's always been like a sister to me!" He stopped talking.

The silence between them was almost audible. It felt as if something was about to explode.

"Because . . ." murmured Jonas, and she didn't know if he was looking at her, because she couldn't bear to look at him. ". . . because — Malena's not the only girl in the world. Because . . ." He took a step toward her.

And then the moment passed. Suddenly, Perry's dad was standing beside them — Mom's Petterson. Jenna hadn't heard him, he'd approached so silently. He looked aggravated.

"Do either of you know where Perry is?" he asked. "I've been searching everywhere for him. When I saw you just now, I thought he might be with you."

"Nope," said Jonas, shaking his head and staring off into the distance.

Jenna shook her head, too.

And you can just go on searching, you pain in the pancreas! thought Jenna. *Because as long as you keep looking, at least you won't be hanging around my mother!* Then she felt her shoulders drop. She hadn't realized how tense she'd been.

"I've been searching everywhere," Petterson said again. "He's not inside, or by the rose garden, or in any of the summerhouses . . ."

Jenna looked up. "Really?" she blurted, caught off guard.

"No," said Petterson. "But if you don't know where he is, either . . ."

"Sorry, sir," said Jonas. His voice sounded matter-of-fact again. "We've been standing here the whole time."

"Well, I'll just have to keep on searching," he said, shrugging his shoulders. "I'm sure I'm worrying unnecessarily."

"Hope you find him!" Jenna chimed in, smiling. *I can be just as two-faced as him*, she thought. *Worrying about your son? Doubtful!*

Only when Petterson had hurried away across the lawn did Jonas look at her again.

"Now he'll get his people to hunt for his own son," he said, and cleared his throat. "Thus endeth the love scene in the love nest. Poor Perry. He's totally avoiding his father 'cause he's in a panic over being shipped off to military school."

"But didn't you hear what he said?" she asked. "Maybe Perry's really gone."

"Gone?" echoed Jonas. "Oh, right, because he's not in the summerhouse."

It's over now, thought Jenna. *That's how fast a magic spell can end, no matter how gently you treat it.* And all because that clumsy oaf interrupted us. *Malena's not the only girl in the world,* Jonas had said. And it was Jonas who had blushed. If Petterson hadn't butted in — if they'd had just one more minute. But now it was over. Now all Jonas could think about was Perry and where he might be.

"It is kind of weird, isn't it?" said Jonas. He didn't look at her. "I'd better go see if I can find him before his dad does."

Jenna nodded. "Oh, definitely," she said.

As he went to leave, Jonas suddenly reached out his hand toward her, in a gesture of . . . what? Jenna didn't know. But then he quickly drew it back, as if he'd just realized what he'd done, and began to run. After a few steps, he turned and waved to her. His face was bright red.

"See you soon!" he called, telling himself he hadn't totally blown his cover.

13

After the first assault on the buffet and the first round of conversation, von Thunberg had asked them to go with him to the hunting room. The walls were covered with trophies that generations of the family had brought home from the hunt: stuffed heads of boar; a collection of roebuck horns arranged like a kind of mosaic; the spreading antlers of a fourteen-pointer; even a lion's head with a magnificent mane, from the von Thunbergs' safaris in Africa.

Four glass-fronted cabinets, one on each wall of the room, contained brightly polished hunting weapons dating back more than three hundred years. Between them hung paintings of traditional hunting scenes.

"Whiskey, anyone?" asked von Thunberg, opening the one cabinet with solid wooden doors. "Gin? I also have sherry for you, Your Royal Highness."

His three guests all shook their heads in silence. Petterson, who had temporarily given up the hunt for his son, leaned on the heavy oak table in the center of the room; Liron stood by the window overlooking the garden, gazing down at the party guests and the grounds, where his son was just waving to Jenna as he left her; Princess Margareta was still standing near the doorway.

"Did anyone get hold of the king?" Von Thunberg's eyes went from Petterson to Liron to Margareta.

"What can Magnus do about it?" asked Liron. He raised his eyebrows almost as high as his hairline. "We've taken every safety measure a country can possibly take . . ."

"Except calling in the military!" von Thunberg stated. "I'm not allowed to mobilize my men, even though for decades it's worked perfectly well."

"Perfectly well?" repeated Princess Margareta. "Von Thunberg! This is now a free country!"

"But when it was under our control at least it was free of smugglers!" von Thunberg exclaimed. "And now every illegal substance you can think of is being brought in, to ruin our youth and, worst of all, to provide the rebels with more than enough money to stock their own arsenals! How can you all stay so calm? They blew up the pylons . . ."

". . . so that Magnus couldn't give his speech," said Princess Margareta.

". . . though everything's almost back to normal again," Liron countered.

". . . except the oil pipeline, and now they've compromised border security! We thought — and Magnus tried to convince everyone — that if the reforms went through and the north was made equal to the south, the rebels would withdraw and we wouldn't need to fight them anymore. No civil war! But look how wrong we were!"

"Magnus never said it would be easy," said the princess. "Never. He knew the transition would bring plenty of new problems."

"Problems!" cried von Thunberg. "You call it problems, Your Highness, when a whole country is starving?"

Liron came away from the window. "I didn't notice anyone starving at your party today, von Thunberg."

"And maybe you didn't notice the pipeline being blown up, either!" von Thunberg retorted. "Or Holmburg's disrupted electricity supply! Or the fact that our customs men were seized by masked bandits at Scandia's largest airport this very day and locked up in a janitor's closet!"

Petterson laughed, and von Thunberg spun around to glare at him.

"I'd like to know what you think there is to laugh at!" he snapped.

"There's something funny about the whole idea — you must admit it, Thunberg," said Petterson. "The janitor's closet, I mean. When I picture it . . ."

"Peter!" said Princess Margareta, shaking her head.

"We can't wait any longer!" von Thunberg said, resuming his argument. "The new constitution still gives the king the right to call in the military in the event of a national crisis."

"There's no way you can call the current situation a national crisis," said Liron.

Petterson glanced at von Thunberg.

"Well, I'd say . . ."

At that moment a cell phone rang. They all listened for a second to see if the ringtone was theirs, then Liron reached into his jacket pocket. "Yes?" he asked, turning away from the group. "For heaven's sake, Carlson, surely you can manage that without me being there!"

He went to the window, an angry scowl on his face.

"No, don't make a big deal about it. It's just some silly kids' prank. It's not likely to start raining on the way back!"

On the other end of the phone, the talk was fast and furious.

"I really haven't got time now for such kids' stuff, Carlson!" snapped Liron. "Fix it, and if you can't, it's not the end of the world." He flipped the phone shut. "My driver," he explained to the room, shrugging his shoulders. "Sorry. He was in something of a state. Someone's broken the windshield wipers on the car."

"I don't suppose you'll be blaming *that* on the terrorists, will you, Thunberg?" said Petterson. "Even if it is the Minister of the Interior's car."

Von Thunberg gave him a withering look.

"I suggest, General," said Princess Margareta, nodding as if to indicate that as far as she was concerned it marked the end of the discussion, "that we talk this over again soon, together with my brother. At the moment, the situation does not seem to me to be so critical as to warrant missing the rest of your delightful party."

"Well said, Your Highness," said Petterson with a satirical little bow.

"Thank you, kind sir," said Margareta.

On his way out, Liron laid a comforting hand on von Thunberg's arm.

Von Thunberg shook it off. "If you can't see what's happening . . . you've only yourselves to blame," he said angrily.

Perry walked up to the main house. The estate was likely to be crawling with guards. He'd seen men with submachine guns near the gate. But they would mainly be watching out for people trying to get in. The rebels wouldn't often get the chance to find all the country's VIPs gathered in one place.

When he reached the house, he went around the corner to the servants' entrance. The guards would not be particularly interested in what came out of there. If he was smart, it shouldn't be too difficult.

He smiled. *Nothing could be too difficult now,* he thought — *absolutely nothing.* The hardest part of all was now behind him, and how easy it had turned out to be! Why hadn't he dared to do it earlier? "Did you really think I didn't like you?" Malena had said, as if he'd been a fool ever to imagine otherwise.

In the little yard in front of the stables there was a large truck with a tarp roof — probably for tables, chairs, and awnings — a laundry van, and several minibuses. There were also several large wire bins on wheels, like the ones they used at school for the dirty linen.

Perry leaned against the wall of the house. Apart from a man putting down a tray, the backyard was empty. The waiters were obviously circulating among the guests. The man left. Now was his chance. He went over to one of the big wire bins.

He had no idea where he would end up — presumably in a laundromat somewhere — or what he would do when he got there. But it had to be worth trying. One step at a time. Anything was better than the military academy. And after all, wasn't today his lucky day?

He pushed the bin onto the lift of the laundry van. If he was going to hide in it, he didn't want anyone wondering why it was so heavy till he was well clear of the place. He pressed a button inside the van, and with a low hum the lift raised the container.

When he heard footsteps approaching, he pushed the bin up against two others at the far end of the van as quickly as he could. He buzzed the lift down again, crept to the bin, climbed in, and pulled the soiled tablecloths over his head. His heart was thumping, but nobody came.

Malena understood why he had to run away. "You've got no choice," she'd whispered. "Once you're gone, maybe your father will realize how much it matters to you! Then he'll let you be and forget about his stupid military academy." Then she had sat there with him, cheek to cheek. "And I'll wait for you," she said. "It'll be really romantic, just like in the movies! Everything will be OK."

He heard more footsteps in the yard, and huddled down under the linens. Malena was right. Everything would be OK.

Jonas jogged gently across the lawn, wending his way between the guests. He didn't care when some of them turned to look at him — he'd long ago learned not to take any notice.

But where could Perry have gone? Had something really happened to him? And why had he left Jenna and rushed off like that, joining the search like an idiot, as if he believed Perry might really have disappeared or been kidnapped?

He slowed down. The sounds from the party were muffled now.

Jenna! he thought. *I was just about to . . . and then I didn't. At least Perry's dad saved me from making a complete fool of myself.*

He looked over his shoulder. Was she still standing in the same spot? Maybe he should go back. He was such a coward! Perry had done it, even with all his shyness and hang-ups — Jonas would never have guessed he'd have the guts — while he himself had chickened out and run away at the first chance.

OK, he vowed, *if she's still standing there when I turn around, I'll go back. No matter how stupid it looks or what she thinks of me, I'll just do it. Bite the bullet. Ask her out right now . . .*

He scanned the lawn; she was nowhere to be seen.

OK! thought Jonas. *So it won't be today. Plan B: I'll see her tomorrow at school. Maybe when we go running. I'll get there really early and wait for her. Where's the best place, so none of the guards at the fence can see us?*

Behind a clump of trees he came to the summerhouse. He had to admit it was a seriously romantic spot. Props to Perry for thinking of it! Maybe they *were* still there. Maybe old man Petterson had simply missed the place. Climbing roses practically covered the glassless windows and the doorway. Jonas poked his head inside and ducked under a hanging branch to enter the little room. The air smelled of fading paint, and the waxed wooden floorboards were shining. He sat down on the wraparound bench.

Tomorrow, then, he thought, and leaned his head back against the wood. *I'll definitely do it tomorrow.*

A dark shadow suddenly appeared in the doorway.

"Ylva!" he said in surprise, sitting up straight.

"Oh, hi, Jonas!" she whispered, as if she hadn't noticed him before. "You're in here! I thought . . ." She stopped mid-sentence and looked down at the floor in embarrassment.

"What?" asked Jonas. He could really do without this on top of everything else.

Ylva looked helpless, standing there in front of him with drooping shoulders and bent head — helpless and fragile in a way he'd never seen before. Ylva was strong, everyone knew that — strong and self-confident. She was captain of the field hockey team, and the toughest player on the lacrosse team, too. But now she stood there like some lost little girl, and through the western window the last rays of the sun were falling on her long blonde hair, lighting it up like spun gold.

"Oh, nothing," she murmured. "It's just that — it's all kind of overwhelming, you know? All those people. The noise. I was just looking for somewhere quiet to get away."

"Uh, me, too," Jonas bluffed. What other reason could he give for sitting there all alone in the summerhouse?

Ylva sat down beside him. A delicate scent, a bit like lemon, joined the smell of roses and paint. It was coming from Ylva's hair. "Do you mind if I sit here with you for a while?" she asked, still not looking at him.

"Yeah, no problem," said Jonas, itching to get up and out of there. But he knew it wouldn't have been kind to leave her on her own after she had just appeared, looking so unhappy and so vulnerable and so totally un-Ylva-like. He didn't get it — the party wasn't *that* bad. And it was her house, after all!

He didn't know what to say, and the silence between them became more and more prolonged. It was a different kind of silence from the one between him and Jenna.

Suddenly, Ylva looked up, as if she'd just made a decision. "Jonas!" she whispered, and at that moment he understood. *Oh my God*, he thought, *this can't be happening*. But he knew what was coming even before she said it. Maybe it *had* been the same kind of silence after all. "Jonas, I . . ."

Her hands were on his shoulders, pulling him toward her, and he couldn't help but move closer. Then she put her hand behind his head, and her face was right up against his, forcing her lips onto his mouth.

No, no, thought Jonas. *I don't want to do this! I just don't understand girls!* But then he stopped thinking altogether. His whole head was swimming, and Ylva's lips were on his and wouldn't let go, and his mouth opened without him even realizing it.

No! He had to free himself — from her hands, from her lips — and he didn't want this feeling, not with Ylva. *Oh God . . .*

"Ylva!" he managed to say. He found it hard to breathe. "Ylva, please! I . . ." He tried to catch his breath. "Please, Ylva. I . . . I don't want to do this."

Now was the time to tell her that he was interested in someone else. But again she was looking so small and defenseless, almost desperate, and how could he make her even more unhappy? "I'm sorry, Ylva. I . . . I just don't feel that way about you."

Jenna had watched Jonas disappear across the lawn. *I'm almost positive he likes me*, she thought, *but why did he run off?* If only that horrible Petterson hadn't chosen that precise moment to arrive! *Malena's not the only girl in the world*, Jonas had said, and he'd blushed when he said it, hadn't he?

She went across to the buffet table. She wanted to talk to Malena. Though could she really say, "Hey, Malena, I saw you before in the summerhouse, you and Perry. Sorry, didn't mean to spy. But anyway, I saw you, and I just wanted to ask . . ."

Could you ask another girl how to do that kind of thing . . . who made the first move, said the first word . . . ?

Of course you can, thought Jenna. *Why not?* And Malena was her cousin. Jenna might not do everything exactly the same way she had — it might all be totally different between her and Jonas — but it still could be useful to know how Malena and Perry had worked up the courage. *And tomorrow at the latest, when Jonas and I meet, or maybe in the morning when I go for my . . .*

No! It should be today. The two of them were simply too shy. She'd seen it over and over again in the movies: boy and girl dithering away and nobody making the first move.

She took a deep breath, then set off determinedly in the direction Jonas had taken. She suddenly knew that she would never forgive herself if she let him go like that. She was Princess Jenna of Scandia, and today she would be successful at whatever she did.

14

The summerhouse loomed up behind the clump of trees. Jenna knew she would find Jonas there. She had told him about Perry and Malena, so that it would be the first place he'd look, logically.

Carefully she lifted up the branch that blocked the nearest window. Her heart was beating so fast and so loud, she was sure Jonas would hear it. But she couldn't flake out again; she was determined to do it: At last she would tell him how she felt. She took a deep breath, then leaned forward to look inside.

On the bench opposite sat Jonas, just as she had guessed. But he was not alone. Ylva!

Malena's not the only girl in the world . . . The words came back to haunt her. How could she ever have thought he meant her?

Jonas's head was facing away, twisted at a strange angle. Between him and Ylva was far too large a gap, and yet . . . they were holding each other. They were . . .

No! thought Jenna. *Not Ylva!*

She turned away. She didn't want to look into Ylva's eyes, which were staring at her, mocking, hard, triumphant, over Jonas's tousled hair. Jenna began to run. Behind her she could still hear Jonas's voice: "Please," he said. "Please, Ylva!" And she ran and ran and ran, and it was as if she had never in all her life known how deep and dark and terrible despair could be.

15

*T*he laundry van traveled through the dusk.
How much longer? thought Perry. They had strapped
the bins to the inside of the van with belts so that their
little wheels wouldn't set them rolling around the floor, but
they kept bumping against each other all the same as the
van drove along the uneven roads, and their metal frames
clashed and clanged.

Perry was well hidden. No one had noticed him. The
gigantic tablecloth that covered him still smelled a little of
detergent, with one large, oily stain that stank of fish. After
what he estimated was a few miles, he ventured to take the
cloth off his head. Here in the back of the van, he figured no
one could possibly see him, and it ended up being so dark that
he couldn't even see his hand in front of his face.

When they got to the laundromat, he could slip away into
the night. The plan was simple but genius, he told himself.

The van rounded a sharp bend, pressing Perry hard up
against the frame of the bin, and finally came to a halt. He

pulled the tablecloth over his head again and tensed his muscles in preparation.

Someone opened the rear door of the van. The halogen lights that illuminated the laundromat's parking lot threw a faint orange glow into the back. Perry peeked out to see two men untying the bins nearest to the door and pushing them onto the lift. Then came the soft hum of the machinery as they were hoisted down.

"We'll just unload them tonight," said a tired voice. "You push the bins, and I'll hold the door."

Perry could hear their footsteps, and the jarring scrape of the metal wheels over a stone surface. It had to be now. This was the best chance he'd get.

Wire clanged against wire as he threw off the cloth and carefully climbed out. He crept quickly to the open door and jumped to the ground.

The air smelled of evening. Old brick buildings lined three sides of the cobbled square, with the fourth side open to the street. Perry kept crouched close to the ground and ran as fast as he could, keeping to the shadows. The two men had disappeared into one of the buildings, and he could hear them pushing the bins, exchanging a few words and laughing.

Almost! thought Perry. And then he saw the moped.

It was standing up against the brick wall, right beside the exit onto the road, and in the light of the streetlamps it glowed a deep red. Although it was an old model, it was polished as shiny as new. It probably belonged to one of the two men.

It's stealing, thought Perry as he looked to see if the moped was locked. But he had no trouble softly pushing it over the rough stones. He didn't start the motor. *It's stealing, but how stupid are people, leaving their keys in the ignition!*

Then he saw the high iron gate. The men must have opened it before driving the van into the yard. No wonder the owner of the moped would have assumed it would be safe inside.

I'll send them some money, I swear. As soon as I can get into my account.

He began to run, pulling the heavy moped along beside him. He wouldn't start the motor until he was good and far away from the laundromat. If the men heard it and came after him in the van, he wouldn't stand a chance.

The narrow road stretched out in darkness beneath an overcast sky. To the right he could see the last lights of a little town. To the left, the road disappeared into a forest. That was the direction Perry pushed the moped.

The men must have finished unloading the bins by now. It was time. He straddled the moped and turned the key. It shot forward beneath him and he only just managed to keep his balance — he'd never ridden a moped before. He could feel the wind blowing through his hair, and he laughed.

Free! he thought. *I'm free! You can forget about your military academy! You'll never lock me up in there. Never!*

The moped glided into the forest, and Perry slowed down. After just a few feet, he switched off the lights and pushed it off the road into the undergrowth. Then he waited.

It was almost half an hour before the laundry van passed him at breakneck speed. The men must have searched all over the square.

He listened, then pushed the moped back out of the under-growth. The night belonged to him now — there was no one else on the road. He knew where he would go. His head and heart felt light, and he was way too happy to be tired.

Before the sun sank down behind the treetops, the first clouds began to gather, gray and heavy, but still so few and far between that, although the guests occasionally glanced up at the sky, no one was particularly worried.

"A wonderful party, as usual, General," said an elderly lady. "Just like the old days. One might almost have thought our Scandia had never changed."

Von Thunberg bowed. "Delighted that you enjoyed it, Baroness," he said.

He was standing with his wife at the base of the broad steps, shaking the hands of everyone leaving the party. Circling the garden, charming Chinese lanterns glowed in the dusk, and yellowish-white splashes of the lights embedded in the foliage created an almost eerie atmosphere. The party was over — this was traditionally how it came to an end. As soon as darkness crept between the trees, the guests would climb into their town cars and limousines and drive home to their own nearby estates. Hardly any would make the long journey back to the city of Holmburg tonight.

"Good night, Countess, Count!" said von Thunberg. "We'll meet again next summer."

"Before that, I hope," said the countess with a radiant smile. "Good night, General."

Across the great lawn, the catering staff was now beginning to stack the chairs and take down the tables. Von Thunberg's brow furrowed, and his wife's face twisted into an angry scowl. Next year they would hire a different company. The staff should have waited until the last guest had departed before they began dismantling the place.

"I'm so sorry," Mrs. von Thunberg said to an old lady with a walking stick, who was watching the activity with raised eyebrows. "I've sent someone to put a stop to it at once. Such behavior, I fear, Your Ladyship, is just one more consequence of the . . ." She hesitated a moment before spitting out the word. ". . . the *democratization* of our country! These days, allowing the staff to get to bed on time seems to be reason enough to end a party."

"I can only assume it's a company that hasn't taught its people good manners, dear Mrs. von Thunberg!" said the bent little man accompanying the old lady. His hand was gently supporting his companion's elbow. "Little *parvenus* who've grown up in the slums and don't know the first thing about society's rules. You'll find them everywhere. All the same, it's been a wonderful party."

Petterson pushed his way toward the front, past the straggly queue of people still chatting as they stood at the foot of the steps. He waited impatiently until the elderly couple had taken their leave, and then he went straight up to von Thunberg.

"Thunberg, please forgive me," he said quietly, "but I can't find my son, and I'm beginning to get worried. May I send my people to search your house? He's definitely not on the grounds."

"Of course," said von Thunberg. "Though I can't imagine . . ."

"Jenna's also disappeared!" said the princess, suddenly standing beside Petterson. "I can't find her anywhere. I didn't think too much of it, but now that you say Perry's gone missing . . ."

"Your people are welcome to search the house for as long as you like," said von Thunberg, smiling past them at the next guest. "Del Halberstrum! We never even had a chance to raise a toast, old chap!"

Petterson and Margareta stepped aside.

"You don't think the two of them . . . ?" the princess began. "But they hardly know each other!"

"It's a strange coincidence all the same," said Petterson. He went over to a man in a black suit, who was standing patiently at the edge of the gravel driveway. "Viktor, take three men and search the house. But be discreet. Don't draw any attention to yourselves."

The man in the suit nodded and disappeared.

"Goodness, might they have been abducted?" asked Margareta. Her face suddenly clouded over with concern.

"Peter? How could that possibly have happened here at the party, with such tight security?"

Petterson shrugged his shoulders. "Maybe my men will find them in the house," he said. He didn't look too confident.

Jenna ran.

She had taken off her sandals and was carrying them by their laces as she ran and ran, faster and faster across the grounds. She ran so fast that her violent heartbeat drowned out her thoughts and, more important, her feelings — *faster, faster!* She could hear her own breathing, her own heartbeat, as if they belonged to a stranger, but it didn't help.

The grounds of the estate were huge, even larger than the school campus — she hadn't realized it before. The landscape had grown wilder now, up- and downhill, with swampy groves of alders in the dips and pine trees higher up; in between were small ponds and meadows full of summer flowers. But Jenna didn't notice any of it.

Run, just run. Beneath her feet she felt grass and moss and pebbles and pine needles, rocks and hard, dry dirt. She didn't even feel all the cuts she was getting on the soles of her bare feet. She felt nothing but despair.

Jonas.

She had never known that sadness could be so huge it could fill the whole world right to the furthest corner, leaving no room for anything else.

Tears flooded her face. Her makeup was a mess of smudges, her mascara streaming in charcoal rivulets down her cheeks. She could not stop crying.

Jonas and Ylva.

She didn't want to stop. She didn't care. Whatever happened, happened. She didn't want to do anything except sink into this sadness and never emerge again into the endless sequence of days, weeks, months that would go on as normal, as though her life had not just been shattered.

I'm just lovesick, thought Jenna, astonished that she was beginning to think again after all as her feet raced along the narrow paths and her heart hammered. *Lovesick*. What a silly word for such a terrible, overwhelming pain.

Hadn't she heard about it, read about it in magazines, a million times before? *Lovesick, heartsick, heartbroken. The sickness passes* — her feet raced — *everyone goes through it. After a few days, you'll wonder what on earth you ever got so upset about.*

But no, Jenna knew it was different for her. She'd never get over this despair that blotted out everything else, till life itself seemed meaningless.

The sun disappeared behind the clouds. Her feet slowed down. The last year had been so difficult, and the only thing that got her through had been her longing for Jonas — though she had never thought he'd feel the same.

And then she had seen Malena and Perry in the summer-house, and suddenly the hopelessness had fallen away like a chain that could be broken through a single weak link. And then Jonas had said, *"Malena's not the only girl in the world,"* and her heart had grown wings.

How could she have been so stupid?

Jenna bent over and rested her hands on her knees. To her surprise, she realized that the tears had stopped running down her cheeks. She was breathing hard and fast.

Not just lovesickness, she thought, as gradually her breathing slowed down. A gentle twilight began to envelop the grounds — the long, late dusk of summer. It must be later than she realized. She'd been running for a long time.

Not just lovesickness, but shame. Stupid her! How could she have thought even for a second that Jonas meant her — Jenna, small and dark and chubby — when there were so many other girls who were more beautiful, more self-assured, taller and slimmer and fairer? Jenna, who never did anything right, who was mocked in the newspapers on a daily basis. Jonas would never want her. Not when there were girls like Ylva to choose from.

But not Ylva! thought Jenna, her stomach in knots. *Why Ylva?* She straightened up and walked on, very slowly now. Since the clouds had gathered, she could feel the coolness of the evening, and the little hairs on her arms stood on end.

Had Jonas realized what she was feeling? Maybe *that* was why he ran away to look for Perry. It hadn't been shyness at all, as she'd so pathetically imagined. No, he'd realized the truth and raced off before the situation could become too embarrassing!

Jonas knew she was in love with him, and he found it so repulsive that he had to literally run in the opposite direction.

Oh God!

She would *never* be able to talk to him again. Was he still sitting with Ylva in the summerhouse at this very moment, laughing about her?

"How could that little fattie possibly think I'd ever be into her?" More laughter, more making out. How could she ever look Jonas in the eye again? And how could she possibly stand to be in the same room with Ylva now — it would be unbearable!

She could hear voices. She must have circled the whole estate. She'd left the wild meadows and was back at the vast, manicured lawns. There was the main house, and the stables, the parking lot, the outbuildings. The gate with its bell tower: the way out.

She couldn't go back to school. She had to leave. There must be an escape route, even though the security guards were patroling everywhere in sight. The catering staff was rushing around, carrying trays of dirty dishes, collecting glasses from wherever they'd been left. There were still a few guests clustered in little groups near the base of the broad flight of steps, having one last conversation, promising to meet again soon, then wandering off together to the parking lot, where their chauffeurs were waiting for them.

Jenna left the shadows of the trees and wiped her tear-stained face. Her hair had come loose from its ribbons, and strands now hung down over her shoulders. As she slipped her sandals back on, she felt the pain in the soles of her feet, but there was no time to worry about that now. A few steps in front of her, two champagne glasses sat in the grass; she leaned over and picked them up, then glanced warily around. It might work. After all, her mother had said she looked like a waitress. The dusk was thickening now, but she could still see various discarded objects lying on the grass: scrunched-up napkins, half-empty plates, an ornate fork. Jenna bent down, picked them up, and bent down again. When she had collected so much she could scarcely hold it all, she hurried toward the catering van.

A man in a black suit, his tie neatly knotted and his short, gelled hair as immaculate as if the party had just begun, looked irritably at her.

"Why didn't you use a tray?" he snapped. "And do you realize how you look?"

Jenna lowered her eyes and didn't answer. She put the glasses and plates in their separate racks, then grabbed a tray. Mom was right about the blue dress. And for such a big reception, the caterers would have had to take on extra staff — especially northerners, who were cheap to hire and hardworking. There was no way the man could remember every face.

But she mustn't go too close to the remaining guests, in case one of them recognized her. There was still some light in the sky, even though the clouds were gathering. She crossed the lawn and bent down to pick up one last glass. That was it. Cautiously she made her way back, but she could see at a glance that nearly all the guests had gone and the parking lot was practically empty.

Behind the stables, tables and chairs were being loaded onto trucks, and the cartons of cookware were being sealed for the return journey. There were women and girls sitting in a minivan, packed together on the seats, with crates and boxes between their feet. Jenna went to the rear door, and a friendly hand gripped her arm and helped her up.

"Come in, child," said the deep, smoky voice of an old woman. "There's still room for you."

All of them looked tired.

"Oh dear, what's the matter? You've been crying! Has one of those spoiled —"

Jenna shook her head. The tears began to flow again. But maybe that wasn't such a bad thing; maybe it would mean they'd leave her alone.

The woman shuffled along the seat. There wasn't much room to spare. She put her arm around Jenna's shoulders and drew her close. A strand of hair fell over Jenna's eyes.

"Go on, honey, you have a good cry!" said the woman.

Jenna sobbed, and someone handed her a handkerchief that had been washed thin. The back door was slammed shut, and the minivan began to move.

"Let it all out, girl," said the woman, and to her surprise Jenna found her kindness comforting. Perhaps the future wasn't entirely bleak after all. As the van drove off the grounds and out onto the road, the women talked about the buffet and how amazing it was to see so much fine food and drink in a country hit by shortages.

But Jenna didn't really listen. She leaned against the soft, motherly shoulder of the woman, and cried till she could cry no more.

PART TWO

16

Joward midnight the weather changed.

Lightning cut across the sky, thunder rumbled continuously, and rain fell from the dark clouds that had gathered earlier in the evening, so heavily that in less than a minute Jenna's thin dress was soaked through.

She saw a bus shelter by the side of the road. Its Plexiglas walls were covered in ancient, ugly ads for a "new" brand of ice cream, and had graffiti scrawled all over them. The acrylic was scratched and chipped in places, but the roof was still intact, and it shielded her from the cloudburst.

In her wet dress, with her arms all goose-pimply, Jenna tried to huddle up on the narrow bench. She needed to rest, at least for a few minutes. Her head was swimming from tiredness, but she was too cold to sleep. Her teeth were chattering so loudly it was almost frightening.

She sat up again.

The van had dropped her and the rest of the waitstaff outside a modern building on the outskirts of a little town. The women had all hurried through the door to form a line at one of the counters inside.

Jenna had wanted to run off right there and then, but the woman who had been so kind to her throughout the journey had held her tightly by the shoulder.

"Hey, now," she'd said. "How can anyone be so tired they forget to collect their pay?"

Jenna had not objected. She had joined the line, and each of the women had been given an envelope for which they'd had to sign. The man at the counter did not even check their names off a list — he must have been tired, too.

Can it really be this easy? thought Jenna. Then she had the envelope in her hand, and the kind woman waved her good-bye and climbed onto a rickety old bicycle. "Are you OK now? Can you get home all right from here?" she'd called.

Jenna had nodded and waved back, then started to walk. She had soon reached the end of the buildings, where a road sign indicated that this was the border of the town. The town's name meant nothing to Jenna — it was only a tiny place, and they had driven for so long that she realized she must be very far north. There were no stars in the sky, and the moon must have been hidden behind the clouds. She had walked, just to get away, far from the sight of any houses or passersby — wandering aimlessly through the night.

And then the thunderstorm had broken. It was lucky for her that she'd come across the bus shelter.

Jenna listened to her teeth chattering. *But it isn't all bad, is it?* she reasoned with herself. *I got away, and now I even have some money.*

The rattling on the roof gave way to a gentle patter. *I mustn't catch cold. I've got to find somewhere to hide, where it'll be dry and sheltered, and where I can stay for a while.*

And then? Jenna twined her arms around her body, trying to get warm. *Que será, será. But I'll never go back. I can't take any more.*

The rain had stopped. The moon came out from behind a cloud and bathed the wet road in a cold, mysterious light.

I'm not afraid, thought Jenna, getting up. *And I've got to keep moving, or I really will catch my death of cold in this wet dress. I'll sleep later, as soon as it's light and the sun has dried me out.*

She felt more awake than before the downpour, and her teeth had stopped chattering. The farther she walked, the warmer she felt. She'd find out where she was heading eventually.

When the short night gave way to a yellowish dawn that promised yet another scorching day, Jenna finally saw a crossroads in the distance. And a signpost — at last!

She walked faster. The signpost had faded from years of sun and rain, and a hunter must have hit it with a stray bullet at some point, because there was a hole where there should have been paint. Even so, the name was clearly legible:

SAARSTAD

What an amazing coincidence! Was this fate? thought Jenna, full of disbelief. Though perhaps it was not quite that amazing. After all, the von Thunberg estate was located in the north of South Island, almost on the sound that separated the two islands of Scandia. Now she knew exactly where she could go to hide.

She clutched the envelope with the money in it, and walked even faster.

They had not left the von Thunberg estate.

"How can I go back to Osterlin while Jenna's still missing?" asked Margareta. There was an undertone in her voice that made it clear to everyone in the room she was on the verge of hysteria. "She's got to be around here somewhere! She can't just have disappeared! This place was so well guarded!"

"*Is*, Your Royal Highness, it still is!" von Thunberg said soothingly. "There's no way your daughter can leave if she's still here. Security is on its way with dogs and searchlights and night vision aids, so rest assured, we shall find the children."

"It was that Pizza Princess business!" said Margareta, burying her face in her hands. "She was so ashamed. And then I had to go and talk to her like I did . . ."

"You think she's run away?" asked Petterson, putting a hand on her shoulder. For a father whose son had also disappeared, he seemed remarkably calm. "But how could she have done that? Thunberg's quite right, the security measures here couldn't be better. I'm more inclined to think . . ."

"No!" said the princess. "No, Peter, no!"

"We need to face facts, Greta," Petterson persisted. "It can't be a coincidence that both Perry and Jenna have vanished at the same time."

"But they could have run away together!" the princess said, almost pleading. "Peter! Why can't you believe that?"

Petterson stroked her hair. "Two of them just slipping through the security net?" he asked gently. "Margareta, be honest with yourself. The rebels have always found ways and means. How can we know who's infiltrated our security staff? True, we haven't received any ransom demands yet, but . . ."

"No!" whispered the princess. She stood up, then paced to and fro. They were in one of the von Thunbergs' reception rooms. The heavy brocade curtains had not been closed, so the glass of the windows reflected the ornate chandeliers. The parquet flooring, with its decorative inlays, was covered with oriental silk carpets that deadened the sound of her footsteps. "Not last year all over again! I couldn't bear that, Peter! The fear! Not Jenna again! It's been nonstop anxiety since the day she was born!"

Von Thunberg cleared his throat. "If I might just point something out, Your Royal Highness," he said. "The security situation in our country is badly in need of improvement. It seems to me very unlikely that the rebels would dare to abduct a princess if they had to deal with military roadblocks at every turn. But of course . . ." He shrugged his shoulders.

"Now is not the time to promote your agenda, Thunberg!" said Petterson sharply. "Margareta, darling. My son has disappeared with her, and —"

At that moment the door swung open. "I came straight from the airport as soon as I got your news, Margareta," said the king, standing in the doorway. "Well? Any updates?"

The princess shook her head. "Not Jenna again!" she repeated in a whisper.

Magnus crossed the room and took her in his arms. "There, there," he said. "It's too soon to tell. Jenna could be sitting somewhere, clueless to all our concerns, happy as a clam . . ."

Margareta pushed him away. "You believe that?" she cried. "After all you went through yourself last year? How can you be so blind, Magnus? And how can we just stand here wasting time? We've got to —"

Von Thunberg interrupted. "Your Majesty!" he said, with an impatient bow. "I can only agree with your sister. We should make a public announcement immediately, issue a missing persons alert for both children. It may not be much help now, in the middle of the night, but tomorrow morning when people get up and it's the first thing they hear on the news, you'll have the whole of Scandia searching for them."

"The press already have photos," added Petterson.

The king nodded. "Right," he said. "An announcement." He looked exhausted. Considering the recent series of events, the last few days had been made up of one long meeting after another. "There's nothing more we can do tonight," he said.

"Forgive me if I disagree, Your Majesty," said von Thunberg. "Let me order my men to take over internal security. Within two hours they can set up roadblocks on all the major routes. Even during the night we can still conduct searches of every known or suspected rebel stronghold. This is a national crisis, Your Majesty!"

"The possibility that my niece has been kidnapped does not constitute a national crisis, von Thunberg," said the king. He leaned against one of the window seats, almost too tired to stand. "Even if it feels like one to my sister and me. A personal tragedy for the royal family is no more important to the nation than the tragedy of any other family. It does not justify military intervention." He looked out across the grounds, which were now in total darkness. "Even if at this moment I might wish that it did," he added wearily.

"Magnus!" cried Margareta. With a few steps she was beside him. "Please, Magnus! It's not just Jenna! Von Thunberg has been asking now for so long . . ."

"To be honest, Magnus, I think he's right," said Petterson. "Look at what happened at the airport this afternoon. The rebels are doing as they please right under our noses — they think they have nothing to fear! If you stay this stubborn, you'll jeopardize all the progress you say you're trying to foster in Scandia."

The king looked at him. "If only I knew the right thing to do," he murmured.

"Please, Magnus!" cried his sister. "Think of Jenna!"

"Think of our country, Your Majesty," said von Thunberg.

"Think of the reforms," said Petterson.

The king gave a weary nod. "All right, von Thunberg," he said. "Do what's necessary. And inform the press. But emphasize that it's only a temporary measure. As soon as the situation calms down again, there'll be no more soldiers on the streets of Scandia."

"Thank you, Magnus," said the princess.

Von Thunberg was already on his way out.

"I don't think we should go back to Holmburg tonight," said Petterson, glancing at the king. "You should get some sleep, Magnus. I fear there are difficult days ahead."

The king nodded. "The last thing I wanted was to have to give orders like these again."

17

As soon as the sun was high enough to give her some warmth, Jenna lay down on the ground behind some bushes, rolled herself up into a ball, and immediately fell asleep.

She woke up when she heard the noise of a vehicle in the distance. There was an ominous tickle in her throat. She must not let it turn into a full-blown cold. The road was narrow and winding, with occasional exits to remote farmsteads on both sides. She wondered who might be driving along here at such an early hour in the day.

Looking over the hedge, she saw it was a milk tanker. She hesitated for a moment; she was tired and there was still a long way to go. All the same, she decided to continue on foot. It was safer. There was no guarantee the driver wouldn't recognize her, even if she didn't look in the least like a princess.

But peeking over the hedge was enough to bring the heavy truck to a screeching halt.

"Do you want a lift?" asked the driver. He had dark hair like hers. "Where are you going?"

"Saarstad," said Jenna, before she could even think about it.

The man leaned across the passenger seat and opened the door. "Get in," he said. "It's not that far, but every mile counts, eh?"

Jenna sneezed and nodded. He hadn't recognized her. How could he, with her straggly, matted hair and her shabby dress?

"Hey, you're soaked through!" he said, putting the truck in gear and pressing the accelerator. The truck moved off. "Were you outside in the storm last night? Here, wrap this blanket around you."

He stopped the truck again, stood up in his seat, and motioned to Jenna to stand up, too. Then he removed the blanket they'd been sitting on and draped it over her shoulders. "There," he said.

Jenna didn't know if she should feel disgusted or not. The blanket was threadbare, and had that musty smell that comes from being used for ages without being washed. But the warmth in it made her realize just how cold she had been. "Thank you," she murmured. She wasn't even aware of her eyes closing.

She was startled out of her sleep by an abrupt jerk of the brakes, and it took her a moment to remember where she was.

"Awake now?" asked the driver with a laugh. "You didn't get much sleep. Sorry." He turned on his radio.

"Are we in Saarstad?" asked Jenna. On each side of the road were wooden houses painted yellow, pink, and red, with well-tended gardens. Ripe berries hung from the bushes, there was not a weed to be seen in the vegetable patches, and the paths leading up to the houses were lined with bunches of daisies and hollyhocks. On the road ahead of them a line of cars stood bumper to bumper.

"Great!" muttered the driver, caught up in his own thoughts. "And we're still only on the outskirts." He fiddled with the radio, switching from one station to another. "No idea what this holdup is all about. Let's see if I can find a traffic report . . ." He sighed. "At this rate there's no way I'll be able to get the milk to the dairy on time. I don't know why every-thing's started running short — suddenly people can't get enough to eat. If there's a cheese shortage as well, you'll know the reason why."

Jenna removed the blanket from her shoulders. "Thank you for the ride," she said. "I'll go the rest of the way on foot now."

The man nodded. "You'll get there quicker that way," he said. "Out you get."

Jenna thanked him again. She waved up at the driver's cab, then walked on past the line of cars toward the center of town.

The short sleep had done her good, and she was warmer now. All the same, she couldn't help sneezing. *I've caught a cold after all,* she thought. *I hope I'm not going to get a sore throat as well. I could do without that.*

She'd gone about a quarter mile when she began to recognize the houses. There was still a long line of cars along the road beside her. Maybe there'd been an accident. It couldn't be too far now to the marketplace where she'd called those horrible coup plotters, Bolström and Mrs. Markas, last year. She remembered the morning smell of freshly baked bread, and children on their way to school.

How frightened she'd been then. Now she just felt sad, though the morning sunshine made her situation seem more bearable.

At the sight of the market square, Jenna came to an abrupt stop. *What's going on here?* she wondered with some apprehension. The square was so full of people, you could hardly see the buildings. Camera operators were standing at the sides with their heavy apparatus perched on their shoulders, filming; reporters were thrusting microphones into the angry faces of South Scandians; and in the center of the square she could see the satellite vans from the country's two most important TV channels.

She moved a little closer, pulling a strand of hair over her face as she went. Recent paparazzi photos of her had shown little more than a gaping mouth, and in the months before that, they'd been portraits of a princess carefully made up for all occasions by the royal stylists. The driver of the tanker truck hadn't recognized her, but that didn't mean no one else would. There might still be people who'd see the ragged little northerner in the damp blue dress and identify her as the Pizza Princess.

Jenna felt the anger rising inside her. In her despair over Jonas, she'd forgotten all about that. *Well, now you're rid of me,* she thought. *Now you'll have to find someone else to write your vicious articles about. I'm no longer available to the media, so tough luck. The Roly-Poly Princess has left the building.*

It was quite a satisfying thought, she noticed, and anger felt better than sadness. At last she'd stopped letting people tell her how to live her life and was doing something for herself. Even if it was only running away. She'd taken her life into her own hands. Yes, she liked the sound of that.

People were packed tight in the market square, watching something — it was surprising how many people there were for such a small town. Jenna heard a loud clattering, followed by yelling. She pushed her way toward the front.

About fifty women in aprons and headscarves were marching around the square, shouting at the top of their lungs, drumming saucepans with wooden spoons.

"Our pots are empty!" they yelled. "Our children are hungry! Down with the government!"

Cameras were filming the scene from all angles. Jenna hid her face behind some man's broad back.

"Our pots are empty! Our children are hungry! Down with the government!"

The women marched up and down, up and down, chanting their slogan. The two at the front were carrying a large banner on which the same words were written.

So Scandia's come to this, thought Jenna. *Mothers demonstrating against hunger. Something's got to be done! How can it be the government's fault? Liron is a good, smart person and he's Minister of the Interior. Surely he can make certain that people have enough to eat?*

She ducked away, and moved slowly through the crowd toward the opposite side of the square. She had to take the road that led to the sea. There was still a short distance to go.

At the side of the square stood a woman holding the hand of a child who was staring at the microphone, its thumb in its mouth. The mother was being interviewed. "Of course it's a scandal!" she said. "Mothers protesting because their children haven't got enough to eat, here at home, in Scandia! This used to be such a rich country!"

"Down with the government?" asked the interviewer.

"Down with the government!" said the mother, and pulled her child away.

Jenna looked back at the marching women, pouring all their energy into the protest. She could see their faces. Suddenly one in particular caught her eye and she blinked in shock.

Mrs. von Thunberg! she thought in utter disbelief. If the woman hadn't been wearing a headscarf and an apron, she could have sworn it was Mrs. von Thunberg!

Jenna sneezed.

Well, Jenna knew better than anyone that people can have look-alikes. But the woman behind Mrs. von Thunberg looked familiar, too. And the one next to her. Hadn't Jenna seen all of them somewhere before? Could it be . . . ? Yes! Yesterday, at the party!

Jenna ducked her head and continued on her way. *I'm losing it*, she thought. *It can't be them. When I think what was served at the von Thunbergs' yesterday — no one was going hungry there! It just can't be them. I'm seriously sleep-deprived, I've got a cold, I'm hallucinating. I need to get to the navigator's house. I'll be able to catch up on some sleep there. After that, we'll see.*

18

Liron wanted to borrow Carlson's car.

"Why?" Carlson asked. He could only bear to drive his own little clunker because he spent the rest of the day behind the wheel of the large state limousine. "It's over ten years old, sir!"

"I just want to remind myself what it's like to drive in an ordinary car," Liron replied. He didn't know whether Carlson believed him. But he couldn't borrow the cook's car again, and he was pretty sure the chauffeur's personal car wouldn't be bugged. "I may be Minister of the Interior, Carlson, but all the more reason why I shouldn't ever forget how ordinary people live, should I?"

"But you don't have to go out in an old wreck like this, sir! Couldn't you borrow one of the other servants' cars?" said the bewildered chauffeur. "I've been wanting to buy a decent car for ages. And I'll do just that as soon as I've saved up enough. It's better to wait and get something really top-notch rather than rush into it and get a load of old junk. That's what I say. Am I right, sir?"

Liron agreed with him, but persuaded him his car would do just fine. He sat down in the driver's seat and turned the key in the ignition. The car coughed and spluttered in response, then moved forward with a little jerk. "It will have to do," murmured Liron.

He exited the grounds of the parliament and merged with the heavy traffic rumbling along the six-lane boulevard that led toward the city center. On each side of the road were wide expanses of lawn, with sprinklers watering the grass. This early in the morning there was traffic everywhere, and progress was slow through the narrow streets of Holmburg, which had been built more than a hundred years ago for horse-drawn carriages and only widened during the last few decades.

In the center of Museum Square stood a nineteenth-century fountain of a shepherdess holding a jug from which water cascaded down several levels of a large basin. It was here that Liron saw the first soldiers. *So soon*, he thought. It hadn't taken von Thunberg long to deploy the army. Presumably he'd had plans drawn up for some time now, and was just waiting for approval to execute the order. The presence of soldiers should have given Liron a sense of security, but instead he felt the hairs on the back of his neck stand on end.

He sighed. Magnus had yielded to pressure and the decision had been made. Now they would have to see how they could live with it. But having the military on the streets made it all the more vital that the crisis was dealt with quickly.

The spotless white buildings on both sides of the street were a sign of the nation's former wealth. Behind the shining shop windows there had once been piles of goods for sale. Now, as he drove past, he could see that they contained nothing except the silk drapes covering the back walls.

And there he was, in his chauffeur's used car, on his way to find a solution to all these problems.

At a crossroads, he made a gut decision. Instead of turning off onto the road that would take him straight across the dam to the meeting place, he drove past it. The next exit took him to one of the newer areas on the outskirts of the city, where from a distance the grim housing projects seemed to dwarf the old church. These prefabricated apartment buildings had been hastily thrown up in order to house the cheap labor from the north who were then so urgently needed to boost Scandia's economy.

Just a year ago, he and Jonas, northerners themselves, had hidden in one of these anonymous buildings. It came as a shock to realize how long ago that seemed, and how unfamiliar the surroundings had become. He was in danger of forgetting how the other half lived. He shuddered at the sight of overturned garbage cans, a shopping cart abandoned in a straggly bush, the graffiti on the walls, plastic bags in the trees, and empty bottles in the gutters.

He drove at walking pace. A military transport stood in the school parking lot, but there was no sign of any soldiers. They'll be sitting inside the school, thought Liron, in the administration office or the hallways. They'll be afraid. They're only boys themselves. They don't want people yelling at them and pelting them with garbage. And they don't want to shoot anyone.

On the pathway in front of a dirty yellow lawn before another bland high-rise stood three youths, smoking. Their pants only reached down to their knees, and their hair was shaved in bizarre patterns. One was holding a can, which he passed on with a nudge to one of the others. A woman with a child hurried past, bowing her head as if that would somehow make her invisible, but the three teens followed her, shouting and laughing. One of them threw his crumpled cigarette pack after her.

I can understand how the southerners feel, thought Liron as he turned down a side street. *Why they're afraid of us. Why they want us northerners to go home. They think we're shiftless — we can't even keep order in our own neighborhoods. What they see is all they know, and they can't believe that if we started out with the same advantages as they do, we'd be ideal neighbors. Maybe one day people will come to appreciate the effects of the new government reforms, but it all takes time — maybe more than we'd like to think.*

A little dark-haired boy with a runny nose and a plastic car on a string was standing at the side of the road, waving his chubby little hand at every passing car. Liron waved back. *Maybe by the time you've grown up*, he thought. *I hope it'll be by then.*

He turned off to the right, passing an overgrown empty lot where the people from the housing projects had dumped their trash: old bikes and fridges, even a burned-out car. Among the waist-high weeds he could see a tattered old sofa with a group of children sitting on it. *It has to be by the time you've grown up*, he thought.

Not far from this empty lot the forest began. It would take a few hours yet to get to the northern sound. The car radio didn't work. He had time to think.

Every so often when he looked in the rearview mirror, he thought he recognized a car — a dark blue Volvo. He pulled over to the right and waited.

A few seconds later, the Volvo went by without braking. *You're imagining things*, he said to himself. Nobody knew he was going for a drive. Besides, he was supposed to be meeting with the undersecretary at that moment — he'd better think of a good excuse for not showing up. So who could possibly be following him?

For the next hour, he felt calmer. Although the rearview mirror did not show anything suspicious, he continued to let other vehicles pass him — private cars, motorcycles, trucks. *If they really are trying to follow me, I'll make it as hard for them as possible.* But he felt almost ashamed of himself for being so paranoid.

Last year, Lorok had driven Jenna, Jonas, and Malena to the navigator's house at breakneck speed. The journey had been so exciting that she hadn't paid any attention to how far it actually was.

When she first left the town, she came to fields of rye and wheat, cabbage and corn, and pastureland with black-and-white cows grazing. Then the fields gave way to forest.

The countryside around Saarstad was hilly. Little lakes glimmered between the trunks of the pine trees, and as she trudged up and down the sandy paths, Jenna grew more and more weary. She was about to sit down on one of the many moss-covered boulders at the side of the road when she heard the first shrieks of the gulls, followed by the splashing sounds of the waves as they crashed onto the shore. It couldn't be far now.

The navigator's house had been her mother's retreat, a place to escape to with Norlin when they were young and in love. It was here that Bolström and Norlin had later held the king and her mother captive, and it was here, last summer, where Jenna had realized for the first time that she was a princess.

It had been evening when Lorok had driven them there; she would never forget it. The gulls were crying as they circled high above the shore; the countryside seemed so quiet and peaceful in the warm glow of the setting sun that it was hard to imagine the battle that had just been fought. She could still picture the windswept pine tree in front of the gable, the jungle of wildflowers in the overgrown garden with its mingled scent of salt and summer pine. And among all this there'd been the wounded — rebels as well as conspirators — and then the reporters with their microphones and cameras.

Today, though, it was noon and the sun was high. A wind was blowing from the sea, driving short, flat, white-crested waves down onto the shore and against the piers of the crumbling dock. With the sun directly above it, the water was almost too bright to look at. A sense of complete calm lay over everything.

A few paces from the house, Jenna stopped. Apart from the time of day, nothing had changed.

The paint was still peeling from the once-yellow wooden walls, with their white window frames, veranda, and corner beams. In the relentless midday sun, the house looked utterly desolate.

Jenna took another step toward it. She could not understand why she suddenly felt afraid. At least tonight she would sleep in the dry. She knew where to find the key. It was not until she reached the door that she saw the broken glass, and the window by the veranda hanging on its hinges. She reached up and ran her hand over the top of the doorframe. The key was waiting where it was supposed to be.

Why was her heart beating so fast as she put the key in the lock? Why were her fingers trembling? The house should be her refuge, so why this sudden fear?

Jenna listened. *The silence*, she thought. *A silence you can hear. Just waves and gulls and the occasional rustle of leaves in a gust of wind. It's the silence that's so frightening.*

She pushed her shoulder against the door. It opened with a groan. In the tiny, almost square hallway, there was a musty smell, and a ray of sunshine came through the broken window and fell on the wooden floorboards. A thousand grains of dust danced in the light.

The doors inside were all open, reinforcing the feeling of melancholy abandonment. *Now, which room should I sleep in?* wondered Jenna. But it wasn't a comforting thought. If it didn't rain again, she would stay outside.

She stepped over the worn threshold into the first room. A tiled stove in the corner, from which one tile had fallen off, showed that this had been a living room. In the center there was a table, once highly polished but now covered with dust. Beside it were two chairs. Jenna began to walk toward them.

When an arm seized her from behind, she couldn't even let out a scream.

19

It wasn't until the afternoon light began to give way to the soft gold glow of evening that Liron turned down the narrow, sandy track that led to the meeting place. Potholes made it difficult to drive and slowed his progress. She was standing in the shadow of the trees, on the edge of a little clearing, waiting for him.

"Nahira," said Liron.

She stepped out from under the branches. "You're later than I expected," she said.

He closed the car door. It was so old that it didn't have an electronic lock. "I thought it would be too dangerous to call you," he said. "I was sure you'd wait."

Nahira scanned the road down which he had driven. "No one followed you?" she asked. "There are soldiers all over the place — they've been here ever since this morning."

Liron shook his head. They listened for a moment. Apart from the wind rustling the leaves on the trees, there was no movement.

"Lorok found it," said Nahira. "I didn't want to meet you there, just in case someone . . ." She brushed a strand of hair from her forehead. "It's what we'd suspected for a long time. All those attacks and shortages are just part of the buildup! They're going to take over the government by force!"

She looks exhausted, thought Liron. *She's been through a lot in the last few years.*

"You need to figure out exactly when and how you're going to make it public, Liron," she urged. "The news could change everything. Once the people of the south realize they've been betrayed —"

Liron nodded. "I know," he said. "Incidentally, that was not a good time when you called yesterday. I just hope no one noticed anything."

Nahira laughed. "Who's Carlson?" she asked. "I'm sure you didn't expect me to understand all your talk about rain on your drive home. But obviously you understood what I was saying, or you wouldn't have come."

She laughed again, but it was not a humorous laugh. She had long since ceased to be the Nahira he used to know. The years of fighting alongside the rebels had made her hard and bitter.

We each chose our own path then, thought Liron. Norlin had left Nahira in order to marry the king's sister, and then as regent he'd betrayed his own country. Liron aligned with the king on the difficult road to reform. Nahira joined the rebels, and eventually became their notorious leader. Not everything she'd done was good, Liron realized, but she always avoided violence. And without Nahira and her men, the king would never have been rescued last year, and Scandia would be a far different place.

"I was talking to von Thunberg and Petterson when you called," said Liron. "Nahira, I think your suspicions are right: One of them is working for the other side. It keeps on happening: A small group of us discuss our plans, and then just a short while afterward . . ."

"Yes?" asked Nahira.

". . . a short while afterward, the rebels attack. Just yesterday the king was set to make a televised speech, and right before he could deliver it, they blew up the electricity pylons, preventing the broadcast."

"You mean one of them is working with *us*?" asked Nahira. "You think *we* blew up the pylons?"

Liron could hear the anger in her voice. He shook his head.

"Of course not!" he said. "Don't misunderstand me. Every time there's an attack, it's blamed on the rebels, but other people are the ones who benefit from it."

"And you think von Thunberg or Petterson might be among those other people?" said Nahira. "Sometimes everything seems so hopeless. If things go on like this, the people who keep saying nothing will change without violence are going to have a field day, don't you think? Liron, the north mustn't lose hope! Otherwise, it really will be my people launching the attacks. If their only option is violence, I won't be able to stop them."

Liron could see the anxiety in her eyes. "I can't hold them back forever," she said. "Or keep promising them a golden future that the north may never see. The reforms must be introduced more quickly—people have got to feel the changes for themselves, or there'll be more bombings." She stepped toward him. "Anyway, I've got something to show you. Once this is out in the open, once you've shown the press and it's on every television screen in every living room in the country, everything could change. When southerners see it isn't the government or the rebels behind all this chaos, then public opinion will shift. It has to."

"I just don't know anymore whose side the media is on," murmured Liron. "Good God, Nahira, how naïve we were last summer! Did we really think everything was going to be all right?"

Nahira walked toward the passenger's side of the car. Liron went back to the driver's door. What happened next was so sudden, there was no time to run.

Lights flashed, and out of the darkness from behind the trees came a line of men in black, guns blazing. Bullets smashed past them into the car, shattering the windows and piercing the frame.

Poor Carlson, thought Liron, *now you won't be able to wait till you can afford your new car* — and he was shocked that such a stupid thought should be going through his head at such a moment. Then someone pulled him to the ground, twisted his arm behind his back, bound his hands together, and placed a hobnailed boot on his neck.

With his cheek pressed against the pine needles on the ground, Liron was able to see under the car. Nahira was running. Bullets ripped into the bark of the trees on the other side of the clearing, splintering the wood. But there was no cry.

Maybe she had escaped.

"No way!" said a voice that Jenna was sure she knew. "Jenna, it's you! Sorry!"

The arm released her and she was able to breathe again.

"Petterson Junior!" she cried, with a mixture of relief, anger, and disgust. Of all people!

"You can call me Perry," he said, holding out the hand with which he had just been attempting to throttle her. "Hi, Jenna."

Jenna stared at him. "What are you doing here?"

"I could ask you the same question," said Perry. "I ran away. In a laundry basket."

"A laundry basket?" echoed Jenna. She noted with some relief that suddenly the house was no longer so scary. The dust danced in the sunlight over the polished table, and the ragged patchwork carpet would only need a good shake. This could be a real home.

Perry nodded. "What about you?" he asked. "I'll bet the security guards are more concerned with finding you than with finding me!"

Jenna sneezed. "I pretended to be a waitress," she said, pointing to her dress. Last night's downpour had turned it into a rag. "I snuck out with the caterers."

"Awesome. And they're always bragging about how 'impenetrable' their security is! 'Absolutely impenetrable!'" Perry scoffed. "But anyone with half a brain . . ."

Jenna was only half-listening to him. She had wandered off into the next room, which contained the beds where presumably the chained-up captives — her mother and her uncle Magnus — had slept last year. A handcuff was still dangling from one of the bedposts.

"We'll put one bed in the next room," said Jenna. "I'll sleep in the living room." *For obvious reasons!* she thought.

"I'll have to go outside," said Perry, "until this place is clean. I can't stop sneezing. Allergies. Come with me."

"And I'll start sneezing if I go outside. But OK, I'm coming." Jenna wiped her nose. *Typical*, she thought. *Something's always wrong with that boy. But I guess I'd better start looking for his good side. Malena must see something in him!*

There were bumblebees buzzing over the wild roses, and butterflies fluttering around the lilacs. Jenna and Perry walked a few feet along the beach till they reached the foot of the jagged cliffs, where at this time of the year wild sweet peas covered the rocks. Among the round washed pebbles, which crunched and rattled under their feet, stood a three-foot-high granite block. Jenna climbed onto the top. "Nice view!" she said.

"Can you see Scandinavia?" asked Perry, and sat down beside her. "Whoa, you can — almost as far as the North Pole!"

"You're not serious, right?" said Jenna. It suddenly felt as if she was on a summer outing to the beach, just like the old days, when her life had been nice and ordinary, the way it should be. A surprising thought struck her and she glanced sideways at Perry. It was almost like being out with Bea. "Why did you run away?"

"Two words: military school," Perry said bluntly.

Jenna wondered how he could be so laid-back about his escape. Then she remembered the scene in the summerhouse. She swallowed hard. She knew how strong you could be if you felt loved. For a few fleeting minutes yesterday, she had felt the same.

"What about Malena?" she asked hesitantly.

Perry stared at her. "How do you know?" he asked. And he actually blushed.

Jenna shrugged her shoulders. "Yesterday, in the summerhouse.. I saw you. Just by chance."

For a second, Perry looked as if he was going to explode, but then he just nodded. "I told her everything," he said. "She understands why I won't go to the academy. Why I *can't* go." He looked her straight in the eye. "I'm no soldier."

"She likes you, doesn't she?" said Jenna.

Perry said nothing for a moment. "Is that crazy?" he finally asked. "I mean, a girl like Malena and a guy like . . ."

"No!" Jenna interjected. "Looks aren't the most important thing!" Then she realized what she'd said. "Not that you're *bad*-looking . . ."

Perry laughed. "I'm pretty realistic about myself, thanks!" he said. "But you know what's really crazy? If I hadn't already been sure yesterday that I was going to run away, I never would have had the courage to tell her . . . and if Malena hadn't told me how *she* felt, I don't think I would have had the courage to run away! How messed up is that?"

Jenna nodded. *You need a lot of courage to escape from under the nose of the Secret Service*, she thought. *And whether you're brave because you're happy, like Perry, or desperate, like me, doesn't make any difference.*

"And? What's your story?" asked Perry.

Jenna looked out across the water. The gulls were gliding above the waves almost without moving their wings. How did they know exactly where the air would carry them? "Oh, all sorts of things," she murmured. There was no way she was going to confess about Jonas, or about Jonas and Ylva. "I just don't fit in. This princess thing. I always screw it up."

"That's bull!" said Perry, and she was surprised at how forceful he sounded. "They *want* you to get everything wrong, Jenna. It's not your fault! The papers could say the exact opposite about you if they wanted to. But there's been a change in people's attitudes, and you're the one who has to pay the price." He looked at her. "They're just using you so that they can get at the whole royal family . . ."

"I know," said Jenna.

". . . so they can attack the government and the reforms . . ."

"I know!" cried Jenna. "I know all that! But knowing it doesn't make it any better! Do you think it helps to know it's not personal when you see hideous photos of yourself plastered across every single paper and all over the Internet? When the whole class is making fun of you? When even the youngest girls in the school start laughing the moment you walk into the cafeteria?" Her voice was shrill now.

"Sorry," Perry mumbled. "I wasn't thinking."

They sat there for a while without talking. Occasionally the shriek of a gull pierced the steady splashing of the waves, and a woodpecker hammered away in the pine forest behind them.

"Now what?" Perry asked eventually. "Before you arrived, I was going to try to make a fishing rod. There are blueberries, too. I don't know if you can hear my stomach, but I haven't eaten anything since yesterday."

Yesterday. Jenna took a deep breath. *Don't think about it anymore. Don't think about anything.*

Now that he'd pointed it out, she realized Perry's stomach was indeed rumbling like a miniature thunderstorm. "Wow," she said. "Malena should hear that. Hot. Not!" But then she grew serious again. "I don't think you'll catch much with a homemade fishing rod. And blueberries, well . . ." She sighed. "But the town's quite a long way away, and by the time we get there, the shops will be closed."

"Not a problem," said Perry, and Jenna could hear the pride in his voice. "I've got a moped. It's back there in the bushes."

"A moped?" asked Jenna.

"I have to watch it with the gas. No money to buy any more. So I guess there's not much point in going into town, anyway. Or do you think the supermarket would put it on credit if you told them you were a princess? Considering the political climate, unlikely! And the way you look, nobody would believe you."

"Oh, you're hilarious — for a guy who hangs out in laundry bins," said Jenna. It really was a little bit like being with Bea. Who'd of thunk it? Substitute besties with Petterson Junior. "Would a princess run away without any money?" She reached into the pocket of her dress and pulled out the envelope. "My wages," she announced. "Compensation for having endured that nightmare party."

"Yes!" said Perry. "You rock! I'm on it." He grabbed the money.

"Hold up!" said Jenna. "I'm going, too. And there might not be any food to buy. They were demonstrating in Saarstad this morning. Against hunger!" She thought of the women marching in the square and her conviction that she'd seen them at the von Thunberg party. She must have been delusional.

Perry shook his head. "Listen, Jenna," he said, and suddenly he sounded serious. "I kid about the princess thing: You can bet that since last night there'll be thousands of them searching for us. And people will look more closely at strangers. It's safer if I go on my own. If they've been putting out missing persons announcements, they're bound to focus on you. You're the famous one. You're freakin' royalty, girl! But since you're already dressed like a maid"— he laughed —"you can clean the house while I'm gone."

"So His Lordship doesn't have to keep sneezing?" said Jenna. "And then you'll come back and be king of the castle, I suppose?" She pretended to be offended. "What a macho man!"

Perry jumped down from the rock, and the pebbles crunched under his feet. "Exactly!" he said. "The man goes out into the big bad world, and the woman stays at home and does the housework." He dodged Jenna's slap and ran off, laughing.

Jenna ran after him. "Sexist pig!" she shouted — but then she had to sneeze.

"Gesundheit!" Perry called back. "And look at it this way: You'll be making the place nice for yourself, too."

Even in Scandia you could still enjoy life, Jenna realized. It was almost like being at home.

20

*B*olström looked out the window at the fading summer afternoon. For the time being, they still had to stay out in the country, but he was sure they'd soon be able to return to Holmburg. That, after all, was the whole reason for coming to Scandia.

"So we're back, Norlin," he said. What a stroke of luck that Liron had let himself get caught red-handed! What a fool the man was! Did he really think that the Minister of the Interior only needed to drive some civil servant's car to avoid being followed? Or to talk on some amateur second cell phone to avoid being bugged? Bolström laughed. "I have to say, Norlin, as far as I'm concerned, there's no place like Scandia. I really don't understand why some people are always so desperate to get away to the tropics." He lit a cigarette. "Not me. And Liron's arrest has just made things even better for us. Now we have the proof to show to the public — that there are northerners in the government who are in league with the rebels! We've even got their plan for the final coup!"

Norlin drummed his fingers on the little side table. "What plan, Bolström?" he bleated. "I haven't heard about a plan. They didn't have any such thing on them when they were arrested."

"Idiot!" said Bolström. "What they did or didn't have on them is entirely immaterial!"

But Norlin was no longer listening. "Do you think they might have a drop of something here somewhere, to soothe the nerves?" he asked. His eyes flickered. "I haven't had any since last night . . . and it was a hard day . . ." His voice trailed off.

"Stop it, Norlin," said Bolström. "Don't be such a pest. Just pull yourself together. Especially now, when things are going so well for us. Don't you want to be back in the palace as soon as possible? Eh, Norlin? It might not be long now!"

He went to the sideboard, poured a glassful of water out of a carafe, and carried it over to the sofa. Norlin dropped it. His hand was trembling as badly as his voice.

"Soldiers everywhere!" said Bolström, ignoring the mess. He poured a glass for himself. "Purely to protect the people — why, what else would they be doing?" He laughed. "But you know what, Norlin? By tomorrow those soldiers will be searching the factories, because the factory workers are northerners, and all of them are secret rebels. You didn't know that, did you? And our soldiers will find lots of weapons, because the rebels are planning a coup. A revolution. The people in the south are already nervous and dissatisfied, and soon it'll be worse. The food shortages, the terrorist attacks, Liron's arrest, and then the weapons! South Scandians will be happy and grateful when the military storms parliament, because the government is doing nothing. And the Minister of the Interior has been —"

Norlin had stood up, and now he paced to and fro. "Do you really think they've got nothing to drink here?" he mumbled. "Nothing at all? We could send someone —"

"Shut up and listen, Norlin!" Bolström snapped. "The one thing I don't like is this business with the children. Again with the children! If the rebels really have kidnapped them, well . . . that would be marvelous! Then we'd be rid of them. But suppose they've simply run away? I don't trust that Jenna. No offense, Norlin, I know she's your daughter. But nevertheless, last summer she was the one who wrecked everything for us. If it hadn't been for your daughter, you'd still have been on the throne . . . Norlin, what are you doing?"

Norlin had begun flinging open all the cupboard doors. "Nothing," he murmured. "Just looking . . ."

Bolström shook his head. "I'll feel a lot more at ease when that girl is back at her school, where she belongs," he said. "I don't want her messing things up for us again. It gives me a minor heart attack just thinking about it."

"Jenna's in Saarstad," said Norlin offhandedly. He flopped onto the sofa and stared vaguely at the table. "In the navigator's house. Give me a drink, Bolström. I can't go on."

With a single bound, Bolström was right beside him. "How do you know that, Norlin?" he asked. "Or are you just guessing?"

"See for yourself!" said Norlin, stretching out his hands.

They were twitching as if someone had run an electric current through them. "And the shakes . . ."

"I'm not asking how you know you can't go on!" shouted Bolström. "Of course you can go on! How do you know where *Jenna* is?"

Norlin ground his teeth. "In Saarstad," he said again. "In the navigator's house. That's where I'd go if I wanted to hide. And she's my daughter, Bolström! She's my daughter!"

Bolström threw his head back. "What sort of crazy argument is that?" he said. "Probably all part of the withdrawal symptoms. Even so . . . it's not a bad idea." He smiled and reached for the telephone.

"Has the navigator's house been searched?" he asked into the receiver, without even saying who he was. "Yes, indeed. Send someone there at once. We have to find the girl. After all, she's . . . our princess." He laughed.

"My Jenna," whispered Norlin. Then he jumped up again. His eyes were wild. "Bolström, give me something! Give me something to drink! I'm Regent! I order you . . ."

Bolström shoved him in the chest. Norlin tottered and fell to the floor.

"Shut up!" said Bolström. "You don't give orders to anyone anymore."

Bea threw herself onto the living-room sofa. As usual, her mother had left some food for her in the fridge, so all she had to do was heat it in the microwave.

But just like every other day after school, she didn't feel like it. And today her last class had been PE, and now it was practically evening. It was scandalous how long they kept teenagers locked up at school.

She fished for the remote control with her foot. On the side table were the three yogurts she'd taken from the fridge instead of the broccoli casserole. After school she always needed a half hour to chill out, and cappuccino, chocolate, and vanilla-mango yogurts were obviously far more soothing than vegetables baked in cheese.

She pulled open the lid of the first container and dipped in her spoon. She sighed. It wasn't a diet yogurt, but after all the stress of the past eight hours, she'd earned the right to some comfort food. A math quiz and a geography test — what sort of school day was that? Was it even legal for teachers to make you do all that in one day? But they didn't care; they just wanted to get all the grades in before summer vacation.

She switched on the television.

". . . can be said that the situation in Scandia is now becoming critical," the anchor on the news was saying. Hundreds of miles away, the foreign correspondent listened through his earpiece, nodded a few times, then raised his microphone.

More Scandia drama? thought Bea, and quickly turned up the volume.

"That's right," the correspondent agreed with the anchor. "Definitely critical, and getting more and more difficult to understand. In the last few days there's been an escalation of incidents. First there were the attacks on the oil pipeline and the central electricity supply, which stirred up speculation that the rebels were mobilized again. For months it had seemed that King Magnus's bipartisan reforms had cut the ground out from under their feet. There were no more attacks or threats, and it was even rumored that the rebels had disbanded. But since Scandia has been subjected to more and more shortages, the mood of the people has begun to change."

The anchor interrupted him. "If you could explain in a little more detail," she said.

Again the foreign correspondent nodded. "The Scandian media believe that the reason for shortages of basic foods and other necessities is economic mismanagement by a new government that's mainly concerned with reform," he said, "but foreign observers are convinced that there must be something else behind this, although it's too soon yet to confirm how all these things are connected."

Bea dropped the first empty yogurt container onto the floor. Chocolate next.

"Initially it seemed unlikely that the rebels were involved, because it's questionable what they stood to gain from the shortages and how they could have organized them. But two hours ago, the Scandian Minister of the Interior was arrested in a remote area of the forest while holding a clandestine meeting with the notorious rebel leader . . ."

"What?" cried Bea, lowering her yogurt. "No way!"

". . . so it's no longer possible to rule out collusion."

"And what about the abduction of Princess Jenna?" asked the anchor. "Has there been any new information since this morning? And might there be some connection with the previous incidents?"

"What?" Bea repeated, staring at the screen in disbelief. Her spoon dropped into her lap. "Not Jenna! Not again!"

The correspondent shook his head, and the anchor said something, but Bea couldn't concentrate anymore. "Stupid Scandia!" she cried angrily, and looked down at the sticky brown stain on the thigh of her jeans.

She jumped up and ran into the hall, where she had dumped her schoolbag just inside the front door. Where was her cell? She had to send a text to Jenna.

Ugh! What had she done with her phone? It wasn't in its case. But there was no way she would have lost it!

She took everything out of her bag — textbooks, folders, handouts, notepads, makeup case — but her cell phone wasn't there.

"Ugh!" she said out loud. "No freakin' way!" And then she remembered. Before gym class, she'd checked to see if there were any new messages. Then Kate had distracted her with her usual panic-stricken questions about the math quiz and what she'd got for answers on questions two and four and everything. So she'd stuffed the phone into her gym bag, but her gym bag wasn't there.

"Thanks, Kate — so annoying!" Bea moaned, though she knew it was her own fault, too, because she should have remembered to bring home her gym bag. And now it was probably lying in a corner of the coach's office, from where it would find its way to Lost and Found. And at this hour, no one would open up the school for her.

"Ugh, ugh, ugh!" she practically screamed, before starting to gather up her books from the floor. So she couldn't send a text message today. Whatever. If they really had kidnapped Jenna, probably the first thing they'd have done would have been to take away her phone. So maybe it really didn't matter, anyway.

When she heard the footsteps on the gravel, Margareta looked up. "Peter!" she said. "Thank goodness!"

She hadn't slept all night. And ever since she got up, she'd been trying to think about other things. How ironic it all was. When they'd been living in exile she'd worried about her daughter all the time. And now that they were back in Scandia, where she felt safe and didn't need to keep an eye on her every minute of the day, Jenna had disappeared.

"Any news?"

Around midday she'd gone into the garden. The gardener hadn't been too pleased when she'd asked him for a pair of shears and a wheelbarrow, but he hadn't dared say anything. She needed something to do if she was to stop herself from going crazy with worry.

"Haven't you seen the news?" asked Petterson. He gave her a quick kiss. His face was gray and bleary-eyed, like hers.

"Have they found her?" cried Margareta. "Why didn't someone come and tell me? Or . . . have there been demands, Peter? Are they asking for a ransom?"

Petterson took her arm. "Shh, shh, Margareta!" he said. "Keep calm. Of course they'd have come and told you if Jenna had been found or there'd been a ransom demand." He stroked her cheek. "No, no, it's something else. Liron has been arrested."

"Liron?" said Margareta, freeing herself. "Why Liron? What has he done?"

"It's a conspiracy," said Petterson, gently leading her to a bench. The branches of a rosebush were hanging over the back, and he pushed them away. "He was caught with Nahira. You know that we've long had our suspicions about members of the government conspiring with the rebels. What other explanation can there be for the general chaos? The food shortages? The fact is, there are people in the government" — he eased her down onto the bench — "who are planning a violent coup, Margareta. We've thought so for some time. They're not interested in reform — that's not enough for them. The reform process is too slow and too limited for their goals. They want revolution. None of us are safe anymore."

Margareta shook her head. "But not Liron!" she said incredulously. "You must be mistaken, Peter! It can't be Liron!" She opened and closed, opened and closed the gardening shears. "He's always tried to change Scandia by peaceful means! You don't know him as well as I do."

"Poor Greta!" Petterson said. "It must feel terrible being betrayed by your friends all the time. First there was —"

"Peter!" she cried.

"I'm sorry," he said. "I won't go on about Norlin. But now it's Liron, and I know you trusted him. They caught him red-handed, Greta, just after he'd met up with Nahira. There are even photos of them together, and some video footage."

"But that doesn't prove anything!" Margareta exclaimed, her voice cracking. *Jenna gone, and now this.* "It might just have been a simple meeting! They've been friends all their lives! Liron owes his freedom to Nahira! If it hadn't been for her, last year, Bolström and . . . and Norlin —" She broke off. "He'd never have been rescued, Peter! He probably owes her his life. So isn't he allowed even to see her?"

"He's Minister of the Interior," said Petterson. "And she's leader of the rebels."

Once again she shook her head. Then she reached for a branch of the rosebush by the bench. The shears snapped shut, and roses fell silently to the ground.

"Don't, Margareta! Stop it!" Petterson grabbed the shears and put them on the bench beside him, out of her reach. "There's more evidence," he said. "They had a plan with them, about how the coup was to be staged. The shortages are all part of it. And it lists the places where they've hidden weapons. The army is searching them at this very moment. I'm afraid there's no doubt about it, Greta: Your friend Liron is a traitor."

Margareta let out a sob. "And the children?" she said. "You don't think they've taken the children . . ."

Petterson put his hand in his pocket and brought out a fine white handkerchief. "Be brave, Greta," he murmured, gently wiping her eyes. "The two of us are going through exactly the same thing. Don't you think I'm just as worried about my son? But I'm afraid we're going to have to accept that —"

"No!" whispered Margareta. "No, Peter, no!"

"I called your brother," said Petterson. He folded the handkerchief and put it back in his pocket. "He's as upset about Liron as you are, and just like you, he couldn't believe it, either, at first." He grasped her shoulders and leaned back so that he could look her straight in the eyes. "But there's no point in trying to deceive ourselves. The truth doesn't stop being the truth just because we don't want to believe it."

Margareta nodded, and sniffled like a child.

"I want to talk to him, Peter," said Margareta. Her voice was still trembling. "Liron. I want to hear it from his own lips."

"So you shall, Greta," he said. "I can understand your feelings. But first he has to be interrogated by the police. Scandia is a democratic country now, and even a princess can't just step in when and where she likes."

She stood up. She looked across the garden, which now lay in a hundred shades of gray beneath the cloudy evening sky. "Tomorrow, perhaps," she whispered. "If only we knew what had happened to the children."

21

*A*fter *Perry had left,* Jenna sat for a moment on the steps in front of the house. The evening sun was descending over the water, turning the sky yellow. The wind that had blown from the sea during the afternoon had died down, and the air was still warm. It would be at least another two hours before it was completely dark, and by then Perry would be back. She'd had enough of being afraid.

She stood up and went back into the house. First she took all the throw rugs outside and hung them over the handrail. *Now I really am behaving like a common housewife,* she thought. *But so what? I can do what I want. And if Perry and me are going to stay here for the night, I may as well make sure we're nice and comfy.*

In a kitchen cabinet she found a bucket, though the accompanying rags looked so dingy that Jenna thought they'd have the opposite effect and actually make things worse. "Can't be helped," she murmured. There were no other cleaning supplies.

She began in the living room. She and Perry would sit here together later this evening. She hoped he'd remember to buy candles, if the shops still had any. There was no electricity. They'd sit and talk while they ate their supper. And they'd make plans for the next day: swimming, picking berries if the sun was shining, and maybe mushrooms if it rained. Then they'd climb into their beds, tired and happy after their long day, and sleep soundly until tomorrow.

It's a bit like a movie, thought Jenna, as she filled a second bucket from the sea. Romantic — sentimental, even — and no Ylva, no nasty tabloids, no one laughing at her. She hadn't even thought of Jonas for hours! She and Perry could live there like Robinson Crusoe, except they'd need to get hold of some money now and then. They couldn't survive for long on a diet of berries, and her wages from waitressing wouldn't last forever.

There was nothing more to do in the living room, so she went outside again. The light was getting dimmer and the colors were beginning to fade. *But I'm not afraid*, she thought, and gave the first rug a good beating against the handrail. A cloud of sand, dust, and dried leaves shook out. It hadn't been cleaned in years. *A radio would be nice now — some music.* It wouldn't feel quite so lonely then, and creepy.

Back in the living room, she pushed and pulled the carpet across the floor until the space looked cozier. It was really nice now, like a proper home. It just needed a candle on the table. She'd find a saucer for it to drip into. And flowers. Flowers always made everything more welcoming.

Jenna put the bucket down and looked in the kitchen cupboards for a vase. A large, empty pickle jar containing some rusty clothespins, rubber bands, and two mildewed coins would do just as well.

She cut some daisies, a thistle, and some chamomile. She wasn't sure about the hollyhocks, because she didn't know how long they would last in a vase and it would be a pity to waste them.

By now she could no longer pretend the darkness was a long way off. It had already turned everything gray, and the sound of the waves had grown louder — almost menacingly loud. *This is our home now,* she thought, *and there's nothing to be afraid of.* When Perry came back, they'd sit for a while on the boulder down on the beach, and they'd listen to the gulls shrieking in the night. Then they'd go back into their nice clean house and have supper. Her stomach grumbled.

OK, Perry, where are you already? I can't sit here forever, dreaming of what it's going to be like. It's way too dark to do any more cleaning, and I'm getting crazy hungry.

At that moment she heard the rattle of the motor. She listened for a second, to make sure it really was the moped, and then ran out onto the veranda, greatly relieved.

Perry got down from the moped and propped it on its stand. Hanging limply from each of the handlebars were a couple of rather empty-looking plastic bags.

"Jenna!" cried Perry. He came hurrying toward her.

Something was wrong. "There are soldiers everywhere! And you'll never guess what I found out! It's all so . . . Come on, I'll show you!"

"You've forgotten the bags," said Jenna.

He turned around and lifted them off the handlebars. "You're never going to believe it when I tell you!" he said, throwing his purchases down on the veranda. "Come on, quick! It changes everything!"

"What changes everything?" asked Jenna. "I'm starving!"

"Then bring something with you," said Perry. He was already back on the moped. "Potatoes and carrots were all I could get, anyway. Hurry up! I don't know what it all means, but come on, Jenna!"

She picked up some carrots. They were gritty, and she didn't know if she really felt like eating them unwashed and raw, but clearly there was no time to cook them. "What about you?" she asked with her mouth full.

Perry had started the motor. "Get on. OK, all set?" he asked. "Yes, pass me one. I'm starving, too."

The moped jerked its way along the narrow sandy path that led through the trees to the nearest road. There was still a whiff of sun-baked pinecones in the air. Jenna chewed at her carrot. The headlight threw a wavering finger of white into the gloom.

Perry accelerated. It was pitch-dark now, but the sky was clear and there was enough moonlight to make out the track stretching out ahead of them. "It's not far!" Perry called over his shoulder. "I can't wait to hear what you think."

Then he turned onto the blacktop road.

During dinner they left on the TV. The news about Scandia had been the same on every channel, with nothing more about Jenna.

"This is driving me crazy!" Bea exclaimed. "First she moans the entire time she's here, so you wonder what's the matter with her, but she won't actually *tell* you anything —"

"Shush!" said her father, holding out the remote control to turn up the volume. "Keep quiet!"

". . . after the local news there'll be a special report on the confusing situation in Scandia," said the anchor. "And now, from the stock market . . ."

Bea's dad turned down the volume again. No one was particularly interested in the financial news just then.

"There really must be something going on in that country," he said, scanning the dish of cold cuts until his eyes alighted on some thinly sliced ham. "If they're doing a special feature."

"Feature, shmeature, I just want to know what happened to Jenna!" said Bea.

During the sports report and the weather forecast, they carried the dishes into the kitchen, then put the plates and glasses in the dishwasher and the leftovers in the fridge. "Almost time! Back we go!" said Bea's father. He grabbed a radish as he went. "We'll clean up the rest later."

On the screen was a man with glasses, whose face Bea had often seen before, though she didn't know his name. He was pointing to a map of Scandia's two islands.

". . . newly democratic island state on the northern edge of our continent," the man was saying, "Last autumn's elections were won by the reformist Justice Party, which contains many prominent northerners. Among them is Minister of the Interior Liron . . ."

"That's him!" cried Bea. "Look, Dad! That's the father of Jonas — the boy who had spaghetti here with us!"

"Shush!" said her dad. "Do you want to watch or don't you?"

". . . arrested after being caught in a clandestine meeting with the rebels," said the journalist. "Even for correspondents in the country itself, the situation is evidently too complex to unravel. We're now going to show you a report from Scandian television about this latest incident."

It was obvious that the report had been filmed with a hand-held camera. The pictures were blurred and the cameraman's breathing and footsteps could be heard on the recording. He jerked along from one shot to another, then zoomed in on a single detail: a man and a woman beside a car. Suddenly there was gunfire, and figures in black hurled themselves at the man while the woman disappeared into the trees, followed by a hail of bullets.

"Lucky the camera was there for the arrest, hmm?" said Bea's dad, tapping a cigarette out of a pack and sticking it between his lips. "Unusually lucky."

"No smoking!" ordered his wife from the kitchen.

"The Minister of the Interior denies that the meeting with the woman, positively identified as Nahira, the rebel leader, was in any way connected with a plot to organize further destabilization," said the journalist. He held a sheet of paper out toward the camera. "However, little credence can be given to this statement, since plans for a coup were found in his car. A court will have to decide whether, in fact, as Scandia Channel 1 is reporting, Liron is guilty of high treason, which in Scandia still carries the death penalty."

"Ohmigod!" cried Bea.

"Shh!" said her mother, who had come in from the kitchen to listen, too.

"It's possible that the meeting had something to do with the disappearance of Princess Jenna, the king's niece, who returned to Scandia approximately one year ago, but as of yet we have no firm information about this," said the journalist. Once again, the screen showed pictures from Scandian TV.

"Of course, no one can say for certain that the princess has actually been abducted," said a man identified by a caption as a spokesperson for the Scandian police. "At the moment all we know is that she has disappeared and we haven't received any ransom demands. But when considered in the context of Minister Liron's arrest and the various incidents of the last few days, kidnapping is a distinct possibility."

Next came another man, identified as the headmaster of Morgard School. "She has had some difficulty adapting to our little school community," he said. "During the last year our girls have gone to great lengths to welcome Princess Jenna and help her adjust to boarding school life. But let's just say she hasn't made much of an effort herself to fit in."

He shook his head with deep regret.

The offscreen interviewer said, "We've also heard that the princess had seemed confused recently, as if she were heading for some kind of breakdown. Did you see any evidence of this?"

The headmaster frowned. "Well, I'm no doctor," he said, "but from the very beginning, when she first came to the school, it seemed to me that in Princess Jenna we were dealing with a rather immature and . . . you might even say . . . disturbed personality." He gave a thoughtful nod. "Although, of course, we've done everything we possibly can . . ."

"Liar!" Bea yelled at the TV.

"Shh!" hissed her father and mother at the same time.

"So she might have run away, then?" asked the interviewer.

"Judging by her character and her mental state, I can only answer in the affirmative," said the headmaster. "One can't rule out the possibility that, despite all our efforts, something simply snapped."

Now the interviewer himself appeared on-screen. "There you have it: Both explanations — abduction or the possibility of a mentally unbalanced girl running away or even attempting to take her own life — appear equally plausible," he said.

"Which is why we ask the people of Scandia to be on the lookout and to join in the search for Princess Jenna, who may well be in urgent need of medical attention."

"You're the one who'll be in urgent need of medical attention if I ever get my hands on you!" cried Bea. "What are these people talking about? They're the ones who are crazy!"

She jumped to her feet. The special on Scandia was coming to an end. As soon as she had her cell phone back, she would try to reach Jenna. She had to know the truth.

22

$\boldsymbol{I}$*n the moonlight,* the wheels of the moped whirred across the blacktop, cutting through the shadows from the trees that lay like beams across the road.

They heard a vehicle approaching. In the silence of the night, it sounded at first like the buzz of a bumblebee. Perry switched off the headlight. By the time the car finally passed them, they had already hidden both themselves and the moped in a dip behind a blackberry bush.

"Phew!" said Perry, heaving the moped over the soft earth of the forest floor to get it back on the road. "Near miss."

"They're going in our direction," said Jenna, coughing.

"What do you mean?" asked Perry, and waited for her to sit on the passenger seat. "They're going in the opposite direction!"

"I mean where we've come from," said Jenna. "The navigator's house."

Perry shook his head. The moped jerked forward. "Only if they turn off," he said. "Otherwise they could be going anywhere. This road leads to all kinds of places, depending on where you turn off. They might be heading for the north–south beltway."

Jenna didn't answer. The moon was now so high that they could almost have managed without the headlight. When they came to a junction, where the road met a broad and rutted gravel track, Perry did indeed turn off the light and the motor. "It's still quite far off," he whispered, "but you've heard for yourself how sound carries in the night. We'll go the rest of the way on foot."

Jenna nodded. She didn't want to ask any more questions. They could hear the noise of engines, squealing brakes, someone shouting. It seemed pretty close, but who could tell just how far voices might carry? She'd see for herself soon enough.

The carpet of pine needles beneath their feet was soft, and muffled every sound. Ahead of them was a cold white light quite high in the sky, suggesting floodlights illuminating a large square. Jenna waited in suspense.

When they reached the edge of the trees, she held her breath. There in front of her were several hangars, as tall as five-story houses, around a huge yard lit by streetlamps. The doors were wide open, and outside them long lines of trucks stood waiting, with the drivers standing and talking beside them.

"What is it?" whispered Jenna.

Perry shrugged his shoulders. He put a finger to his lips and gestured to Jenna that she should follow him to where they could get a view of the whole scene.

"I don't know, either," he whispered, "but I've got a pretty good idea. Why have they come secretly in the night? Why not during the day?"

"Stolen goods?" whispered Jenna. The shudder that ran down her spine was almost pleasant. This was exciting! Like one of the mysteries she used to enjoy reading.

"No!" whispered Perry. "Think! It's obvious, isn't it?"

Now they could see several figures, bathed in the ghostly glow of the streetlights, hurrying silently back and forth, carrying boxes into the hangars. A smaller van reversed out through one of the gates.

"Isn't it?" hissed Perry.

Jenna pulled her cell phone out of her pocket. She'd have to be quick, so that she couldn't be located by its signal. She switched on the video. Now they had proof. Who knew whether or when it might be useful?

"Turn it off!" Perry insisted in a whisper.

Jenna did so. At that moment, she felt a tickling in her nose. Last night's storm and her thin dress! Why did she have to go and catch a cold? She pinched her nostrils, but it didn't help. Oh no, not now! Not when it was so important to keep quiet!

Ridiculously loud, her sneeze echoed all around the stock-yard, and the men stopped dead in their tracks.

They had taken a single car. Three men would be enough. The driver had only needed brief directions. He knew the way to Saarstad, and from there it was only a few miles to the navigator's house.

In the darkness they'd almost missed the sandy track that led from the main road to the sea. The driver swung the car around just in time.

"Headlights off?" he asked.

"Not yet," said the high-ranking security officer next to him. "If he's right and she's there, she'll be asleep now, anyway. We'll approach on foot."

The navigator's house lay ahead of them in the darkness. It was just a black silhouette against the dark gray backdrop of the sea, where the ever-moving waves reflected the moonlight in crests and streaks. There was no light in the windows, and no sound that they could hear.

"Shh!" said the leader, and gestured to his men to stand still. "Now, you go right, and you left. And be careful! There might be someone else in the house — not just the girl."

But all was still. "The door's locked," whispered the youngest man. He was eager to prove himself. "But let's see . . ." He ran his fingers over the top of the doorframe. "Here's the key!"

The second they cautiously stepped into the little hall, they knew they wouldn't find anybody. The silence was total. They went quickly into all the rooms, shining their flashlights into every corner.

"Nothing!" said the driver. "He was wrong. Just because he's her father . . ."

"But she was here!" said the young man. "Definitely!" He pointed to the bunch of flowers. "Or at least some girl was. See? Freshly picked."

"Well, she's gone again now," said the driver.

The young man shook his head and picked up a plastic bag from the veranda.

"Potatoes and a couple of carrots. She's coming back," he said. "She wouldn't leave her food here otherwise. And she wouldn't have picked a bunch of flowers if she wasn't planning to stay."

The officer nodded. "Good thinking," he said. He pulled his cell phone out of his pocket. "Unfortunately, sir, the subject is out at the moment," he said. "But we presume that she'll be back soon. There are enough indications . . . Precisely. Then we'll bring her in."

He put the phone back in his pocket. "I'll give you the signal," he said. "And men, be very gentle. We're not dealing with a criminal here. This is our princess, and she's not being accused of anything worse than mental instability."

"And overeating," murmured the driver.

"That's no reason to use excessive force," said the officer. "So let's not get excited. Now, each of you find your own hiding place."

The sneeze was so loud that for a moment the whole yard seemed to freeze. A forklift screeched to a stop, and something fell to the ground. Jenna only caught a glimpse of the sudden standstill before they were up and away. Every head had turned toward the place where she and Perry had been hiding behind the trees.

Jenna was grateful for all the hours she'd spent running round the campus at Morgard. *Proof!* she said to herself. *Everything has its purpose.* Behind her she could hear Perry already beginning to pant.

"Hurry!" cried Jenna. There was no point in keeping quiet now, or in trying to hide. The men's shouts were echoing behind them "You can do it, Perry! We're almost there!"

Even before Perry reached the moped, she had pulled it up and turned on the ignition. As soon as he jumped onto the seat in front of her, breathing heavily and trembling all over, the machine leaped forward onto the road.

"Go, go, go!" cried Jenna. "Faster, Perry, faster! They're on foot — they can't catch us!"

Perry accelerated, and the moped raced along the road as the angry shouts behind them faded away. Soon, there was nothing to be heard except the noise of the moped and their own heavy breathing. They had escaped.

Jenna felt light-headed. It really *was* like one of those thrillers! All they had to do now was convict the gangsters.

"Can't you hear?" Perry cried, breaking into her fantasies. "They're coming after us in their trucks! Hold on tight, Jenna. If they catch us . . ." He turned the throttle, but they were already traveling as fast as the little moped could go.

The noise of engines behind them was getting louder. "Faster, Perry, faster!" Jenna urged again. In stories, the heroes never got caught.

The moped gave a great howl, as if trying to summon up all its strength; then the engine spluttered and died.

"Perry!" cried Jenna. Why had the engine cut out? "What happened?" She realized, panic-stricken, that they were slowing down.

Perry turned the ignition again and again, but the motor remained silent.

"Gas!" he whispered in despair. "We're out of gas! I didn't fill it up earlier. I wanted to save money, and I didn't think we'd be . . ."

He made a sudden decision, and steered the moped between the trees. It began to skid, but he straightened it up. The uneven ground slowed them still more, but for a little while they continued to freewheel through the moonlit night.

"That's it," said Perry, and got off. "At least they won't be able to see us from the road now."

He crouched behind the trunk of a pine tree. The ground between the trees was covered with low-growing blueberry bushes. It was absurd: Just a few hours ago, Jenna would have been delighted. Berries meant food. But now she would have given anything for some tall cover, with or without berries.

The sound of the trucks seemed to be drawing threateningly close.

"But they'll see our tracks in the sand!" said Jenna desperately. "If they just look at the side of the road, they'll see exactly where we turned off into the woods."

At that moment, the moon disappeared behind a cloud.

Perry gazed at Jenna. She saw that there was a smile on his face. "Shh!" he whispered, as if someone in the passing trucks might hear them. There was a drone of engines, a whole convoy of them. And then the sound faded away into the distance.

For a few seconds, Jenna did not dare move. Her heart was beating as hard as if she had just run her first marathon.

"But why?" she asked. "Are they blind?" The moon came out again from behind the cloud. Its light suddenly seemed as friendly as a fairy tale. *Hansel and Gretel*, she thought. "Why didn't they see our tracks?"

Perry pointed up at the sky. "Because of that!" he said softly. "Now let's get out of here! If they come back and start searching for us again, and the moon's still shining . . ." He shrugged his shoulders. "Then we're done for. And believe me, I *still* don't want to go to the military academy."

"But where to?" asked Jenna. "Where can we go?"

"Home!" said Perry. "To the navigator's house. They'll stop looking for us soon. And they don't know where we came from. They must be scared of the police, too. They're probably rushing to empty their warehouses." He had started walking.

"So you think they're criminals?" asked Jenna. Her heart was beating more normally now. Perry had called the navigator's house *home*. She had shaken out the carpets and picked flowers.

"I don't know who they are," said Perry. "But whatever they're up to, it can't be legal. Those hangars? Otherwise they wouldn't be unloading all that stuff in the middle of the night!"

Jenna agreed.

"But I've got my suspicions," said Perry. "It could also be . . ." He glanced across at her. ". . . the rebels. All the shortages? Maybe the rebels take all the food, all the supplies, to this depot to hide them. That's what they keep saying in the papers. Maybe they're right."

"But where would the rebels get it all from to begin with?" asked Jenna. "The food and everything? And all those trucks? Here on South Island. Think about it, Perry."

They walked faster. "How should I know?" said Perry. "But it sure seems like there's some connection, doesn't it?"

He stopped and made another sudden decision. "I'm going to call my father," he said. "We have to tell him exactly what's going on. Then he can tell the police, and they can find out what it all means."

Jenna looked at him. She knew that they could be traced as soon as they used a cell phone. And yet she understood that he had to do it. The criminals had chased them, and as long as they were still at large, she and Perry might not be safe.

"Why don't you call the police yourself, directly?" she asked.

Perry hesitated. "Don't laugh at me," he said, "but my father . . . As far as he's concerned, I'm just a loser. The biggest disappointment of his life. But if I uncover something like this now . . ."

"Oh, Perry!" said Jenna. She understood perfectly. Her mother was just as disappointed in her. This was a chance to prove they'd discovered something that even the Scandian police didn't know about. "OK, then," she said. "Do it."

As they walked, Perry took his phone out of a pocket in his jeans and brought up the number on the screen.

23

*O*nce the shooting had stopped, Nahira hid for a while in the bushes. She couldn't go to Lorok, who was waiting for her in the pickup — that would have put him in danger, too. She just had to hope that he'd turned the truck around and drove away as soon as he heard the shots. But he was such a young hothead, she was afraid he might try to play the hero.

She listened to the sounds that were coming from the clearing. Mainly shouted orders, but at least no screams of pain. Then, very quietly, she climbed to the top of an oak tree — something she had not done for years. Up there she made herself a seat out of a fork in the branches and waited, in the hope that she would be safer where she was than down below. Only if they sent a search party with dogs would her hiding place risk exposure. Her trail ended at the foot of the tree, and a glance upward would be enough to deliver her into the hands of any pursuers.

But when dusk fell, she began to have doubts. Why hadn't

she heard anything for so long? Why no voices, no footsteps, no shouts, even in the distance? Where had all the soldiers gone?

They couldn't have given up the hunt so easily, thought Nahira, trying to flex her limbs in her uncomfortable perch. One of her feet was threatening to go to sleep. *No one followed me. It was just bullets. But why didn't they come looking for me after that?*

She looked down. There was an almost inaudible rustling in the dry leaves. A mouse. Or maybe a rabbit. *They tried to shoot me, but after that they stopped searching.*

I'm safe.

Before lack of light made it too difficult, she slowly let herself down, branch by branch. *I was better at this when I was younger*, she thought, and couldn't help laughing. *But then, who'd have imagined I'd need to climb trees again?* She jumped down to the ground and stretched her limbs. She'd been living in hiding for so long that her whole body, eyes, ears, nose, were alert when there was even the slightest chance of danger. Sometimes her heart would start beating faster even before her eyes and ears had perceived the approach of trouble.

But now her heart was calm, and her breath was even. *They're not looking for me. I'm safe.*

Not until she reached the road and still had seen no sign that she was being followed did she take out her cell phone. "You can come and get me," she said softly. "As agreed. See you soon."

She looked up at the blue-black sky. Up here in the remote north of South Island, there were so few settlements, and so few streetlamps or houses or lights of any kind, that the night belonged entirely to the stars.

But at home on North Island, the sky is even more lovely, thought Nahira, leaning against a tree while she waited. *Nowhere in the world are the nights so beautiful as they are on North Island. Behind all those single stars the Milky Way still shines, like a white veil, millions of light-years away and yet just a minute in the timetable of the universe. I should look at the sky more often. Sometimes it's a good thing to realize just how small we are, and how insignificant in the great web of the world.*

She shook herself. This was absurd — the shock of what had happened earlier must have been greater than she'd tried to make herself believe. Once she started to tell herself how small and insignificant she was, the next step would probably be to accept that there was nothing she could do. But it was for precisely the opposite reason that she'd first joined the rebels. To do something. To change things. To *improve* the great web of the world — or at least the little web of Scandia.

"What a romantic I am!" she murmured. She glanced up again at the stars shedding their seductive light, oblivious to her change in mood. "Where's Lorok?" Then she heard the engine.

"Nahira, thank God! I practically peed myself with fear!" cried Lorok, opening the passenger door of the old pickup truck. "I heard gunfire. Why didn't you come?"

"Because I didn't want to lead them to you, dummy," said Nahira, flopping down into the seat. The springs had long gone, and as they drove away she could feel every inch of the rough ground below. It had almost been more comfortable sitting up in the tree. "Don't tell me you sat there waiting for me all this time?"

"Of course I did," said Lorok. "You didn't think I'd just leave you behind, did you?"

Nahira groaned. "That *was* pretty dumb, Lorok," she said. "They could have found you while they were hunting for me." She was silent for a moment. "They *didn't* find you, did they?" she asked.

"Am I or am I not here?" asked Lorok, turning down a narrow road.

"So they didn't come looking?" asked Nahira warily. "You didn't hear a search party? Bloodhounds?"

The truck stopped behind a hill. The hut, nestled in a hollow amid birch trees and tall grass, was dilapidated: Tiles were missing from the roof and glass from the windows. The shiny new satellite dish on a recently cut tree stump stood in striking contrast.

Lorok shook his head. "Nothing," he said, jumping out of the truck.

"Nothing," said Nahira thoughtfully. "Nothing."

The front door opened. "At last!" said Meonok. "Come in. I know what happened." In the one room of the darkened hut, standing on a base of empty fruit cartons, was a flickering television set.

"You know what they want you to think," said Nahira. "Is there any coffee?"

Meonok looked at her uncomprehendingly. "What do you mean?"

"Can't you at least answer my question first?" said Nahira. She was tired. Sometimes she wished that in addition to their courage these boys also had a little bit more common sense. "Have you made some coffee?"

Meonok nodded and poured her a cup. A small cloud of steam rose from the mug, and just the sight of it made Nahira feel better.

"Turn up the sound," she said, glancing at the TV. "Well, well, they actually filmed the arrest!" She took a cautious sip, and the coffee burned her tongue, but she felt more alert now. "Just as I thought. They were all prepared."

A man in uniform held a sheet of paper out toward the camera, and in bold block letters were the words *PLAN FOR THE COUP*. He folded it up again.

"And what's that?"

"That's the plan they found in Liron's car when they arrested him," said Meonok. "They keep showing it over and over again. Apparently, it's proof that Liron was planning a coup with us. They say the Minister of the Interior is a traitor, and he's going to be accused of high treason. And if they find him guilty . . ."

"A coup!" said Nahira. "Liron had no such plan with him!" The coffee cup was now empty, and she put it on the table.

"How could we be so stupid? They probably had his phone bugged the entire time. Both of them."

"That's how they knew about the rendezvous," said Lorok.

"I shouldn't have called him," said Nahira. "But I thought it was crucial for him to show the depot to the media."

"That's why they didn't even have to follow him," said Lorok. "They only had to wait for you both at the place you arranged on the phone."

"Curse all these phones and devices and GPS!" said Nahira. "Curse the Internet! They can track you whenever they want. There's no privacy anymore!"

"Calm down, Nahira," said Meonok. "I don't think it was any better in the days of smoke signals. When people sent each other letters, they always risked interception, you could always steam them open. And with radio signals, they could crack every code. Don't tell me it was harder in the old days to spy on people."

Nahira sighed. Over and over again the same images flickered across the TV screen, as if they needed to be imprinted forever on the minds of every single Scandian: Liron getting out of the car, walking toward her, and then the soldiers racing out of their hiding places, and her running away from a hail of bullets.

So why hadn't they hunted her down?

When she'd seen the footage for the fifth time and knew every word of the commentary by heart, she finally understood the reason. There was no other possible explanation. Nothing else made any sense.

They didn't want to catch her.

"Of course," she murmured.

They had Liron, and that was all that mattered to them, to show that members of the government were secretly in league with the rebels. But if their ultimate aim was to topple the government — and it certainly was — then they had to go on stirring up people's fear of the rebels, just as they'd almost succeeded in doing a year ago. They mustn't capture the rebel leader too soon!

"Because then people would no longer be afraid of the rebels," she whispered. "They deliberately missed me and let me escape. So that they could say I was still at large."

She looked at Lorok and Meonok. "What a disappointment!" she said with a sigh. "I was so proud of myself for having escaped from half a battalion of soldiers, and all the while I was just carrying out their plan. They think they can manipulate us like chess pieces! But I have a few ideas, too. Boys, we have some planning of our own to do."

On the moped, the journey hadn't seemed very far, but on foot it seemed endless.

When the forest gradually became more familiar, Jenna began to feel the full effects of her tiredness. She had hardly slept for two days now, and it would be morning again before she could finally lie down.

"I'm just dying for my bed!" she said to Perry. Since talking to his father, he'd been walking faster, and when she looked at his face, she saw that he was smiling.

"My father could hardly believe it!" he said. "He was speechless!" His smile grew broader. "And then of course he insisted that I come home. 'Only if you promise that I don't have to go to your fascist military academy,' I told him. At least now he knows his son isn't a total idiot! Ha! By now the police should be raiding those hangars."

"Aren't you tired, Perry?" asked Jenna.

He shook his head. "Too excited," he said. "Are we going to boil some potatoes?"

"How?" asked Jenna, yawning. "There's no electricity. And anyway, I don't want to eat — I just want to crawl into bed. Without even brushing my teeth."

"Oh no, I forgot to get toothbrushes!" said Perry. "Assuming they had any. OK, you're excused, then." He ran his hand over the top of the doorframe, and found the key. "Good night, Jenna."

But that was as far as he got.

"Or should we say good morning?" said a male voice. It sounded amused.

Then three men jumped out, and Jenna knew there was no point in running. She was too tired, anyway. So now back they would go. To school. To Ylva. It had all been for nothing. She shouldn't have even bothered picking the flowers.

The young man who had seized her was bending her arm

behind her back. "Ouch!" said Jenna. But she wasn't going to let them treat her like this. "Let me go!" she protested.

The older man who had spoken first, and was evidently the leader of the group, laughed. "I'm afraid we can't," he said. "Even though you're a princess, we're not able to grant your wishes today."

Out of the corner of her eye, Jenna could see Perry trying to shake off his captor, but he had no chance against someone so much bigger and stronger than him.

"So now you're going back to school," said the older man. "And maybe to see a doctor or a psychologist, you crazy little princess! And it seems to me you're just as crazy, boy. What made you think we wouldn't find you?"

They were right; it *was* a ridiculously obvious hiding place, thought Jenna, surprised at how wide awake she was now — wide awake and feverish. *Why did I think I'd be safe in the navigator's house? Any fool would know that's the first place they'd look for me. And it's no consolation that Perry's as stupid as I am.*

In the car, they sat jammed together in the backseat with the youngest of the three men, barely more than a boy himself. When they'd driven out onto the main road, he'd offered them something to drink. Jenna sneezed, then held her head up high. *There's no danger*, she thought. *Nothing to be afraid of. It's not like last year. We're not prisoners. They're not threatening us, or preparing to torture us. They're just taking us back to school.*

Like that wasn't bad enough.

She could picture the school cafeteria, or the classrooms, which would all fall silent as soon as she walked in. She could see Ylva's face and hear her harsh laughter. "Well, and there I was thinking I'd have the room all to myself!" she'd say. "Without the constant *eau de northerner*! But the poor little Pizza Princess can't even run away right. What *can* she do?"

But there was still her other life — she should concentrate on that now. There was Bea, and her few other friends from her old school, even if everything else had changed. And when she was totally grown-up, in just a few more years, no one could stop her from going home.

She felt the tears rising. She could not even *begin* to let herself think about Jonas now. She wanted to think about Bea, about dinner at Bea's, how they'd both climbed out the window. She fished her cell phone out of her pocket. The men hadn't even taken their phones, but then, why should they? She and Perry were just two runaways being brought back to school — mixed-up kids, that was all.

"First chance I get, I'll run again," hissed Perry. "They can't lock me up forever in their stupid military jail!"

The man in the passenger seat turned around and laughed. "That's got nothing to do with me, kid," he said. "You can work it out with your father. But if you were my son, well . . . in the old days there was such a thing as the cane."

"Yeah, maybe in the Middle Ages!" said Perry furiously.

"In case you hadn't noticed, we're in the twenty-first century now. And I wasn't talking to you, anyway!"

It's even worse for Perry than it is for me, thought Jenna, switching on her cell phone. No one tried to stop her. She opened the address book, then pursed her lips and zapped through her pictures in search of the pizzeria photos. She'd tell Bea she'd come and visit her soon, and ask if that was OK.

The phone of the man in the passenger seat let out a shrill tune, and he pulled it out of his pocket. "Yes?" he answered in a bored tone.

Jenna had flipped through all her pictures and reached the videos. They were all dark, and you could scarcely make out what was going on in the one she'd taken tonight: the hangars under the streetlamps, the trucks and the figures scurrying around the stockyard.

The man on his cell phone listened, then gave a start and quickly turned in his seat. Jenna couldn't make out his expression. "That changes everything," he said. Now his tone was sharp. "Of course. We'll see to it."

With a loud click, he shut his phone.

"There's been a change of plans," he said. He gazed straight ahead at the road. "We're not going to Morgard. At the next junction, turn left."

"Why not Morgard?" asked Perry. Jenna could hear the mounting panic in his voice. "I won't go to the military academy! Don't even try it!"

"Shut your mouth!" said the man in the passenger seat, the

anger audible in his voice. He nodded toward Jenna. "Take her cell phone!"

The young man grabbed for it.

"Why?" cried Jenna. She held her arm as far away from him as possible in the confines of the car. At least she was going to send Bea the photos from the pizza place, even if she couldn't write her a message. She pressed the SEND key. "It's mine! It's none of your business!"

The young man pulled her arm, then bent her fingers back. "Perry!" screamed Jenna. But Perry didn't even try to help her. *Coward!* thought Jenna.

"Do you know who we are?" Perry asked, leaning toward the back of the passenger seat. "What do you think you're doing, treating us like this? You'll be in serious trouble with my father. *Serious* trouble, I promise you."

The man turned around with a contemptuous expression on his face. "Oh really?" he said. Then he grabbed Jenna's cell phone and switched it off.

"Yours, too," he said to Perry.

Stand up for yourself, Perry! Jenna was thinking. *Don't be such a wimp!*

But Perry made no attempt to resist. He handed over his cell phone, looked at Jenna, and shrugged. "We'll get them back soon," he murmured. "Why fight over it? You don't think my father's going to turn a blind eye to this, do you?"

"Turn right," said the man in the passenger seat. The forest opened out, and for a few minutes they drove through fields.

There was thick mist hovering over the ground now, hiding the road and swallowing up the headlights. Dawn was breaking. "Who knows? You might get a good old-fashioned caning after all!" The man turned to look at Perry, and laughed. "Yeah, that's a pretty safe bet. You may even end up wishing that's *all* you were getting."

Jenna turned cold. Something had changed. This latest threat definitely had nothing to do with Perry's stupid military school.

24

"*Yes, we've got them,*" Bolström said into the receiver. "Now don't get all upset, Captain. Why did you tell me about it in the first place? Everything's perfectly fine, so just calm down," The man at the other end was evidently very agitated. Bolström rolled his eyes. "Yes, of course," he said. "I'll be in touch." He slammed down the receiver. "Idiot!"

He went to the window and closed the curtains. It was slowly getting light outside. The heavy red velvet smelled musty.

"But of course we do actually have a problem now, Norlin," he said. "You do realize that? A serious problem." He looked at the other man in the room. There was dust on the paneling and the brocade wallpaper, as if the room had not been used for a very long time. The men sat at a delicately ornate writing desk on equally delicate chairs that looked as if they would collapse under their weight. The lamp on the desk was lit.

"How come, Bolström?" asked Norlin. He was holding a glass of cognac in his hand, and the bottle was standing beside him. Bolström had given up trying to keep the man on the wagon. "It can all quite easily be . . ."

"Quite easily?" said Bolström. "Really? How so?"

"When our mission is accomplished," said Norlin. "When we've saved our beloved country." Now that he had the drink again, he seemed almost clearheaded. The trembling had stopped, and there were no beads of sweat on his brow. "No one will ask any more questions. We just have to make sure that it all happens fast — faster than we'd originally planned."

Bolström's hand jerked in the direction of the bottle, then he took a deep breath. "The booze has softened your brain, Norlin!" he said irritably. "So, after we've saved the country, the children suddenly turn up safe and sound and everything's wonderful. Is that what you think? But what happens when they tell their story to the press, huh? To the world at large? What if someone talks? How will the people react? They may start by cheering us for rescuing them from conspiracy and economic mismanagement and terrorism. But do you imagine they'll keep on cheering when they hear it's us who've actually been organizing —"

"Those two children won't talk!" said Norlin. But his voice sounded uncertain. "I'm sure that once they're back home, they won't tell . . ."

"Nonsense!" snorted Bolström. "Complete and utter nonsense, Norlin! Of course they'll talk! How are you going to stop them? And what will happen to us when they do?" He was breathing heavily. "The children are dangerous, Norlin.

Surely you can see that, can't you? They could wreck every-thing! Blast! I should never have stayed out of the country for so long!"

"But we can't keep them locked up forever!" said Norlin uneasily, and poured himself another glass. "After we've taken over the country, they'll have to go home, if not beforehand. You'll have to think of something, Bolström." He began to grovel. "You've always found a solution before."

Bolström nodded grimly. "Trust me, I've got one now as well," he said. "As long as they're alive, these kids are a threat to us, my dear Norlin. You understand what I'm saying?"

"No!" yelled Norlin. "You don't mean . . . No, Bolström, no! Not my little Jenna!"

Bolström laughed. "Right now they're more use to me alive than dead," he said, "in the short term, that is, though just how short remains to be seen." He leaned toward Norlin. "You'd like to be regent again soon, wouldn't you, Norlin? Eh? But there's a price to be paid." He slammed his hand down on the desk.

With trembling fingers, Norlin reached for the bottle and took a large gulp.

They'd been driving for a while. Occasionally, Jenna's head had sunk onto Perry's shoulder, or vice versa. It was amazing that even in a situation like this you could actually go to sleep if you were tired enough.

As the sun rose and the air in the car began to get warmer, Jenna woke up.

"Aren't we there yet?" she asked with a yawn. She tapped the seat in front of her. "Where are you taking us?" And then the fear returned.

The car jerked to a halt. "Stupid animals!" said the driver. Ahead of them, two shaggy dogs were driving a flock of newly shorn sheep along the sandy road. The bleating was so loud that anyone who hadn't been woken up by the abrupt braking of the car would certainly have woken up now.

Perry yawned, too. "Morning already?" he asked in surprise.

A confused sheep tried to break off and run into the trees on the right, but the larger of the two dogs herded it back into the flock. A lamb veered off to the left, and its mother let out a shrill cry.

"Stupid animals!" said the driver again. He drummed his fingers on the steering wheel. There was no way he could move on.

The man in the passenger seat impatiently wound down his window. "Hey, shepherd!" he yelled. "Hey, old man, how long is this going to take?"

Leaning on his crook, the shepherd stood at the edge of the forest, looking at his flock. He appeared to be counting every single animal, as if he knew each one of them by sight and was making absolutely sure that none of them got lost. His hat was pushed back on his head to reveal gray hair that looked as if it had once been black.

"Not long now, sir," he called out apologetically, and gave a signal to one of the dogs. Only then did he look at the car.

"They belong to Mr. von Soderberg, sir. Lovely sheep!"

"Lovely sheep!" growled the man in the passenger seat. "We're in a hurry, man!"

The shepherd raised his hand. "Can't go no faster, sir," he said. "Not many more to go. Lovely sheep!"

"Curse these stupid old men!" said the man in the passenger seat. "Probably never even been in a car! We need to get off this road before we're too far into the day."

"Where are you taking us?" Jenna asked again. The last of the sheep were now crossing the road, with a small black dog zigzagging behind them.

"You'll soon find out, Princess," said the man. He wound the window up again. The shepherd tipped his hat and called out something that they couldn't hear through the glass. Then he disappeared into the forest with his flock.

"And here we are!" said the man. The car turned down a path that looked too narrow to be passable. Branches scratched the doors and scraped across the windshield.

Then suddenly the path broadened out. After the drive through the shadowy forest, the brightness was blinding, and Jenna shut her eyes against the glare. The morning sun was reflecting off the water, and little flashes of light were dancing over the crests of the waves. Once again, they were beside the sea.

Jenna knew at once that she'd never seen this place before. A weathered wooden hut stood at the edge of the forest. There were plants growing out of its foundations. It looked as if it had been abandoned for a long time. A few feet in front of it, a narrow dock jutted out into the water. Just like the one at the navigator's house, it had boards missing and one of the piers was broken, so that the end of the structure hung down at an angle into the water.

"What is this place?" asked Perry.

The man in the passenger seat laughed. "No five-star hotel, I can assure you that," he said. He checked to make sure the central locking was secure, then keyed in a number on his cell. "We've arrived, sir. But we need to be relieved as soon as possible. My men need sleep badly."

Jenna couldn't hear what was being said on the other end. The man closed his phone.

"What do you mean 'relieved'?" she asked. "And I want my phone back! When my mother hears how you've treated us . . ."

The man released the lock and got out. "You'll stay here till I tell you to get out," he said.

Suddenly there was a gun in his hand. Was it real?

"Out!" the man ordered Perry.

The hut was in a terrible state inside as well. Many years of neglect had left their mark. Cobwebs hung from the ceiling as thick and white as mesh curtains, and low enough to brush against Jenna's hair. On the floor were coils of rope covered in bird droppings. A broken lobster trap stood under the single window, in which a missing pane of glass had been roughly replaced with a piece of cardboard.

"Welcome!" said the man. "Do sit down wherever you feel most comfortable. And get it into your heads that there is absolutely no point in trying to escape." He waved his pistol. "As you can see, I have my little friend with me."

He pulled the door shut behind him. It seemed almost incredible to Jenna that there was actually a key to lock it with.

"Perry?" she said. She could hear just how weak her own voice sounded. Perry had gone to stand at the window, and was looking through the three remaining panes of glass. They, too, were covered with cobwebs. "Perry, do you understand what's going on?"

Very slowly, Perry turned toward her. He shook his head. "I'm scared!" he whispered. "At first I thought they were just bodyguard types who'd been sent to find us and take us back to school. The whole country must have been searching for us, so it's not exactly a surprise that they found us! Isn't that what you thought, too?"

Jenna nodded. Barely visible through the cobwebs, the head of the youngest kidnapper now appeared outside the window. He grinned at them, and made a V-for-victory sign with two fingers before disappearing again.

"It was the phone call," said Jenna. "That's when their behavior changed. Do you think it suddenly occurred to them that they could demand a ransom? Then they decided to kidnap us instead?"

"Could be," Perry said slowly.

"It's the only explanation that makes sense," said Jenna. "So now what are we going to do?"

Perry sat down on a coil of rope.

"Wait," he said. "Wait for them to ransom us. Our parents will pay. What else can they do? So we might as well get some sleep."

The gulls screamed outside the hut. Jenna found a fishing net spread out on the floor, and lay down. She tried to tell herself that the men could only get money for them if they were still alive, so they weren't in any real danger. She wanted to stop being scared. She was so tired of being frightened.

Her eyes closed.

25

*B*ea *had never gone* to school this freakishly early before. The place was empty, and there were only three cars in the parking lot. From one of the ground-floor classrooms came the occasional sound of a weary voice: Some poor sucker was having a private tutoring session before classes began.

Bea pulled open the heavy main door. Of course, the custodian was already up and about, but his cubicle was empty. Usually he'd be sitting there behind the glass partition with a steaming cup of coffee and a bacon sandwich. "Hello?" she said. "Anybody frickin' home?!"

"What's the matter?" asked Philippa. Bea hadn't heard her coming. "What are you ranting about so early in the morning?"

"He isn't here!" moaned Bea. "Oh, for the love of —!"

"Tsk, tsk, don't let any of the teachers hear you going off like that," said Philippa. "Why do you want him, anyway? Is he your *secret love*?"

"Shut up, Philippa, this is important!" snapped Bea. Maybe the man had an appointment — even custodians go to the doctor — or he might be somewhere in the school, looking at a broken window. If she was lucky. "You don't have Jenna's number, do you?"

"Have what?" asked Philippa.

"Jenna's cell phone," said Bea. "That's why I'm here."

"You think the custodian's got Jenna's phone number?" asked Philippa incredulously. "You can't be serious!"

Bea groaned. "Would you please try to keep up! I left my phone in the gym yesterday, and the number's in it, duh! So now I can't call her . . ."

"Oh, I get it. You're worried about Jenna because of all that stuff on TV yesterday!" said Philippa. "I saw it, too." Now she sounded excited. After all, it wasn't every day that a former classmate became a princess, or got kidnapped, or appeared in a special news program on television. "But she's your best friend! Don't you have the number written down on a piece of paper somewhere? You could just call her from a landline."

"Do *you* write cell phone numbers down on pieces of paper?" Bea asked sarcastically. "Doesn't that kind of defeat the whole point of them *being* cell phone numbers? Why do you think they invented all these devices? So that we'd no longer *have* to write every last bit of information down on little pieces of paper!"

By now the rest of the students had started streaming into the building behind them, talking and laughing — the little ones pushing and shoving, the big ones yawning. And still the custodian's post was empty.

"Maybe someone else has got her number," said Bea, without too much hope.

No matter what, it's probably a waste of time, she thought. *If she's run away, she'll have switched off her phone so that the signal can't be tracked. And if she's been kidnapped, that'll be the first thing they'll take from her. Whatever! I still have to try.*

But no one else in school had Jenna's number. Of course they didn't. It was only when she started asking around that Bea realized Jenna hadn't given her new number — a Scandian number — to anyone but her. As Princess of Scandia, she would only have been allowed to give it to her closest friends.

Unbelievable! thought Bea, still beating herself up for leaving her own phone behind the day before. During French, she was told to answer a question and she didn't even know what page they were on. During chemistry, she discovered that she'd mistakenly brought her geometry notes instead. But the teachers were nice to her. They had all heard about Jenna's disappearance, and they knew that Bea and Jenna had always been inseparable.

"She'll be all right," said the chemistry teacher, without mentioning a name. It was meant to be comforting.

As soon as the bell rang, Bea rushed out of the chemistry lab and hurried downstairs. If the custodian had just been fixing something in the building, he was sure to be back at his desk by now.

The men hadn't given them anything to eat; they probably had nothing for themselves, either. It was obvious that they, too, had been surprised by the phone call last night and the sudden change of plans. Jenna thought longingly of the potatoes and carrots still lying there in the navigator's house. Her mouth watered.

Very little light made its way through the cobwebbed window, but there was enough to follow the movement of the sun. Jenna looked at her watch. "It's nearly lunchtime," she said. "Perry, I'm starving!"

"And I'm not?" said Perry. "I can't stop thinking about the Thunbergs' buffet!"

"Yes, but that was weird, wasn't it?" said Jenna thoughtfully.

"The men out there won't want us to starve to death," said Perry confidently. "Then they couldn't get a ransom for us."

"You don't think they're going to do anything to us?" she whispered. When she managed just for a moment to stop thinking about how hungry she was, the unavoidable question kept popping into her mind. "That's what happens when they kidnap people. You see it on TV. If the ransom money isn't paid . . ."

"You think your mother would refuse to pay the ransom?" said Perry. "Or my father?"

"Or when the victims have seen their kidnappers," persisted Jenna, "so they could identify them, testify against them later. Then they kill them. Don't they?"

Perry stood up. He went to the window, tried looking out, and came back.

"Listen, Jenna," he said. "You know as well as I do, the whole of Scandia will be looking for us. This is not your average kidnapping. We're not just the children of some millionaire." He sat down beside her on the net. It was full of sticky scales, and it still gave off a faint odor of fish. "You're Princess of Scandia, Jenna. So you can be sure that the entire Scandian police force will be on the job as soon as any demands are made. Maybe the army, too. And I'm the son of a princess's boyfriend . . ."

"Perry!" said Jenna.

"It's true," said Perry. "And the kidnappers know that — they're not stupid. They know they've got to wrap up this scheme as quickly as possible. And if they harm a single hair on our heads and they get caught . . ." He drew his hand across his throat. "Curtains!"

"Curtains?" Jenna repeated, perplexed.

"It's an expression," Perry said with a shrug.

"So they won't harm us?" Jenna asked. She really wanted to believe it.

"Only if they're cornered," said Perry, absentmindedly peeling the scales away from the blue plastic mesh. "And only as a last resort. But the police know that, too. That's why they'll be supercareful, believe me." He put his hand on her shoulder. "Jenna, let's not drive ourselves crazy. We've got to keep it together. Who knows? We might need to make a sudden break or something."

It was at that moment they heard the car. Even though they couldn't see it, the engine sounded so smooth and quiet, they knew it must be a large one. They both got up from the net.

"See?" said Perry. "I bet this is our food, and then we'll try to find out —"

The key turned in the lock.

"Hello, Jenna," said a man's voice. With the sunlight behind him, she could only see his silhouette and not his face. Even so, the memories flooded back instantly, and she felt herself going cold.

"Bolström!" she said, retreating. She stumbled over a loose rope and almost fell. "I thought you were . . ."

Abroad, she finished the thought. Bolström. If he was behind this kidnapping, what did it mean? She knew from last year just how unscrupulous, how ambitious, how dangerous he was.

"How nice that you remember me, Jenna," said Bolström with a sneer. "You've grown. And if I may say so, you've become prettier, too."

Jenna froze.

"And this must be young Petterson!" Bolström continued, turning toward Perry with a charming smile. "I'm so sorry we have to meet under such unpleasant circumstances, Peter. I knew your father very well when we were children. We went to school together." He laughed. "But when I think back to how devoted he was to all things military even then, I fear you're not exactly the son he would have dreamed of, eh?"

Perry stood stock-still and glared.

Bolström laughed again. He seemed to enjoy Perry's anger. "Not one for words, either, I see. Well, regardless, I must apologize for the inadequate accommodation. There was nothing more comfortable at our immediate disposal, but I hope you're settling in. You may have to put up with this humble abode a tad longer, though I fear it may leave a little to be desired — especially at night." He smiled.

"What do you want?" Jenna demanded in a shrill voice.

"What do you think, little Jenna?" asked Bolström. "Are there so many possibilities?" He reached into his jacket pocket for a rolled-up newspaper. "You're not without imagination. How much do you think you're worth to your mother? And your uncle, the king? And as for your little friend here — you are friends, I hope? — how much do you think his father will pay for him?" He laughed. "We're talking about an eight-figure sum, I should think, Jenna, which will provide me with a comfortable old age. Even if I have to pay off a few assistants." He pointed outside, from where the sounds of the men gulping down food had been coming since he arrived.

He gestured impatiently at Jenna and Perry, sending them to the wall opposite the window. "Very good, very good," he said. "Now, a little closer together, please. Yes, that's perfect." He came toward them and handed the newspaper to Perry. Jenna suddenly understood what was going on.

"You want to photograph us," she said. "With today's newspaper. So that our parents know we're still alive."

"What a clever girl you are, Jenna!" said Bolström. "I can understand why your father is so proud of you. Incidentally, he sends you his warmest good wishes."

"Stop it!" Jenna shouted. "Don't talk about my father!" She began to cry.

Perry put his arm around her shoulder. "Don't," he said. "Don't cry, Jenna. Don't give him that satisfaction."

Jenna wiped her eyes on her sleeve. But they were already red, and the tears were already on her cheeks. She would look terrible in the photo.

"Quite right, my young friend," said Bolström. "And very gallant. Now smile. Smile!" The tiny camera clicked in his hand. "Ah well, it'll have to do. But remember, this photo will be in all tomorrow's newspapers — and not only in Scandia. I'm sure you'd like to spread a little charm, wouldn't you?"

Perry made an angry move toward him, but then stopped himself and stepped back again.

"And now one with a flash," said Bolström, and Jenna involuntarily closed her eyes. "Good, that's lovely. Now we can only hope that your parents come up with the money quickly. I'm sure you don't want to sit here in all the gull droppings any longer than you have to, hmm?"

He was virtually out the door when Perry called after him, "What about food? Aren't you going to give us something to eat?"

Bolström raised his hands in mock horror, as if he were embarrassed. "Food, oh dear me!" he said. "When the men have had enough, I'm sure they'll give you their leftovers. Let's just hope they're not too hungry themselves!" He laughed one last time, then shut the door behind him.

"Perry?" whispered Jenna. She was almost pleased to see that he, too, had started to cry.

26

"Slowly, slowly!" said the custodian in his distinctive eastern accent when Bea opened the door to his post. Everybody loved the custodian. Nothing ever flustered him. He would separate fighting sophomores with a calm "What going on here?" and would give extra gold stars for the younger students to stick on their tests when their teachers weren't looking. Bea should have stayed out in the hallway and spoken to him through the Plexiglas partition, but he could see that she simply couldn't wait. "Is world coming to an end?"

"Almost!" said Bea. "I left my bag in the gym yesterday — or maybe it was the locker room . . ."

The custodian nodded and turned to the cabinet behind him. "Is plenty choice for you!" he said, opening it up. "I no understand how you young people never take your things! You have so much money? Your parents no yell at you?"

Bea shrugged her shoulders. "I do take my things," she said. "It's a —"

"Not this one," said the custodian, holding up a pink backpack with fairies and princesses all over it. "That belong to a fifth-grader, yes? They leave it on purpose. To get new one. Fifth grade too old for fairies."

"Mine is —" Bea attempted again.

"And not this one," the custodian continued his inventory. "This one" was a dark blue bag on which someone had used a thick black marker to write the names of all the teams in the NBA. "Is boy. Also forget on purpose. Maybe mother tell him off. Ah, but this one . . ." And there in his hand was Bea's burgundy-red messenger bag. "This one look as if it wait just for you."

"That's it!" cried Bea, grabbing the bag. She rummaged inside.

"Something wrong?" asked the custodian.

Bea shook her head. She pulled out her T-shirt, then her track pants, then one sneaker, then the other. She reached deep down into the bag, and then she tipped it over on its side and shook it empty.

"Nothing!" she said. "My phone's gone! Somebody stole my cell!"

"It was switched on?" asked the custodian.

"No, I never turn it on in school," said Bea. "That's *totally* verboten. If someone texted me and the teacher heard it — buh-bye! Though it seems to be buh-bye now, anyway . . ."

The custodian smiled. "Was very new model? With the apps and all this things?"

"Yeah, right," said Bea. "Like my parents are millionaires. No, it was just a cheap little cell phone. They'll still freak, though, when I tell them it's gone!"

"You see, you lucky!" said the custodian. "When thief see cheap phone, maybe he throw away. Then maybe you get back."

Bea stared at him. "Oh, yeah, that's going to happen. As if."

"Can happen, yes!" said the custodian. "Pigs can fly."

"But I need it *now*!" mumbled Bea. "Thanks anyway." Slowly she trudged back out into the corridor and then up the stairs. She was all for folksy wisdom, but for real? She didn't believe in flying pigs.

When Bolström's car had gone, Jenna and Perry said nothing for a few minutes. Then Perry went to the door and rattled the handle. The men were still on the other side, eating and talking. He heard them laugh.

"Don't bother," said Jenna. "You won't be able to open it, and even if you did, they'd catch you right away. I'm not hungry anymore, anyway."

Perry came back. "That jerk," he said.

Jenna was surprised at how calm she suddenly felt. Her fear and despair seemed to have gone. "Why do you think Bolström's mixed up in this?" she asked.

Perry shrugged his shoulders. "I don't even understand what he's doing back in Scandia," he said. "For a year now, he's been pretty much the most wanted criminal in the country. Though maybe that means he's got nothing more to lose."

"But why is it Bolström of all people who found us?" she asked. "That can't be a coincidence! I mean, our parents must have had hundreds of people searching for us, so why is it Bolström who —?"

"Because he must have been the first to think of looking in the navigator's house," said Perry. "You sort of have that place in common, considering. He must have realized that this was his chance to make buckets of money and then maybe disappear with it for good."

The door opened, and a man they hadn't seen before put a tray down on the floor. Evidently there had been a change of guards. "Enjoy your meal!" he said. "Lots of tasty scraps." He laughed and closed the door.

Jenna didn't even look at it. "I'm just thirsty," she said. "Perry, they will pay up, won't they? My mother and your father."

Perry nodded. He passed her a bottle of water, and took one for himself. "And fast, I hope," he said. "Then, if Bolström has only kidnapped us for the money, he'll leave the country ASAP. And then we'll be free."

"But I still don't understand what that phone call in the car was all about," said Jenna. "If Bolström sent the men to look for us in Saarstad so he could demand a ransom, why did they initially want to take us back to Morgard? It doesn't make sense."

Perry nodded in agreement. "Yeah, I know. That's what worries me."

"Well, you're the genius," said Jenna. "At least Jonas always says so. You figure it out!" As soon as the words were out of her mouth, her heart missed a beat. *Jonas*, she thought. *Oh no! Why did I have to start thinking about Jonas?*

During Bolström's brief absence, a layer of powdery gray dust had accumulated over all the flat surfaces in the room. On a chaise longue that was much too short and narrow for his squat body lay the curled-up figure of Norlin, fast asleep. Every so often he let out a short, startled snore; then he tried to wriggle over onto his other side, realized in his sleep that he would fall off, grunted, snuffled, and began to breathe evenly again. On the floor next to the chaise longue was a half-full bottle of cognac, with a completely empty one not far away from it.

As he walked past, Bolström kicked the empty bottle, which rolled a short distance until it caught against the curved leg of the chaise longue.

Bolström picked up the telephone, dialed, and leaned against the ornate desk.

"Now listen," he whispered into the receiver. "No, I can't speak any louder. The drunken sot's asleep, and under no circumstances do I want him to hear this. And by the way, not a word to the Captain, either, or at least not the whole story. You know yourself —"

The person on the other end interrupted him.

"Yes, yes," said Bolström. "I'm well aware of that. Norlin's becoming more and more of a liability. After we've 'saved the beloved country' — as he likes to put it — of course he'll have to go." Without looking, he groped behind him on the desktop for his cigarettes. He lit one. "We'll think of something. I've got no problem with that. The children are the main threat . . ." He took a long puff on his cigarette.

The person at the other end was speaking. Bolström exhaled, and a smoke ring rose to the ceiling. He looked pleased with himself. "Agreed, indeed, they have to disappear for good," he said, "but not yet, golden boy. Come on, think! For now, we go on informing the media of our demands, every day." He let out a grunt as the other man interrupted him again. "No, not money! Once we've saved the country, what will we need money for? The floodgates will be open and we can take whatever we want. What we're demanding now is a swap: the children for Minister Liron. Admit it: That's a stroke of genius."

Again he inhaled and listened. "Exactly, now you've got it," he said. "Then it'll be obvious to everyone that it was the rebels who abducted the children, so if anyone still has any doubts, that'll be the final proof that the rebels and the northerners in the government have been conspiring together. With the Minister of the Interior. Ha, what a traitor! Imagine the outrage!" He tapped his ashes nonchalantly onto the floor. "And when the children are found later — the *bodies* of the children, dear boy — then it'll be clear to every citizen of Scandia that the kidnappers — the rebels — were the ones who killed those poor, innocent babes. Perfect! Absolutely perfect."

He laughed. "Right you are," he said. "Bit of a detour there, but ultimately it's all working out in our favor." He listened for a moment. "Of course. Then it'll be time to get rid of Norlin. And guess what? The rebels will be responsible for that, too. I'm telling you, dear boy, things couldn't have gone better."

He took one last puff and then stubbed out the cigarette on the desktop. A nasty black burn mark stained the white lacquer. "And then we march in," he said. "But we may need to act very fast, and very soon."

27

*J*onas was not surprised when he was summoned to see the headmaster. The only surprising thing was that it had taken so long.

The previous evening, he had watched the news in the dorm's lounge and learned for the first time about Liron's arrest — no one had thought it necessary to tell him in person, although the school must certainly have received a telephone call. After the video footage of the arrest and, in particular, of the "plan for the coup" found in Liron's car, there had been a deathly silence. No one had said a word to Jonas. It was as if he had suddenly turned invisible. He had just gone to his room and packed his bags.

He hadn't folded his things neatly, just chucked in whatever he lay his hands on: clothes, books, the pictures from the wall above his bed. He'd had to throw his full weight onto the top of the case in order to get it closed.

So now where do I go? he'd wondered. *Who'll take me in?*

He'd hoped the king might call him, or Princess Margareta.

Surely they would know that Liron was innocent and offer him shelter. Wouldn't they?

But by the morning, when his phone had still failed to ring, he'd known there would be no word from them. *Jenna's disappeared*, he'd realized. *How could her mother possibly spare a thought for me? And Malena's only allowed to call from her boarding school on the weekends, so what can I do till then?*

He'd paced up and down his room, five steps each way. Since Perry had disappeared, too, he'd had the room all to himself. He didn't want to go outside, or go to class, and have everyone stare at him. And nobody came to find out where he was.

His father's voice echoed in his mind. "If something happens to me, just think about these three questions," Liron had said. He'd probably been expecting a moment just like this. Except Jonas didn't even know where to begin. "What came three years after the kingdom of Scandia conquered North Island? What was for a long time the tallest building in Scandia, and why? What do dwarfs and wonders have in common?"

Every so often during the last several months he'd thought about the questions. He'd tried looking things up in the encyclopedia in the school library. The Internet was too risky, because PCs could be bugged and searches could be traced. The questions, no matter how weird they seemed to him, were secret, and no one else must know.

But the longer he thought about them, the more stupid he felt. North Island had been conquered in 1732 — every

Scandian child learned that in grade school. So three years later was 1735, but that year wasn't mentioned in any history book or encyclopedia.

The other two questions weren't any easier. The tower of the city hall, built in 1621 by a German architect, was 300 feet high. But what was the point of asking *why* it was the tallest building? It was the tallest because it was the tallest building! In the encyclopedia, he'd read that at that time South Island was a member of the Hanseatic League, and people from Sweden, Germany, and Russia had lived in Holmburg then. Could the puzzle be connected with that?

The craziest question was number three, about dwarfs and wonders. What the heck could they have in common?

Up and down, five paces up, five paces down. The first two questions were connected with Scandia and its history, but the third was a complete curveball. Maybe he was supposed to put the three answers together somehow. Maybe the combination of all three contained some vital information.

"Only if something should happen to me," Liron had said. No matter where he went, Jonas had to find out what these questions meant, and what the answers were, in order to see where they were leading.

But first things first — he'd been summoned to see the headmaster. On the way, he continued to puzzle over the questions. Then he knocked on the door and was told to enter.

"You know why I've sent for you," the headmaster announced, without even saying hello. "To start, you'll hand in your school uniform. I see you're not wearing it, anyway. Our uniform is a mark of honor."

Jonas nodded, and tried to read the expression on the man's face. "I don't think any of it's true," he began. "And no one who knows my father—"

"It doesn't matter a jot what you think," said the headmaster. Was he enjoying this conversation? Or did he find it awkward? He'd been head for many years — back in the old days, then under Norlin, and now under the new government. He was headmaster of Morgard, and any personal beliefs were of no concern to anyone. His task was to take the school in whatever direction was necessary at the time. "You will understand that I cannot allow your fellow students to share a classroom with the son of someone guilty of high treason." He opened a file and leafed through it. "Furthermore, I don't know who will now be responsible for paying your tuition."

Jonas looked him straight in the eye. There had been no hope, anyway. He'd had all night to prepare for this conversation, and so nothing could shock him.

"No worries, dude. I'm good with being an outcast. Got lots of practice," he said, and waited. The headmaster was too shrewd to react.

"A car will take you to the railway station," he said. "From there I presume you'll know where to go. I hereby abrogate all responsibility for you." He closed the file.

Jonas pointed to it. "Are you going to throw that away?" he asked. "Because you're sure it's final? Because you're sure I won't be back?" He fixed his gaze firmly on the headmaster's eyes. He wasn't going to let him off the hook. The headmaster would have to be the first to look away. "Or maybe you'd better hold on to it? To be on the safe side. In case the wind changes. In case you have to welcome me back with open arms." His voice deepened with contempt. "What sort of man are you? You're always saying you want to set an example for the students. And yet you always go whichever way the wind blows. So what are we supposed to be learning from you?" He laughed. "Liron will be proved innocent. If there's one thing *I'm* sure of, it's that. He's been framed, and one day you'll all learn the truth. But don't bother to apologize then, Headmaster. Unlike the Terminator, I *won't* be back."

He turned and went toward the leather-padded door without bothering to listen to what the headmaster shouted at him.

As he pulled the door shut behind him, Jonas felt remarkably clearheaded. He hadn't allowed himself to be intimidated or even to complain. He had stood up for himself, and he had stood up for Liron.

He grabbed his bags, which someone had brought from his room to the steps under the portico. The car that was to take him to the train station was already waiting there, its engine running.

Liron taught me that, he thought, tossing a bag in the trunk. *Never let anyone look down on you. And most important of all, no one can make you feel small if you refuse to let them. I taught that to Jenna, too.*

It was a lesson Liron had taught him during the time they'd been on the run, living in a squalid little apartment in the projects, two northerners among all the other northerners in Holmburg. *"Every man can keep his dignity. Even if they take everything else away from you, that's yours to keep forever."*

At the time, Jonas had thought the words too grand for the conditions — the run-down kitchen with its worn-out linoleum floor, and the dismal concrete buildings outside their window. Almost absurd. High-sounding words for people down so low.

But all through the night they'd echoed in his head. *Who I am is up to me and me alone, and it doesn't matter what other people think. I won't ever let anyone make me feel small.*

Suddenly, from behind one of the portico's columns, a girl came toward him. Jonas was startled.

"Ylva!" he said. He hadn't seen her since Sunday evening in the summerhouse, and for the last few hours Liron's arrest had driven everything else out of his thoughts. Still, he didn't know just what his feelings were yet.

Ylva took a step toward him. A suitcase stood between them. Her face now wore the expression that everyone at school was so familiar with: self-confidence and pride. There was none of the uncertainty and vulnerability that had bewildered him two days before.

"Jonas," she said. She knocked up against the suitcase, and stopped. "It was obvious you'd have to go." She looked toward the car and the driver, who was leaning against the open door, listening to headphones. "Jonas, I had to speak to you before you left!"

Jonas waited. "What do you want to say?" he asked. "Actually, don't bother. I can guess. Strangely enough, your feelings for me have cooled, is that it? Now that my father's a traitor. Now that I'm not such a good catch anymore — the Minister of the Interior's son." To his fury, he noticed that his voice was trembling. The talk with the headmaster had been easy. This was far more difficult.

"Don't be ridiculous!" said Ylva. She pushed the suitcase to one side. "What kind of girl do you think I am?" She glanced over her shoulder toward the driver. "I just wanted . . . Jonas, I just wanted to apologize. It wasn't very nice of me. But during the last few weeks, I noticed that it was actually Jenna . . . Anybody could see it! The way you looked at her. And I wanted to . . . I'm not in love with you, Jonas. But I wanted to spoil it for her. I just think Jenna's so . . . She's no princess, that's all." She took a deep breath. "Jonas, I'm not in love with you, and I wasn't in love with you on Sunday, either."

Jonas stared at her. "How dare you?" he yelled. "How dare you say you were just using me in order to get at Jenna?" He should have realized just how stupid he'd been. But what did he know about girls? The only one he really knew was Malena.

Ylva shrugged her shoulders. She didn't seem ashamed. "I wasn't going to tell you at all," she said. "I'd have gone on playing the game. I'm sorry, Jonas. That's what I was going to do. It wasn't very nice of me, I know, but I mean . . ." She shrugged. "People do these things, don't they? And after the news broke yesterday . . ."

"You wanted to make sure I didn't go around telling people that Ylva von Thunberg was in love with me!" said Jonas. "Is that what you were worried about? Unbelievable. Well, no stress, Ylva, your sterling reputation's safe with me."

He picked up his suitcase and went toward the car, but she stopped him with a gesture.

"That's not what I came for," she said. "It was a game, and it was just for fun, all right? But there are much more important things to talk about now. I don't believe it, Jonas." Suddenly she looked very determined and even a little excited. "This business with your father. And that was why I wanted to be honest with you, before you left. Something isn't right, Jonas. It should be obvious to everyone!"

Jonas stared at her again. "What do you mean?" he asked.

"The plan!" said Ylva. "The one they held up to the camera. Where it says in big block letters *PLAN FOR THE COUP*. It's like out of a cartoon or something! You don't seriously think anyone would be stupid enough to take a plan like that along to a secret meeting, let alone give it a title! These days, nobody even needs to write anything down on paper. That's obvious to me, and what do I know about this kind of stuff? You see what I'm saying?"

Jonas nodded. Why hadn't it occurred to him, too? Even if Liron really was the traitor everyone took him for, he'd never have been so careless as to carry the evidence around with him.

"Your father's been framed," said Ylva. "Last night I couldn't sleep, I just kept thinking about it. I'm sure there's something behind all this, only I don't know what it is." Very gently she put her hand on Jonas's arm. "And I'm sorry for what I did at the party, Jonas," she said. "I just wanted you to know."

"OK," murmured Jonas. "I'd better go."

Ylva stepped back. When the car drove off, she gave him a small, stiff wave. *She's got more guts than the headmaster,* thought Jonas with surprise. *She doesn't care if other people see her saying good-bye to me. What she did on Sunday was totally vile, but she's got guts all right. And she dares to think for herself.*

None of the other students was anywhere to be seen.

28

After saying good-bye to Jonas, Ylva went slowly upstairs to the students' lounge. Lunch period was over, and there was no one in the corridors. Early in the morning the cleaning ladies had cleaned the rooms, and their shift was long over. The housemother would be sitting in her office, and now that all the girls were in class, the dormitories would be empty.

In the lounge there was a dirty cup on the table next to the sofa. The girls were supposed to be responsible for keeping the place tidy, but someone always forgot something. Ylva pulled the door shut behind her. She didn't want anyone to notice that she hadn't gone back to class. She looked at the clock above the fireplace, then switched on the television with the sound turned down.

She threw herself onto the sofa and looked at the screen. It was almost time for the midday news, and just before it began, the station was running a clip of a silent chorus of smiling

blonde girls in national costume who were presumably singing a folk song. Something strange was going on. Ever since
yesterday, when she'd watched the news, she'd felt uneasy. If
her suspicions were right, if the Minister of the Interior had
indeed been framed and wasn't conspiring with the rebels,
then who'd set the trap for him? And how come the television
people had been there on the spot to film it all? Who was in
a position to manipulate the media?

Do I really want to know? Ylva asked herself. *Why? What if
I find out something I wish I didn't?*

The girls on TV had stopped singing. Ylva turned up the
sound slightly. *I want to know because I need to get to the truth,*
she thought. *And because I can't stand the idea that I'm being
duped. I never could stand people doing that to me. But why do
I think it's happening now? Why do I keep getting this feeling
that something's not right?*

The images of Liron's arrest and the commentary that went
with them were familiar by now. Since last night they'd shown
nothing else. ". . . ransom in the usual sense," said the anchorwoman, smiling her perfectly made-up smile into the camera.
"Instead, the rebels say that they are holding the children
hostage, but are willing to exchange them for Minister Liron."
A photo appeared on the screen, showing pathetic little Jenna
and Peter Petterson Junior, holding up today's newspaper. The
princess's face was tearstained. *Typical,* Ylva thought dismissively. *No self-discipline.*

"Enough of her!" Ylva muttered, reaching for the remote.

And yet there was still something off. Surely she couldn't be the only person to have realized it.

They had disappeared on Sunday evening, pudgy Jenna and wimpish Petterson Junior, whose father was so ashamed of him, and rightly so. But how could the rebels have already known on Sunday evening that they'd need to kidnap Jenna and Perry in order to exchange them for the minister? He hadn't even been arrested at that point. So why kidnap them? Just to get a ransom? No, it didn't add up.

"And finally, some images of what's happening in towns all across the country at the moment," said the anchorwoman. "The following footage was compiled yesterday morning in Saarstad, on the northern sound of South Island. Because of the dramatic arrest of the Minister of the Interior yesterday, we postponed broadcasting it, but despite the escalation in the Princess Jenna situation, we would not want to overlook the suffering of the Scandian people."

Ylva aimed the remote control at the TV. She had no desire to see yet more interviews with yet more people complaining that they couldn't get any shampoo. But then a group of about fifty women appeared on the screen. They were wearing headscarves and beating pots with wooden spoons. It was pathetic. "Our pots are empty!" they cried. "Our children are hungry! Down with the government!"

"Oh boohoo, no shampoo," murmured Ylva sarcastically. They looked like country bumpkins in their scarves and aprons. Peasants. One of them, right at the front, actually looked like her mother. Without the scarf and apron, with some makeup, she'd be . . .

"Mama!" gasped Ylva. She dropped the remote control down on the couch.

She recognized the shoes. What peasant woman could afford shoes like those? And the woman next to her mother looked just like . . .

"This demonstration by the mothers of Saarstad was only the first in a series of protests held all over the country," the anchorwoman was saying. "Mothers everywhere are protesting the . . ."

Ylva picked up the remote and turned off the TV. She didn't need to see any more.

She took out her cell phone. After so many years at Morgard, she knew the taxi company's number by heart. And she didn't care if she was breaking the rules. The headmaster would never dare expel Ylva von Thunberg from his school, anyway, even if she did disappear on a weekday without telling anybody.

She went to her room to pack her makeup and some money before the taxi came. She had to go home. She had to talk to her mother.

At some point after they'd eaten, Jenna fell into a restless sleep. When she woke up, she saw that Perry was also asleep, using a coiled rope as a pillow. Judging by the light coming through the window, it was afternoon.

Jenna stretched and yawned, then reached for the tray. The water had all gone.

Next to her, Perry, still half-asleep, propped himself up on one elbow. "No more water?" he asked, also yawning. "I'll tell them."

Everything was quiet outside the hut. All they could hear was the splashing of the waves. But when Perry beat on the door with his fists, footsteps hurried toward them.

"Hey!" shouted a voice. "What are you doing? You'll bring down the house if you pound on it like that!"

"And hey to you, too," said Perry. "You can take the tray, and bring us some more water."

The footsteps went away, then came back, and the door opened. "Two bottles," said a young man. They hadn't seen him before. He had shaved the hair above his ears, leaving just a strip of blond bristle on the top of his head to show he was a southerner. "But don't go guzzling them, or there won't be any left. Then I'll have to fill them up with seawater."

"Who do you think you're talking to?" Perry said angrily. He grabbed the bottles. "Do you realize who we are? When you've got your ransom money and we're free —"

The young man laughed and blew out his chewing gum. "Then what?" he asked. "Huh, kid? Then what are you gonna do?"

"C'mon, Perry," said Jenna, trying to pull him back from the door. "It doesn't matter." She was afraid of the fair-haired man, though she didn't know why.

"Doesn't matter?" the man repeated. Suddenly he looked furious. How could his mood change so quickly? He sucked his chewing gum back into his mouth. "It does matter, Pizza Princess! You don't seriously think we're going to let you go, do you?"

"Perry, no!" cried Jenna.

But Perry had already hurled himself at the guard. "You'll be sorry!" he shouted, hitting the man's chest. "You'll be —"

The young man gave him a push. He put so little effort into it, he might have been swatting a fly, but Perry stumbled and fell on one knee.

He shouted a stream of curses.

The guard just laughed. "You made a big mistake, little man," he said. "Spying on the depot. After that, why would we want to set you free?" He tapped his forehead, then picked up the tray. "Don't know? Can't figure it out?" he asked. "Well, you've got time." He shut the door and turned the key.

Still on the floor, Perry watched him go. He cursed some more, then got up and brushed off his pants. There was dirt and bird droppings stuck to his knees. "I don't get it," he said. "How does he know about the depot?" He looked at Jenna with consternation.

Jenna swallowed a large mouthful of water. She never knew it could taste so good. "No idea," she said. "Or maybe . . . It could be from my phone. Remember? The video was on it."

Perry sat down again on his rope and twisted the top of his water bottle. "Oh yeah," he said. "I should have thought of that myself." He drank until there was hardly any water left in the bottle. "The video. But why is that a reason not to let us go? It's not logical, Jenna."

Jenna stood on tiptoe at the window. She could hear the waves splashing against the pebbles on the shore, and a guard was walking back and forth in front of the door. Two other men were talking outside. There was no point trying to break out. She and Perry wouldn't stand a chance.

"Um, because . . . No, you're right. It's not logical," she murmured, going back to her own rope. She wriggled around to make herself comfortable. "If it was the rebels that set up the depot, why would it matter to Bolström that we found it? It wouldn't put him in any danger. If anything, it would support his whole anti-northern thing."

"Exactly," said Perry. "So what is it about the depot that makes Bolström so determined to stop us from talking about it? Why should he refuse to let us go even after the ransom is paid? But it can't have been him who set up the depot. He's on the run himself."

Jenna shrugged her shoulders. "I don't know," she murmured. "And I don't care. I'm getting scared, Perry. They're not fooling around. If he's not going to let us go, what's he going to do to us?" She was beginning to feel sick just thinking about it.

Perry made a dismissive gesture. "We've *got* to figure it out, Jenna," he said. "We've got to understand what's going on. It's our only hope of getting out of this."

He closed his eyes. *Superbrain*, thought Jenna. *Genius at work*. Except that it wouldn't be enough to grasp what was behind all this. He also had to find a way for them to escape.

"Got it!" Perry slapped his forehead, then looked at Jenna. "How could we have been so dumb? But if it's what I think it is . . ." He shut his eyes and shook his head. "Then it's a lot worse than we thought. Then there might be no hope at all."

29

*D*uring the drive to the train station, the driver never said a word to Jonas.

No one wants to talk to me now, thought Jonas. *I'm the son of a traitor.*

He heard the news on the car radio: He already knew that Jenna and Perry had disappeared, but the fact that they were being held hostage, to be exchanged for Liron, had come as a shock. What did it mean?

The driver made eye contact in the rearview mirror, looked at him contemptuously, then turned his attention back to the road.

At the station, the man did not even take the luggage out of the trunk for him, but just popped the lid from the driver's seat, then watched the boy struggle, shouting, "Watch it!" a couple of times when it looked as if Jonas's suitcase might scratch the paint. He drove off as soon as Jonas had slammed down the lid. He'd already been paid back at the boarding school.

Guess it was worth the fare to get rid of me, thought Jonas.

The station looked like most stations in small South Scandian towns: dark red brick with white frames around the tall, narrow windows. The entrance was exactly in the middle. In the old days, the station manager used to live on the upper floor, but now those windows were full of cobwebs.

Jonas went into the station. There was no agent. It was a small town, and the prosperous South Scandians generally traveled by car, anyway, since they found it more comfortable and convenient. Instead, passengers bought their tickets at the automated dispenser with its flashing screen, and withdrew cash from the ATM sponsored by Scandia's largest bank.

Jonas heaved his bags into the middle of the room, where two benches sat back-to-back. He sat on the edge of one of them. A little boy was standing on the other, and he peered curiously at him. He was about four years old, and obviously regarded the benches as a kind of jungle gym.

"No, Albert, get down at once!" said a young woman sitting on the other bench with a load of bags and packages, next to an older woman.

The boy started climbing over the back of the bench, but his mother pulled him down.

"No!" yelled the boy.

Jonas smiled at him.

Above the entrance to the one platform hung a clock. *I'll take the first train that comes*, thought Jonas. *It doesn't matter where I go. I've got to wait till Malena contacts me. She has to call. She's never going to believe that Liron . . .*

He stiffened. The three questions. He was still no closer to answering them. How could Liron have thought he'd be able to solve these riddles on his own?

Perry, thought Jonas. *The Superbrain. He could have figured it all out, but I wasn't allowed to tell him. And I'm no good at these kinds of mind games. How could Liron have thought I was? He's seen my grades!*

There were still ten minutes to go before the next train. Why had the two women come to the station so early? The little boy was fidgeting and whining. His mother gave him a cookie.

Perry. He hadn't wanted to think about Perry — or about Jenna. Had the rebels really abducted them? Just to trade them for Liron? That would make Liron not just a traitor but responsible for Perry and Jenna being taken hostage.

No. How could he even think that for a minute? Liron was not a traitor.

But then who had Perry and Jenna? Who else could it be but Nahira? And how were they being treated?

Perry and Jenna. Why hadn't the kidnappers taken him instead of Perry? The thought gave him a warm feeling inside. *I wouldn't have cared if they did kidnap me — not if I was locked up with Jenna. But now she's alone with Perry . . .*

Jonas glanced again at the clock. *I'd have been better off getting myself kidnapped than sitting here at the station, not knowing what to do.*

Or should he try calling Jenna's mother, Margareta? Or her uncle, the king? Would they help him even if they didn't trust Liron?

If only I had their numbers, he thought. *But I don't, so it's pointless even thinking about it.*

The hand on the clock crept slowly from minute to minute, marking each movement with a *click*. The little boy was still sniveling on the bench behind him.

"No, Albert, leave Mommy alone! Mommy's going to get some money," said the older woman.

Jonas heard the boy clambering down from the bench, and then saw him running after his mother toward the cash machine.

"Me!" he shouted in a voice that would have drowned the sound of an incoming train. "Me, Mommy, me! Let me do it!"

The woman pulled a wallet out of her bag. "All right, come here," she said. She lifted the boy up and gave him her card. "Put it in there now, Albert." The card disappeared into the slot, and she put the boy down before entering her PIN.

"Oh goodness!" she said to the other woman. "All these wretched numbers! Cell phones, passwords, online banking . . . I always get something mixed up. Luckily I wrote it down somewhere . . ."

She started rummaging in her bag again.

"That's a risky thing to do," said the other woman. "What if someone steals your purse?" She glanced at Jonas, as if he might be a potential bag-snatcher. "You should make up something to help you remember — then you wouldn't have to write it down."

The machine hummed and money poked out of the dispenser.

"Me!" yelled Albert again. "Me, Mommy, me, Mommy, let me!"

His mother lifted him up again.

An idea began to form itself in Jonas's head.

"How do you make up something to remember? Like when you play the lottery?" the woman asked over her shoulder as she put the boy down and took her money from him. "All the family birthdays, that kind of thing?"

Jonas stood up. Of course. Why hadn't he thought of it before?

He went out through the main entrance to the station and looked around the parking lot. He'd left his suitcase by the bench — the women wouldn't steal it.

Frantically he pulled his cell phone out of the duffel bag that was hanging over his shoulder. At last he'd found the answer.

Ylva had not told anyone that she was coming. She was certain her mother would still be at the estate, because there had been a few things to take care of after the party, and she'd been running around in Saarstad yesterday!

"All that way?" the taxi driver had asked when he'd picked up Ylva at the school entrance and she'd sat in the back and told him her destination. He'd sounded suspicious.

"Did I not say it clearly enough?" she'd asked. The von Thunbergs knew how to talk to inferiors, who would realize at once from the tone, the look, the slightly raised eyebrow, just who they were dealing with. "Afraid I might not be able to pay? Do I look poor to you?"

The driver had shaken his head and put the car in gear. During the journey, she'd gazed out at the countryside. Thinking wasn't enough — she needed to ask some questions.

The taxi climbed the gravel drive to the house and came to a halt at the foot of the broad flight of steps.

"Is this it?" asked the driver. He looked at his meter. This one fare would earn him more than he would normally make in three or four days — or, in bad times, a whole week.

"Wait a moment," said Ylva. She got out and summoned the housekeeper, who came hurrying out of the double doors with an immaculate hairdo and a bewildered face.

"Please pay the driver," said Ylva, and walked past her into the house. She had intended to add, "And please tell my mother I'm here," but instead she raced upstairs.

Music was coming from the second floor, which meant that her mother was exactly where Ylva had expected her to be. Her parents had their living quarters on the first floor, but about two years ago her mother had set up a studio in an unused room on the floor above. At that time, for some reason, all her friends had been taking up painting in addition to golf and tennis. To Ylva's amazement, her mother now spent her mornings in this sparsely furnished room, with her hair severely tied back and an ever more colorful artist's smock over her perfectly fitting designer jeans.

Just now, the theme was Africa, as Ylva could see at a glance. On her last visit to the studio, it had been still lifes.

"Ylva!" cried her mother, taking her brush away from a yellow canvas. The joyful surprise in her eyes changed almost immediately to anxiety. "Darling! What happened?" She put the brush down on the palette and wiped her hands on a cloth. She took a step toward her daughter, but stopped when she saw Ylva's expression.

"You tell me," said Ylva, leaning against the doorframe. Would she also live like this one day? Golf and tennis and watercolor giraffes? *I'd rather shoot myself,* she thought. Once upon a time her mother had been class president and captain of the field hockey team, too, though not at Morgard. So what was it that made people into what they became?

"I don't understand, darling," said her mother. She was still wiping her hands, over and over again, on the cloth between her fingers.

"I saw you on television," said Ylva.

At last her mother dropped the cloth. "Oh?" she said.

"The cameramen should have known better," said Ylva. "Even the best headscarf is no use if they get a close-up of your face! Or maybe they didn't know exactly what was going on. And you should have worn different shoes! Honestly, Mother, have you forgotten what people like that wear? Have you never looked at your cook's feet?"

Her mother seemed shocked. Maybe she was trying to decide whether she should deny the accusation.

"How did you get involved in something like that?" Ylva went on. "What was it all about? Whose idea was it?"

"Ylva!" her mother said. "How dare you talk to me like that?"

"Tell me whose idea it was!" cried Ylva. "I want to know what's going on!"

"Baroness von Eskyll spoke to me at the party," said her mother, looking like a sulky child who thinks she's being unfairly told off. "To all the ladies, in fact. She asked if we didn't think it might be fun to —"

"Fun?" exclaimed Ylva. *"Fun?"*

". . . to skip our usual Monday morning book club and go to Saarstad instead. The poor hungry people there are suffering so much, she said, and we should hold a demonstration to show our support. We owe that to Scandia, she said. All those unfortunate souls who can no longer buy anything in the shops —"

"But up until Sunday you were obviously able to buy anything and everything you wanted!" said Ylva. "Unless I was *imagining* all that food at our garden party!"

"Yes, but one also has to think of other people," said her mother, almost pleading. "One mustn't always think just of oneself, Ylva — that's our duty as aristocrats, to take the side of the ordinary people —"

"That's a load of baloney!" said Ylva. "So you thought you'd just go and pretend you were a poor peasant woman? That you were hungry? You didn't think that was fraud? It never occurred to you that you were a fake?"

"One must think of Scandia," said her mother. "Perhaps not everyone knows how terrible conditions have been in our country since this new government started ruining everything! And we have to show them — that's what Baroness von Eskyll said. How bad things are, and how hungry everyone is!"

"Oh, thank you, Mother, thank you so much," Ylva said, turning on her heel. "And you never even noticed that you were part of a game, did you? With rules you knew absolutely nothing about? You never thought they might be using you?" She slammed the door behind her.

"Ylva!" cried her mother.

Ylva opened the door again. "Just go back to painting your African sunsets!" she cried. "Although you know nothing about those, either! But at least you can't do any damage with them!"

Then she ran down to her bedroom and locked the door behind her.

30

Immediately after school, Bea went to the police to report the theft of her cell phone. She had to answer a list of questions that the police receptionist read off a computer screen, and then she had to sign a statement.

"If the phone was switched on, you've lost it," said the policeman. "So don't get your hopes up. If it was off, there's still a chance." The school custodian had said the same.

The policeman gazed thoughtfully at her, his eyebrows knitted. "Why do I get the feeling that I know you?" he asked. "Have you lost your phone before?"

"Nope, first time," said Bea. "I'm not that careless!"

A smile lightened the policeman's face. "Wait, now I remember," he said. "Last time it was your *friend* you reported missing, right? And you kept saying you'd seen her on TV. And she looked like a princess." He typed something into his computer. "I thought then: The things teenage girls get into their heads!" He laughed.

Bea wanted to leave.

"And the craziest thing about it was that it was true, right?" He looked up from the keyboard. "My partner and me, we've seen a lot of strange stuff in our time — that's what the police are for — but someone reporting a missing *princess* . . ."

Luckily the door opened at that moment and a very agitated woman in a torn dress came storming into the police station. Bea didn't wait to find out what had happened to her.

"Thanks much!" she called over her shoulder. Whoever heard of a stolen cell phone being recovered, anyway?

Ylva sat down on her bed. Pink silk covers with gold trim — a princess's bed.

"And you're *my* princess," her father had said when she was little. It had been one of the wonders of her childhood that it had almost been true. "Almost" was also the word her father had used. He had told her how close the von Thunbergs were to royalty, and all they had to do was find a prince for her somewhere in the world, because a von Thunberg would be just the right person for a prince to marry. And then she really would be a full-fledged princess.

"Unbelievable!" said Ylva.

She remembered the fairy tales her nanny had read her every evening before she went to bed, or on gray winter afternoons over a cup of cocoa, or on rainy summer days in the garden house. She remembered all the princesses who really were what she *almost* was, and one day ought to be. They were beautiful and gentle and kind. That was the most important thing, because only a kind princess was a real princess, as all the fairy tales kept repeating, and if a princess was mean or stuck-up or stupid, then either she'd be punished or she'd have to change before she got her reward — the handsome prince and the kingdom.

She stood up, pushed the covers back, and threw herself down on the bed.

Little Ylva had been all of these princesses, night after night, rainy afternoon after rainy afternoon: beautiful and gentle and kindhearted. But at the same time she'd been all the princes who had rescued, freed, and finally married the princesses. Because princes were also brave and strong, smart and kindhearted.

Ylva pressed her face into the silk covers. Why hadn't she thrown them out the window ages ago? Whenever she'd slept in this room over the last few years, she'd vowed to do just that. The pink was hideous. But she hadn't been here very often. Most of the time she was at school or at the von Thunbergs' town house in the city. She spent the holidays skiing or sailing or somewhere in the sun. Perhaps she didn't have the heart to get rid of the pink covers, anyway. They were part of the memory of those princess days, when everything was right with the world and she was Princess Ylva who was always perfect, whatever she did.

When had it all changed? When had she first realized that life was not a fairy tale?

There was a knock on the door. "Ylva?" said her mother.

"Ylva? The headmaster just called to tell me that you left the school without permission. I told him you were here."

Ylva said nothing.

"I told him you were ill," her mother added hesitantly. "Ylva? He said he'd let you off this time."

"Brilliant!" said Ylva sarcastically.

When had she first realized that princes weren't all kind-hearted, and swineherds weren't all swine, and above all that life wasn't always fair? And when had she first tried with all her might *not* to think about it?

The bedcovers had a slight scent of detergent, or fabric softener, or something. After every stay, the housekeeper would have the room cleaned. There could never be any trace that was truly Ylva's, with her own smell, with stains she could recognize and remember making.

And then Jenna had arrived at the school. At last, a real princess. Ylva remembered very clearly how the headmaster had announced her arrival, and she had introduced herself as the roommate who was to help the new princess get accustomed to life at Morgard. It hadn't bothered her in the least that it meant separation from Paula, who had been her friend since they'd first come to the school.

"You can understand why I have to do it, can't you?" Ylva had said, and Paula had agreed, because everyone in the school knew that nobody was better suited to the job of looking after a new princess than Ylva von Thunberg.

But then Jenna had turned out to be Jenna. Plump, dark, and

pathetic. Not like a princess at all — not beautiful, not smart, not kindhearted. Ylva's nanny or the cook's daughter — any other girl in the school, for that matter — was more like a princess. What kind of cruel joke was life playing on her? How could someone like Jenna be a princess? She was supposed to be wonderful, better than everyone else: How else could you justify one person being placed above the rest? And if life could play tricks like that, what did it mean for Ylva?

She'd begun to hate Jenna. This princess was the final proof that everything she had once believed about the world was nothing but a fairy tale. She'd begun to hate her, and she'd shown her hatred. It served Jenna right.

"Ylva?" cried her mother through the door, and knocked a bit louder. "Is everything all right, darling? You're *not* ill, are you?"

Ylva sat up. She had made her decision. *Maybe life really isn't like that*, she thought. *Maybe it isn't like the fairy tales. But it's going to be like that for me. I want it to be like that for me. All my life I've been almost-Princess Ylva, beautiful and smart and kindhearted. And no one's going to change it.*

She picked up the remote control and turned up the volume of her TV so loud that her mother would realize there was no point in expecting a response. There was a cooking show on Scandia 1 and a talk show on Scandia 2. Even after the change of government, Scandian television had stayed the same as ever. But, whatever you thought of the new regime, they had made it possible for everyone in the country to see what they wanted to see, including foreign channels — if the reception was good enough. And they'd provided telephone and Internet connections. For a few moments Ylva watched an old movie in a language she didn't understand. Then she switched to a news channel in English. English was OK.

"Ylva?" cried her mother through the door.

Let her go back to Africa, she thought.

At the corner of the station building, Jonas looked around. No one was watching. There were two women with shopping bags gossiping on the opposite side of the street, and there were just three cars in the large parking lot.

What came three years after the Kingdom of Scandia conquered North Island?

1732 plus 3 equaled 1735. He had been making it way too complicated. He wasn't supposed to find connections between the questions or figure out what the answers *meant*. It was the numbers themselves. His father had given him a telephone number that he was to call if something should happen to him. A telephone number that Jonas shouldn't even know he had, and that he would never be able to reveal to anyone if he were subjected to interrogation — though by whom? Liron had been certain that if there was a crisis, Jonas would figure it all out.

He keyed in the first set of numbers.

Which was the highest building in Scandia for a long time, and why?

Liron must really think I'm a genius, thought Jonas. The town hall was the tallest, because it was 300 feet high. He keyed in 300.

A train pulled into the station, and Jonas knew by the direction it had come from that it was going to Holmburg.

What have dwarfs and wonders got in common?

The answer was so simple: Seven. He keyed it in.

There was a pause while the display showed CONNECTING. Then he heard an automated woman's voice saying, "The number you have dialed is currently unavailable. There is no further information about . . ."

Jonas pressed the END button. Could he have got it wrong? What other kind of number would Liron have wanted to give him?

It was too long for a PIN or a safe-deposit box or a postal code. It couldn't be a house number, and it couldn't have anything to do with web banking. So what else could it be?

He went back inside the waiting room. His suitcase was still standing next to the bench. The train beside the platform began to move, and swiftly gathered speed.

Jonas sat down on the bench. Maybe it *was* an account number. But what use would an account be if Liron was locked up?

It just had to be a telephone number. He must have done something wrong.

He took the cell phone out of his pocket and dialed. Again the automated voice informed him that the number was not in service. Maybe it was someone's number last autumn, when

Liron had first posed the three questions, but they'd since changed it. If so, his last hope had gone, and he had no idea what to do next.

It had to be a cell phone number. In Scandia they all started with 173. Then suddenly he knew. The answer hit him like a bolt of lightning, and even before he'd finishing keying in the number again, he was certain that someone would answer. Cell numbers had nine digits.

1735300 . . . plus 7 dwarfs *and* 7 wonders . . . so 1-7-353-0077.

As he waited for the connection, Jonas's heart was pounding. In a moment he would know who it was.

"Hello?" said a voice. Jonas recognized it immediately. He wasn't even surprised.

31

It was a while before Jenna understood.

"What do we know about Bolström?" Perry asked.

"Why?" asked Jenna, but then she told him all about last summer — how Bolström had kidnapped the king and lied to the country that he was dead so that Norlin (she had to swallow hard just mentioning the name) could seize power.

"Exactly," said Perry. "And why did Norlin suddenly have to become regent? Who was behind it?"

"You know that already," said Jenna. "It was because the king wanted to pass that law — giving the north equal rights with the south."

"So taking that thought one step further," said Perry. "Who stood to gain by kidnapping the king, pretending he was dead, and putting Norlin in as regent?"

"The ones who had most to lose from the new law, I guess," said Jenna. "The rich southerners, the aristocracy, people who own oil wells and real estate and mines . . ."

"Right!" said Perry. "But no one could ever prove anything, could they? And no one dared suggest it out loud, because there was no evidence. They were all so happy when Magnus came back alive and well to sit on the throne again. They were all disgusted with Norlin. But behind it all, behind it all . . ."

". . . at least one of them must have been working under-cover with Bolström and Norlin," said Jenna, nodding at Perry. "The very fact that Bolström and Norlin were able to get away so easily — someone must have helped them. Well, Genius-boy, did you really figure all this out by yourself?"

Perry shook his head. "Jonas told me the theory," he said. "But no one could do anything about it, since there was no proof."

"So it's the same people still trying to stop the reforms!" she whispered. "And now that their campaign's really taking hold, they're working with Bolström again. And the depot . . ." She stared at him.

"Yes, of course!" he cried, then clapped his hand over his mouth and looked toward the door. When he spoke again, it was in whispers. "It all fits together. If the rich land-owners make sure that the harvest goes to secret depots instead of the market, and the factory owners do the same, and the transportation firms take the goods to these depots instead of the shops —"

"Which they can, easily," said Jenna. "We couldn't understand how the rebels would be able to cause shortages. But if the owners themselves —"

"Bingo!" said Perry. "And meanwhile, they blame the government for mismanaging the economy! That's how they've turned the people against the government, so that everyone starts wishing for the so-called good old days."

"And then by the next election people won't vote for Liron's party," said Jenna, "at least not in South Scandia."

Perry laughed caustically. "I don't think they'll want to wait that long," he said. "And that explains what the guard was saying. If Bolström really is working for these people, how could he possibly release us? We'd tell the media everything we've seen." His tone grew darker. "Jenna, we're in real danger."

Jenna felt herself go cold. "I never should have shot that video," she said, shaking her head. "If I hadn't, they wouldn't know what we saw."

"There was no way you could have known," said Perry. Jenna was grateful that he wasn't blaming her. "And there might still be a way out," he added.

"But how?" she asked wearily. She remembered Bolström from last year, and she knew that he would stop at nothing.

"We're only in danger because they discovered the video on your cell phone," said Perry. "Right? They know what we saw, and they want to make sure we don't tell anybody. Because once we did . . . once the people of Scandia learned the truth . . ." He stopped. Jenna hoped he wouldn't go on.

She didn't want to hear it. She'd already had the same thought herself. "The fact that we discovered their depot is our death sentence, Jenna. But suppose someone else, who's not part of their plot, also knows about the depot? And suppose that someone else went to the media with the information? In other words, suppose there was nothing to gain by getting rid of us? Because at the very least they'd have to kill this other person, too, as well as everyone else that he'd told, and that wouldn't be so simple . . ."

"Your father!" whispered Jenna. "You called him and told him that night!"

Jonas had always said that Perry was a superbrain. And now his superbrain might save them.

"Then we've got to tell the men outside!" cried Jenna. "Now, Perry! That your father also knows about the depot, so it won't do them any good to kill us." She banged on the door. "Perry's father knows!" she shouted. "Hey, you out there! Perry's father knows what's going on in the old factory, too! And he must have already told the police! You can't keep it secret any longer!" Her fists began to hurt, but she hardly felt the pain. "It won't help you to silence us! Perry's father knows!"

Someone outside the door laughed.

Jenna lowered her arms. Her hands were burning and she'd skinned her knuckles. "Then we'll tell Bolström tomorrow, Perry, if he comes," she said. "If these people are so stupid that they can't see what it means . . . But when Bolström learns that your father knows . . ."

". . . and that they can't hush it up anymore, even if they silence us . . ." said Perry. But Jenna could hear the doubt in his voice. "Yes, we'll tell Bolström, if he comes. He'll know what it means."

They were sitting at the large dining table in the princess's private apartment at Osterlin. King Magnus had his arm around his sister's shoulders. She appeared to be staring at the door, as if it would open at any moment and her daughter would appear. But in fact she was gazing into empty space.

Petterson was standing at one of the windows, drumming his fingers on the sill. Since he and Margareta had received the demand for Liron in exchange for the children, he had become very ill at ease. Now and then he ran his fingers through his sweaty hair, which was sticking up in a kind of crest.

"We've *got* to make the exchange, Magnus," said Margareta. "Give the order to let them have Liron!"

"I can't do that, Margareta," said the king with a helpless gesture. "At least not on my own! I've just bypassed parliament with my order to mobilize the military, and it's supposed to be parliament and the elected government that makes these decisions."

"Some of whom may well be secretly conspiring with the rebels!" protested Margareta. "We've got the evidence now to prove it!"

"We've got what *may* be evidence, Margareta — *may* be — that Liron was in contact with the rebels," said Magnus wearily. He raised his coffee to his lips without drinking. "*One* of the ministers! Just one! But the government is still the government. I can't bypass them again."

Petterson turned toward him. "The government's a mess, Magnus!" he exclaimed. "The nation is looking to *you* for leadership!"

"I still can't believe that Liron was planning a coup with the rebels to topple his own government," said Magnus. "I've known Liron for years. Of course he's always sided with the north, but he was always against violence."

"But he said it over and over again," said Petterson. "'The reforms are going too slowly.' If he got control, he could push them through."

Margareta looked angrily at him. "Why do you keep talking about Liron?" she snapped. "It's Jenna that matters to me. Magnus, imagine it was *your* daughter that had been abducted. How can you be so coldhearted?"

Petterson joined them at the table. "At least you should try to persuade the government for the children's sake," he said, wringing his hands. "I agree with Margareta."

The king was surprised to see that even Petterson seemed to be losing his ice-cold composure. "You're overestimating my powers," he said. "Petterson, I know you're as worried about your son as Margareta is about her daughter, and I'm worried about them both, too. But we mustn't lose sight of Scandia's interests. I can't give in to the rebels. The country's already on edge, with soldiers everywhere. Von Thunberg was a bit too eager, in my eyes, to let his men loose on the country."

"You can rely on Thunberg," murmured Petterson.

"In a situation like this, how can you —?" cried Margareta.

The king stood up. "I'll see what I can do," he said.

3 2

All morning, messages had been passing to and fro, as far afield as North Island. Everyone who received the news immediately passed it on, and so by midday Nahira knew that there would be enough men.

"Tonight," she said to Lorok. "Ten men will do it. They feel safe, so I don't think we'll need more than ten."

"It's been hard enough to get ten!" said Meonok. "You've let things slide during the last year, Nahira. You were relying on the new government to settle everything, and now you can see that you need to stay on the alert. We kept telling you, Lorok and me, but you —"

"Enough!" Nahira cut him off. "We can talk about that another time. There are more important things to be done now." She knew very well that increasingly she was losing her authority. You couldn't be a rebel leader if you didn't give your people something to do — an attack, a kidnapping, or last year even a bomb. You couldn't hope to keep them together if they didn't understand why they had to wait. Tonight at last there would be a chance to act. "Midnight," said Nahira. "Give them the coordinates."

The two men keyed into their cell phones.

Nahira thought of Kalijoki. Only the old ones continued to follow her without question and with total trust. The old ones and the even older ones! They'd long since stopped fighting, but they were still of vital importance to her.

"And tell them the signals," said Nahira.

Lorok and Meonok nodded as their fingers flew over the buttons.

At that moment, Nahira's own phone rang. *The first protester,* she thought. *Wants to tell me what's wrong with the plan. Wouldn't have happened in the old days. Back then, my word was law.*

For a second she thought of cutting off the call, but then she pressed the receiver button. She didn't want it to come to protests, or a possible move against her. As long as they were still talking to her, she could keep hold of the reins.

"Yes?" she said.

The voice at the other end was trembling.

Outside the grimy window, the sky had turned gray. There would still be some time before nightfall, but already Jenna felt more desperate. Again and again they had tried to convince the guards that Perry had told his father, but the only response had been laughter, a kick at the door, and the order to shut up.

Bolström had not come back.

"But he'll come tomorrow," said Perry. "With the morning paper." He looked down vaguely at the torn fishing nets on the floor.

"What if he doesn't?" said Jenna. "What if he never comes back? He might just get one of the guards to take our photo tomorrow. So who can we talk to then? Perry, are you listening to me?"

Perry didn't respond. For some time he'd been drawing in the dust with his index finger, without looking up. Even now he didn't seem to hear her. He was drawing circles and wavy lines, then angrily rubbing them out with the flat of his hand before beginning again. Jenna gave him a nudge. "Perry, what is it?" she asked.

He raised his head and looked at her, but to her horror she realized that he didn't see her. His lips moved silently, as if he were speaking to himself.

"Perry!" she cried, and felt goose bumps spreading over her arms.

He stared into space.

"Perry, what is it?"

When at last he managed to speak, his voice was flat and expressionless, and his eyes were fixed on some point in the distance that didn't exist for Jenna.

"What did the phone call mean?" he asked. "The phone call in the car. It was only after that call that they changed their tactics and started to treat us as prisoners."

He turned to Jenna, and she could see such despair in his eyes that she wanted to put her arms around him.

"But we talked about that yesterday, Perry," she said. "I think it's all clear now. We know that Bolström . . ."

Once more he seemed not to be listening.

"It was the *caller* who told them we'd seen the depot," whispered Perry. "They didn't find it out from your phone, Jenna. They didn't take the phones away from us till later! After the call. It was the *caller* who told them!"

Jenna looked at him. She still couldn't comprehend why he was in such a state.

"Then maybe it was someone from the depot who called them," she said. "That's logical, isn't it? After all, they saw us!" She tugged at his sleeve. "But that doesn't change anything, Perry! Once we tell Bolström that your father knows . . ."

Again his gaze wandered off into the distance. Then he turned to her almost in slow motion. From outside, Jenna recognized the high trill of a blackbird's song. "So why haven't the police stormed the place? Twenty-four hours have gone by, Jenna. It's almost twenty-four hours since I told my father."

She couldn't bear the pain in his eyes. "What do you mean?" she asked. She still didn't get it. "Maybe your father didn't tell the police right away. Or maybe the police haven't done anything right away, haven't found the place . . . Or maybe . . ." But even she could see how unlikely all that was.

No.

No, not that, too.

Horrified, she finally understood.

"Jenna," he said, "I think . . . I think . . ." Then his voice broke. He lay down on a coil of rope and began to cry.

All afternoon Bea had been unable to concentrate on her homework. She'd left the radio on in the kitchen, and whenever the music stopped and someone spoke, she rushed in. But the short news bulletins made no mention of Jenna. She would have to wait till the full evening news on TV.

"Bea!" her mother called from the living room. Bea looked at her grammar book. Tomorrow was the French final exam, and she still didn't understand where these wretched pronouns were supposed to go. Which one came before which? Why couldn't the French stick their pronouns in normal places, like everyone else?

"*Y!*" she moaned. "So stupid! What are you supposed to do with *y*?"

"Bea!" called her mother. "You wanted me to tell you — the special feature's on in a moment!"

Bea took her French book with her into the living room. A dumb thing to do. Like she'd be able to learn anything while she was watching the news.

Her mother was sitting at the end of the sofa watching a fat little man in an ill-fitting suit pointing to the weather map.

"Special programs two days in a row," she said. "Things must be heating up in Scandia."

"You don't remember the rules about French pronouns, do you?" Bea asked without too much hope. "*Y* and *en*, and all that stuff?"

"Sorry, honey," said her mother. "I only took French for three years."

Bea sighed. Cell phone stolen, best friend kidnapped, and now French final exam. "It's just not my week," she muttered, and let the book slide to the floor.

The screen showed the host in the studio, repeating what he'd already reported the previous evening, with the same familiar pictures in the background.

"Will you say something about Jenna, *s'il-vous plaît*!" cried Bea, leaning forward.

She heard the front door open. "Any news?" her father called. He looked at the TV, and sat down in his muddy shoes. "Anything about —"

"You could have wiped your feet," complained Bea's mother. "Just look —"

"Silence, je vous en prie!" cried Bea, not even realizing she'd just used one of the weird pronouns. "I want to see this!"

". . . since yesterday morning, the streets of Scandia have been filled with soldiers," a reporter was saying into his microphone. Bea recognized the foreign correspondent from last night. "Forty-eight hours ago, King Magnus declared a national state of emergency and brought in the military to keep the peace in Scandia. Discussion continues to rage as to whether this is the right move to pacify a country in which unrest is escalating by the day. On the streets of the capital city of Holmburg we asked . . ."

There were now armed soldiers in the background. People with frightened faces spoke into microphones.

"What about Jenna?" said Bea. "Do they think a princess is so unimportant that —"

Her father motioned her to keep quiet. "Shh, Bea, for heaven's sake. This is important, too!"

". . . evidently the first successes," said the correspondent. He didn't look too happy about what he had to say. "Today, soldiers searched a number of factories after receiving reports from the locals that North Scandian rebels were hiding there. A few arrests were made, but the most important discovery, allegedly, was of large stores of weapons. Unfortunately, reporters have not been allowed access to view the weapons for themselves."

"Make sense of that if you can!" said Bea's father, taking off his right shoe. "That's completely illogical! Just now, when the country's bringing in a whole raft of reforms—"

"Dad, shut up!" cried Bea.

". . . most extraordinary," said the correspondent. In the background was a cemetery. Soldiers armed with shovels were digging up graves. "In the cemetery of the little town of Ylarook, on North Island, further caches of weapons were found in a number of coffins. The police and army would certainly never have found them had they not been tipped off by local citizenry."

"They can say what they like!" growled Bea's father. He looked as if he wanted to crawl into the set to take them all on. "But there's no way they can —"

". . . latest news on Princess Jenna," said the host in the studio.

"Shh, Dad!" yelled Bea.

". . . perhaps the biggest surprise of all," said the correspondent. The scenes behind him began to repeat themselves. "Last night it was still not certain whether the princess had run away or had been abducted, but over the course of this afternoon the situation was made clear. The press, Princess Jenna's mother, and her frequent companion in recent times, Peter Petterson, who is the father of the other missing child, have all received the same demands from the kidnappers." A photo appeared on the screen showing a tearstained and exhausted Jenna together with a boy that Bea didn't know. They were both holding a newspaper.

"Oh God, Jenna!" exclaimed Bea.

"They have provided photos showing the two young people with today's newspaper as evidence that they are still alive, and they are demanding in exchange the release of Minister of the Interior Liron, who was arrested for high treason yesterday. The North Scandian Rebel Movement has claimed responsibility for the abduction. However, a far more serious threat to the country is the fact that rebels have been working in league with at least some members of the present government. Yesterday's arrest was seen by many as proof that the

Minister of the Interior has been planning a coup with the rebels . . ."

"That's incredible!" said Bea's father.

"Incroyable," Bea echoed.

"And now back to the studio," said the correspondent.

"Will they do it?" asked Bea. "Dad? Will they make the exchange? What will the rebels do to Jenna if they won't cooperate?"

Her father shrugged his shoulders. "If you ask me," he said, "there's something very peculiar going on. We can only hope for the best."

Bea stood up. "I'm going to my room," she said.

Her mother bent down. "What about your French book?" she said. "You left it behind!"

"Oh, forget French!" said Bea. There would be no more pronouns this evening.

33

For a while, Jenna just sat looking at Perry. She didn't dare go to him, or take his arm to comfort him. Because if his suspicions turned out to be true, what comfort could there be?

Only when it was completely dark, and the voices and laughter of the guards had gradually faded away, did she finally sit down next to him. She felt utterly helpless.

"Perry?" she whispered. He had hidden his face in his arms. Maybe he'd fallen asleep. "Perry? It may not be like that at all. There could be a completely different explanation."

Perry slowly raised his head. Jenna saw to her relief that his eyes were now dry. But there was also a coldness in them that made her shiver.

"And what sort of explanation might that be, Jenna?" he asked. "We've been through it all. If my dad is part of this plot —"

"But why do you insist on thinking he is?" Jenna pleaded. "It doesn't have to be that way!"

"Doesn't it?" said Perry. "Last year you saw how *your* father was mixed up in a plot against the king. Why does someone *have* to be a good person just because he's a father? Criminals have kids, too. And do you know how much oil the Pettersons own on North Island? And bauxite mines? Not to mention our huge flocks of sheep and our farms . . ." His voice trailed off. "There's no way my father could want the reforms."

In the forest, the unsuspecting blackbird repeated its song. This was the time of night when the horned owl flew off in search of its prey.

"He wouldn't allow it," said Perry. "The idea that he might lose out. That one day he might even lose everything. He'll be afraid, just like the rest of them, that the reforms are only the beginning. He'll have gone in with the people who are planning the coup. Not the rebels, Jenna — the opposite. All the time that Bolström was in exile, they must have stayed in contact. Who knows what they're planning now? And I went and told my father that we'd discovered the depot . . . God, how naïve! How totally, shamefully stupid!"

"But he still wouldn't hand over his own son to Bolström!" insisted Jenna. "Perry, your father wouldn't do that!"

Perry shook his head. "Maybe he didn't think it through," he said. "Maybe he panicked, and the only thing on his mind at that moment was 'How can we stop those kids from blowing our cover?' Maybe in all the excitement he just felt he had to warn Bolström, and only realized later what that would mean for me."

The blackbird was still singing. *Oh, be quiet*, thought Jenna.

"Then Bolström informed the men who'd captured us," said Perry. "That was the call to the car. *My father* is the one who betrayed us, Jenna, and I'm to blame. Why did I trust him?"

"Perry!" whispered Jenna. The harshness of his expression frightened her. "Maybe he isn't . . ."

"There's no maybe," said Perry, and Jenna could see that in the last few hours something had changed in him. Perry was no longer the boy she'd met in the navigator's house. Why couldn't he lie to himself just a little? *He understands too much — that's what Jonas always said — and once he's understood something, he can no longer ignore it.* Jenna stroked his arm. She didn't want to think about Jonas.

"Well, we've got something in common, then," she whispered. She couldn't help him. She couldn't take this terrible burden off his shoulders. But maybe she could console him a little with the knowledge that he was not alone. "My father's a criminal, too."

Perry didn't seem to notice the hand on his arm.

"Yes, they're both criminals," he said. "But last year when he had to decide whether to let you go or kill you, your father chose to save your life, even though it meant his own downfall. But *my* father, Jenna . . ." His voice began to tremble. "My father has betrayed me. He's sacrificed me. His property, position, and reputation are more important to him than my life."

"Oh, Perry," said Jenna.

The blackbird in the forest had stopped singing.

Petterson had left Osterlin to go to his own estate, where he could talk freely. He'd pretended that the groundskeeper had called to tell him there was something wrong with his favorite mare — a valuable animal — and that he had to see her for himself in order to decide what was to be done.

"Your son is being held hostage and you're worried about a horse?" Margareta had shouted at him. "Peter, I don't understand you!"

"What difference does it make whether I wait here or at home?" he'd answered. "I'll come back, Greta, though maybe by then it'll all —"

"No!" she'd screamed. "No! How can all of you be so . . . ?"

He would have to hurry back to her. He didn't even park the car in the garage.

He rushed up the stairs to his study and closed the curtains. A pointless thing to do — even if someone saw him on the phone, how would they know who he was talking to, and what about?

"Bolli!" he said when the call was answered. "Bolli, I want to know —"

Bolström said something.

"But I told you straightaway!" said Petterson. "It was obvious something had to be done to stop the children from talking about what they'd seen! But now you're holding them prisoner and using them as hostages! I've seen the photo."

Bolström tried to interrupt, but Petterson wouldn't let

him. "Yes, it's fine that you've put even more suspicion on the rebels, and yes, it would be even finer if we actually got hold of Liron! But you don't honestly think they'll make the exchange, do you?" He was breathing hard. "And in any case, you wouldn't go ahead with it, would you? You're not going to release the children, even in exchange for Liron. If you were, you wouldn't have needed to lock them away." He waited a moment. There was silence on the other end. Bolström did not contradict him. "So what are you going to do? With the children, I mean? *What are you going to do with my son?*"

The answer was cool and calm.

"Is that a promise, Bolli?" asked Petterson dubiously. "You swear you'll set them free when it's over?" What else could he say? He knew Bolström only too well. Even at school, he'd been as cruel as he was brilliant. He'd tormented anyone he could torment, just for the sake of it. And he'd had a nickname for everyone — a name that fit, but was often mocking. Petterson himself had been lucky: You could live with being called "Captain."

"I don't know if I can trust you, Bolli," he said softly. "And whatever impression you may have had in the past, I am far from indifferent to the fate of my son, even if he is a wimp." He listened for a moment. "Tell me as soon as you're ready."

When the conversation was over, Petterson went to the window and gazed thoughtfully outside. Somewhere in this darkness, Bolström was holding his boy and the princess prisoner, but he wouldn't say where. When they'd saved the country, and the reins of government were firmly in their hands, Bolström would set the children free — or so he said. How stupid did Bolström think he was, then? Would what they knew no longer pose a threat? No one must ever know that the hunger being suffered now was not the work of the rebels but of himself and Bolström. Bolström was far too clever not to realize the danger if the children talked.

Slowly he went downstairs. He must go back to Margareta. She was already furious with him. For the moment, the children were safe, because Bolström still needed them. There would have to be new photos every day.

But afterward? Once power changed hands?

And, worst of all, there was nothing he could do about it.

34

They sat, wide awake, on the ropes and nets, waiting for the morning, even though everything was sure to be the same as it had been the day before. Why was Jenna longing so much to see the sunrise?

A few times she had tried to sleep, but just a few feet away Perry sat so stiffly upright that the very sight of him immediately jolted her awake.

Perry's theory had to be right. It was the only explanation that made sense. And how could he sleep when he'd been betrayed by his own father?

If there had been a church clock anywhere nearby, they would have heard it toll the hours. If it had been lighter in the hut, they might have been able to see their watches. But for now they just sat there.

A confused blackbird let out a high trill, which was answered by another. The sound was comforting, though.

"Stupid birds," murmured Perry. "It's the middle of the night."

For a moment all was still, and then a third blackbird responded.

"Maybe it's almost morning now," said Jenna. "Maybe we slept on and off after all, and the time's gone by. Lots of birds start singing before sunrise. I wonder how they know, when they don't have clocks." At a time like this, Jenna also wondered how she could even be thinking about birds.

The blackbirds continued to hold their conversation. Perry jumped up.

"These birds have no more clue about the sunrise than we do!" he whispered. "If you get what I'm saying, Jenna. Let's just hope that the guards are asleep."

At that moment they saw the beam of a flashlight ranging over the window. At least one of the guards was on duty. Since nightfall, the man had been patrolling around the hut, sometimes close to it, sometimes farther away. The blackbirds fell silent.

Perry sat back down again. "Then again, maybe not," he murmured. "They probably wouldn't be that stupid."

Now Jenna understood. "You mean the blackbirds," she whispered.

"No blackbirds in the world sing at this hour," Perry answered softly.

For a while, all was silent. Then both of them sat bolt upright.

The blackbird sounded close enough for them to reach out and grab it.

"The guard on patrol!" Perry hissed anxiously. "He's bound to realize —"

Then everything happened very quickly.

They heard a shout, footsteps, someone falling to the ground, more footsteps. There must have been a lot of men. Crashing sounds, but no gunshots. Then the door was kicked open.

"Everything all right?" said a gruff but cheerful voice. Flashlights suddenly threw a ghostly brightness over the shore and the forest, and in their glow Jenna saw a face that she knew was somehow familiar.

The old man turned around. "Have you taken everything off them?" he shouted. "Especially their phones? Check that none of them have managed to send out any messages!"

Seven other men — the youngest not much older than Jenna and Perry, and the oldest so stooped he was almost doubled over — were outside the hut, tying the hands and feet of the guards and gagging them. There were four cell phones lying in the sand nearby.

"So far, so good, Kalijoki," said the youngest rebel. "They were snoring like pigs. I never thought my first mission would be so easy."

Perry leaned against the doorframe. "Blackbirds sleep at night," he said. His voice was trembling.

"Fortunately so did the guards!" said the old man, laughing. "But you're right, we should have thought of something a bit more subtle. If the fellow who spent the whole night wandering around the hut with his lamp knew the first thing about nature . . ." He shrugged his shoulders. "They watch too many movies, these kids," he said. "Don't know enough about the world they live in." He beckoned to the boy to bring the cell phones, and they disappeared into the deep pockets of his shepherd's cloak.

"All right, let's go," he said. "We might get some sleep tonight yet, eh?"

The rescuers pushed the guards through the narrow door-way past Jenna and Perry. Jenna didn't want to look at them.

"Once they're in, take off their gags," ordered the old man. "We don't want them suffocating. And no one'll hear them, no matter how loud they shout. Let's hope that one of their group will come along in the morning and find them. Otherwise, they'll get mighty bored sitting here all day." He laughed. "Are you two good to walk? We have to go a little way on foot."

Jenna nodded. *Kalijoki*, she thought, recognizing him at last. *The old man whose sheep had blocked the road.*

"Thank you!" she whispered. "Thank you for rescuing us!"

"Piece of cake," said the old man.

Jonas had found it tough going, lugging his heavy suitcase. The uneven slabs of pavement had made its little wheels rattle, and the whole time he had been afraid that the handle would snap under the weight.

But he knew he couldn't wait for the car in town, or in daylight, so he dragged his bags to the agreed-upon meeting point, just three hundred feet from the sign marking the entrance to the town. He sat down there on an old stand for milk churns that was weathered by many years of wind and rain.

When he saw the bobbing lights approaching over the stones and potholes of the forest track, he jumped down. The pickup truck came to a halt.

"Hey, Lorok," said Jonas.

"Hi, kid," said Nahira's most loyal follower. "You really want to take that thing with you?" He nodded toward the suitcase. "Think you're going on a cruise?" He laughed.

They didn't speak during the journey. And Lorok still drove like a maniac.

"This is it," said Lorok. "Out you get."

The shack looked derelict. Only the satellite dish on a tree stump showed that anyone was living there. Jonas slid down from the seat. "Thanks," he said.

In the doorway of the shack, with only the flickering light of the television behind her, stood Nahira. "Jonas!" she said.

Before he had even reached the shack, Jonas had to ask. "Did you really kidnap them? Do you really want to swap them for Liron?"

Then he came close to her. For a moment she seemed to want to ruffle his dark hair, but she let her hand fall. "Come on in," she said. "Of course we didn't. What do you think we are? But that's going to change in the next few hours."

Jonas looked around the room. There were three mattresses on the floor, and the sound was turned down on the television. Obviously Nahira and her people hadn't been using this hideout for long, and they clearly had no intention of staying much longer.

"It was very risky, Liron giving you my number," she said. "Your father has taken too many risks altogether. He kept saying that the same people who tried to seize power last year would do it again, and yet he went on acting as if he didn't believe it himself."

"He didn't exactly give me your number," said Jonas apologetically. "He concealed it in a riddle. But why did you meet yesterday? He must have realized how dangerous that would be!"

Nahira looked at the screen. The midnight news. "It's the day *before* yesterday now," she corrected him gently. She left the sound off the TV.

Then she turned to him. "This time it was my fault," she said. "I'd found something out — or rather Lorok did — that seemed to provide proof of what we suspected. I wanted to show him. So I was just as careless as he was."

"But he . . . There's still the death penalty for high treason," said Jonas.

Nahira looked away again. "We don't know how we can rescue him," she said wearily. "Liron's only hope is that this whole business will be over soon. That the plot will be exposed and everyone will know he didn't do anything wrong."

"And how's that going to happen?" whispered Jonas. "When we don't even know —"

Meonok burst into the room. The door slammed against the wall behind him.

"They got 'em!" he cried, pumping his fist triumphantly in the air. "And they're bringing 'em here!"

"Who?" asked Jonas. "Who have they got? Who's got who?"

No one answered.

"Are they all right?" asked Nahira.

Meonok shrugged his shoulders. "Going to throw them a party?" he asked.

"That's not exactly in the budget," Nahira said. "The way things are at the moment, we haven't even got anywhere for them to sleep."

The TV was showing the same pictures it had for the past two days.

"For who?" asked Jonas. "Nahira, have you got Liron?"

Nahira shook her head, and gave him a tired look. "I'm sorry, Jonas," she said. Then she signaled to her men. "We'll have to do as we've done before — cut some fresh branches. Lorok, Meonok, make a camp for three."

"Now? In the dark?" protested Meonok. "Can't they just sleep on the ground?"

"The boy can help you," said Nahira. "Hurry up, so you finish before they get here."

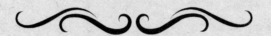

PART THREE

35

*J*enna stumbled when she stepped down from the truck in the darkness. The clearing swirled before her eyes, and if first Perry and then Nahira hadn't grabbed her arm, she would have collapsed to the ground.

"She hasn't slept for days," she heard Perry say, as if trying to excuse her. After that she didn't hear anything else.

When she woke up, it was morning. Perry lay next to her, fast asleep on a bed of pine branches, the scent of which had accompanied her in her dreams. In his sleep, Perry had put his left arm over her shoulder, as if to protect her.

Poor Perry, thought Jenna. *Poor, brilliant little Perry. Now I know what Jonas meant when he called Malena his sister. You've been my brother during these last few days — and that will never change.*

Carefully she removed his arm from her shoulder and sat up. In the tiny shack to which they had been taken last night, everyone was trying to be quiet in order not to wake the newcomers. Now Nahira was there, smiling at her and putting a finger to her lips, pointing toward Perry.

Jenna nodded.

Through the open door she could see Meonok carrying the television set to the pickup truck. Nearby, Lorok was busy lifting a satellite dish off a tree stump. It looked incongruous here in the forest clearing. A third man hurried through the narrow doorway, carrying a cable.

"We have to go!" whispered Nahira. "It's too dangerous here. Since last summer we've moved from one place to another practically every day. It's a pain, but we have to."

Perry opened his eyes and stretched.

"Just don't ask, 'Where am I?'" said Jenna as he looked at her, half-asleep and bewildered. "You're not Sleeping Beauty."

He yawned. "More like Hansel and Gretel, by the looks of things," he said. "Though I could sleep for days. Anyway, where are we?"

Lorok poked his head through the door. "We're ready now," he said.

"We're off," said Nahira, motioning to Perry to stand up. Jenna could see that she was on edge. "We're almost off. No shower today, and you'll have breakfast on the way."

Perry yawned and stretched again. "OK by me," he said, getting up. "As long as that whole kidnapping thing is over." Then he seemed to recall what he had figured out the day before. "At least as long as that's over," he murmured again, but his face had fallen.

Jenna was scarcely listening. She had a feeling that she knew the third man who was helping Meonok to load the truck. Oh! How could she have . . . ?

"Jonas!" she cried, and jumped up. Then she stopped in her tracks. *Ylva!* she thought. *How could I forget that, even for a second?*

Jonas stood against the back of the truck, his arms folded defiantly across his chest, gazing out over the clearing. He turned toward her, his face expressionless. "Hello, Jenna," he said without even smiling. Then he turned away again, and helped Lorok fasten the sides of the truck.

Jenna's face turned red. She could ask later what he was doing here. But how could she have forgotten about Ylva?

Now he's freaked that I'll throw myself at him again, thought Jenna, feeling the redness deepen. *Like at the garden party, when he had to literally run away from me. Oh God! He's trying to show me that he doesn't care so that I don't get the wrong idea again.*

She mustn't think about it! Not now. She'd seen Jonas with Ylva, oh so gracefully sucking face, so he didn't have to stress that she'd make things any more awkward. Just for a moment on Sunday she'd thought he shared her feelings, but now she knew better. As soon as she had the chance, she would show him that he was safe from her, no worries.

From the truck, Lorok signaled that they could go. Jenna stood tall and walked toward the clearing. Toward Jonas.

"Cool to see you," she said with the smile that she had

learned to put on for the cameras — though rarely with much success. Lorok cupped his hands to lift her onto the back of the truck. "We're so relieved to be out of that terrible fisherman's hut, aren't we, Perry? And what's been happening with you?" Perry had waited for her to climb in first; now she stretched out her hand to him, and without Lorok's help he clambered up and joined her.

To her surprise, Jenna found the fake smile easy to keep up. Shouldn't she really be feeling happy, after all? Relieved? Wasn't she glad that they'd rescued her? And she was still alive!

Who was Jonas, anyway? What did it matter who he was in love with, or who he was hooking up with, or what he thought of her? *Lovesickness!* she said scornfully to herself. *What's that compared to being afraid for your life?* Her lips tightened. It was no use. Her head was saying one thing, but her heart . . . *Stop that!* she told herself. *You're Princess of Scandia, and you've just been freed from your kidnappers. You're still alive, which is all that matters.*

"Hello, Perry," said Jonas. Surely it wasn't necessary for him to look as coldly at his best friend as he had at her?

Perry laughed. "Funny seeing you here!" he said, punching Jonas's arm. "How come? Did you hear what happened to Jenna and me?"

Nahira was the last to climb on the back of the truck. Meonok closed the flap and fastened it. "We can go," said Nahira. She sat down opposite Jenna and Perry.

Jonas sat with his back to the driver's cab. "Everyone in Scandia knows about it," he said without looking at Perry. Then he gazed out at the passing forest.

"Crazy, right?" said Perry. "Hey, Jonas, is something wrong?"

"We must hurry," Nahira interjected. "As soon as the plotters find out we've taken their hostages, they're bound to take action. And quickly, too."

Jenna looked up. "Action?" she said. Nahira's voice had sounded tense.

"I wonder if they've found out yet," said Perry. "Your men took the guards' phones. They've got no way of telling anyone."

"True," said Nahira. "But sometime during the morning, their contacts will realize what's happened. Then the question is what they'll do."

Perry nodded. Jonas kept his eyes so fixed on the forest, it was as if he was preparing for a presentation in biology class on the growth patterns of pine trees. Jenna forced herself to look at Nahira. *What's lovesickness? Don't be such a drama princess, Jenna. Better to think about the serious political situation at hand, what needs to be done now.*

Then she remembered. "We made a discovery, Perry and me! Nahira, did Perry already tell you about it last night? In this old factory by Saarstad. We've got to —"

"I know," said Nahira. "Lorok found out about it, too. That was why I met with Liron. But we were careless — unforgivably careless!"

"Why didn't you go to the press, then?" cried Jenna. The truck bounced through a pothole, and she had to cling to the side. "Instead of meeting with Liron? They could have taken photographers along, and then everyone in the country would have known . . ."

"Jenna!" said Nahira. "Me? And the press? I'm the leader of the rebels! Who would have believed me? I'd have been locked up before anyone could have gone to the depot!"

"Then let *us* do it now," said Jenna. "Perry and me! Take us to a police station — or a television station! We'll tell them what we saw —"

"To give them the heads-up so that they can clear out the depot pronto?" said Jonas dismissively. Now he did look at her. "How naïve are you two? Haven't you noticed the way the media have been reporting things for weeks on end? Whose side they're on — ever since last year? These people will clear out whatever they can clear out, or even pack the place with weapons to show that the rebels had set up the depot and are planning an armed revolution!"

Jenna hesitated. An image came to mind. "On Sunday I saw the editor in chief of the *Scandia Times* at the von Thunbergs'," she recalled. "At the party. Where there was so much to eat." She looked at the others. "But all this time, his paper's been reporting that the people of Scandia are going hungry, because the rebels . . . Jonas is right. We can't go to the media."

"They're also claiming they've found weapons every-where," said Nahira. "You wouldn't know about that, but the news has been full of it since yesterday. In factories in the south, farmhouses in the north, even in a ceme-tery! The people in the south feel threatened again. Fear's spreading all over Scandia. So everyone is more than will-ing to believe whatever the papers and television tell them about the rebel menace. And that's what the plotters are building on."

"So there's no way of informing the country about what's going on in that old warehouse?" asked Jenna. "There must be at least one paper in Scandia, one TV station that isn't —"

"We've got no choice," said Nahira with an impatient shrug. "But the danger is that we might achieve the exact opposite —"

"Because then the conspirators will be warned," said Jonas, once again staring out at the passing forest.

"Probably," said Jenna. "But the plotters already know that Perry and I found the depot. And now we're free . . ."

Up until then, Perry had said nothing. *He's thinking of his father*, thought Jenna. *Nobody understands his feelings better than I do.*

But now he looked up. "You're talking as if Scandia is the same country it was a year ago," he said. "But it isn't. We've got foreign TV broadcasters here now, foreign newspaper bureaus, and the Internet. Every Scandian has access to the outside world. So if we try to get the *international* press . . ."

"Yes!" cried Jenna. "They've all got correspondents here in Scandia. If we took *them* to the factory . . ."

"You've got their phone numbers?" Nahira asked ironically.

"I'll call Bea!" Jenna insisted. "She can arrange it for us. She'll do it, or her father!" She looked at Nahira.

Nahira hesitated.

"It's worth a shot, Nahira," said Perry. The truck hit another pothole, and he was thrown against Jenna. "What other options do we have? If my theory about the southern aristocrats is correct, then the situation is critical. Now that we've escaped, who knows, they might even launch their coup today."

"Today," murmured Nahira. "Today . . ."

"At least let Jenna try to contact Bea," said Perry.

Nahira raised her head, and passed one of her cell phones to Jenna.

Jenna opened it. She'd known the number by heart for years. At first it had been Bea's father's, until Bea had taken it over from him. *Mom's old number and Bea's*, Jenna thought. *I'll never forget those two, though Mom's got a different one now.*

She heard it ringing. And then came that familiar voice, which she had heard hundreds of times through the years — friendly but impersonal. "The person you have called is not available . . ."

"Oh, Bea, where are you?" said Jenna in frustration. "Maybe she's still at school. I'll try again later."

"Send her a text asking her to call you," said Perry. "Right away!" He looked at Nahira. "Or do you think we should try the Scandian press anyway?"

Nahira shook her head. "We should still have a few hours at least," she said.

Jenna clutched the cell phone. "So now what, Nahira?" she asked.

Jonas went on gazing at the passing trees. By now he must have gathered enough material for two presentations.

36

In the morning, Bea didn't feel like going to school.

"I didn't get a wink of sleep all night," she said when, after three wake-up calls, her mother mercilessly pulled off the bedspread. "Mom, please! I'll be too tired to learn anything, anyway!"

"Don't you have a French exam today?" said her mother, disappearing through the door before adding over her shoulder: "Next time it'll be a wet towel!"

Bea couldn't remember ever having a night like that. She'd always laughed at the sight of her mother sitting slumped at the breakfast table with eyes glued together, saying, "Didn't sleep a wink!"

How was that possible, Bea used to think. Nights were for sleeping, which was exactly what she did, like any other sensible person. Always. Until last night. She was certain that she'd been awake for every single terrible minute. She'd tossed and turned from left to right, from right to left, till the sheet beneath her had got so crumpled that no one could have slept on it. So she'd straightened the sheet and shaken the bedspread. After that she'd closed her eyes again, breathed deeply and regularly, counted sheep, and then — just when some fragment of consciousness had let her know that she was about to cross the border into sleep — back into her head came the jumble of images: Jenna with a crown on her head; Jenna with a gag in her mouth; Jenna with cheese on her chin in the pizza restaurant. Then Jenna at school — and suddenly the headmaster shooting at her with a gun, with the music that introduced the TV news in the background, and then smacking her rhythmically on the head with a French grammar textbook while he shouted, "Adverbial pronoun *y*, genitive *en*! And that's for the pizza!"

But that last part must have been a dream. So she *had* had some sleep, at some point. Before her mom could carry out her threat of a wet towel, Bea heaved herself slowly out of bed.

What happened in school that morning was a blur. She fell asleep during history, and no one woke her. She snapped at the math teacher when he asked her a question, and he simply shook his head and said nothing. They all knew the situation.

After the third period she excused herself and went home on the pretext that she'd had a fever the day before and her headache today was unbearable. The young chemistry teacher was concerned and sympathetic. But things couldn't go on like this indefinitely; she had to pull herself together. Jenna was still in the hands of the kidnappers — the morning news had confirmed as much — and Bea couldn't do anything about it.

Back home, she dropped her schoolbag on the floor. She was almost too tired to unlace her shoes. She'd go and lie on the sofa in the living room, switch on the TV, and sleep, or — if she still couldn't drop off — watch the news. But preferably sleep.

As she walked past the answering machine, she noticed the red light flashing. Wouldn't be for her. Friends would call her cell, or send text messages or e-mails. Nobody would call her on the landline, especially in the morning.

She pressed the button anyway.

The voice that boomed out of the machine seemed familiar, although she couldn't have said who it was. "It's your lucky day, Miss!" said the voice. "What I'm doing isn't exactly by the book, but we've known each other for a long time, right? They found your phone in a trash can!" There was a short pause, during which the policeman was presumably taking a good look at her phone. "Hardly surprising nobody wanted it, it's practically an antique. Lucky for you your parents didn't get you a more up-to-date one!" He laughed. "This one runs on coal, right? Anyway, you can come to the station and get it anytime."

Bea stared at the answering machine. How could a person snap so wide awake in just a few seconds? She laced her shoes back up, and grabbed the key. Now at last she could try to call Jenna.

Bolström would have preferred to talk with all the top men around a conference table behind closed doors this morning, instead of having to do everything by phone or e-mail, as he'd done for the last year. There was always the danger of mis-understandings during difficult negotiations like these. Sitting together, being able to look into people's eyes, was always the most effective way — especially when it came to persuading someone who didn't want to be persuaded. A smile, a frown, a clearing of the throat: Even the best conference calls could never replace a face-to-face conversation.

But today, time was too short. They had to act now. He couldn't wait for people to come from all over the country, from their mines, their oil wells, their farms on North Island. By the time they arrived, it could be too late. Everyone who mattered would now hopefully be waiting by their telephones. They'd all hear what the others had to say, and that would have to do.

Everyone, that was, except Petterson. Unfortunately, Petterson had to be excluded from this particular conference call. Who knew what he might do, loyal though he normally was? Since this concerned his son, it was obvious — if regrettable — that he couldn't be relied upon. No one could possibly have anticipated a development like this, which threatened to ruin all their plans.

It wasn't until around half past eight that Bolström heard something had gone wrong. The guards at the fisherman's hut were supposed to check in with his men every two hours, day and night. Whether the two a.m. call had come through, no one knew for sure, because the men on telephone duty had been asleep. *We'll deal with them later*, thought Bolström. Men who failed in their duties had no place among his people. But now there were other, more urgent matters to attend to. When the four o'clock call didn't come, the men — who swore they were awake at the time — assumed that the guards at the hut had done the same as them, and fallen asleep on duty. Even when the six o'clock call failed to materialize, they still thought their colleagues at the hut must simply have overslept. And they acknowledged they didn't want to blow the whistle on them, and they didn't want to wake Bolström, either, although by now they were, admittedly, beginning to get a bit concerned.

Only when there was no eight o'clock call did they suspect that something must have gone wrong. They'd waited another quarter of an hour, then tried all four numbers. After that, they knew for sure. The only problem then was who should tell Bolström. They'd drawn sticks, because nobody dared to give him the news.

"Tarnation!" roared Bolström. "Send someone there at once! But tell them to be careful. It could be a trap!"

It was hard to imagine who might have set one. The rebels, possibly. Had they freed the children? No, that was absurd. They were scattered everywhere. Could it have been government forces, the police, the press, the military? No, the power centers of the country were now on his side — they'd all had enough of appeasing the north.

Shortly after nine o'clock, he heard that the guards had been found tied up in the hut and the children were gone.

"Tarnation!" Bolström yelled again. "How could this

have happened? Now there's no time to lose!"

If I hadn't advanced the plan in the last few weeks, he thought, *and if the military weren't deployed all over the country, ready to strike — even though they might not know it yet — where would we be now? Suppose I hadn't come back to take charge of everything? Useless idiots! But we've all got to work together. I need them all. And I have to be in charge.*

He switched on the speakerphone. He didn't want to have to hold the receiver to his ear the whole time. He needed his hands free for coffee and cigarettes.

"Is everything ready?" he barked. "It's an emergency! We've got less than twenty-four hours now. Tonight at two. Holmburg. Parliament. The palace. I'm sure the people are ready for it."

Someone interrupted. "Of course those two children are the second priority," said Bolström. "Search the whole area for them, and don't be squeamish. Tell the men there's a price on their heads, dead or alive."

People started talking all at once. *Fools!* thought Bolström. *Fools, the lot of them! They'd like to think they can get everything they want without dirtying their hands.*

"What difference does that make to our plans?" he snapped. They stopped talking. There was always silence when he spoke. "If the children are found dead, people will say it was the rebels, and that's precisely what we intended all along." He dragged on his cigarette. "And finally," he said, flicking off the ash, "there's Norlin."

Someone said something at the other end.

"No, it has to be done now. Norlin's got to go before anyone gets the chance to talk to him!" he said. "Who knows what he might come up with? He could ruin us all. But you can leave him to me."

He'd finished his cigarette. "In summary," he said, "at two a.m., we march in. Meanwhile, Norlin disappears. And so do the two children. Until then, the media will continue to show yesterday's photos of the hostages. People may wonder why there are no new photos with today's paper — doesn't matter. One answer could be that the rebels have already killed the children. Then, if they're actually found dead this afternoon, it'll simply be confirmation that the rebels were responsible, and everybody will hate them all the more for it, as well as be frightened by how ruthless they are. And all that can only be to our advantage when we march on Holmburg tonight."

Bolström went back to his desk. "We'll stay in contact," he said. Then he disconnected the call without waiting to see if anyone else had anything more to say.

Norlin had not yet made an appearance. Bolström's men could probably dispose of him in his bedroom without the drunken buffoon even waking up. How convenient. That was one less problem, at least. Who'd have thought that Norlin's boozing could turn out to be so useful?

Out in the hall, a figure in a silken robe hurried toward the staircase.

37

The windmill stood well back from the road, near the sea — too near, perhaps, to withstand the gales. One frame was broken, and the sails of the other three hung down in tatters. It had been a long time since the grindstones had turned, and the cobbled forecourt where cartloads of grain had once been unloaded now lay bare and desolate.

So when Meonok opened the door, Jonas was almost startled to hear the noise of voices and see the dense cloud of smoke hanging beneath the low ceiling before it floated up the narrow staircase. At least twenty men were leaning against the unplastered walls, or sitting on the worn wooden steps that led up to the next floor. Some were young, some old, but, like him, all of them had dark hair and the typical features of the north.

"Nahira!" cried one. "At last!"

They all looked toward the door through which Nahira had entered the room, followed by Lorok, Meonok, and the three

young people. Jonas would not have been surprised if someone had started to applaud.

"I'm grateful that you've all come," said Nahira. "And I'm
grateful that you're still ready and willing to pursue our cause.
You all know what's happening in our country. We're still not
getting our share in the north, but even the initial reforms
have been too much for the southerners. They're afraid of what
they might lose in a country where everything once belonged
to them. They're not content to sit and watch it happen. That's
why we're here now. That's the whole point of our meeting."

The room had fallen silent. Everyone was listening
intently.

"They're planning a coup, as we've suspected for a long
time," said Nahira. "They've prepared the way by fostering
resentment among the people against the new government.
And they've arrested Liron to prove that the government is
actually being run by us, the rebels! So everyone in the south
will not only be supportive if the government changes, they'll
even approve if it's done by force."

"It was careless of you, Nahira," said one of the older men,
"to meet with Liron." As a murmur of agreement rippled
around the room, Nahira interrupted him.

"You're right, Inuk," she said. "It was unforgivably careless.
But something has happened now to change the whole situation. The conspirators are no longer in control of their own
plans. They've got to act now, and act fast. Thanks to these
young people"— she turned to Jenna and Perry, and motioned

to them to step forward —"the conspirators have run out of time. We believe they will have to act tonight — earlier than they'd intended. And so this is our opportunity."

Now she'll tell them about the smuggled goods in the old ware-house, thought Jonas. *And about Bolström, and how he held Jenna and Perry hostage. And about the rescue.*

He looked at Jenna. Her head was resting on Perry's shoulder, and Perry had put his arm around her. They were so comfortable with each other. Anyone could see they belonged together.

So why did Jenna tell me that story about Perry and Malena? Jonas asked himself. But maybe it wasn't a story. Maybe Jenna and Perry didn't fall in love until they were prisoners together. Things like that can happen.

For that brief shining moment at the party on Sunday, he'd even thought he and Jenna might . . . No, that was stupid, stupid, stupid. Jenna was a princess, and Perry was no ordinary southerner. Perry was an aristocrat, whose father owned mines and oil wells and plantations. While he, Jonas, was Liron's son, just a poor northerner like everyone else gathered there in the mill.

". . . and all the fishermen in their boats," Nahira was saying. "Get the message to all of them. We don't know where the enemy is coming from, or when. Everyone must be prepared."

"There are too few of us, Nahira," said Inuk, "especially if the military is involved. The Scandian army has thousands of troops; the air force can send planes over our towns; the navy can blockade the ports. There just aren't enough of us!"

"I know that," said Nahira. "But there are other ways of fighting. Just bring as many as you can."

Slowly the men stood up.

Just three paces away from Jonas, Jenna raised her head from Perry's shoulder and ran her hand through her tousled hair. When her eyes met Jonas's, she quickly turned away.

He'd been so stupid on Sunday. But he'd learned his lesson. The hard way.

38

There were three people already at the reception desk in the police station. An elderly woman was waving her arms around while the policeman whose voice Bea had recognized on the answering machine was trying to calm her down.

"From my bag!" shouted the woman, holding up a large, old-fashioned shopping bag. "Over there, in the supermarket! Just as I got to the checkout . . ."

Another policeman had his head down, typing at the far end of the desk, while a man holding the hand of a little boy gave a statement. Bea looked from one policeman to the other. She couldn't wait.

"Pardonnez-moi!" she said, trying to worm her way past the elderly lady. "Hello, it's me, I've come for my poor little lost cell phone! Could you maybe just let me —"

Her policeman gave her a stern look. "You can see I'm busy, can't you?" he said. "Give me the bag, please, madam." He leaned over and peered into its large middle compartment, before pulling out a bunch of keys.

"Oh please please please please please!" said Bea, shuffling from one foot to the other. "It'll only take a second!"

The policeman ignored her.

"A hundred dollars!" cried the old lady, her voice on the verge of cracking. "I'd only just been to the bank, Sergeant. I was going to buy a birthday present for my grandson!"

Bea could hear how upset she was.

"Next thing we'll do is call the bank," said the policeman. He hadn't finished with the bag yet. "You might have left your purse there."

He was now searching the side pockets. The old metal zipper got stuck.

The woman shook her head in despair. "I can remember quite clearly!" she said. "I took the money out of the dispenser, put it in my purse, and then I deliberately put the purse . . ."

She stared at his hand. In it was the purse. He held it out over the counter.

". . . in the side pocket," she murmured. "I'm so sorry, Sergeant! Oh dear, I'm ever so sorry, Sergeant! Because there was so much money in it! I deliberately put it in the side pocket, so I could zip it up. Oh dear!"

The policeman gave her a friendly smile and handed the purse over.

"And when you went to pay at the supermarket check-out, you'd forgotten where you put it, right?" he said gently. "It can happen to anybody. Just as long as you're all right now."

The old lady looked as if the embarrassment was almost worse than the original loss.

"How can I ever repay you?" she said, putting the purse back into the middle compartment of the bag with trembling fingers. "I've caused you so much trouble!"

"We're always happy to help. That's our job. No reward necessary."

The old lady wanted to say something else, but by now Bea had really had enough.

"You left a message on our answering machine!" she declared.

"Good-bye, madam," said the policeman, waving to the old lady as she turned in the doorway to thank him. "The world isn't such a bad place as we sometimes think it is, is it?"

Only then did he turn to Bea.

"OK, young lady. Now it's your turn. It all takes time. First things first, right?" He smiled and went into the next room. When he came back, he was holding something in his hand. "There we are, then. I'm making lots of people happy today. Sign here, please."

Bea reached out. It really was her cell phone.

Impatiently she switched it on. "*Merci* very much," she said, without even looking at the policeman.

"Just a second!" he said. "What's the big rush? I need a signature. As I said, first things first."

"OK," said Bea. She picked up the ballpoint pen. "And thank you for calling me!"

The policeman took the form as Bea looked at the phone's display: TWO MESSAGES. ONE MISSED CALL.

Without looking up, she went toward the exit door and brought up the list.

Jenna's number — she knew it! Her fingers were trembling. Then twice a number she didn't recognize, but also a text from Jenna. She hoped it hadn't been sent before the kidnapping.

"Must be from the love of your life!" said the policeman. "Couldn't even wait to get home, hmm?"

The display flickered. Jenna had sent a video. What was it supposed to be? Obviously it was night, and someone was rushing around, but the image was blurred. A truck, then another, men carrying things . . .

Bea looked at the number. Yes, the video had definitely been sent from Jenna's phone. She watched it a second time, but still couldn't figure it out. Why had Jenna sent this? And why hadn't she written something to go with it?

She clocked back onto the main menu. The call had also come from a Scandian number, and the text: **Call me NOW!!! —Jenna**

Bea looked at the display. She could hardly read it, she was so excited. Did Jenna mean this number or her own? She'd try the unknown number first, since the instruction had come from there. She hit the CALLBACK button.

It only took a few seconds, and then at the other end she heard Jenna's voice, as clear as if she were sitting in her old room around the corner, like back in the pre-princess days.

"Jenna, OMG!" cried Bea. Her fingers were trembling so much now that she almost dropped the phone. "Are you free or what? Where are you? What's happening? That country of yours is crazy!" She didn't even notice the two policemen looking up at her.

"Bea!" cried Jenna down the line. "Bea, is it really you?"

"Yes!" said Bea. "What's going on, Jenna? Are you safe?"

"Listen, Bea," said Jenna in an urgent tone. "You must do exactly what I tell you, and do it now!"

"*Oui oui*, Your Royal Highness," said Bea.

"Seriously!" cried Jenna. "Every second counts! There are people here plotting a coup. They might even be marching on Holmburg this very minute! But —"

"You mean the same people as last year? What's-his-name Bullhorn?" said Bea with a frown. "But I thought —"

"Bea, love you, but stop interrupting me!" cried Jenna. "They've set up a depot where they're storing all the goods that have run short in Scandia — in an old warehouse. Now you've got to —"

"Ah, so *that's* the video!" said Bea. "The one you sent me, with a nighttime —"

"No, what I sent you was us in the pizza place!" said Jenna. "But —"

"The pizza place? Have you completely lost it?" said Bea. This was getting stranger by the second. "Maybe your crown is a tad too snug . . ."

"Bea!" yelled Jenna. "Listen, please! Things here are critical! This isn't a game! You've got to tell a newspaper or a TV station to send someone there immediately —"

"Newspaper?" said Bea. She started looking around for the cameras, thinking maybe she was on one of those reality prank shows. "Now?"

"Or television," said Jenna. Bea could hear that her voice was getting more and more desperate. "They've got to go to the abandaoned warehouse on the northern end of South Island, near Saarstad. Then they'll see for themselves. All the big international media outlets have got correspondents in Scandia now!"

The line crackled.

"Bea, are you still there?" cried Jenna. "If you can't get hold of a newspaper or TV reporter, then go to the police! They've got to help you! Can you hear me, Bea?" The signal had got so bad that her last words were barely audible.

"Affirmative!" said Bea. "The police — they're right here. How did you know?"

But there was silence at the other end.

"Cut off," said Bea to the policemen. "Unless she hung up. No, she wouldn't do that."

The two policemen looked at her. "We don't believe in listening in on other people's conversations," said the one who had given her back her phone. "But we didn't have much choice. Is there something the matter with your sweetheart?"

"Best friend," Bea said, shaking her head. "I'm supposed to alert the media. I'll show you the pictures."

The policeman sighed. "Pictures? Don't tell me you want to try out for one of those talent shows!" he said.

But Bea was already standing at the desk, playing Jenna's video. "No, no, I did that last year. Ended up being a total scam," she said dismissively. The second policeman joined them to look at the small screen. Maybe they'd be able to make more sense of all this.

39

Ylva had stayed in her pink room practically all the day before. Her mother kept calling and banging on the door, but she hadn't responded.

In the evening, her father had come home. She'd let him in. His men were now all over the country, and Ylva could see that he was worried about what might happen next.

"Believe me, it's all coming to a head," he'd said. "The rebels with spies inside the government! Who'd have suspected Liron? And they've got arms caches everywhere!"

Ylva had said nothing.

"These northerners want it all," her father had continued. "And the king and the government do nothing. Sabotage everywhere, shortages, people starving . . ."

"Are you sure the rebels are really behind it?" Ylva had asked with just a hint of sarcasm. "Are you sure it's not your wife again, banging her wooden spoon?"

"What?"

Then Ylva had gone to bed. Let him ask her mother what she meant.

She had been lying on her pink princess bedcovers since she woke up, not knowing what to do. The television was on, with the sound turned down, but all it was showing was Scandian forests followed by Scandian folk singers, interspersed with the familiar photo of Jenna, Perry, and the newspaper. Why should she bother going back to school? And what should she do at home? Nothing was what it seemed to be. She thought about her mother in that phony housewife's apron, and then zapped the remote control until she got an international news channel. The Far East. The Middle East. Famine in Africa. Floods in Southeast Asia. Earthquakes in the Caribbean. So much suffering, yet here she was, an almost-princess.

"Ylva!" her father called through the door. She knew right away that something had happened. "Ylva, I've got to go!"

She jumped up and unlocked her door. Her father gave her a hug.

"It's started," he said. "The rebels are marching on Holmburg."

"What?" asked Ylva.

"I've just received a phone call," said her father. "Battle orders. I wanted to say good-bye before I leave. Be careful, Ylva. This is civil war, and you know what that means."

To her surprise, Ylva saw that he was sweating. Was he afraid? Or excited?

"We're going into Holmburg," he said. "We have to take Parliament House and the palace. These are momentous times, princess. Look after yourself and your mother."

Ylva stared at him. She thought of her mother with that headscarf. And of the blatant heading on the plan for the coup. Nothing was what it seemed to be. "Are you sure this is right?" she asked. "Daddy, the business with Liron . . ."

"Good-bye, Ylva," said her father. "I just didn't want to go without saying good-bye." He turned, waved his hand, and closed the door.

Ylva fell back on the bed and stared at the television screen. Was there really going to be war now? Civil war, people killed — how many killed? Who would govern afterward? Far East, Middle East, starvation in Africa, floods in Southeast Asia, earthquakes in the Caribbean . . . She turned up the volume. From now on, she'd stay tuned to the international news channels. She couldn't stand the suffocating coziness of the Scandian stations.

". . . the shortages in Scandia," said the anchorman. "Our foreign correspondent has been shown a video taken on a cell phone . . ." (dim pictures of barely recognizable trucks in the distance) ". . . which would seem to suggest that the cause of the shortages in Scandia is by no means what the citizens have been led to believe. The situation in the country now appears in a totally different light."

Had she understood correctly? Ylva turned the volume up even louder, as if that would change anything. Now the correspondent himself appeared on the screen, pointing excitedly to the scene behind him of large hangars, men running, trucks and satellite vans with the logos of international broadcasting companies. ". . . still trying to contact our Scandian colleagues," he was saying. "But despite our efforts, not a single Scandian TV station has a representative here! And yet it would seem that this has been going on for weeks . . ."

Ylva jumped up. So it wasn't the rebels! She *knew* it!

"Although the citizens of Scandia have been led to believe that members of the new coalition government were conspiring with the rebels, and deliberately causing the widespread shortages of food and other supplies," said the correspondent, "it seems clear now that what lay behind all this was a plan to turn the people of Scandia against their new government, and in due course even to . . ."

Her father! She had to tell him!

"When our French colleagues arrived, they filmed a large number of trucks loaded with weapons that were being taken to the hangars, evidently in order to give the impression that this was a rebel arsenal," said the correspondent. Ylva could hear his excited voice behind her now as she leaned out the window. "Only last year, Scandia experienced . . ."

Had her dad gone already? Or might he still be saying good-bye to her mother? Maybe she could still catch him. The car was standing by the steps, its engine idling, with the driver at the steering wheel.

". . . our cameras," said the correspondent. "In fact, our German colleagues have already . . ."

Her father emerged from the front door and stood at the top of the steps. He was wearing his uniform, and now began slowly to go down toward the car.

"Dad!" shouted Ylva.

". . . incredible!" said the correspondent. "The French cameraman has . . ."

"Daddy!"

He heard her. Thank goodness, he heard her! He turned and, as he opened the car door, he looked up. The engine was running.

"Dad, come back! It's all a lie! It's a lie, Dad! I've just seen on television —"

As he got in, he waved, and then he closed the door. Even before it was shut, the car leaped forward and was on its way.

"Daddy!" cried Ylva.

It was too late.

She stood at the window. The car was racing down the driveway. And it was all one huge lie.

"The Scandian security forces have confiscated their cameras," said the anchorman in the studio. In the background was a photo showing uniformed, armed men attacking the foreign television crews. "A CNN cameraman has been clubbed on the head and is badly injured. We can only say that the situation in this island country is becoming more and more confused. It does seem certain, however, that the attacks and incidents of the last few days have been the work of very different forces from those first reported by . . ."

Ylva grabbed the telephone and dialed her father's cell number with flying fingers.

The other end was dead. She should have expected that — under the circumstances, he would have switched off his personal phone.

The television had returned to the Far East, the Middle East . . . Ylva zapped back three channels. On Scandia 1, four contestants were trying to guess the name of Zeus's wife: a) Vera; b) Hera; c) Pallas Athene; d) Maria. On Scandia 2, a duo in embroidered Scandian costumes was singing a folk song and gazing enraptured into each other's eyes while behind them the sunlight sparkled on a Scandian lake.

"I don't believe it!" screeched Ylva.

She toggled back and forth between the two channels. On Scandia 1, the next question was: "Who composed *Eine kleine Nachtmusik*?" On Scandia 2, the duo had been replaced by a middle-aged tenor with a spray tan, trying to look twenty, while the lake had been replaced by waves beating against the shore.

"But they *must* know what's going on!" cried Ylva.

Had she been dreaming? The international news channel was showing the floods in Southeast Asia. "And now back to the extraordinary reports coming in from the island state of Scandia," said the anchorman. She recognized the images, scanned back to Scandia 1 and 2 — still the quiz, still the singers — then back to the foreign news again, the nervous correspondent, soldiers rushing toward him, then a blur, and the anchorman in the studio.

". . . by the Scandian security forces," he said, and Ylva clicked back again. The game show had given way to a cooking program, and the singers and their Scandian landscapes had been replaced by three women on a sofa in front of a studio audience: a talk show.

"I don't believe it!" she yelled again. One last time, she went back to the international news channel.

"After today's events, however, it does seem certain that . . ."

Why wasn't Scandia 1 showing what was happening here? They should have been the first to broadcast it! And why did the security forces seize the foreign reporters' cameras?

Did her father know? Was it possible that he was one of the people behind the whole plot? Or was he just as stupid as her mother, banging her pot with her wooden spoon?

"I don't think he knows," murmured Ylva. "Daddy would never . . ."

She jumped up. Everyone in the country could see this if they wanted to. But who would think of switching to a foreign newscast? Scandians watched Scandia 1 and Scandia 2, and Scandia 1 was showing a cooking program, Scandia 2 a talk show. So who else in Scandia would know what was going on?

She had to do something. She couldn't let her father march on parliament and the palace just because he thought the country was under threat from the rebels, when in fact . . .

She dialed a second time, although she knew she wouldn't get through. There was only one thing she could do now. She had to look up the number of the local taxi company. The only one she knew by heart was the one by Morgard.

All her life she had thought of herself as Princess Ylva. She wasn't going to stop now.

40

He would have to give up smoking. Eventually, when all this was over. There must have been at least twenty stubs in the ashtray. He was always telling Norlin to lay off the booze, but he couldn't keep away from the pack in his pocket. Not that smoking was as bad as drinking, but it still annoyed him that he couldn't get it under control.

"Blast it all, what a disaster!" he yelled into the phone. "Which channel? We should have thought of that when the kids got away! We should never have let ourselves rely on the loyalty of our own media!" He looked for the remote control and began switching channels. "Just as I thought! I always knew it would be our downfall if we let all these foreigners into the country without rigid controls! A free press . . ."

At the abandoned factory, the security forces were confiscating a journalist's camera. Down came the billy club.

"And now we all know how the rest of the world is going to react, thank you very much! What did they have to do that for?" He was breathing heavily. "Just as long as it's over before the citizens learn about it . . ."

But Bolström knew that, in the long run, that was impossible. Every Scandian household had a television, and almost everyone could now receive international channels. The only question was who was actually watching, and how quickly the news would spread. Maybe over the Internet. But as long as the Scandian press kept quiet, nothing was likely to happen yet.

Abroad, of course, they would think the worst, but what did he care? If by tomorrow morning the government he'd set up was sitting in parliament, it wouldn't matter two hoots that the foreigners now knew what had been going on in Scandia.

Someone was saying something on the telephone, but he didn't listen. He knew that there were enough people abroad — enough governments, to be frank — who'd be secretly toasting his success. And as soon as he'd saved the country, he'd make sure the borders were closed and the phone networks controlled as quickly as possible. Cutting off access to satellite television and the Internet might be more tricky. The people probably wouldn't like that. No, it wouldn't be easy, but after only one year away he should be able to regain a grip.

"And of course we still need to get those two kids!" he hissed into the receiver.

The last match. He hated lighters. He needed that hissing sound, the tiny explosion when the sulfur scraped against the side of the box. "What do you mean, everyone can see there aren't any rebels on the march? Who can see that? How? Let them all think the rebels are marching somewhere else! You've got the soldiers: Use them, and fast!"

He threw the empty matchbox onto the table. "I need to be kept informed at all times."

The door opened. Two bodyguards stepped into the room.

"What?" said Bolström. They hadn't knocked, so it must be something important.

The men looked at each other, and then one spoke. "Norlin's gone," he said. He looked scared, as if he was afraid he might be blamed. "He's not in his bedroom."

"We can't find him anywhere," said the other man. "We've searched all over."

"What?" yelled Bolström. Not this on top of everything else. "Then search some more! You know what will happen if he talks? I hope I don't have to put out a bounty for him as well, do I?"

The men shook their heads and beat a hasty retreat. Bolström inhaled again, then picked up the phone. Why was it all going so wrong? If he didn't do everything himself . . . The whole country was full of idiots.

Malena sat on a boulder at the edge of the school grounds and looked down into the valley. It was full of heather and white clover, and she thought she could smell the scent of raspberries up here under the burning midday sun. It was from here that she'd run away last year, ducking behind one bush after another until she was finally out of sight of the school and no one had been able to find her. How far away it all seemed, and how unhappy she'd been.

And now? Was everything all right now?

She listened to the voices behind her on the field, the shouts and the laughter. *At school I'm cut off from everything*, she thought. *Perry and Jenna disappeared two days ago, and I have no idea what's happened to them.*

Her school banned the use of any kind of phone during the week so that the students would form a community of their own, without constantly communicating with parents, relatives, and friends back home. *Forget community!* thought Malena. As if a cell phone would make any difference.

And there was no television, either, during the week, because without it, they wouldn't sit there passively, wasting their time. They'd talk to one another, and play games, and compete in every sport that Scandians participated in, and join the orchestra, the choir, the theater troupe, the film club . . .

But I'm sure they would have told me if Jenna and Perry had been found, thought Malena. *Everyone knows how worried I am. After all, Jenna's my cousin — they all know that. They'd tell me. If I've heard nothing, that must mean nothing's happened.*

She started throwing pebbles down into the valley. At first they clicked against the rocks, but then they disappeared silently into the bushes farther down the slope. "Malena?" said a high-pitched, slightly out-of-breath voice behind her. It was a little girl with messy braids. Her tails of her school blouse had slipped out of her skirt waistband. "I was told to come and get you, Malena. Telephone."

Malena felt a tightening in her chest. What did the call mean? Something good or something bad?

"Is it my father?" she asked, jumping down from the rock.

The little girl shook her head and shrugged her shoulders at the same time. "Don't know," she said timidly.

As she hurried past the girl, Malena recalled how she had felt at that age. Little girls had to be polite to big girls, run errands, hold doors open. One day little girls would themselves become big girls, and other little girls would do the same for them. Malena remembered how strange it had seemed at first: She was a princess, so how could anyone tell her what to do just because they were five years older?

But then she'd grown to love the custom. She had admired the big girls and envied them, and she'd longed for the time when she would be one of them. But that had long since ceased to be something special.

She hurried along the cool corridor of the school building, and knocked on the door of the headmistress's study. Soon she would know.

The headmistress looked up and smiled at her. "Malena!" she said, pointing toward the telephone. "It's Ylva von

Thunberg. She sounds very upset. I thought I'd better make an exception and let you speak to her."

Malena was taken aback.

"Hello, Ylva?" she said.

"I think you should go home at once," said Ylva. "I think something's about to happen."

41

*J*he *branches cracked* beneath Norlin's feet. He just had to get away from there! It was a good thing that Scandia was full of forests so thick and impenetrable you could hide for days in them — weeks, even. He could grow a beard. He could give himself a new name.

At some point he would have to eat. At the moment he couldn't imagine ever feeling hungry again, but there'd be berries and mushrooms. He wouldn't starve.

He sat down on a stump. He hadn't even had time to get dressed when he'd overheard Bolström: *"Norlin's got to go before anyone gets the chance to talk to him."* He'd left in his robe — this ridiculous silk dressing gown with a Chinese dragon embroidered on the back. He could grow a dozen beards, but if anyone saw him in his robe, they'd never swallow the story about him being a poor woodcutter.

But he'd had no choice. All that mattered was that he'd got away in time. Good grief, who'd have thought that Bolström . . .

"He could ruin us all. But you can leave him to me."

His hands were trembling and his heart was thumping. Was it fear? Or was it the lack of alcohol? Where in the forest could he get something to drink?

But that wasn't crucial now — no, he had to concentrate. Where should he hide? How could he get away?

Drat! He had to keep going, even without a drink.

"But you can leave him to me."

Why hadn't he thought about this before? How could he have believed Bolström's fairy tales about him returning to the palace and being regent again? Shouldn't he have realized it would be impossible after what had happened last summer?

But he'd shut all that out. He'd tried to forget it. And instead he'd escaped to the magic world of the bottle.

Why had he let it go so far? When he'd heard what Bolström planned to do with his daughter, he should have woken up to the truth — realized the lengths to which Bolström was prepared to go. But all he'd done was offer up a feeble protest and turned back to his brandy.

He looked at his trembling hands as if they belonged to someone else. He was being torn apart. He needed a drink. Everything else would work out then. He *needed* it! He wouldn't be able to go on for another second without that merciful oblivion, that heartwarming comfort. He needed it!

Norlin leaped to his feet and rushed backward and forward, punching the tree trunks with his fists, groaning. There was nothing, nothing in the world now, no plans, no fear, only this burning desire.

When he saw the village, it was all he could think about. Someone would give him something to drink. Or he'd smash a window and rob a shop. A village meant rescue from the craving in his head and in his body. A village meant drink, and drink meant the feeling of peace that would restore him to himself.

But a village also meant revealing himself to people. No longer hiding.

When the two men jumped down from their rickety truck, he was almost relieved. They grabbed him in his ridiculous silken robe. They'd shoot him, and then at least it would all be over. He couldn't stand it for another second.

"You don't happen to have a little drink . . . ?" he whispered.

The men pushed him up onto the truck without saying a word. Maybe they hadn't heard.

His hands were trembling so much he could hardly hold on to the side as the truck raced away. His teeth were chattering. *Just let it end quickly.*

The meeting at the mill had disbanded. Jenna could only guess where all the men had gone. They'd be telling the fishermen of North Island, and all the rebels that were left in the south. They would walk nonchalantly past the soldiers on the streets, and secretly put their people on the alert.

Jenna had gone outside. The ragged sails of the mill rattled in the wind. She didn't even want to look at Jonas, who had been leaning, grim-faced, against the banisters when she had last seen him, positioned as far away from her as possible. What on earth had she said on Sunday that made him so cold and distant? She hadn't even touched him. If only she could remember it all more clearly, but so much had happened since then. She must have done something to make him behave as if he didn't know her, as if he didn't even *want* to know her.

Lorok and Meonok had carried the satellite dish to a beech tree and had set it up against the trunk, so that the television was now on inside the mill. Maybe she should go in and watch the photo of her kidnapped self every half hour, with game shows in between. It might at least be a distraction.

When she opened the door, she saw at once that Jonas was no longer downstairs. Maybe he had climbed up to the next floor or had gone out while she'd been standing with her back to the door, gazing out over the forest. Only Perry was there, sitting cross-legged on the floor, testing which TV channels they could get.

When the blurred, brownish pictures flickered across the screen, Jenna gasped. "My cell phone!" she cried.

Perry stopped surfing. "No way!" he breathed.

There it was, the video she had taken at the old ware-house — even more blurred in this larger format, but still distinguishable. "How did they get that?" Jenna stammered.

"Your friend Bea," said Perry, without taking his eyes off the screen. "She came through — big-time!"

Bea, Bea, fabulous Bea! *That* was why she'd laughed when Jenna said she'd sent her photos of the pizza place. In her moment of panic before the kidnappers took away her cell phone, she must have sent the wrong pictures.

The short video was followed by daylight scenes, with a commentary. There were armed men in uniform attacking a foreign news team. "A CNN cameraman has been struck over the head . . ."

"They found the factory!" shouted Perry. "Nahira, they found the factory! Jenna's friend did it! They're showing the pictures all over the world!"

"Really?" cried Nahira. "On the news channels?"

"Then they can't do anything now!" said Jenna, and from her own relief she realized just how frightened she had been. "Now the whole world knows what's been going on in Scandia. Isn't that right, Nahira? There's nothing they can do!"

Nahira didn't respond. She was talking into her cell phone a mile a minute. It was Perry who answered Jenna.

"It means that they'll have to act even faster," he said. "The conspirators couldn't care less what people abroad are saying. They just have to limit what people here get to know. Now they'll be going into action as soon as they can."

"You mean it's all useless?" asked Jenna. "Bea telling the media, and people all over the world seeing the proof?"

Perry shrugged his shoulders. As if in order to prove his point, he switched channels to Scandia 1, where singers were twirling and dancers gliding across a meadow, their faces radiant in the sunshine. "See?" said Perry. "Nobody's going to learn anything from Scandia 1. And once the plotters have taken Holmburg, they'll block access so that no one can receive any foreign channels — just like in the old days. Then they'll decide exactly what information people are going to get. But still . . ."

"But still what?" asked Jenna.

"Now they'll never really be able to deny it," said Perry. "Too many people in the rest of the world know what they've done — and one day it will all come out."

"One day?" cried Jenna. "It needs to come out *now*! I don't want them to take over Holmburg! And I don't want to spend the rest of my life on the run from them, Perry! Isn't that what it'll mean? If the conspirators win?"

They could hear the sound of vehicles pulling up outside, and Perry turned toward the door. "Yeah, that's what it'll mean, Jenna," he said. "For you and me both." She could feel his tension as he listened. "I'm sure they're already hunting for us. Bolström will have put a price on our heads." He put his arm around her. "We'll have to go into hiding."

Jenna, too, turned to watch the door. She knew that Lorok and Meonok were standing guard, but still they were not safe. She listened to a truck door slam, and the shouts that followed. Her head felt strangely light. Perhaps she was catching a fever . . .

"Nahira!" shouted one of the men. "We've caught someone! Come and see who we've got!"

Then they dragged him into the mill. One sleeve of his shiny Chinese silk dressing gown was torn, and his unshaven face was covered in sweat. His hands were trembling.

Jenna turned away and rushed up the stairs. At the top she collided with Jonas. But she didn't even care.

When they were in Holmburg, Petterson preferred to stay in his own apartment, but this time he made an exception because Margareta was in such a state.

They'd traveled back to the city the night before — Magnus had insisted on it. In a situation of such confusion and urgency, the king couldn't possibly stay out in the country, he'd said. But now that he was back in the palace, what could he do? Everything seemed calm in the city — almost too calm. If it wasn't for the soldiers everywhere, you'd never know anything was wrong or that Scandia was under a state of emergency.

But there they were, stationed in all the squares and on the main roads, holding their guns loosely in their arms, chewing gum, and looking slightly embarrassed, as if they didn't really know what they were doing there themselves.

Petterson had retreated to his room, pretending that he had a headache and wanted to lie down. He closed the door behind him and went straight to his suitcase. The code for the lock was Perry's birthday. How could he have been so sentimental as to choose that?

His cell phone was tucked inside a sock. It had felt too dangerous to carry it around with him, but he couldn't wait any longer to check his messages. It was almost twenty-four hours since he'd last spoken to Bolström, and since then he'd had no news. The display still showed nothing: no texts, no voice mails. He held it up close to his eyes. What the devil was going on?

"Almost twenty-four hours!" he murmured. Why hadn't Bolström made contact? He had always been the first person Bolström discussed things with. He'd even been assigned the delicate task of infiltrating the royal family, which he'd accomplished masterfully. And now silence.

Slowly he sank down on his bed. The search for the children had produced nothing all day. Why? Were Peter and Jenna already dead? Was that why Bolström had not been able to photograph them with today's newspaper? That must be it. The news broadcasts must be right. The rebels had killed the children because they saw no prospect of them being exchanged for Liron.

Except that the rebels weren't the rebels.

Petterson dialed Bolström's number with trembling fingers. No reply. What else did he expect?

He turned on the television concealed in a cabinet opposite his bed. *What should I do now?* he thought. *What is Bolström planning next? If he's killed my son and knows that he won't be able to trust me anymore, what does he intend to do with* me *once the country has been "saved"?*

"One life more or less doesn't matter to him," murmured Petterson. On Scandia 1 some idiots were dancing across the screen with ribbons in their hair. On Scandia 2 the host and a well-known actress were cooking some exotic dish, smiling enthusiastically into the camera. "What a joke!" murmured Petterson. He switched to the international news channel.

He had to wait a few seconds. Evidently there were disasters happening all over the world, but eventually a map of Scandia with its two islands appeared on the screen. The anchorwoman's voice was urgent.

". . . assume that the abducted children have been killed, as there has been no more communication from the kidnappers for more than a day," she said. In the background was a new picture, and Petterson caught his breath. "Based on the discovery of an abandoned warehouse stocked with supplies, it now seems clear that the shortages in the country have been caused deliberately, and were not in any way connected with the rebels sympathetic to the cause of northern equality . . ."

"No!" Petterson spat.

"The military are now heading for the capital city of Holmburg from all over the country," said the anchorwoman, and the image shifted to a live shot of the channel's correspondent, on the ground in Scandia. ". . . looks like a military coup," he was saying. "Many of my colleagues in the foreign press have already closed down their bureaus and left the country. In the meantime, the . . ."

Petterson could feel the fear rising, and his heart was pounding. He couldn't just sit here waiting till the soldiers arrived and aimed their guns at the palace. Who knew what they would do with him? He was sitting in a trap.

"No, no, no!" he cried. Why hadn't Bolström contacted him? "Blast you, Bolli, call me! This is my coup as much as yours!"

His cell phone remained stubbornly silent. What he heard instead, though, was a stifled cry from behind him.

Margareta had opened the door and was standing there holding a tray on which sat a glass of water and a bottle of aspirin.

42

*N*ahira gazed at the man in the silken robe. "Norlin," she said.

How many years was it since they had last met? During the incidents last summer she'd seen him on television with his hair dyed white and blue contact lenses concealing his dark eyes. Now his hair was growing black above his pale, bloated face.

Once she had loved him. Once they had even been engaged, when they were both fighting for the cause of the north. Then he had decided to leave her and join Princess Margareta in a life of luxury. And finally, last year, he had forced his way onto the throne. Meeting him again under these circumstances was grotesque.

"Nahira!" said Norlin. His voice sounded like a plea, his hands were trembling, and he looked old. "Nahira, you must have something here to . . . I need . . ."

"What?" asked Nahira. What was he talking about? They had captured him, and he ought to be grateful her men hadn't killed him. So what was he rambling on about now?

"Something, Nahira, you must have something —" His voice broke off. She could see the sweat pouring down his forehead. "I can't go on, Nahira. Once we were . . . Something, you must have something . . ."

Nahira couldn't take her eyes off him. Was this the same Norlin who for a short time had actually ruled the country? "Lorok," she said. "See if we've got some liquor for him somewhere. He's no use to us like this."

Within seconds, Lorok was back with a bottle. "We were keeping it to celebrate our victory," he said reproachfully.

Nahira took it from him. "If we succeed in beating the conspirators, there'll be other places we can get supplies for our celebration party," she said, unscrewing the top. "Here, drink."

It was amazing to see how quickly the alcohol took effect. Norlin seized the bottle with trembling fingers and raised it to his lips. As one gulp followed another, his body began to relax, his hands stopped trembling, and, when he finally put the bottle down, his eyes were almost clear.

"Thank you, Nahira," he said. "You've saved my life. I've got this little problem at the moment, which I shall attend to as soon as —"

"Shut up!" said Nahira. She couldn't stand the way he turned pompous the moment he'd regained some sort of control over his shakes. "Just keep quiet, Norlin! Saved your life? Who knows how long we'll let you keep it."

Norlin smiled. He raised the bottle to his lips again, but this time took just a single sip, which he kept in his mouth for a reflective moment.

"You were always against bloodshed, Nahira," he said. "And when I tell you what I know —"

"Well, that I *am* interested in," said Nahira, leaning against the wall. Out of the corner of her eye she could see Perry and Jonas, Lorok and Meonok. Where was Jenna? It was hardly surprising that she found all this unbearable. "What are you doing running around Scandia in your bathrobe? And what are you doing here of all places?"

"Perhaps you could let me have a chair?" said Norlin.

Nahira rolled her eyes. He actually believed in the royal role he'd been playing! He was pathetic.

"I'm on the run from Bolström and his men, Nahira. They've betrayed me! They simply used me last year, those traitors . . ."

"I know what happened last year," said Nahira. "What I'm interested in is now. Today. This moment. What is Bolström planning? That is, if you've managed to retain any of it into your pickled brain."

Norlin didn't seem in the least offended. "He wants to kill me!" he cried. "As soon as he's taken over the country — 'saved' it, we say — I shall only be in his way. He's not even afraid to —"

"Norlin, you fool!" cried Nahira. How could she ever have loved this man? Even if it was years ago, decades ago, how could she not have seen the hidden side, the real Norlin? "For heaven's sake, just for once think of something other than yourself! I'm asking you about the country. *What does Bolström intend to do with Scandia?* If you want us to spare your life, then tell us what you know!"

Norlin looked confused. "After we've saved the country?" he murmured. He tried to put the bottle to his lips again, but Nahira snatched it out of his hand.

"Not after!" she yelled. "Before! Now! How does he plan to stage his coup? And when? What is to happen where and when, Norlin? We need places and times!"

Norlin nodded. His eyes were fixed on the bottle as he spoke. "Tonight at two o'clock," he said. He reached out his hand. "They're going to march on Holmburg. They're going to take over the parliament building. And the palace. What'll happen to the king and his family will depend on how they respond. If they're loyal to the friends of the motherland . . ."

"He makes me sick!" Jonas interrupted.

". . . then they'll be allowed to live and the king will stay king. But if they resist . . ."

"Me, too," added Perry.

". . . then unfortunately Bolström will be forced to adopt certain measures . . ."

Nahira did not wait to hear any more. She had already taken her cell phone out of her pocket. "Yes, at two o'clock in the morning!" she said. "The fishing boats are in the bay? We'll meet at the dam. That's the only land route — they'll have to come in that way." She listened for a moment. "Of course there aren't enough of us! But can you see any other way?" She closed her phone and looked at Lorok. "Let's roll," she said. "Meonok, lock this wreck in the mill and leave him his bottle."

Slowly she climbed the steps, through the second floor and up the narrow stairway to the gallery. Jenna was sitting there on the wooden floorboards, hunched up, her head on her arms and her arms around her knees.

"Jenna," said Nahira, running her hand over Jenna's hair. "You must come with us. There's no point in hiding yourself away. There's no hiding place from life."

When Jenna raised her head, Nahira saw to her surprise that her eyes were dry. "Why do I have to have a father like that, Nahira?" she whispered.

"Come on, Jenna," said Nahira. "We need you because you're you. It doesn't matter who your parents are."

She put her arm around Jenna's shoulders. As the two of them went down the steps, they could hear Norlin beating the door of the granary with his fists. "What's the meaning of this?" he was shouting. "Are you leaving me here to die? Let me out!"

Jenna turned her head, and Nahira could see that her lips were trembling.

"He doesn't count, Jenna," she said. "The only one who counts is you."

Then she took her to the waiting car.

Margareta was crying. The king had his back to a fireplace in which no fire had burned for many years.

"Well?" he asked.

Margareta knew she should be grateful that the palace servants were still loyal to them. Given what she was now beginning to understand, that kind of devotion could by no means be taken for granted.

She looked at Petterson. He was sitting in a deep armchair, with two servants behind him. Old Bergson was holding a kitchen knife in his gnarled fingers. He looked ridiculous. They had not told the palace guards: Who knew which side they were on?

"Well?" asked Magnus again. It was astonishing that Petterson was making no attempt to escape or even to defend himself.

"I know nothing," he murmured. "I've told you a thousand times, Magnus! It's the truth! Bolström isn't speaking to me anymore!"

"But he's got the children, hasn't he?" cried Margareta. At first, when she'd realized Petterson had been deceiving her all this time, she'd felt only anger and pain. How could it happen? Why her? Once it had been Norlin, and now it was Petterson. Then she'd thought of Jenna again, and fear had overtaken despair. "Are they still alive?"

Petterson shrugged his shoulders. He looked as if he didn't care about anything.

The king moved closer to the chair. Petterson cowered back as if afraid the king would hit him. "I shall never forgive you for what you've done to my sister, Petterson," he said. "But we'll deal with that later. For the moment, we have more urgent matters to attend to. You will now tell me exactly what's going to happen next. When are the conspirators going to strike? And where? Who else is involved?"

Petterson leaned forward as if he was about to stand up, but Bergson immediately held the knife to his throat and he sank back. The knife was old, as Margareta could see from where she was sitting, and its handle was worn and rough. But it could still be a deadly weapon.

"How should I know who's involved?" said Petterson. "Nobody made a list! But it must be obvious even to you, Magnus, that there are many sympathizers who are afraid of losing their property and their future, and of what might happen next in this country. Did you think we would just sit back and let you take away everything that's been ours by right for generations?"

"Nothing is ours by right," said the king. "Nothing is yours or mine. What we have is a gift. Can't you get that into your head?"

Petterson laughed, and the knife came closer to his throat. *Poor old Bergson*, thought Margareta. *He's almost wishing there was a reason for him to stick the knife in, though at the same time he's hoping he won't have to. Such a quiet, gentle old man.*

"A gift?" Petterson sneered, and now he actually caught hold of Bergson's arm. The old man hissed like a snake, and Petterson jerked his hand back. "A gift? How sentimental can you get, Magnus? Has the great romantic Liron addled your brain with his talk of equal rights? What's ours is ours! Because our ancestors worked for it for centuries! Because the land has always belonged to us, and we —"

This was too much for the younger of the two servants. He had short black hair, and was likely of northern descent. "Because *your* ancestors worked for it, you traitor?" he cried, and Margareta saw that he, too, had a knife. In his powerful fingers, its short serrated blade looked infinitely more dangerous than the worn-out one in Bergson's gnarled hand. "Did *your* ancestors work in the bauxite mines? Work in the fields till they were permanently stooped to bring in the harvest before the rains came? Did *your* ancestors die before their children had grown up, because the dust from the mines had settled in their lungs? *Your* ancestors worked for it? Say that once more and . . ."

"Arinoki," said Magnus. "Put down your knife. As for you, Petterson, you need to tell us what Bolström is planning and give us the names of your coconspirators. And what about the media? What would happen if I wanted to make a speech to the nation now?"

Petterson laughed harshly. "Try it!" he said.

Magnus looked at Margareta, who sat as if turned to stone.

"How could we have been taken in for so long, Margareta?" he asked. "How come we didn't notice anything?"

Margareta raised her head. "Did we really notice nothing?"

she murmured. "All I know is that I didn't *want* to see it."

"Sit still, you traitor!" yelled Arinoki. Petterson pushed his arm aside and stood up.

"Bolström is going to march on Holmburg, Magnus," he said. "I don't know when. But I do know that you won't be able to do a thing about it. I'm sure the telephone wires have already been cut. And I'm sure that the only people still serving in the palace guard are in alliance with Bolström. And I know that most of the army are on his side, too. Perhaps not the rank and file, but the officers — southern aristocrats like us. Their men will obey them. And your attitude toward the saving of our motherland, dear Magnus"— again he pushed aside Arinoki, who was making vaguely threatening gestures with his knife —"will determine what is to happen to you. To you, your family, and the monarchy." Again he laughed. "If you go out on the balcony with Bolström and wave to the crowd . . ."

"As if to say we're in favor of this coup?" cried Margareta. "Then you'll let us live? Is that it? Is that it?"

"You always had such a romantic soul, Greta," said Petterson, curling the corners of his mouth. "If you hadn't, you'd never have left Norlin and lived like a commoner abroad. But during the last few months I've enjoyed playing the part of your paramour. It wasn't quite such hard work as I'd feared."

Margareta jumped to her feet and slapped his face. Then she began to beat his chest with her fists. "You sick . . . disgusting . . ."

Bergson grasped her wrist. "Your Royal Highness!" he whispered, and then, shocked at himself, gave a little bow.

Margareta got a grip on herself. She stepped back and breathed deeply. "You're right, Bergson," she said. "It's not worth demeaning myself for a man like that."

Magnus came and stood by his sister. "So that's it, then," he said. "Either we welcome the coup and cooperate with you, or you'll kill us." Thoughtfully he wandered across to the French doors. It was still daylight. At this time of year, the summer evenings were full of warmth, and in the center of the circular flower bed in front of the palace, couples sat on the marble sides of the fountain, watching the soldiers parade back and forth in their brass-buttoned coats outside the wrought iron gates. "And then you'll lay our bodies out in state, and bury us with full honors, five-gun salutes and all the pomp and circumstance. Because the people still love us, as you well know, so you'll claim it was the rebels who shot us in the back."

"If you're so clever, Magnus," Petterson said with a sneer, "why didn't you think of all this before?"

Magnus ignored him. He unbolted the French doors and stepped out into the gentle evening sunlight. "Margareta!" he called.

They stood together on the balcony from which the kings and queens of Scandia had greeted the cheering crowds for centuries, looking down on the flower bed and to the boulevard beyond, where just a thin trickle of evening traffic streamed. From beyond the garden they could hear the sounds of the city by night, and on the horizon, behind the silhouette of the old city, rose the grim towers of the borderline quarters where the northerners lived. Below them, by the flower bed, a tourist was taking a photo of his sweetheart against the background of the palace and its ceremonial guards. He had no idea what he had got himself into.

"Margareta," the king said, taking her hand. "I shan't let them . . . shoot me in secret." He turned his head and looked back into the now darkening room. "Everyone will have to witness it, Petterson! You'll have to do it here on the balcony, in full view of the public, so that later you won't be able to deny what happened. And the news will spread, Petterson. You can't turn the clock back, no matter how much violence you use and how much blood you spill."

Margareta pressed up close to him. Behind them, Petterson was again sitting in the gloom, guarded by the two servants, but outside, the sounds coming from the city had changed. A strange noise was mingling with the hum of the evening traffic, the occasional car horn, and the church bells. An unfamiliar, inexplicable sound.

Magnus pulled Margareta closer to him.

For a second, she wondered if perhaps this might be the right moment to put on her crown. For the first time in her life she would have done so without a feeling of embarrassment.

Then, shocked, she gave a short start. Someone had silently crept up beside her.

"So now we're three," said Malena.

43

During the drive to Holmburg, Jenna laid her head on Perry's shoulder. She kept her eyes closed, and didn't see the strong light of afternoon gradually giving way to the gentle shimmer of dusk. She didn't see the swallows circling high in the sky. She didn't hear the high-pitched whine of the dragonflies and mosquitoes.

"Ow!" yelled Perry, slapping his arm. "Bloodsuckers!"

Jenna pretended that she was already fast asleep. She didn't want to see or talk to anybody. Why did Lorok have to pick up Norlin of all people? Since last year she had managed to put him out of her mind a lot of the time. Now suddenly there he was again, and with him came this feeling of despair.

How pathetic he was! And how humiliating for her to have a father like that!

"Ow! Jeez!" yelled Perry again, jumping in his seat this time. Jenna's head was jerked back off his shoulder. "Can't you go and bite somebody else? Jenna, for example. I'm sure she's absolutely delicious! Or Jonas over there?"

Jenna could feel the draft as he waved off the insects. No one would believe it now if she went on pretending to be asleep. She opened her eyes, and for a fraction of a second found herself staring straight at Jonas — but then he turned quickly away.

"We must be there by now!" Perry moaned. "I count twenty-six bites just on my legs!"

Nahira looked across at him and smiled. "I hear your father wants to send you to the military academy," she said. "I'm not so sure that would be the right place for you, Peter. Fortitude doesn't seem to be your strong point."

A shadow passed over Perry's face. "Don't talk to me about my father," he said. "Has anyone got anything to keep off these mosquitoes?"

Nahira shook her head. One of her phones rang, and once more she gave out her instructions, softly and precisely.

I've got to stop thinking about Norlin, thought Jenna, straightening her back. *Perry's no better off than me. And what lies ahead tonight is much more important.*

"Are they all coming to the dam?" asked Jenna. "How many will there be?"

Nahira shrugged. "Maybe fifty," she said. "Maybe a hundred? It's hard to say. There aren't many of my supporters left."

"Fifty men against an army?" said Perry with another curse and a slap on his arm. "That's madness, Nahira."

"We're going to block the dam," said Nahira. "Can you think of a better way?"

Jenna tried to remember the dam, which supported the only land route into the capital from the rest of the country. It was only about a quarter-mile long and centuries old. Long ago the road had been narrow, but over the years it had been continually widened so there was now a six-lane highway passing over the water and into the city. But it was still a bottleneck. Every morning and afternoon there were traffic jams at rush hour. There were plans to build a bridge and a tunnel, eventually. But for now there was no other route that the soldiers, tanks, and trucks could take.

"If there are fifty of us, we can form a chain across the dam," said Nahira. "If there are a hundred, we can form a double chain."

"A human chain against tanks?" cried Perry. "Is that the best you can do? Do you all want to be martyrs? You won't hold them up for a minute!"

Nahira didn't respond. She glanced across at Jonas, but he merely looked down at his feet.

"Do you want us to think back on today and remember how we never even *tried* to stop them?" she asked wearily. "If I did that, Peter Petterson Junior, I'd never be able to look myself in the eye again. I have to do whatever I can."

"Yeah, but if you try that, you'll never look *anyone* in the eye again," said Perry. "Because you'll be dead!"

Again Nahira didn't answer. The pickup truck was now moving smoothly over the paved surface of the highway. "Nearly midnight," Jonas noted, without looking up.

Jenna realized to her surprise that she hadn't thought about Jonas for a while. Was there anything left in the world that she *did* want to think about? In the dying light of the summer night, she could see the towers of the city looming black against the sky. They could only be a few minutes away from the dam. "Nearly there," she murmured.

At this hour, the highway was almost deserted. Every now and then a single car would pass along one of the six lanes, either to or from the city. There was no sign of any tanks. "Stop!" called Nahira, banging on the rear window of the driver's cab. But Lorok had already started to slow down, and now he let the truck slide slowly onto the hard shoulder of the road. "No one here," Nahira explained.

For a moment, Jenna stayed sitting in the flatbed of the truck. Here at the dam there were lampposts lighting the road. In their cold white beams the motorway seemed so empty you'd have thought no vehicle ever passed this way. The whole place had an air of desolation.

But on the far side of the water, countless dots of light were twinkling comfortingly: the illuminated towers of the palace and city hall, and a moored ship with a string of bulbs shining in all the colors of the rainbow. A billboard flashed an advertisement for a new model of car, followed by a well-known brand of jeans, followed by something else. And here and there, Jenna could see the friendly glow of lights in living-room windows, where people would be yawning and wondering if they should go to bed, or nodding off in front of the television, or playing a board game with their family.

As if today was just another day, she thought, slowly getting down from the back of the truck. *How beautiful our capital is, and how peaceful it all seems.*

Jonas and Perry were standing by the driver's cab, ten feet away from each other, both looking back at the forest. They would be coming from that direction if they were heading for the city. Nahira, Lorok, and Meonok all had their phones to their ears.

How beautiful our capital is, Jenna thought, *and how peaceful it all seems, and how pictures can lie.*

44

At first Magnus hadn't understood what was going on. Malena, standing wearily beside him, had thrown him a confused and questioning look when the first of them had appeared, heading along the boulevard from the direction of the city. To start with they came on their own, in twos and threes, and in the golden light of the old streetlamps the trio on the balcony saw that some of them were carrying flags stuck under their arms, as if they were embarrassed, and also rolled-up banners.

"What does it all mean, Magnus?" whispered Margareta.

The room behind them was empty now. Bergson and Arinoki had taken the laughing Petterson away. Magnus hadn't asked where they were taking him. All that mattered was that they had gone, since soon the tanks might be training their guns on the balcony. When they fired, no one must be hit by a stray bullet.

The trickle of people coming along the boulevard slowly grew into a flood. Now there was a dense crowd moving toward the palace, and the astonished, almost incredulous Magnus saw that there were more and more people joining them.

"It's midnight!" he said. "Where are they all coming from? What do they want?"

Malena looked as if she was on the verge of collapse. "They're carrying Scandian flags," she whispered.

No leader emerged from the crowd. No one had told these people what to do, and there were no megaphones, no loud-speakers. Each one individually had made the decision to come to the palace square, but now that they'd reached their destination, they looked around as if they were waiting, hesi-tating, wondering whether they had done something stupid and should just turn around and go back home. Two men who had begun to unfurl a banner looked around and then rolled it up again. Maybe all of them had expected to be met at the pal-ace, to have someone tell them what to do once they'd arrived. They had certainly thought they were going to do something great, and yet now there was nothing. If there hadn't been more and more people coming after them, the first arrivals might already have left the square.

"They've seen it on television," said Magnus. "Or maybe they found out online."

Malena looked at him. Suddenly her expression was alert, even excited.

"They've come to protect Scandia," she said. "Papa! Of course! They're all here because they know that a coup has been planned and they don't want it to happen! And they're

South Scandians, Papa. Look, most of them have got fair hair!"

Magnus nodded. "They won't be able to stop it," he said wearily. "Once the tanks roll in, they'll be in terrible danger."

"But they know that!" cried Margareta. "Do you think they're so naïve? And will their own countrymen fire on them? Magnus! You must speak to them!"

Magnus looked at her. "And what should I say?" he asked.

Margareta's eyes flashed angrily. For a moment it seemed that she had forgotten her daughter, the abduction, Petterson, the treason. "What should you say?" she cried. "Everyone down there would know what's to be said! But someone has to *say* it! And you're the king!"

"I haven't got a microphone," said the king, taking a pace backward. "Or a loudspeaker, or a megaphone!"

Margareta stepped toward the front of the balcony. Seeing her, the moving mass on the square below seemed to freeze, and then wild applause broke out, people cheered, and suddenly the flags were unfurled.

She looked back at her brother. "When this palace was built, there were no loudspeakers," she said. "But the kings of Scandia always addressed their people from here all the same. If you won't do it, I will!"

Malena came to stand beside her.

In the square the cheers and applause redoubled. The people had seen them now. Someone had brought along a bugle, and blew it as if he was on parade. Banners were unrolled:

Scandia United!; Our Goal: Equality — Quality — Jollity; Two Islands, One Country, No Limits! Margareta remembered these banners from the elections last year: Now, in this grim moment of crisis, they seemed out of place, and yet at the same time just right.

"People of Scandia!" she cried out. A hush fell over the square.

"She wants to say something!" people said to one another. "Quiet! Princess Margareta is going to speak!"

"Scandians from the north and Scandians from the south!" she said, but her voice was too soft. She cleared her throat.

"Scandians from the north and Scandians from the south!" repeated her brother from behind her, and it carried over the whole square. Once again there were cheers and loud applause.

"The king!" they shouted. "It's the king!"

"We stand here together . . ." said Magnus. There was total stillness in the square. Not even the flags fluttered. ". . . to avert a danger we hoped would never again threaten our country. Never! I am proud of all those Scandians who have come here tonight in order to defend the belief we all share: that only a just and united Scandia can be a happy Scandia. A country in which every citizen feels responsible for his or her fellow citizens, regardless of whether they come from the north or the south. Only in such a country can there be a prosperous and peaceful future for all."

The silence was so complete that any cough or sneeze in the square could be heard up on the balcony.

"I am proud of each and every one of you," Magnus stressed, his voice trembling slightly. "And I am grateful to be king of such a wonderful nation. But now I must ask all of you to consider. You know what is coming. You know that the tanks that are about to roll into this square are not part of some computer game. They are real and they are deadly." He drew a deep breath. "So I beg you to think carefully whether you wish to remain here. Think of your children, of your families. When the tanks arrive, some of you will pay for your courage with your lives, and none of us can know who will make this ultimate sacrifice. To leave now will not be an act of cowardice. You must think seriously about this."

Now there was movement in the crowd — a new sense of unease and annoyance. "We know the risks!" shouted a young man. "We know this is no game! And when they see all of us here" — instead of addressing the balcony, he now turned to look at the crowd — "the soldiers, they won't dare to shoot! Not at us, their own people!"

There were murmurs of agreement on all sides. Magnus waited until the crowd had quieted down again before continuing. "That is what we all hope," he said. "But we can't know for sure. These things can happen. These things do happen, and *have* happened, over and over again in the world. Brother shoots brother" — he paused for a moment — "friend shoots friend. No one can be certain. So there is no shame in leaving here now."

No one moved.

"But my sister, my daughter, and I will stay," said Magnus. "And we shall wait. With you."

There were thunderous cheers. If the tanks were now rumbling toward them from the dam, the people's shouts would have drowned out the sound.

Then someone started singing, and others joined in until the whole square was filled with their song. It was a North Scandian song of summer, but a song they also loved in the south.

45

The traffic on the dam had gradually dwindled to nothing. Just an occasional car came from the city, looking almost lost on the broad highway, but not a single vehicle crossed the dam to go into Holmburg.

Had the road farther out been blocked to clear the way for tanks and troop transport? If so, the people who were now beginning to arrive must have found a way around any barriers. One by one or in small groups they headed toward Nahira, their weapons in their belts or in their hands. Jenna saw scythes and axes, knives of all sizes, and at least one man carrying an air gun. So these were the dreaded rebels? It was laughable — they were farmers and shepherds, laborers and factory workers, and they'd brought their tools with them. How could Nahira possibly think they'd be able to hold up an entire army? Fifty, sixty, at most seventy men and women without real weapons? What could they do against tanks and machine guns? It was stupid even to go on hoping.

Nahira now stepped out of the darkness into the middle

of the road. She stood in the center lane and raised her arms for silence. In the cold light of the streetlamps, her tiny figure cast a long shadow.

"Thank you for coming!" she said. "All of you. But there are only a few of us, and we should not deceive ourselves. Against the soldiers and their tanks we don't stand a chance. We are too weak. We don't have proper weapons. All we have is ourselves and our courage." A silence had fallen over the crowd. "So lay down your scythes, your axes, your knives, and your guns. We shall gather here in the middle of the road. The soldiers should know that the people standing before them will not use force. The people standing before them have nothing to oppose the army with except their lives, and their hopes for a better future."

"No weapons at all?" cried a young man, grasping his ax even more tightly. "Have you lost your mind, Nahira? They have tanks. They have —"

"That's precisely the reason," said Nahira. "They have tanks. We have our hope for justice and our dream of a better life. We shall wait."

"There aren't enough of us!" cried a woman with a scythe. "Nahira, it's insane. How can we possibly . . . ?"

But the first of them had already begun hesitantly to lay down their weapons. The pile of things they had brought to defend themselves with grew higher and higher. And the higher it became, the more pathetic it looked, and the more helpless they appeared.

"Nahira!" whispered Jenna. They had to stop this. Perry was right: It was madness.

And then they heard the rumble of the tanks. The chains grating over the asphalt. The sound was unmistakable.

"They're coming," murmured Jonas. Jenna hadn't even noticed that he was standing next to her. Maybe he hadn't realized it himself. "Oh God, they're really coming."

Then, out of the bushes in which they themselves had been hiding, stepped a slender figure. Her long blonde hair shone even in the pale light of the streetlamps.

"Ylva!" gasped Jenna. What was *she* doing here?

Ylva didn't look at her, or at Jonas. As the rumble of the tanks drew ever nearer, Ylva marched straight up to Nahira.

"If you don't mind," she said, "I'd like to stand with you."

Once again they'd spent the whole evening glued to the television.

"That's mine!" Bea kept shouting when the blurred pictures of the trucks and the hangars flickered across the screen. "Look! From my cell phone!"

"Yeah, yeah," said her father for the third time. "I think we've got the message."

Nevertheless, she knew how proud of her he was. After all, it had been thanks to her that these reports were going around the globe. Ordinary Bea from Nowheresville. Thanks to her, and thanks to the policeman who had sent the video from her phone to all the newspapers and TV companies.

46

*B*ea had totally lucked out by being at the police station when she'd called Jenna. Who would have put a semihysterical girl straight through to the chief political editor? But with the authority of the state behind him, the policeman had been connected automatically.

"Hate to think what the phone bill will be," the policeman had said. "But what the heck, it's all for a good cause, right?" And he'd gone on to call the next one, and the one after that.

Now they were watching yet another special news program about Scandia.

"Breaking news!" said the anchorman. The shock effect of the words made Bea realize just how close she'd been to falling asleep. It was almost two o'clock in the morning. At this time on a normal weekday, she'd have long since been in bed.

"As these scenes, which our reporter filmed from his hotel window, clearly show, Scandians are flocking by the thousands to the palace square. It seems that the whole country has now heard about the imminent threat of a coup, and even the South Scandians, who have lost and will lose many of their privileges because of the reforms, are in an apparent majority on the side of the king and the elected government."

"What is he talking about?" asked Bea.

The reporter now left his room to mingle with the dense crowd of people in the street, who were all heading in the same direction. He held his microphone out to an elderly man.

"You don't think we'd actually let ourselves be tricked like that, do you?" he said. "We'll never believe another word they tell us! Have you heard what they did? The shortages? It wasn't the rebels at all! Do these plotters seriously think we'll let ourselves be governed by people who've betrayed us like that? Ha! The scoundrels. We won't let them get away with it!" And then he disappeared into the crowd.

The familiar face of the reporter now appeared on the screen. "And so it appears that, by opening up their country with the reforms of the past year, the government took a step that might now be crucial to its survival," he said. "Access to foreign television channels and the Internet, which had been denied to the Scandians until recently, has allowed every citizen to find out what's being reported beyond the state-controlled stations of Scandia 1 and 2. And the commitment of the people to defending and promoting these reforms is both surprising and dramatic. If indeed the tanks should enter the city tonight . . ."

"I bet they will," said Bea's father. "We know what those plotters are like!"

". . . they will have to point their guns not only at the government, but also at their own people. Whether the plotters expected such a development remains to be seen. How will they respond? How much blood are they prepared to shed when the world as well as the rest of the Scandian nation is watching? Everyone now knows that this is an artificial crisis deliberately staged by a secret cabal claiming they want to free the people from the strife that they themselves created!"

Bea leaned back on the sofa. "And all thanks to me!" she said. She'd never been interested in politics — who was? But now, suddenly, she had helped change the fate of an entire nation.

"OK, freedom fighter," said her mother. "Isn't it about time you went to bed?"

Bea shook her head. "Not until they say that Jenna is safe. What happened to her? Don't they know?"

Her father said nothing.

"Then I suppose I'd better brew some coffee," said her mother. They were in for a long night.

Until now Jenna had only seen tanks on television. Since she had been a princess living in Scandia, there hadn't been any more military parades, and now, as these mighty machines came rumbling toward her, she held her breath. Out of the darkness of the forests they were advancing, four abreast, slowly and massively. Their searchlights lit up everything before them as bright as day. She knew that they were all helpless in the face of such power.

Next to her in the human chain stood Perry, holding her hand tight. On her other side was a North Scandian boy with bags under his eyes, who had somehow come between her and Jonas.

Next to Jonas was Ylva.

The tanks were so much darker and larger than Jenna had imagined, and her fear suddenly grew equally large and dark. Why was she standing here? They would never be able to save the country. The tank treads split the asphalt, and the barrels of the guns moved from left to right, like the antennae of giant blind insects hungrily seeking their prey.

The machines were coming nearer and nearer, but they weren't slowing down. It was as if the soldiers in the turrets really were blind, as if they didn't see the people waiting ahead of them, hand in hand in the glaring light.

"Now!" whispered Jenna.

The first row of tanks had reached the pathetic pile of weapons. Metal splintered under the chains, and scythes and axes, sickles and knives, were crushed to powder, air guns and pistols ground to dust. But the massive hulls didn't deviate an inch from their path. They rolled forward, crunching the weapons as if offering the people in front of their gun barrels one final proof of their terrible power, one final chance to get out of their path.

"Mom!" Jenna murmured, and felt her legs desperately wanting to run away. But Perry's hand held her fast, and on her other side the fingers of the North Scandian boy pressed equally hard — maybe to encourage her, maybe to warn her.

Only thirty feet to go. Only twenty. Only ten. They were really going to do it.

And then the column stopped. The guns were still aimed at the people in front of them, but the terrifying noise suddenly ceased. The silence only increased Jenna's fear.

Along the hard shoulder of the road, racing at breakneck speed past the stationary tanks, came an armored car. Even before it screeched to a halt just a few feet in front of the people on the dam, the passenger door flew open and a man leaped out. In the bright light, Jenna could see gold braiding and stars on his uniform and his cap. She heard the crackle of a megaphone.

Von Thunberg, thought Jenna, and threw a sideways glance at Ylva.

But Ylva did not try to release herself from the human chain.

"Please clear the road!" boomed the general. "Attention! Attention! Please clear the road at once! If you don't, we will have no choice but to —"

"No!" said Nahira. Unnoticed, she had stepped out of the crowd, and now stood in front of the general, tiny and tired, but driven by an inner strength. "Why would we have come, General, if we were prepared to leave at the first threat, or the first shot you fire at us?" She turned and looked straight into the faces of her followers. "We stay!" she cried. "We stay!"

Someone in the chain began to clap, but then stopped abruptly when no one else joined in. After that, the quietness seemed even more menacing. But nobody moved, and the silence was so complete that you could almost hear it.

"Please be sensible!" shouted von Thunberg. His voice sounded strained. "Please clear the road! Otherwise we will be forced to —"

"Forced?" cried Nahira. "Forced? Who is forcing you, von Thunberg? Isn't it entirely your own decision what happens next?"

One of the tanks inched forward, then stopped again. The people on the dam cried out and reflexively took a step backward; some stumbled, but the chain of hands did not break.

And so they stood, the gun barrels pointing directly at them. Jenna was trembling.

Von Thunberg had turned to Nahira. "Can't you see what will happen if I give my men the order to proceed?" he shouted into his megaphone. "Can't you see how afraid your people are? Tell them to clear the dam — if they're still willing to listen to you! Are you prepared to take responsibility for what's going to happen if the tanks roll on?"

Nahira shook her head. Her voice was loud enough to be heard even without a megaphone. "Oh no, General!" she cried. "The responsibility will be yours and yours alone! It's you who will give the order! We're doing nothing except standing here. We're not attacking anyone. We don't even have any weapons. *You* will be responsible for every injury, every death, *you* alone, and you will have to live with that for the rest of your days!"

The general was about to raise the megaphone to his mouth again, but Nahira cut him off. "No," she said, quite softly now, "no, not just *you*. But all those young soldiers in your tanks. They'll also have to live with it, von Thunberg, and I don't know how they will cope with that. So don't try to shift the responsibility onto us. It's not ours."

Von Thunberg still held the megaphone in his hand.

"It's not a matter of individual people, as you well know," he said. "It's for the whole country. It's our beautiful Scandia that you rebels are trying to destroy. I'm going to give the order now to advance. Your people still have the chance to leave. For the sake of the country!"

The general raised his arm.

At that moment a figure detached itself from the human chain.

"Stop!" cried a shrill voice. "It's always a matter of individual people! Always! What else is it about, Dad? What else matters?"

"Ylva!" cried the general, shocked. His arm sank down. "Ylva, what are you doing? Come here! Come here at once!"

If there was one person in the world that Jenna hated, it was Ylva von Thunberg. Blonde, arrogant, smart, she had made this past year a living nightmare, and worst of all she had taken Jonas from her.

And yet, in spite of all that, Jenna now felt something different.

Defiant, Ylva stood there in the middle of the road. *All that's missing is a flag she could wave*, thought Jenna, *like the woman in that famous painting of the French Revolution.* But Ylva didn't need a flag.

"So was it always just words that you said to me?" she cried. "Just words, Daddy?" And as her father approached her, hesitant and confused, the circle of rebels closed silently and protectively around her. "Only words, about princesses who love their people so much that they're ready to do anything for them? Only words, about the noblemen and the rich who share their wealth with the poor? Only words, about princes who sacrifice their lives for the sake of justice?" She took a deep breath. "Was it only words that you spoke to me before I went to bed each night, when I was small and ignorant enough to believe everything you told me? My strong, brilliant, kind father? Were they just stories then, but this is real life?" Her voice was trembling. "Is that it, Daddy? How could I have been so stupid as to believe you?"

All around her, the rebels stood as if frozen to the spot. No one spoke; they scarcely dared to breathe. Yvla continued. "And so now you'll turn your guns on these people who want nothing more than the justice you always spoke about? Did you always lie to me? Was it all lies, Daddy?"

With these last words, her voice cracked. Jonas went to her and held her in his arms.

So now there are three of us, thought Jenna. *Three! My father, Perry's father, and von Thunberg. It's unbearable. Betraying the country, and betraying their children.*

"Ylva!" cried the general. Still he tried to come closer to her, but still the rebels barred his way — silent and unarmed. "My child! You've joined the wrong side! We're here to free the country, my men and I! We have to enter Holmburg! We have to march on parliament, Ylva, and on the palace. The government and the rebels are destroying our country!"

"The government and the rebels?" repeated Nahira in her tired voice. How tiny she looked next to von Thunberg. "I am Nahira, leader of the rebels, and now it will be easy for you to capture me at last, unless you prefer to shoot me along with my people. But before you do, explain one thing to us, General. Why are you lying to yourself and to your soldiers? Even now, though the truth has for hours been filling the television screens in every living room . . ."

Jenna could see the bewilderment on von Thunberg's face, and she realized that Ylva saw it, too.

"It's not the rebels, Dad!" cried Ylva, releasing herself from Jonas's arms. Her face was stained with tears, and her voice sounded questioning. Jenna sensed that, quite unexpectedly, a ray of hope had illuminated Ylva — the hope that her father might know nothing of what had happened, might himself have been deceived, and therefore might not after all be the traitor over whom she had wept. "You must have heard! They must have told you! You've got a telephone in your car — you're updated on any new developments . . ."

"What?" asked von Thunberg, and Jenna saw the astonishment in his eyes. It was real. "What are you talking about, Ylva?"

"You mean you haven't heard?" cried Ylva. Her face grew brighter. "Am I supposed to believe that? Your soldiers haven't heard, either? No one has told you, and you're left to storm into Holmburg with your tanks and your guns? Dad! If they've kept secret from you what the whole world has known for hours, isn't that proof enough in itself . . . ?"

Jenna saw one of the soldiers in von Thunberg's car hurriedly talking into the microphone that was fixed to his helmet. He started gesticulating with his arms, and von Thunberg went to him and leaned over the dashboard. Time stood still.

Then the general turned, almost in slow motion. His arms sank to his side. He said something to the soldier, who nodded and spoke again into his microphone. Later, Jenna could not remember exactly what happened during the next few minutes. The enormity of her fear beforehand was now matched by the greatness of her hope. Suddenly, everything had changed. The tanks lowered their guns, and the hatches of the turrets all opened at the same time, like some strange sort of ballet. The faces that now began slowly to appear were young, South Scandian, confused, but most of all — as Jenna saw with mounting joy — they were infinitely relieved.

Jenna was trembling, and sank down to the ground where others were already sitting, as exhausted and relieved as she was. Rebel men and women, old and young, some of them weeping, some laughing, arms hugging knees, back-to-back, united in the feeling that the danger was past, but also that there was something else to come. She could see von Thunberg talking to Nahira. He took Ylva in his arms. The guns were still lowered.

So Ylva's father is not one of them, thought Jenna. *Perry's father is, though, and mine. But it would have been a miracle if something as terrible as that had happened to Ylva von Thunberg, too.* And yet Jenna realized that they would all be forever in her debt for stopping this invasion, and maybe even for saving their lives.

The first soldiers began to climb out of the tanks. They stood, embarrassed, by the side of the road, just a few feet away from those at whom they had just been aiming their guns — Scandians just like themselves. When eyes met, the soldiers were the ones who lowered their gaze. Suddenly one of them let out a cry.

"Gustafson!" he shouted, and leaped toward an old man in the crowd, which parted to let him pass. "Gustafson, it's me! Aarvid! Little Aarvid, from the farm next to yours!"

Then he threw his arms around the old man's shoulders, and they slapped each other's backs, laughing and sobbing at the same time, like two old friends bumping into each other after a long separation, and not as if one of them had just been on the verge of killing the other.

"My neighbor! My neighbor!" cried "Little Aarvid," who was at least six feet tall. Suddenly other soldiers began to smile, too. Tentatively at first, but then with increasing affection, they went over to the people in the human chain and shook their hands. If someone had had a bottle of champagne to pop, the whole scene would have appeared to be one big party.

Another officer now took charge and began to issue orders. The soldiers climbed back into their tanks, but the hatches remained open, and the young men looked across the water to the dark streets of the city they no longer had to attack. Without even asking permission, the rebels climbed up and joined them. They made themselves comfortable, holding on to the gun barrels and laughing.

In this way they all rode together into Holmburg — not to conquer it, but to put an end to all the lies at last.

47

When they crossed the dam, the suburbs on the other side lay in silence, but behind the walls of the houses, Jenna could sense the fear. As people heard the tanks roaring through the streets, their shocked faces peered out from behind curtains. But then through the cracks they saw the rebels waving and the soldiers laughing, and with joyful relief they opened their windows and waved back.

"White flags!" one of the rebels shouted. "Give us white flags!" And down they fluttered from windows and balconies — a shower of bedsheets, crumpled or ironed, old and worn thin or brand-new, enough for every tank. Knotted around the gun barrels, they flapped peacefully, if a bit sloppily, to show everyone in the city even from a distance that the dangers of the night had passed.

Jenna sat in the back of the pickup truck between Jonas and Perry — perhaps a little closer to Perry. Ylva had also insisted on traveling with them. But why wasn't she sitting next to Jonas? Why the distance between them in this, her hour of triumph, when she had proved to Jonas she was on his side? And why was Jonas looking away from her?

They're embarrassed, thought Jenna. *You can't kiss a boy when the whole world is watching. They're just embarrassed.*

The closer they came to the palace, the denser the crowds grew. When they reached the main boulevard, the sky was already turning pink in the first light of the new day. Jenna was astonished to hear the sound of singing.

The people lining the boulevard were singing the old Scandian folk songs that she had struggled so hard to learn during the last year — songs from the north and songs from the south. Not everyone was singing in the same key, and not everyone was singing in tune. But they sang with all their hearts, with defiance, and with the certainty that right was on their side. There were out-of-tune guitars and flutes; Jenna could see a banjo and hear a clarinet, then a saxophone, and a little boy perched on his father's shoulders was banging two saucepan lids together.

"Perry!" she whispered, light-headed with exhaustion and relief. "We did it!"

Then she saw that he'd fallen asleep, and that Jonas was laughing. She gathered up all her courage, and laughed back.

When the tanks with their white flags reached the circular flower bed in front of the palace, they stopped at the sides of the square as if to form an honor guard. Then, through the avenue of fluttering bedsheets, came the pickup truck, with

Nahira, Lorok, and Meonok in the driver's cab, and Jenna, Jonas, Perry, and Yvla in the back. The wrought iron gates opened wide.

Someone lowered the flap at the back of the truck; someone helped Jenna climb down; someone escorted her up onto the balcony, where her mother burst into tears as she took her in her arms. There was thunderous applause. "Jenna!" whispered her mother. "Thank God!"

Jenna could see a blurred ocean of faces down below in the square. "Perry's father!" she said. "Mom, Perry's father is . . ."

She had never longed so much to go to sleep. In a real bed in a real house, and without fear. But she was a princess. She took a deep breath, turned, and waved to the people, who were still singing and cheering and throwing hats and flowers up in the air. Many of them had pulled up pictures of lighters on their cell phones and MP3 players, and were waving the electronic flames.

"Perry's father . . ."

"I know, Jenna, I know," said her mother, stroking her hair. *She's even more tired than I am*, thought Jenna.

"Only now," shouted her uncle the king, "only now is Scandia truly free and united! Because you yourselves, the citizens of our country, have chosen freedom and unity!"

As Jenna listened to the applause, and hoped that the people in the square would hurry up and go to bed so that she could get some sleep at last, she saw Perry embracing Malena as if he never wanted to let her go. *At least they don't mind if the whole world sees them*, she thought, and looked for Jonas and Ylva. This, surely, would be the time for them to do the same.

But Ylva was standing quietly and proudly next to Nahira, and when Jenna eventually spotted Jonas, he was staring incredulously at his best friend, Perry, with a broad smile lighting up his face. Then suddenly he was beside her.

"Hello, Jenna," he said. As if he'd only just seen her, as if they hadn't spent the whole day traveling together on the pickup truck, as if they hadn't stood just a few steps away from each other facing the tanks.

"Hi," said Jenna without turning. She went on waving to the singing, cheering crowds and didn't look at him. But she could feel the blush creeping up her neck and into her cheeks, and she hoped that at least the people down below wouldn't notice, even if Jonas next to her could hardly miss it.

"Let's not be stupid, Jenna!" whispered Jonas. He waved to the people, too. Was he really turning red? Red like her? "Jenna, I thought . . . We could have been killed just before. Let's not waste any more time being stupid!"

Her eyes wandered across to Ylva, and to her surprise she saw her laughingly stretch out her arm toward Jonas and, as if to encourage him, give him the thumbs-up.

"Jenna!" whispered Jonas.

Who would have thought they could kiss when the whole world was watching?

"Look!" cried Bea. "Look! It's him!"

All night long they had sat together watching the television reports from Scandia. The coffee had been drained, and in the early morning twilight her father had finally fallen asleep in the armchair, to be followed soon after by her mother. Had Bea slept, too? Maybe just a wink, but definitely no more than that. The news channel was still transmitting events from Scandia, but outside it was already getting light, and she knew there was no way she could possibly go to school after such a night.

"It's him, Mom! Dad! The spaghetti-and-meatballs boy! I *knew* it!"

She could see Jenna in his arms — the little player! The Player Princess! She might have let on when she was visiting them! Hadn't Bea actually asked her? And the sly girl hadn't breathed a word!

Bea's cell phone played an old Beatles tune.

Txs 100x!!! Jenna had written. **W/out u . . .** But that was the end of the text.

Bea yawned. "I'm going to bed," she said. "Don't even *think* about telling me to go to school!"

Her mother sighed. "Today's an exception," she said. "And what was that?" She pointed to the cell phone.

Bea laughed. "Jenna tried to send me another text," she said. "But somehow that girl never gets it right!"

"She's probably very tired," said Bea's mother. "But it was a real stroke of luck, wasn't it, that she sent you the wrong pictures to begin with. Who knows if anyone would have believed you without that video? Yes, she's probably just tired."

"Who isn't?" said Bea. "But when I'm awake again, *she's* got to tell *me* all about *him*!"

48

"At least let Jonas in!" said Jenna sulkily, and sneezed loudly into a fresh tissue. "You can't leave me lying here all alone in my room while the rest of you are out there celebrating our triumph!"

Her mother was standing at the foot of the bed with a thermometer in her hand. "Still 100.4," she said severely. "It's just the flu. But you have a fever, so you should stay in bed, and that's final. What you need is plenty of sleep. Then maybe by tomorrow you'll be all right again."

Jenna coughed. Mom always talked to her like this when she was ill. But back before she became a princess, the worst that could happen was that she'd miss a day of school — not a nationwide victory celebration! Mom was being totally unfair. Jenna had obediently stayed in bed all day just so she could enjoy the fun that night.

"Then at least let Jonas come in and see me!" she pleaded. Though she wasn't a hundred percent sure she wanted him to see her — not like this, in her pajamas, red-nosed, puffy-eyed, bed-headed. "Please, Mom, please!"

"Absolutely not!" she said emphatically, and handed over a mug of hot lemon tea. "You want to infect him, too?"

"Well, I already kissed him," said Jenna defiantly. "On the balcony. So he's already caught all my viruses!"

When you've got a fever, maybe you lose a few inhibitions.

Mom laughed. "Then you can dream about him," she said. "That'll do you more good than any medicine."

Jenna sipped at the steaming mug of tea. It was much too hot. Mom had never understood that honey lost all its vitamins if it was dissolved in such hot water. But at least Mom could tell her what had happened today. Jenna slid back under the covers, putting the mug on the bedside table. "So, what's the latest?"

Mom understood. "They went and arrested him," she said softly. "At the mill. Now he's in prison. Don't be sad, Jenna. I wish I could have given you a better father. But in those days I was young and stupid."

Jenna nodded. Mom shouldn't be apologizing. It had all been way worse for her. First Norlin, then Petterson. *Poor Mom*, she thought. *Who knows if she'll ever trust a man again?* Jenna decided not to ask what had happened to Petterson.

Then she thought again of Jonas. Fortunately, she had not inherited Mom's bad luck!

"And eventually they'll find Bolström," said Margareta. "I'm sure they will, and the two of them will be put on trial, along with Petterson and von Thunberg and all their accomplices."

"What about Liron?" asked Jenna with a big sniff.

"He's here with Jonas," said her mother. "Now blow your nose! Is that how you were brought up? Otherwise you'll get blocked sinuses on top of your fever, and we don't want that!" She sighed, and pushed another tissue into Jenna's hand. Then she watched Jenna give a mighty blow, after which she threw the tissue with unerring aim into the wastebasket. "Finding the accomplices won't be so easy, though. What's the evidence? Who's going to confess to being part of it, now that the plan has failed? But the real heroes are you children. Magnus and I are so proud of you."

Jenna sneezed. "I don't feel like a hero," she said grumpily, and rolled her eyes.

Mom laughed. "Sleep well, my little snuffler. Tomorrow everything will look different."

She turned off the light and pulled the door shut behind her.

Jenna rolled over on one side. How could life be so unfair? She'd helped to protect the country against the conspirators, and now she had to lie in this dark room all alone while everyone else was out partying. Was that gratitude? Was that any way to treat a princess who was also a hero?

"What a bummer!" she murmured, and had a good cough.

At that moment, the door opened very quietly. Jenna only

noticed it because for a second a thin shaft of light fell on the carpet. Then the room was dark again.

"Jenna?" whispered a voice that she would have recognized anywhere. "Jenna, are you awake?"

"Bea?" said Jenna in amazement, and bolted up in bed as the light went on. "What are you doing here?"

"I so knew you wouldn't be asleep," said Bea, and stopped three paces away from the bed to give a little bow. "I'd have been surprised if you were. Just please don't give me your virus, Your Highness. I want to live it up while I'm here. How often do I get the chance to hang out in a palace?"

"But how did you . . . ?" Jenna started to ask, before being rattled by another bout of coughing. "What are you doing here?"

"Your moms invited me," said Bea, pulling up a chair so that she could sit close to the bed. "To join in the celebration! Because I helped you with the TV people, et cetera. But then she told me you were ill, so I said, in that case, I'd come and see you . . ."

". . . but then, let me guess, she said I needed to sleep," said Jenna. "Classic! Pass me a tissue, please?"

Bea looked for the box. "So I just sneaked away," said Bea. "Since that time we climbed out the window, I've really felt like doing it again. You know, a crazy adventure! Seriously, Jenna, it's so just like in a movie!"

Jenna giggled. "Oh, totally. Especially the part at the end when I catch a cold," she said. "How anticlimactic!"

Bea shrugged. "Even royalty can catch cold," she said. "Moving on. The boy. Details, now. Why wouldn't you admit it last time?"

"Oh!" said Jenna. Should she tell Bea the whole story? After all, she was and would always be her BFF . . .

"One day there shall be a double wedding!" Bea pronounced dramatically, draping a clean tissue over her head like a bridal veil, then passing Jenna the mug of lemon tea. "Now drink up, my child. Yes, you and Sir Spaghetti-and-Meatballs, and Malena and that Mr. Brainiac she's besotted with. I shall be your bridesmaid, and wear a fetching designer frock the color of which is yet to be determined. How completely and utterly romantic!"

Jenna couldn't help but smile. "Mom's forbidden Jonas to come and see me," she said, taking a gulp. The lemon and honey drink had cooled down a bit by now.

Bea nodded thoughtfully. "When that woman's right, she's very, very right," she said, giving Jenna a searching look. "Frankly, my dear, you look dreadful. Although with true love, that's not supposed to matter. Personally, I wouldn't want to take the chance!"

Right then there was a cautious knock at the door. "Jenna?" whispered the voice that would have made her immediately turn red if the fever hadn't already done the job.

"Ooh, busted!" Bea whispered. "Now we'll find out whether he really loves you."

In the doorway stood Jonas, Malena, and Perry, all three

with trays in their hands. "I see you've already got a party going on in here!" said Malena. "Can we join you?"

"We figured that if you weren't coming to the party, then the party should come to you," said Perry, and put his tray down on the desk. "We only brought the best. Who'd like some *crudités*?" he said in a pompous voice. "Buffalo wings? Waffle fries?"

Jenna wasn't even listening to him. She wished she could disappear under the covers.

"Well, Jenna," said Jonas, sitting down at the end of the bed. "I have to say your hair looks as stunning as a toilet brush." The expression in his eyes was everything she could have wanted it to be. Then he gave her foot a quick squeeze through the blankets.

"I look awful," she mumbled.

Jonas nodded. "That you do," he said.

"Jonas!" cried Malena. "You mustn't say such things!"

"Why not?" said Jonas, grinning at Jenna. "She knows I really think she's beautiful!"

Perry made a gagging noise. "Stop!" he said. "Or I'll puke. You've been watching too many bad movies."

"I think so, too," said a voice from the doorway.

Jenna looked over. No doubt her fever had crept up a few more degrees in all this excitement, but she didn't care. "Ylva?" she said.

"I've brought the drinks," said Ylva, carefully depositing a tray on the floor. "If you don't mind? Since all the interesting people at this party seem to be hanging out in here . . . Anyway, I just wanted to tell you . . ."

"It's OK," said Jenna, looking toward the end of the bed, where Jonas had now settled in comfortably. Life was perfect. "You don't have to —"

"But I want to," Ylva persisted. "Jenna, I'm sorry. I behaved very, very badly."

"If it's going to get this serious, I'm out of here!" said Perry. "Is it? 'Cause I'll go join the conga line with the old folks, I swear."

"Oh no!" said Malena.

"Oh no!" said Jonas.

"No, definitely no!" said Jenna.

"Who'd like a soda?" asked Ylva.

Jenna sighed. What a good thing it was that Mom had told her to stay in bed!

ABOUT THE AUTHOR

*K*irsten *Boie,* author of *The Princess Plot* and its sequel, *The Princess Trap,* was born in Hamburg, Germany, where she still lives today. Before becoming an author, Kirsten worked as a grade-school teacher. She began writing after the adoption of her first child, and since then she has published more than sixty books for young readers. She is the recipient of the prestigious German Youth Literature Award, and many of her books have become international bestsellers.

WHAT WOULD YOU DO TO SAVE SOMEONE YOU LOVE?

At the hospital, upset and scared after her dad's heart attack,
Isla meets Harry, a boy who really understands her—but he's
sick, too. If she can save the injured swan they see outside the
window, could that somehow help Harry, and her dad?

★ "Compelling. Sensitive."—*Booklist*, starred review

★ "Beautiful...Mystical...Superb."—*School Library Journal*, starred review

EXPERIENCE THE EPIC SAGA FROM BEGINNING TO END

THE ICEMARK CHRONICLES

WHAT IS THE SECRET THAT MARKS HER?

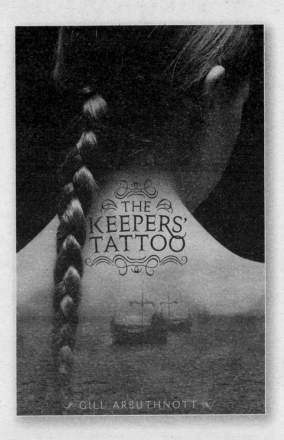

From birth, Nyssa has been branded with
mysterious words. To uncover their meaning, and
to stop a tyrant in his tracks, she must find the other half
of the message, written on a twin she's never known.